The Last Gift
by
Daris Howard

I0598545

Publishing Inspiration

The Last Gift
by
Daris Howard

Copyright © 2014
by
Daris W. Howard

ISBN-10: 1629860107
ISBN-13: 978-1629860107

www.publishinginspiration.com

Publishing Date: June 2015

Publishing Inspiration LLC

Table of Contents

I dedicate this book to my son, Gavin. After I had written it, I put it away for seven years because the topic was hard for me. His encouragement motivated me to prepare the manuscript for publication.
Daris Howard

Senator Davis

Rachel could feel her blood boiling as Matthew yelled at her, "You know you have money, and part of it rightfully belongs to me!"

Her children were hiding in the old Minnesota farmhouse, doors locked as she had told them. And, though she knew what it would bring, she stood her ground and answered forcefully, "What money we have I need for my children and Mother Davis. If you need money, get a job!"

They exchanged more fiery words. Finally, Rachel could take no more. She looked at him defiantly as she spoke. "Get off of our property, or I will call the sheriff."

Matthew raised his hand to strike her, just as she had expected. She squinted and braced for the blow, but instead, Matthew suddenly spun around. Barely daring to open her eyes fully, Rachel saw a man standing there. He was holding Matthew's arm tightly, and as he spoke, his hazel green eyes were narrowed and piercing.

"I had better never ever see anyone being abused on my property! Is that understood?"

Matthew was stunned. "I, uh, just . . . " Finally, he regained his composure. "Your property? Then you must be Senator Davis." Matthew's whole countenance changed as, smiling, he offered his hand. "My name is Matthew Davis. Might we be related?"

The man ignored Matthew's outstretched hand and looked at him with disdain. "I am not related to you."

Matthew dropped his hand to his side, and the smile disappeared from his face. Matthew glanced briefly at the man, then back at Rachel.

Senator Davis coolly observed Matthew and Rachel. Rachel looked into the man's eyes, but they seemed to burn right through her, and she turned away. Something about him tore at her heart, and she didn't know why. Her rattled emotions and kindled anger stopped her from thinking clearly.

Matthew seemed uncomfortable with the silence. "Am I correct in assuming you are Senator Davis?"

The man's solemn face was etched with a slight frown and showed little emotion. Yet something in his curt voice, his austere face, and his rigid demeanor rang familiar to Rachel. Senator Davis slowly nodded in response to Matthew's query and spoke with no emotion.

"I am Senator Davis, but I will be leaving the Senate this year."

Matthew gushed on in a drippy sweet voice. "We heard that the person who bought our land was a popular senator from Washington state, and we are so honored to . . . "

He was cut off abruptly by Senator Davis. "I'm a busy man, and I came here to see Martha Davis. Is she here?"

Rachel responded, "Yes, Mother Davis is here. She's in the kitchen at the back of the house."

Senator Davis turned directly to Matthew. "Would you mind getting her for me?"

Matthew nodded. "Won't you come into the house?"

Senator Davis shook his head and spoke sternly. "No. I'd prefer to stay here in the yard."

Throwing a quick glance at Rachel, Matthew headed toward the house. He knocked and demanded loudly of the children, "Unlock this door!" Then, with an embarrassed glance back over his shoulder at Senator Davis, he meekly added, "Please." The door remained latched until Rachel called to the children and told them it was okay. As soon as the door was open, Matthew disappeared into the house.

Senator Davis didn't move or say anything, and Rachel felt that, perhaps, she should also go into the house. Yet she could not move, struggling to understand her feelings. Senator Davis stood unmoving, keeping his back to her. Her anger started to ebb, and her mind started to focus. Suddenly, a memory sparked in her mind—a memory almost too painful to remember—a memory of a fateful, tragic decision she had made many years earlier. Her heart jumped as her breath came in a rush. Could it possibly be? Could she truly know this stranger?

It seemed impossible. What she had dreamed of and hoped for these many years could not be coming true. Or could it? Was her mind playing tricks on her because she wanted something so desperately? Surely that was it. She had harbored an impossible hope for so long that it had to be interfering with reality. Yet her heart told her it was he, the man she longed for, even as her mind questioned the plausibility of it.

She had to know. She spoke quietly, softly, almost under her breath, hoping that if she were wrong, he would ignore it. "Jacob?"

Slowly, deliberately, Senator Davis turned until his steely eyes again seemed to be looking right through her. After an awkward silence, he finally spoke in a voice that was quiet, stern, and free of emotion. "Rachel, it's been a long time."

At the sound of her name coming from his lips, the past memories flooded her heart with such force that she stepped forward to hug him before she even thought about what she was doing. He quickly stepped backward, away from her, and the disapproval showing on his face brought her to an abrupt stop.

"Rachel, I am married, and so are you."

Rachel wilted at the disdain in his voice as she spoke. "I'm not."

Her voice sounded strange, even to herself, as she trembled and tried not to cry.

The change in Jacob was instant, and confusion filled his voice. "You're not? But I thought that you must have remarried if . . . " He stopped mid-sentence as he looked toward the house, where Matthew had gone.

Rachel spoke quietly. "He left me for other women, and I would never take him back."

"But he was asking for money?"

"He found out that Mother Davis sold her house, and he feels he should have some of the money."

Jacob's face flushed red with anger. He didn't say anything, so she continued. "Jacob, a day hasn't gone by that I haven't regretted the decision I made those many years ago, and . . . "

He interrupted. "That's water under the bridge, and it's probably inappropriate to even speak about, considering the circumstances. I'm sorry about your divorce, but it's not my concern."

His coolness toward her was worse than if she had been slapped, but she was driven to explain more. "Actually, the divorce was the best thing that has happened to me in a long time. He never was faithful, and the children and I put up with his abuse for far too long. I was already planning to divorce him when he filed."

Then Rachel thought of something else. "Jacob, you said you thought I must have remarried. You knew I had divorced?" Jacob didn't even pretend that he planned to answer. Rachel wanted to pursue it further, but Matthew reappeared with Mother Davis, leading her by the hand until she was standing in front of Jacob. Matthew announced to her in a very businesslike manner, "Mother, this is Senator Davis, the man to whom you sold the house."

Mother Davis, leaning close, reached up to touch Jacob's face. "Jacob, is it really you?"

Jacob's whole demeanor softened. His voice was gentle and kind, and he smiled that smile the Rachel remembered well from so long ago. "Yes, Mother. It's me."

Matthew instantly became angry. "Jacob?" He stepped forward and shoved Jacob. Matthew stepped between Jacob and Mother Davis, snarling angrily, "How dare you come back here pretending to be

3

something you're not!"

He swung at Jacob, but Jacob sidestepped the blow, and in a quick motion, he grabbed Matthew's arm, twisted it, and threw him to the ground. Matthew was momentarily stunned but soon recovered and scrambled to his feet. "Why, you dirty . . . "

He took another swing, which was again blocked, and once more Matthew was thrown to the ground. This time, Matthew stayed there, cursing and making threats toward Jacob.

Jacob seemed unflustered as he looked down at Matthew. "I'm no longer intimidated by you or your threats, Matthew."

Suddenly the sheriff appeared. When Matthew saw him, he scrambled to his feet. "Sheriff, I want you to arrest this man for assault and battery."

The sheriff turned to Jacob and gestured toward Matthew. "Senator, would you like to have this man arrested for assault and battery?"

"Not me!" Matthew complained angrily, pointing at Jacob, "Him! Didn't you see the way he attacked me, throwing me to the ground?"

"What I saw," replied the sheriff, "is you attacking him, and him defending himself. Further, it's a felony to attack a U S senator."

Matthew's face flamed bright red with anger. "Stop with the U S senator stuff! Don't you know who this is? This is my stupid little brother, Jacob. He comes in here pretending he owns the place, pretending he's some great senator, and everyone believes him!"

"First," the sheriff said, "he does own the place. You sold your ranch, and he bought it, and your mother sold the house, and he bought it. He wasn't sure if you would cause problems, so he asked me to come out with him. He asked me to wait in my truck unless there appeared to be a problem. And, apparently, there is."

"I sold the ranch to some multimillionaire senator!" Matthew screamed. "Not to my stupid little brother!"

The sheriff seemed to be losing patience. "Your brother is that multimillionaire senator." He turned back to Jacob. "Senator, would you like me to make an arrest here?"

Jacob spoke as calmly as if he were visiting with a friend at a party. "Thanks, Sheriff, but not this time. I would like a report made, in case I have any further difficulty and need to press charges. I also plan to get a court order to bar him from trespassing on my property again."

Matthew was livid. "You can't stop me from coming out here! This is my wife and my family!"

Jacob turned to face him. "From what I understand, she is no

4

longer your wife. And from what I saw when I arrived, I think she would be better off without your visits."

"Even so, they are still my children!"

Rachel, who had been quiet until this time, finally spoke. "You gave up all visitation rights in order to avoid paying child support."

Matthew was very much a man who had always gotten his way. He stood there looking venomously at those around him. "What about visiting my mother?"

Rachel, feeling more confident, answered, "You have never come out here to visit, except to ask for money."

Again, Rachel saw Jacob bristle at the thought of Matthew's attempts to get money. Jacob spoke with authority. "We won't keep you from seeing Mother if you choose to take her to dinner or something. But you don't need to come here to do that." Then, turning to the sheriff, Jacob continued. "Sheriff, I'd appreciate it if you'd escort this man off of my property."

The sheriff grabbed Matthew's arm, but Matthew jerked away. "I can take care of myself!" He turned to Jacob. "If I had known it was you buying the ranch I never would have sold it!" With that, he stormed away.

The atmosphere seemed to soften dramatically after Matthew drove off. The sheriff shook his head. "I can hardly believe the two of you are brothers."

"Actually, Matthew made sure we can't legally make that claim anymore," Jacob said.

The sheriff looked at him quizzically, but Jacob just shrugged. "It's a long story."

Nodding, the sheriff returned to his own vehicle, which Rachel noticed was parked down the lane. The dust cloud blowing up from the road indicated his departure. After he left, there was an uneasy silence, as if no one knew quite how to proceed.

Finally, Jacob turned back to his mother. "Mother, I'm sorry about all of that."

She spoke softly. "Not as sorry as I am, Jacob. Somehow I always dreamed that he would welcome you back with open arms and that you could forgive him. But, in all reality, I knew it would probably be like this."

Rachel tried to help ease the tension by suggesting they all go into the house to visit. She desperately wanted to hear about the last eighteen years of Jacob's life, and to, in turn, share some of hers. He answered her cooly. "There is no need for that. I only came to visit with Mother."

His terseness with Rachel, in many ways, cut her deeper than any abuse she had received from Matthew. She knew she deserved Jacob's scorn, but she didn't deserve it from Matthew.

The tears Rachel could see welling up in Mother Davis's eyes matched the ones in her own. She couldn't blame Jacob, but somehow, when she had dared to dream of seeing him again, it hadn't been like this. She could not respond, nor dared she say more, fearing further rebuke. She was relieved when Mother Davis spoke.

"Please, Jacob. We understand how you feel, and we don't blame you, but it doesn't help." She paused briefly, and when Jacob didn't respond, she continued. "Won't you at least come in and meet the children? They *are* your niece and nephews."

"No, they aren't!" Jacob retorted. "I have no brother!"

"Jacob," Mother Davis answered quietly, "will you punish the children for the sins of their parents?"

No one said anything for some time, but when Jacob did speak, he was much more subdued. "Perhaps it wouldn't hurt to just say hello."

Mother Davis reached out her arm, and Jacob linked it through his and carefully led her back to the house. Rachel preceded them, glancing back over her shoulder now and then. Jacob's tenderness with his mother made her heart swell within her. Matthew had always been so callous and demanding of everyone, even his own mother. Rachel loved Mother Davis as if she had been her own mother, and she had even stood up for her against Matthew's abuse. Now, seeing Jacob's gentleness made her feel jealous.

But jealous of what or whom? She couldn't be jealous of Mother Davis. Was it possible she was jealous of Jacob's attention? Jealous of his kindness? Jealous of . . . was she jealous of his wife, whoever she was?

Rachel opened the door, and Jacob gently led his mother into the house. He paused and looked around, taking in his surroundings as if he were a man waking from a dream, unable to reconcile the imaginary with the real.

"It hasn't changed much," he said, seemingly as much to himself as to anyone else.

Rachel felt very self-conscious about her house. She considered that he, being a United States Senator, had probably been in some beautiful mansions and associated with people who were rich, famous, and powerful. With all of his money, his own home was probably elegant.

The children moved to stand by their mother, and Jacob's attention shifted to them. Pointing at the two oldest, Rachel introduced them. "Jacob, I'd like you to meet my two sons. This is John; he's eleven. And this is David; he's seven." Then she reached behind herself and gently pulled her little daughter into view. "And this is Emily. We call her Emmy. She's almost four."

Jacob smiled a big smile as Emily slid back behind her mother and peered shyly out at him. His smile reminded Rachel of how she remembered him.

Jacob knelt down and motioned to Emily. "Hello, young lady. You know what? I usually have something in my pocket for good little children."

He reached into his pocket and pulled out a Tootsie Roll, holding it out toward her. She looked up at her mother. Rachel nodded her permission, so Emily moved slightly toward him. He continued to speak softly. "I always wanted a pretty little daughter of my own. I have five sons but never got a girl."

She inched slowly, cautiously toward him. Rachel was afraid Emily would grab the Tootsie Roll and then scamper back, but Jacob encouraged her with his calm voice and steady gaze. As she took the candy from him, his kind smile seemed to take away her timidness. She looked directly at him and spoke calmly. "You stopped that mean man from hitting Momma. Are you her friend?"

Jacob shot a glance at Rachel as if he was unsure of what to say. Rachel wanted to answer and say that they were friends, but she did not know if Jacob would agree. She waited to see what he would say. He patted Emily on the head. "We used to be." He paused momentarily then spoke again. "But that was a long time ago."

Rachel had to bite her lip to keep it from quivering, hearing him speak of their friendship as long past.

Jacob continued. "Did you know that I knew your mother when she was just your age?"

Emily's eyes grew wide. "Really?"

"Yes. Is it hard to imagine that your mother and I were once your age?"

Emily just giggled, so he went on. "The first time I remember meeting her, I noticed that she had those unusually pretty blue eyes and long dark braids, just like you do. And she was just your size."

Emily looked back at her mother. "Really, Momma?"

Rachel nodded and Emily turned back to Jacob. "Wow! That must have been a long, long time ago."

Everyone else laughed, easing the tension in the room considerably. Rachel thought about how long it had been since she had heard Jacob's laugh and how nice it sounded.

Emily drew closer to Jacob, and he knelt on one knee, pulling her onto the other. She looked up at him. "What's your name?"

"Well," he said slowly, "I guess you can call me Uncle Jacob."

"Are you our father's brother?" John asked.

"No!" Jacob answered quickly. Then, a little slower, he added, "Not anymore."

John looked at his mother, but she just shook her head at him, warning him not to pursue it any further.

"Jacob," Mother Davis said, "why don't you stay for dinner?"

Jacob shook his head. "No, Mother. I just came out here for some business."

Mother Davis shook a scolding finger at him. "No business until after dinner."

"But, Mother, I don't think . . . "

"I am making homemade bread. It won't take long to cook, and we have raspberry jam."

Rachel could see Jacob wavering in his determination. He glanced at her and started to protest again, but Mother Davis interrupted once more.

"The bread dough is probably all over the counter by now. You just make yourself comfortable while I get it in the pans. It will take just a short time to rise. Doesn't homemade bread sound good?"

Before Jacob could even answer, she started back to the kitchen. As she did, he lifted Emily down, stood, and reached out touching Mother Davis's arm. "Mother, do you need help?"

She laughed. "I've lived in this house so long that I don't need to see to get around." She patted his arm. "Why don't you read a story to the children? They would like that. I used to read to them before I lost my sight."

Mother Davis shuffled off to the kitchen. Jacob looked at Rachel and shifted uneasily, so she told Emily to go get some books and then slipped in to help Mother Davis.

When she entered the kitchen, Mother Davis was efficiently punching down the bread dough, humming as she worked. Rachel knew this was a habit Mother Davis had when she was trying to ignore someone. Why was she trying to ignore her? Then it hit her. "Mother, you knew he was coming, didn't you?"

Mother Davis continued to hum. Rachel felt exasperated. "Mother, you did know, didn't you? How did you know he was coming?"

Mother Davis continued to work as she answered. "This is not the time, Rachel. We'll talk later."

Afraid her presence would make Jacob uncomfortable, Rachel only stole glances into the other room from the doorway. Emily was curled up in his arms, and John and David were sitting close while Jacob read. Seeing the four of them there together warmed her heart. She wished it could stay like this forever.

She stayed in the kitchen with Mother Davis while the bread rose and baked. The older woman stubbornly refused to talk about anything of importance, sticking to mindless chit-chat. Neither of them seemed inclined to approach Jacob as if so doing would drive him away. Rachel set the table, and when the bread was ready, she stepped to the door. She waited until Jacob finished the story before she called them.

Emily slid from his lap and grabbed his hand. "Come on, Uncle Jacob. You can sit by me." He smiled, but his smile faded quickly when he turned and saw Rachel.

They moved into the kitchen, and Emily guided him to a chair. As Mother Davis took the bread from the oven, Jacob stepped up to help her, but she gently told him he was a guest and should sit down.

He took his seat next to a smiling Emily. When everything was ready, Jacob bowed his head. John and David looked at their mother with uncertainty.

It had been so long since Rachel had been at a table where a prayer had been offered. Matthew had said anything religious was a waste of time, something only for those who were weak. Momentarily, Jacob looked up and glanced around the table questioningly.

Rachel knew of Jacob's strong feelings about God, and though she shared those feelings, she had raised her family without them, not wanting to endure Matthew's mocking. Now she felt intensely ashamed for that decision.

Mother Davis seemed to sense what was going on, and, as she often did, knew just what to do. "Jacob, it has been a long time since you've been in our home. Would you favor us by blessing the food?"

Jacob again bowed his head, and Rachel answered the questioning looks from her children by following suit.

Jacob offered a simple prayer that, to Rachel, seemed to be the most beautiful prayer in the world. Perhaps it was just because it was nice hearing him say it. When he finished, Emily said, "I liked that."

Jacob answered with a friendly pat on the head. When he looked up into Rachel's eyes, she turned away. Even with Matthew gone these last years, she hadn't tried to go to church or teach her children about God. She could sense that Jacob knew it. She could only guess what he thought of her.

Her uneasiness lessened considerably when Mother Davis pushed the bread in front of Jacob to have him cut it. The atmosphere of the room changed as the knife cut through the loaf and the comforting smell of warm bread wafted into the room. Emily wouldn't let anyone help her except Jacob, giving explicit instruction on buttering, applying jam, and quartering her slice. She said he did it just right. She kept up a constant chatter about everything from her favorite dolly to why she liked raspberry jam, even if the seeds got stuck in her teeth.

Rachel had never seen Emily so animated and friendly to someone she had just met. She obviously liked Jacob. He seemed fond of her, too. John and David seemed to like him as well, though it was hard to tell with Emily's incessant chatter. Rachel had hoped Jacob might talk about his own life, but he wasn't getting a chance, and finally, in exasperation, Rachel spoke in a slightly scolding tone. "Emmy, you need to eat your food and quit talking his ear off."

Jacob patted Emily on the head and teasingly pulled one of her pigtails. "It's okay. I like hearing Emily talk."

Emily then continued on unabated. At one point, when Emily had to take a breath, Rachel determined she'd try to get Jacob to share something about his life.

"So, Jacob, how did you get to be a senator?"

Jacob just shrugged. "It's a long story."

Her attempt to get him to talk was fruitless. He didn't seem inclined to open up. She knew it was because of her. She was on the outside of the wall he had built around himself. Emily took over the conversation again, leaving no other opportunity to make any more inquiries.

Rachel felt totally exasperated with Emily, and she wanted to get the children in bed so she and Mother Davis could talk with Jacob alone. She truly would have liked to have him to herself, but she knew he would never allow that.

As soon as dinner was finished, she told the children to get their pajamas on. "Oh, Momma," Emily complained, "do we have to?"

"Yes, Emmy, you have to."

"Can Uncle Jacob tell me a story and tuck me into bed?"

Rachel looked at Jacob questioningly. He smiled at Emily. "Sure. Why not?"

Emily brought him her pajamas, and he started to help her change. While he did, John asked, "How did you learn to defend yourself like you did against Father?"

Jacob seemed embarrassed by the question and just shrugged. "I took some Taekwondo and jujitsu classes in college. It saved my life once when I was attacked by an angry, knife-wielding constituent."

Rachel could see John admired Jacob's ability in this area, and it concerned her because John and David were too caught up with fighting. Jacob seemed to understand that as well because he spoke further.

"You know, John, I studied martial arts only as a means of defending myself and those I care about. I would never use it to attack someone else. A man should never do such a thing."

Rachel appreciated Jacob's words. He seemed to know a lot about her family, but how? She turned and saw Mother Davis smiling, and remembered her humming in the kitchen. She thought about Mother Davis selling her house to Jacob. Could she have been in contact with him these many years?

After Jacob slid Emily's nightgown over her head, he pulled her onto his lap. "Now, young lady, what story would you have me tell you?"

"Your favorite story from when you were little."

Jacob looked off as if thinking. "Well, let's see. One of my favorites was about a man in the Bible whose name was Jacob, just like mine."

"What's the Bible?" Emily asked.

Jacob turned and looked at Rachel before he answered. "The Bible," Jacob explained, "is a book about God."

Emily's eyes got big, and she said, "Oh!" as if she had just discovered something.

Jacob began to tell the story of Jacob's twelve sons and how Joseph was sold into Egypt. He told all that happened and how Joseph had stayed true to what he knew was right and how eventually he was able to save his family. When he finished, Emily said, "Joseph must have had a good mommy."

"Yes," Jacob answered. "He must have had a good mommy."

"What was her name?" Emily asked.

Jacob was quiet for a moment. He looked down at the floor as he responded. "Her name was Rachel."

Emily bounced up and down excitedly. "Hey, that's what Gran calls my mom!"

"Isn't that amazing?" Jacob answered. He patted Emily on the head. "I suppose that will just mean that you, John, and David will have to be like Joseph."

Trying to delay the inevitable bedtime, Emily begged for another story, but Rachel told her she needed the sleep. She quit complaining and started to giggle when Jacob hoisted her up onto his shoulders. He gave her a ride to the bathroom to brush her teeth then lifted her into his arms to carry her to bed. As he set her on her bed, he asked, "Do you want me to help you say your prayers?"

"What are prayers?" Emily asked.

Jacob's voice was warm as if speaking of an old friend. "Prayer is the way we can talk to God. We tell Him things, and He listens to us, and even though we can't see Him, He helps us."

"Has he ever helped you?"

Jacob brushed Emily's bangs back from her eyes. "Yes. Years ago, when I left here, I was much like Joseph, alone and discouraged, and God helped me. I don't know what I would have done without Him."

"Oh!" Emily said.

Jacob knelt by her bed, and she did likewise. He said a few words, and she repeated them. They continued this way until they finished. He then lifted her gently into bed. He tucked the blankets around her and sang her a lullaby.

When he finished, he kissed her forehead, and when he turned, he was smiling a serene smile, which faded the minute he saw Rachel. If he was trying in the slightest to hide how he felt about her, he wasn't doing a very good job.

Rachel sent John and David off to bed, after which she, Jacob, and Mother Davis returned to the living room. Rachel hoped she could finally hear about what had happened to him, but he clearly didn't want to stay and got right to the point.

"Mother, the reason I came here is to talk to you. I wanted to tell you that Anna and I are building a new home here, and it should be done by Christmas. We would like to have you come live with us. We are going to build on an apartment just for you. It will be entirely self-contained so that you can maintain your independence, but we will be there to help you if you need it."

"But Jacob," Mother Davis protested, "this is my home."

"Mother, the stairs are steep and hard for you to climb. This apartment would be all on the ground floor. You would be with family."

Mother Davis spoke sternly. "Jacob, I'm with family here!"

Jacob looked at Rachel, and she could almost read his thoughts and feelings from the frown on his face. He turned back to Mother Davis. "Mother, we wouldn't be far away, and you could visit anytime you . . . "

Mother Davis cut him off in mid-sentence. "Jacob, I don't want to go anywhere else. I know this is really your house now, and you could make me leave, but I would prefer to live here until I die. This is the home your father built for us, the home where I raised you and your brother. This is the home that has all of my memories. This is the home where Rachel and I have struggled for the last eighteen years. And especially with my eyesight gone, I don't want to go to some place unfamiliar."

"But Mother, the stairs are . . . "

"I don't mind the stairs. They make my heart feel good."

There was a long pause. Apprehension and loneliness crept into a corner of Rachel's heart. She didn't know what she would do if Mother Davis was gone. She had been such a good friend. Yet Rachel could also understand Jacob's feelings. For eighteen years he had had no family, and he surely still felt rejected by those who should have been his family.

Jacob was silent, and Mother Davis seemed to sense his feelings. She smiled kindly at him and spoke softly. "Jacob, please understand. I don't love you any less because I want to stay here. I am old and need to keep some semblance of normalcy in my life. Please don't make me leave."

Jacob sighed deeply. "Mother, I would never make you do anything you didn't want to do. You are free to live here as long as you like."

There was a question that was eating at Rachel. She was afraid to ask, but she knew she had to. "Jacob, where are you building your home?"

He looked directly at her and stiffly spoke the answer she was already too sure of. "We are building up on Pine Ridge, overlooking Jensen Lake. I have also bought the Jensen ranch from Camilla and much of the woods and ranches all around."

Rachel breathed short quick breaths to keep from crying. The memory of something that was to be hers, and that now would belong to another, choked her heart with a mixture of grief and jealousy. The next senseless question came out without her even thinking, words she actually spoke to hide her disappointment.

"Jacob, what other land do you own?"

Jacob's sudden, loud, angry response surprised her.

"Rachel, is that all you care about? Is your only concern how much property someone owns?"

"No, Jacob, I didn't mean . . . "

"Is a person worthless if he doesn't have money or farms or ranches? Is your friendship only purchased by the highest bidder?"

"Jacob!" Mother Davis spoke sharply. "That is enough!"

"You're right!" Jacob said, with sharpness of his own. "It is enough! Thank you for dinner. I must be going."

He stepped quickly to the door and almost jerked it from its hinges as he left. Rachel followed him out, her heart pounding in her chest. He walked briskly away, and she called after him. He stopped but did not turn to face her. She swallowed hard to get her voice to work. She had to speak. The words and feelings had welled up in her heart for so long, and if she didn't speak them after all of these years, she knew she could never look herself in the mirror.

"Jacob, I'm . . . " She swallowed hard again, but nothing could keep the tears from her voice. "I'm so very sorry about what I did."

He still refused to turn to face her but spoke into the night, almost as if to himself. "I guess it doesn't really matter anymore, does it?"

He started to walk away again, and she called after him. "Jacob! Jacob, stop! Please, stop!" He stopped but still refused to turn to her. The tears were now pouring down her face, and trying to hide her overwhelming feelings was futile. "Please, Jacob! I know that if there is anyone in this world who has a right to say I deserve what I got, it's you! But please don't. For eighteen years I have said it to myself. I still view you as the best friend I ever had, and I can't bear to hear it from you, too."

Jacob was quiet for some time, unmoving, still facing away from her. The silence was uncomfortable, but Rachel didn't dare say more. Finally, when Jacob did speak, his voice was quieter but still callous. "No one deserves what you've been through." He paused for a moment, then continued. "But no one deserves what happened to me, either."

With that, Jacob strode swiftly into the night, leaving Rachel sobbing on the porch.

Mother Davis's Secret

It took Rachel a long time to gain control of her feelings. When she finally did, she stepped back inside and quietly shut the door. Mother Davis was still in her chair, her knitting sitting on her lap, her hands idle, and tears coursing down her cheeks.

Rachel knelt down beside her and looked up at her. "You knew he was coming, didn't you?"

Mother Davis nodded. "Yes, but I didn't think it would be like this." She started to cry openly as she spoke. "Somehow I thought he would come back, and we'd all be so happy to see each other that . . . "

Her voice trailed off into sobbing. Rachel stood and put her arm around the elderly woman's shoulders. Mother Davis leaned against Rachel for some time. Finally, Rachel pulled up a chair facing Mother Davis.

"Mother, how did you know he was coming?"

"He wrote to me."

"He wrote to you? When? I never saw a letter."

Mother Davis shook her head. "He didn't send his letters here."

"Letters? You mean there was more than one?"

Mother Davis nodded. "I got the first one about a year after he left."

"How? Where did you get them?"

"About a year after Jacob left," Mother Davis explained, "he sent a letter to Camilla, asking that she not contact our family or let any of us know he had written. He asked her how his father was. When she wrote back and told him that his father had passed away, Jacob was heartbroken. He said he didn't blame his father for what he had done because he knew his father didn't really know what he was doing.

"His grief caused him to want to contact me, and Camilla agreed to be a go-between. One day, Camilla invited me over to visit. You can imagine the shock I had when Camilla gave me a letter from Jacob. In it, he told me he would continue to write and send letters through Camilla, but he said that if I ever told anyone else about him, especially Matthew or you, he would never write again."

Mother Davis paused briefly, and looked up at Rachel, then lowered her eyes again as she continued. "I wrote him back and promised

15

that I would never tell anyone else anything except Camilla. His letters have been sporadic, never more than a few times each year, and usually regarding some milestone in his family."

Mother Davis smiled. "I always knew Camilla had a letter when she called and said it was time for a visit."

Rachel could hardly believe what she was hearing. "Mother, all these years you knew where he was and what he was doing, and you never told me?"

"Rachel, I couldn't. I had promised him, and I always failed him before. Besides, I didn't know all that much. He told me only bits and pieces, and almost all of the information was about his wife and children."

"When did he marry?"

"The news of his wedding was the main reason for the first letter."

Rachel could hardly believe it. "So he must have married around seventeen years ago?"

Mother Davis nodded. "His first son was born about a year later, so his oldest would be about fifteen or sixteen."

"How did he get to be a senator?"

Mother Davis shrugged. "I didn't even know he was until recently. I knew he had purchased the farm, and when word got out that it was a senator who had bought it, I put two and two together. But he never wrote me anything about it. His letters were almost entirely about Anna and the boys."

"How did he know when my parents were killed in the car wreck?"

"I sent an overnight letter to him. He never shared his phone number with me."

A lot of things started to come together for Rachel. "That is how you knew there was a man who would buy your house and still let you stay in it, isn't it?" she asked.

Mother Davis nodded. "I knew we could trust Jacob. Even though he might not owe either of us anything, I knew he would help us. He paid almost twice what it appraised for to give us more to live on."

Rachel was quiet. She was exhausted by the gamut of emotions she had experienced, from fear of Matthew to sorrow from painful memories.

Mother Davis seemed to sense Rachel's frustration with her and spoke kindly. "Rachel, I'm sorry. I wanted to tell you. I know how badly you wanted to know. But I was so afraid that, somehow, Matthew would find out and punish us, or that Jacob would find out that I told you and quit writing."

Rachel took some deep breaths and tried to act like it didn't matter, though she knew it did. "So, what can you tell me about him?"

"Only a little. I'm not sure I can get it all straight. Perhaps, since you now know, it would be okay for you read his letters."

"You still have them?"

"Not here. I didn't dare. They are at Camilla's. We can get them tomorrow."

Rachel didn't think she could wait until tomorrow, but Mother Davis was tired, and stubbornly refused to talk more about it.

Rachel was glad she had the next day off from work. She got up to make breakfast, picking up the phone a half a dozen times to call Camilla, but each time she realized it was too early to be polite. Rachel decided that seven o'clock would be the earliest she should call, but by six thirty she could stand it no longer. Besides, she rationalized, Camilla had been a farmer's wife and was used to getting up early.

Camilla sounded cheerful, as usual, and agreed that Rachel could come read the letters, but only after Mother Davis got on the phone to tell her it was okay. Rachel had no sooner sent the boys to the bus then she was kissing Emily goodbye, leaving her in Mother Davis's care, and hurrying out the door herself.

When Rachel arrived at Camilla's house, Camilla looked as though she had been up for hours. The smell of cinnamon rolls filled the air. Camilla invited her to have one, but all Rachel could think of was the letters. "Surely you can eat one cinnamon roll," Camilla said.

Rachel loved Camilla. She was a sweet, elderly widow. She had been friends with her own mother, along with Mother Davis, since before Rachel was born. Rachel knew that once Camilla started talking, it might be a while before she could get away. But Camilla didn't seem in any hurry to get the letters, so Rachel agreed to a cinnamon roll, hoping it might hurry things along.

Rachel had to admit that the hot cinnamon roll, topped with brown sugar frosting and walnuts, along with a cold cup of milk, was really good. If it weren't for her anxious desire to read the letters, she could have enjoyed it more. Camilla settled in for a visit as if she didn't have a care in the world.

"That Jacob is a good young man. You know he bought our farm?"

Rachel nodded and Camilla continued. "With Ed's hospital stays, and his being in the nursing home those last years, I had lots of bills to pay, and I didn't know what to do. I finally knew I had to sell the farm, not knowing where I'd live. That good young man bought my farm, and he said I can stay here rent-free for as long as I want. Can you believe that? Of course, he made me promise not to tell anyone, especially you or Matthew, but I guess the secret's out now. I told Martha that he bought it, and that was what gave her the idea to sell her house to him. I understand that he paid twice what is was worth to give you something to live on."

Rachel nodded. It seemed that, once Camilla had found out that Rachel knew that Jacob had been in touch with her all those years, she had a lot to tell. Rachel asked Camilla what she knew of Jacob's life for the last eighteen years.

"Oh, I don't know. You'd have to read the letters for that. But I remember, once when he was a boy, he was . . . "

She continued on with stories of Jacob in his youth as if it were yesterday. Rachel began to fidget. She began to worry that it would be time for her boys to get home from school before Camilla ever let her see the letters. In the middle of one of her stories, the phone rang. She excused herself to get it.

Rachel could overhear Camilla's side of the conversation. "Yes, she's here . . . Right now . . . Okay, I'll tell her."

Camilla returned to her seat. "Martha says there is a man there, a lawyer, who was sent over by Jacob. She says you need to come home right away."

Rachel gasped at the thought of Jacob sending a lawyer, but her thoughts returned to the letters. "Camilla, can I take the letters with me so I can read them?"

"Well, I don't know. I'd have to ask Martha since she's the one who made me promise to keep them here."

A quick call to Mother Davis and permission was granted. Rachel, letters on the seat beside her, was soon hurrying down the road as fast as her rusty old car would go. Her thoughts were going much faster. What could Jacob be sending a lawyer for? Was he planning to make them move out of the house? He had said Mother Davis could stay as long as she wanted, and Jacob was always a man of his word. But did she really know Jacob anymore? He was so upset with her when he left. It must have something to do with that. And, since she needed to come home, he must be angry with her. Maybe he was going to ask them to start paying rent. She didn't know if they could afford that for very long. By the time she arrived home she had imagined so many terrible things, she expected only the worst.

When she hurried into the living room, a sharp-looking man in a business suit stood to greet her, introducing himself as James Briar of Briar and Thornton Law Office. She tried to act calm. "Is there some trouble?"

The man laughed. "Not for you."

His laugh and easygoing demeanor set her at ease, but it was Mother Davis who filled her in.

"Rachel, Jacob has asked this man to draw up papers to make sure Matthew doesn't come on the property and harass us again."

The way Mother Davis said it, Rachel knew it hurt her that such action had to be taken, though she sounded as if she was resigned to the fact that it was necessary.

"Yes," Mr. Briar added. "He wanted us to ask you if you would like a restraining order against Matthew so he can't bother you or your children at all."

A wave of relief swept over Rachel. Jacob was still the good man she had known. She felt ashamed that she had doubted him. "How much will it cost?"

"It won't cost you anything," Mr. Briar said. "Senator Davis will pay for it. But it could take up to a week to get it before a judge."

Rachel happily agreed to it even though she could see the sadness in Mother Davis's eyes.

Mr. Briar asked lots of questions. He had to know what kind of harassment had taken place along with many other details. She also had to sign a sworn testimony.

Mr. Briar stood to leave. "There really shouldn't be a problem getting this in place. Both Senator Davis and the sheriff signed statements saying they had witnessed the harassment. You will get a call from our office when it has been served to your ex-husband."

As he reached the door, he turned back to Rachel. "You know, you're lucky to have Senator Davis for a friend."

Rachel nodded, but she wondered if Jacob actually thought of her as his friend. She knew he was a man who always tried to do the right thing. Perhaps that was the only reason he was doing it.

After Mr. Briar left, Rachel mentioned that she wanted to read the letters from Jacob, so Mother Davis offered to keep Emily from disturbing her. Rachel went into her room and shut the door. She organized the letters according to date and started to read.

The first letter was addressed to Camilla, as Mother Davis had said. From there she read bits and pieces of Jacob's life, beginning with his marriage to Anna. Rachel could tell from his letters how much he loved Anna. Rachel read about the birth of their first son, Abraham, one year later. Then, in almost three-year intervals after that, there were Isaac,

Joseph, Peter, and James. Rachel calculated their ages. They would be from about sixteen down to four.

His letters were almost all just facts. He obviously loved his family and was proud of them, but he never shared feelings or thoughts. She sensed that he had built a wall between himself and his family and friends in Minnesota made of the bricks of hurt and loneliness he felt, and she felt heart-wrenching anguish knowing she was responsible for most of those bricks.

Mother Davis was right; the letters were only regarding milestones in their family. But they hardly said anything about Jacob at all. There was nothing about his work or life other than a quick mention that he met Anna at college. They didn't say anything about his being elected a senator, or anything like that.

Rachel did note the return address change from Washington state to Washington, D.C. after six years, but there was nothing more. When she finished, she knew a fair amount about Jacob's family, but very little about his life. What had happened to him? How had he made his money? How had he become a senator in such a short time after leaving home, all while raising a family?

She went to Mother Davis with some of her questions, but she had no more answers than what the letters already told.

"You can bet," Mother Davis said confidently, "that he earned his money in an honest way." Rachel knew Mother Davis was right, but questions continued to plague her. She just had to find out more.

Determined to find additional information, she promised Emily an outing to the library. She knew she could have Internet access there. Once at the library, Rachel Googled "Senator Davis Washington."

There were thousands of links about him, but most of it was regarding his voting record. He had been a congressman before becoming a senator. He was apparently very popular in both positions, though some big interests didn't like him. He was given the highest rating for ethics and couldn't be bought. She found an article questioning why he would not be running again at the peak of his career. He had said it was for personal reasons but said no more. Rachel assumed that it was because his mother was getting older and he felt he needed to be with her.

Rachel also found an article regarding Jacob's family, meaning his parents and siblings. He had only said he had no family, and apparently no one had looked any deeper. He had been so popular that no one expended much effort to dig dirt on him. Interestingly, they turned their attention to his wife, Anna. Her family seemed to be highly respected.

Rachel read many articles about Anna's family. She tried to tell herself it was just out of a desire to know, but she couldn't avoid the feelings of jealousy that made her hope to find something that would cause her to dislike Anna. But she could find nothing.

With her curiosity only mildly satisfied, Rachel wanted to continue her search, especially to see if she could find a picture of Jacob's family, but he had somehow managed to protect his family from the public. She felt somewhat embarrassed that she wanted so desperately to learn about him. He was married, she reminded herself, and she needed to get over her feelings for him.

She checked her watch. Emily was getting restless, having missed her afternoon nap, and the boys would be getting home from school soon. Reluctantly, Rachel logged off.

Pine Ridge

Jacob had a way of getting things done. Before the end of the week, Rachel had received the phone call telling her the restraining order was in place. In addition, men in heavy equipment had started building a winding lane along the stream that ran up to Pine Ridge. Obviously, no expense was spared. Gravel was hauled in, and Rachel could tell they were preparing it to be paved. A tidy white fence was built along one side, while half-grown trees were planted on the other.

Before the road was even finished, construction on the house had begun. The night after they started digging the hole for the foundation, Rachel took an evening stroll up the hill. Mother Davis seemed to understand Rachel's feelings about the new house and helped distract Emily so Rachel could slip off without her.

Rachel walked slowly along the path that wound from her house through the meadow and up to the ridge. She had traversed it many times over the past eighteen years to reminisce, but now it had more significance. She knew she would not be able to go up there much longer.

When she arrived at the top of the hill, she found the spot where she and Jacob had laid out their blanket for that picnic many years before. She was glad the house was being built far enough away that this spot was not yet disturbed. She sat down and looked out over the lake and listened to the sounds of the evening, the music of nature. Suddenly her churning emotions boiled over, and she started to sob, her tears flowing freely.

The memories flooded back as if it had been yesterday. She remembered sitting there on that blanket with Jacob's arm around her. He had told her his dad had promised him this piece of ground overlooking Jensen's Lake and assured her that he was going to build them a home right there. She had leaned against him, and together they had watched the orange glow of the setting sun.

She recognized that she had come up there all those times over the past years to try rekindling the feelings of that day, trying to erase the pain from the mistake she had made. Indeed, there was a home going in now, and it belonged to Jacob, but she wasn't going to be part of it. It would belong to someone else, just as he did.

She was again up on the ridge watching the sun set, but this time she watched all alone— alone with the big equipment and her regrets. Her heart was heavy as she returned from the ridge that night.

She wandered up there every night after that. She knew she was trespassing, but she went anyway. In the long shadows of the evening, she walked around the skeleton of the house, trying to imagine what it would be like. The builders seemed to be hurrying to get it framed in before winter. As the walls rose, she meandered through the rooms trying to imagine the purpose for each one, pretending it was her house, and she was hosting a party.

There was one vast room that she imagined would handle banquets, musical performances, or dancing. Her mind wandered back to the first formal dance Jacob had taken her to. That was the first time he told her that he loved her. Since their families' farms adjoined and their mothers were friends, it had been natural that they'd become playmates at an early age.

Jacob, almost two years her senior, always sought her out at recess even though he was teased for playing with her. He was her best friend, and she was his.

She could remember him standing up for her against a whole group of much older boys who had been bullying her. He fought them all, and though he was outnumbered and severely beaten, he stood his ground, and the other boys eventually backed down and left her alone.

She and Jacob had been an inseparable duo. She recalled their tree house in the big oak behind her house where they had played for years, even pretending they were husband and wife.

Her mind snapped back to that first formal dance again. He had come to pick her up, looking so handsome. He had told her she was beautiful, which made her feel beautiful. He had always treated her like a queen, and he had always been the perfect gentleman. Everyone, including Rachel, had expected them to marry right after she graduated.

But then Jacob's father had started developing dementia, which created a serious problem. Mr. and Mrs. Davis had tried for ten years to have a child, and when Matthew had finally come, they had been so excited. They had given him everything. When Jacob was born ten years later, Matthew hated sharing the attention and despised Jacob. Matthew always made life miserable for Jacob, taking everything from him that he cared about. Their father's dementia gave Matthew the perfect opportunity. He tricked their father into signing the farm over to him. Luckily, the house was in their mother's name or he would have had that, too. Matthew took everything, leaving Jacob with nothing, not even the promised property on Pine Ridge.

But there was one thing that meant more to Jacob than anything else, and Matthew couldn't take that. That was Rachel. She could vividly recall when Matthew started bringing her presents and seeking her company. She was flattered to have the attention of a man twelve years older than she was. She had recognized that it was merely for the satisfaction of taking her away from Jacob, yet she allowed it to continue.

She could well remember Jacob begging her not to go with Matthew or to take his presents. But she had eight brothers and sisters, and her family had had so little money that the presents were too tempting to turn down. She also realized that if she married Jacob, they would have nothing to start out on. She had grown up with little money, and she desired more. Jacob had pledged his love and promised her that he would take care of her, but she held back from committing to him.

Inexplicably she had reveled in Jacob's jealousy, feeling powerful and in complete control—as if she were the master of it all.

Confused, Jacob again begged her not to go with Matthew, saying he could not stand to watch it and would leave, not returning until he was married to someone else. Doubting he would ever truly leave her, she had challenged it and even teased him that it was an idle threat. Her own mother had pleaded with her to reconsider what she was doing, saying that she was unfairly playing with Jacob's feelings, fearing the consequences might be grave. Her mother loved Jacob and didn't like Matthew. Rachel ignored the warnings, empowered by the attention of the two men.

Truthfully, she had never thought she would marry anyone but Jacob. He had always been her best friend, and she had never had the same feelings for anyone else.

She would never forget the night she let Matthew kiss her. He had brought her such expensive gifts and was so demanding. She hadn't been excited about the kiss—in fact, it disgusted her. But, when she turned and realized that Jacob had seen it, she felt ashamed, and she knew she had made a big mistake. Devastated, Jacob stormed out of the house. She considered running after him but was too ashamed and embarrassed. Oh, how she wished she had. She decided that she would apologize to him when she saw him the next day.

But that opportunity never came. Typically he would come over to her house at six o' clock, right after work. But six o' clock came, then seven o' clock, then eight o' clock, and still Jacob hadn't come. When she called his home, Jacob's mother tearfully said he had left and that even she didn't know where he had gone. She said that all he mentioned was something about going off to college somewhere far away.

The searing memory of that night haunted Rachel. Something would trigger a pleasant memory of Jacob only to be dashed to pieces by the flashback of that kiss, that horrible, horrible kiss—a careless, foolish indiscretion that had wiped out so many wonderful hopes and memories, replacing them with nauseating pain.

Rachel tried to find Jacob. She talked to every one of his friends but learned nothing more than the fact that he had boarded a bus heading west, and that was the last anyone had seen of him. She did everything she could think of to find him, but the deed had been done, and Jacob was gone.

It angered Matthew that she was trying to find Jacob. Matthew's whole demeanor toward her changed. He gloated and treated her like he owned her. He no longer asked what he wanted but demanded. She no longer felt in control of anything. Without Jacob she was lost and afraid, uncertain and confused. With him she had been sure, vivacious, and strong.

Her parents tried to talk her out of having anything to do with Matthew, and though she wished him out of her life, she was afraid of him. One night, when her parents were gone, he came to her home and forced her to go with him.

She had wanted to get out of the car and run, but he had threatened her. He drove them more than three hundred miles away to a wedding chapel. It was a nightmare. They were married by a justice of the peace with no family present. She had paused when she was asked if she would take Matthew as her husband, but his hand clenched her arm tightly, scaring her into saying yes.

After the ceremony was even worse. She felt used and dirty. Matthew thought of her as nothing but an object for his pleasure. She didn't love him, and she knew he didn't love her. Though her parents seemed resolved to what had happened and tried to accept him as their son-in-law, it was hard for them because he was so disrespectful and mean to them. And he seldom let her visit her family.

Unlike Jacob, who was extremely industrious, Matthew wouldn't work for anything. He still lived with his parents and moved Rachel in there as well. They had only been married a month when he started spending nights with other women. She could remember the first time he hit her. He hadn't come home for two days, and when she questioned him about it, he hit her and told her it was none of her business. She wished she had left him then, but she was too ashamed and wondered where she could go. She was also afraid of what Matthew would do to her.

In order to buy food she had to get a job, and all she could find was work as a checker at the grocery store. Each time she received her paycheck, Matthew took it, complaining it was not enough for all of the things he wanted, accusing her of taking too many days off from work. He would spend it frivolously, and she struggled to pay the bills with what little he left her.

She often wondered what it would have been like if she had married Jacob. Once, when she suggested to Matthew that Jacob would not have treated her as poorly as he did, Matthew struck her over and over and forbade her from mentioning Jacob again. But all of the threats in the world couldn't stop her from thinking and dreaming about him.

She dreamed that Jacob would come and whisk her away with him. But reality always set in, and she knew that, even if Jacob came back, he wouldn't take her. Ignoring the obvious, she still yearned for the impossible.

She and Matthew had been married for less than a year when Father Davis died. She had hoped beyond hope that Jacob would be at the funeral, but he wasn't. She doubted that he even knew about it. She wondered where Jacob was and what he was doing. She wondered what he thought of his own family. His own father, even though he wasn't in his right mind, had signed the papers disinheriting him and disowning him. His own mother had not stood up for him, backing down to Matthew's demands. And his own brother had taken from him everything that he cared about. However, Rachel knew that she was the greatest disappointment of all to Jacob, for she was what he cared about most, and what she had done was the reason he left.

Rachel loved Father Davis. She and Mother Davis had lovingly tended to his needs as he had become totally unable to take care of himself. But as much as she loved him, her tears on the day of the funeral were more for Jacob and herself than for Father Davis.

She felt so completely alone that day. The man she truly loved and hoped would be there was not. And Matthew didn't even stick around to be with the family after the funeral. He was off somewhere or with someone; she hardly dared guess. A few members of her own family came, and they were some support, but her loneliness and disappointment were almost unbearable.

She should have left Matthew then, but she had grown to love Mother Davis and was worried about leaving her alone with Matthew.

It was a lot of years before she and Matthew had children, probably because he was gone most nights. She had the mistaken idea that a child might make him love her and even make her love him, but it just made things worse. He was furious when he found out she was pregnant, beating her both physically and in spirit. The night John was born, Matthew was out with another woman, so she clung to her mother and Mother Davis.

She tried to avoid pregnancy after what happened when John was born. When she found out she was pregnant with David, she was too frightened to tell Matthew. She waited so long to tell him that she couldn't hide it any longer. When she did tell him, he unleashed his fury, beating her mercilessly. He claimed the baby wasn't his and accused her of being with someone else. How angry that made her! He knew it wasn't true, and it was so hypocritical when he was the one that was unfaithful.

Mother Davis tried to intercede on Rachel's behalf and was beaten, too. Rachel wanted to file charges against him, but Mother Davis begged her not to. Matthew, scared that she might, brought her all sorts of presents and promised he would be better, a promise that lasted only a few days.

When David was born, Matthew was again off with someone else. Mother Davis and Rachel's mother were again her only support. But that was the last baby Rachel's mother was to see born. A few years later, just after she became pregnant with Emily, her parents were killed in a car wreck.

When Matthew came to her parents' funeral, all of his conversation centered around whether there was any inheritance. Rachel's brothers and sisters either totally despised Matthew or were afraid of him. He was so controlling that he would hardly let her talk to them. She had Mother Davis, John, and David, but there was still an empty spot in her heart. She couldn't help but think of Jacob. He had loved her parents, and they had loved him.

She harbored a glimmer of hope that he would come, but he didn't. But there was something. Her sister, Marie, brought it to her attention. She quietly moved Rachel away from Matthew and pointed out a beautiful rose plant that was in full bloom. It was the most beautiful flower at the whole funeral. The card took her breath away. It said, "For all the love you gave me, and for being like parents to me as a boy. I send my love. Jacob Davis."

"Jacob!" she gasped.

Matthew immediately turned. "What did you say?"

Marie slipped the card into her pocket. "She said Janob. It's a new type of All-American rose. Isn't it beautiful?"

Matthew was suspicious, and Rachel saw him looking for a card, but when he didn't find one, he let it go. Marie later whispered to her, pointing at the rose, "I think you should take that one home and plant it."

Rachel thanked her. "But maybe you could keep it for me until Matthew forgets about it," she replied.

Marie agreed.

The funeral was a wonderful tribute to the great lives of Rachel's parents. Everyone who knew them loved them—everyone except Matthew. He knew they didn't feel he treated their daughter well, even though Rachel had told them very little about the abuse. They just knew.

Rachel's mind kept wandering off during the service. Jacob had sent flowers. Where was he? Was he married? What was he doing? It had been almost fourteen years. What had happened to him? How had he found out about the funeral? She hardly dared ask her brothers and sisters if they knew anything for fear Matthew would find out. Marie checked for her but found no information.

Just knowing that Jacob had sent flowers, that he was still alive, that he knew of things there, gave her strength. This knowledge also gave her courage, and she determined she would divorce Matthew. She was petrified to tell him that she was pregnant again, but she was even more afraid that her sons would grow up to be like him. John was seven and had already exhibited signs of being a school bully, acting out what he had seen from his father.

She was ashamed she hadn't left Matthew the first time he struck John. John was only two and was crying, and Matthew hit him for it. When she threatened to call the police, Matthew became angry and threatened her, but he eventually became scared and cried and promised that it wouldn't happen again. But it did happen again, over and over, and it was always the same. Why hadn't she found the courage to stand up for her sons when she had been angry at Mother Davis for not standing up for Jacob?

When Matthew found out about John's problems at school, he would hit him and order him to stop hitting other kids. Rachel pointed out that it was hypocritical to hit John to try to teach to him stop hitting others, but Matthew slapped her for daring to question him.

Shortly after the funeral, when the family was trying to decide what to do with their parents' property, Matthew demanded that it be sold so each could have their share. Some wanted to rent it so they could come back home to the old farmstead now and then. Matthew became loud and obnoxious until the others gave in. Marie later told her that many in the family agreed to the sale because they didn't want to deal with Matthew in the future.

The farm was purchased almost immediately after it was put up for sale. Rachel had cried the day she and her brothers and sisters cleaned out the old house and divided up things. Matthew said, "Only take things we can sell and not some stupid sentimental junk." By the time they were done, her brothers and sisters and their spouses would have nothing to do with her or Matthew, and she couldn't blame them.

True to form, Matthew was angry about the things she had chosen from her parents' home. They were simple things that meant a lot to her. What probably angered him most was that he was sure some of them were tokens of Jacob's love for her parents and for her. Matthew destroyed almost everything, showing no concern for her feelings. And then, when the forty-thousand-dollar check came, her inheritance from the sale of her parents' farm, he took it from her. It was written to her, so Matthew beat her until she gave it to him, and then he illegally signed her name to it so he could cash it. She had planned to use the money to buy clothes for her children, pay bills, buy food, and purchase other things they so desperately needed.

Left with two black eyes, a bloody nose, and no inheritance, she went to Mother Davis and told her of her plans to divorce Matthew. At first, Mother Davis tried to dissuade her, but Rachel was adamant that it was wrong to let Matthew continue to strike David and John, and Mother Davis had to agree. When Matthew returned from cashing the check, he brought presents to try to appease Rachel. But she threw them back at him and told him to get out of the house.

When Rachel worked up the courage to file for divorce, she found he again had the upper hand. He was always more interested in money than anything else, and he was afraid she would end up getting half of the farm. He reasoned that if he filed for divorce first, she would have no right to anything.

He also had money for a lawyer and she didn't. Ironically, it was her inheritance money he used. He told her he would take the children if she tried to get any money from him. Wanting to get him totally out of her life, she agreed that she wouldn't go after any property if he would give up all rights to the children and never come around again. He wasn't interested in the children anyway and readily agreed, even giving up visitation rights. She was careful to include in the deal the baby with which she was pregnant. Her sole concern was for her children, and Matthew knew it and used it to his advantage. The divorce was finalized out of court, with him having all of the money and her having sole custody of the children.

Matthew sold the farm immediately, still afraid that Rachel might be able to get part of it. She was brokenhearted to see it sell, but not as much as Mother Davis was. She cried and cried about it. But then, strangely, she was over it and never said another word about it.

Rachel now realized that Jacob had gotten word to his mother that he had purchased the family farm. What would Rachel have thought if she had known that, in some ways, Jacob was so close, even though he was so far away? She thought about him every day and often talked to Mother Davis about him.

The next few years were hard. Rachel continued working her job as a checker at the grocery store, which paid minimum wage with no benefits. As she gained weight with Emily, her feet hurt from standing all day. She tried to keep her emotions in check, fearing she'd be fired if she didn't. But at night, all alone, she cried. Many times it was while she was sitting on Pine Ridge. She didn't miss Matthew at all, but she cried for what could have been, and she knew she was actually crying for Jacob.

When Emily was born, she took only a week off from work without pay because the medical bills had mounted up. Camilla came that night to watch the boys so Mother Davis could be in the hospital with Rachel, but Rachel desperately missed her own mother. Even more, she missed Jacob, and when beautiful little Emily was placed in her arms, she remembered crying softly, wishing that this little daughter could have been his.

As the next few months rolled on, she began to find renewed strength. She realized Matthew had not just beaten her, but he had beaten down her self-esteem. She started gaining more resolve and determination to raise her children appropriately. She started trying to teach them right from wrong, though she didn't bring religion into it. Somehow, deep in her heart, she knew she needed to start taking them to church, praying, and doing other religious things, but she felt God had abandoned her. As she thought about it now, she realized it was she who had abandoned God.

She did everything she could to take care of her family, but the bills kept mounting. The hospital expenses for Emily's birth seemed to put them into an ever downward spiral. She had to skimp on almost everything. She knew part of her sons' problems at school were from the teasing they received because of their poor clothes, but she had no money to buy them more. She tried to stitch their clothes as best she could, but more than once she cried when the boys came home with black eyes, feeling it was her fault.

To make matters worse, there were back taxes on the house, and the state was threatening to take it from them. In the midst of this crisis,

Mother Davis proposed selling the house. Rachel was frightened. The house, with its rickety outbuildings, wasn't worth much because of years of neglect and disrepair, but it was all they had. Rachel asked her where they would live. Mother Davis seemed unflustered, saying she knew of a man who wanted to buy the house and outbuildings for the land and would allow them to still live there.

Rachel thought Mother Davis was confused. Why would anyone do that? But Mother Davis assured her it would be okay; he just wanted to secure the property so no one else could buy it. Mother Davis would not divulge his identity and simply said, "He is the same man who bought the farm."

Rachel couldn't understand why Mother Davis trusted the man and tried to dissuade her, but her mind could not be changed.

The sale took place, and Rachel was sure someone would come and tell them they had to move, but that never happened. And when Mother Davis told her how much they received from the sale, Rachel was shocked.

They put the money into an account from which Rachel paid all of the bills. She could see the money going fast and tried to be careful. She bought the children a few new clothes, but not many. They grew so fast that clothes didn't last them long.

Things turned around for a while after that. But then Mother Davis's eyesight started to fail. They spent quite a bit of money trying to help her, but it was to no avail.

It had been almost four years since Rachel had seen Matthew, when he suddenly showed up. He had found out his mother had sold the house, and he felt he was entitled to some of the money. Rachel told him to get off of their property or she would call the sheriff. He had left, but not without some threats of his own. Her threat to call the sheriff deterred him for a short time, but she knew he'd be back.

She was afraid and didn't know what to do. For the first time in a long time she started praying to God for help, but she actually wondered if he would help her after all she had done.

She was right about Matthew not being deterred. It wasn't long before he was back. She saw him pull into the yard, told her children to lock the door and stay in the house, and went out to confront him. He was more threatening than ever, but she knew she needed the money for her children, for Mother Davis, and to continue paying mounting hospital bills. At that point, she didn't know that Mother Davis had already given him most of what was left. If Rachel had known, she would have been even angrier.

31

That was when it happened. She told him to get off of their property, and he retorted that it obviously wasn't hers, or even Mother Davis's for that matter, because he knew it had been sold. She said as long as the new owner allowed them to stay, it was theirs, and if Matthew didn't leave she would call the sheriff. He raised his hand to hit her and, suddenly, there was Jacob.

Not knowing immediately who he was, she was stunned to think a total stranger would stand up for her. When he said it was his land, she felt a sudden surge of gratitude to this man who had already shown such kindness by allowing them to stay in the house.

When she realized who he was, and he spoke her name, eighteen years of emotion flooded through her. For that whole time she had hoped and dreamed of his coming home and of her falling into his arms, but he had squelched her impulse to hug him and shown he detested her and the memory of her.

Rachel's thoughts returned to the present. She looked at the house that she was standing in, this new house that would belong to Jacob and his family, and suddenly the thought that it could have been hers overpowered her, and she sank to the dusty floor and sobbed. She sobbed until her whole body was exhausted.

When there were no more tears left in her, she knelt there in the stillness of the night and did something she had only recently started doing. She prayed.

"Dear God, I know I don't have a right to expect Jacob to love me anymore. I know he is married to someone else. I know that it is probably too much to expect him to ever think of me as his friend again. But, God, please help him to at least not hate me. Please. I just can't bear it."

She couldn't say any more. She had spoken the prayer from the depths of her heart, more than ever before in her life. She wondered if God felt about her like Jacob did since she had turned her back on him, too. She lay there on her back in the house, looking at the twinkling stars. She stayed there for a long time.

Her heart gradually grew calm in the serenity and the stillness of the evening, and she felt that God had heard her.

Anna

Rachel kept a vigil on the house on Pine Ridge, watching the walls climb higher as her spirits sank lower. Soon it was closed in, and she couldn't go inside anymore, yet after tucking her children into bed each night, she made her way up there to look in the windows. It was going to be a beautiful home, though it was smaller and simpler than she expected it to be considering how rich she had heard Jacob was.

When she wasn't at work, she watched the workers coming and going all day. It seemed that half of the county was up there at one time or another. Rachel had doubted it could be ready by Christmas as Jacob had indicated, but she changed her mind as she watched the frenzied pace of work on the hill.

Landscaping was being done right up until the time the ground froze in late November. Fences had been erected, and shade trees, shrubbery, and an orchard had been planted. Nothing was landscaped right next to the house yet since lots of equipment came and went. A large area was leveled and left bare, leaving Rachel to wonder what it was for.

She often stole moments to spend in their picnic area from long ago. She was afraid that during all of the construction it would be changed or destroyed, but it was left untouched.

As Christmas approached, the pace quickened still. She came home from work about a week before Christmas and saw a furniture truck near the house. It made two more trips that evening, and when she looked in the window, she saw that the house contained shiny new appliances, couches, chairs, and big screen televisions.

Jealousy tugged at her heart. She couldn't remember ever having a new appliance. Every one she had purchased had been found in the want ads or at a thrift shop. Her stove had one plate that didn't work and one that only got warm. Her washer rattled as if it would fall apart, and she had to dry clothes on a drying rack because her dryer had quit altogether. Her living room furniture had been there since before she had. The chairs were worn, and the couch leaned to one end. She tried telling herself it didn't matter, but she knew it did. She would have loved having something better. She had hoped to buy a few things with the money from the sale of the house, but with all of the bills and with Matthew taking much of it, that dream was gone. Rachel was furious that Mother Davis had given in to Matthew and given him money, but by the time Rachel found out, it was too late.

Just a few days before Christmas, a heavy snow fell. The next day, a commercial lighting company came and hung Christmas lights. That bothered Rachel more than anything. The lights, shimmering around the house and bouncing off of the bright snow, made it look homey. Before that she had been able to tell herself it was just another house. But as she walked around it that night, with it all lit up and sparkling, she felt a tightness in her chest that seemed to choke the air out of her.

Pressing her nose against the window, she saw wreaths and garland draping everywhere, stockings already hanging over the fireplace, and a tree standing in the corner with gifts stacked high under it. Each one was beautifully wrapped in bright, colorful paper with a bow on top.

She didn't stay long that night. She couldn't stand the way she felt.

When she walked into her own house, it was all she could do to stem the tears that were welling up in her eyes. Mother Davis set aside her knitting. "Well?"

Trying to act cheerful, she replied, "It looks like it's done. I'd say we should be welcoming neighbors any day."

Mother Davis seemed to sense that Rachel needed some time alone and excused herself to go to bed. Rachel looked over at her own pathetic Christmas tree. It was more of a shrub than a tree. She had salvaged it from the discard pile at the tree yard. It was so dry she didn't dare turn on the ugly old string of red lights for fear it would catch fire. She wasn't sure it would have a single needle left on it by Christmas.

The few presents beneath it were wrapped in newspaper, and all of their contents had been given to her or were purchased at a secondhand store. She gently touched a branch on it, and it was so brittle that it broke off into her hand. She dropped to her knees and sobbed. After some time, struggling to gain control of herself, she wiped away her tears. She felt funny. She felt almost as if she hated Jacob and his family. But how could she hate him? This wasn't his fault. She had made the decisions that brought her to this point. And she didn't even know his wife. How could it be her fault?

The next day, December twenty-third, there was no school. She arrived home late to a doorway full of children bubbling over with news. Emily didn't even wait for Rachel to reach the house but threw the door open and ran out to greet her.

"Mommy, there was a moving van and cars and everything up at Uncle Jacob's house! I think they're here!"

Rachel could see two cars and a pickup near the well-lit house. She was sure Emily was right.

Early the next morning, Jacob was at their door. Rachel greeted him pleasantly, but he was all business. "Hello, Rachel. Is Mother here?"

She nodded and offered him a seat, but he said he wouldn't be long. When she returned with Mother Davis, he was kneeling down chatting with Emily.

"Uncle Jacob, we saw your house being built!"

He smiled. "Oh, really?"

"Yes. Momma would go up there every night to look at it after we were in bed."

Rachel felt a flood of embarrassment wash over her as Jacob raised his eyes to look at her. He then turned back to Emily. "Did she like it?"

"Yeah. But she said it was far too pretty for a normal person to live in."

Rachel wished she could find a hole to crawl in and hide. Jacob just patted Emily on the head. "Well, you come up and visit us sometimes in our *too pretty* house, won't you?"

Emily nodded enthusiastically. Jacob stood and stiffly asked, "Rachel, could I have a word with Mother? Alone?"

Rachel led Emily by the hand into the kitchen. She didn't mean to listen in on Jacob's conversation with his mother, but the walls of the old house were thin and held no secrets.

"Mother," Jacob said. "We would like to have you come up for Christmas."

"What about Rachel?" Mother Davis asked.

"She can get by without you for a day."

"You know very well that is not what I meant. You have Anna and your family, but Rachel needs me. I don't think I want to go any place she is not welcome."

Jacob's voice rose slightly. "Mother, if you don't want to come to my house, just say so."

Mother Davis's voice sounded as if she might cry. "Jacob, you know that is not what I meant. I know you feel we deserted you, and I so want to meet your family. But what family you still have you are now deserting."

Jacob's voice was terse. "Oh, this is my fault now, is it? She chose what she wanted all of those years ago, and it wasn't me. Now it's my fault because I don't choose to spend time with her?"

"Jacob, she is sorry for what happened. She's been through

35

enough. Can't you see that? Why can't you forgive her? And what about the children? They should be able to meet their cousins and their aunt. They admire and love you—especially Emily. How do you think they feel when they see the way you act toward their mother?"

"I wouldn't mind having the children come. But when I am around her, the painful memories come back. I don't see why I should be expected to have my Christmas ruined."

"And I suppose Anna feels the same way?"

Jacob's took a deep breath, and his voice was suddenly subdued. "No. Anna is excited to meet everyone. Strangely, Rachel most of all."

"Then why don't you let her?"

Jacob didn't even answer. From her place in the kitchen, Rachel could see him, instead, step to the door. "I'll just tell her you declined."

With that, he walked outside. Rachel stepped into the living room and could see the tears rolling down Mother Davis's wrinkled cheeks. Summoning all of her inner strength, Rachel ran out the door and called after him.

"Jacob! Jacob, please stop!"

Jacob stopped, but as before, he didn't turn to face her.

"Jacob," she said, "I understand how you feel about me, but please, don't take it out on Mother Davis and my children. Please invite all of them. I can just stay here and read a book or something."

Jacob didn't say anything for a long time. Finally, slowly, he turned, looked at her, breathed a big sigh, and said, "No, Mother is right. What would your children think of me if I didn't invite you?" He was quiet for another moment then continued. "Rachel, forgive me. We would love to have Mother, your children, *and you*, come for Christmas."

Rachel felt scared. She was afraid to meet Anna, and she would be there knowing Jacob didn't want her there. "Are you sure?"

He smiled weakly. "Anna would never forgive me if you didn't come."

Rachel was still unsure about going, but she wanted Mother Davis to go, and she wanted her children to meet their cousins. As frightened as she was, she would go for them. Then Rachel thought of all of the presents under Jacob's tree compared with her own and suddenly realized how her children would feel watching their cousins open lots of presents when they had so few. She tried to keep her voice steady as she spoke. "How about after we are all through opening presents?"

Jacob nodded. "We usually eat dinner around one o' clock."

"Can I bring anything?'

"Not besides your family," Jacob said, almost smiling. "Anna always plans enough food to feed a third world country."

With that, he turned and was gone. Rachel trudged back to the house. Her children could soon talk of nothing else. Everyone greatly anticipated the next day—everyone except Rachel. She was so anxious about what Jacob's wife would think of her that she felt sick inside.

Christmas morning was dismal to her even though her children were kind to thank her for what little they received. When Emily asked her when they would be going to Uncle Jacob's, Rachel told her it would be at one o'clock. For the rest of the morning, the excited little girl kept coming and asking what time it was and how much longer it would be. To Emily, it couldn't come soon enough, but for Rachel it came all too quickly. It seemed it was no time at all before they were loading into the old station wagon. If it hadn't been for Mother Davis, they probably would have just walked the path through the meadow.

Before the car had even pulled to a stop, Emily was pounding on John to let her out. He had no sooner opened the door and stepped out than she was bounding up to the door.

Rachel had hoped to find a picture of Jacob's family on the Internet but had never had a chance. She was almost afraid to see what his wife looked like. She had conjured an image of Anna in her mind. She was probably drop dead gorgeous, trim, and perfect model—the absolute millionaire's wife with stunning clothes and a perfect figure. She envisioned Anna with dark black hair down to her waist, just as Rachel had. Anna would surely be graceful and absolutely perfect in her manners. Rachel consoled herself by saying that most millionaire wives were probably brainless airheads.

As Emily raced to the door, Rachel called out for her not to ring the doorbell until they were all there. Rachel helped Mother Davis out of the car and led her carefully up the walk, assisted by John on the other side. Emily kept calling for them to hurry, and after everyone was gathered on the doorstep, Rachel told her she could ring the bell.

Emily, in her excitement and impatience, pushed it four times. A scurry of feet could be heard in the hallway, and then the door opened slightly. Behind it there stood a boy about Emily's age. He was blond with beautiful blue eyes. Emily squealed with delight to find a potential playmate. Then the door behind him was pulled open wide by a woman who spoke in a loud, happy voice. "Well, James, don't just stand there. Invite them in."

Rachel stood in shock as the woman pushed the door wide. She was nothing like Rachel expected. Though she was slender, she was not petite. Her blond hair was pulled back in a bun, and she didn't look at all like a model, but like she could be anybody's mother. She looked at them with blue eyes that mirrored James's. Rachel soon found herself in the foyer of the house she had admired for so long, being hugged like a long-lost sister who had wandered home after many years.

"So you're Rachel," Anna said. "It's nice to finally meet you."

Rachel was so surprised that she stumbled all over her words trying to respond in kind. Anna swept Mother Davis into a big bear hug, too. "Why, you must be Mother. As young as you look, I would have thought you were Jacob's sister. But it's obvious why Jacob is so good looking." Mother Davis giggled like a schoolgirl.

Rachel saw Jacob standing back, letting Anna greet them. He had a slight grin on his face, and she wondered if it was her own shock that caused his amusement.

Anna embarrassed David and John with a warm hug, and then she pulled back to look at them. "My, what handsome boys. I bet you have to beat the girls off with a stick." Rachel watched as John and David blushed.

Behind Anna stood four handsome boys, all with their mother's blond hair, blue eyes, and big smiles. The first stood taller than Anna, and the second was nearly as tall. Anna turned to introduce them. "This is Abraham. He is sixteen. Isaac is thirteen. Joseph is ten. Peter is seven. And . . . " She stopped and looked around. "Where did James go?"

Abraham laughed. "He took Emily to see his Christmas presents."

Rachel looked around and, for the first time, realized Emily wasn't there. Anna laughed. "Well, anyway, that was James who opened the door."

She laughed again with her contagious laugh. Rachel had not wanted to like Anna, feeling it would be easier that way, but she found herself instantly drawn to her. Anna was so friendly and kind. Rachel finally found her voice and introduced her sons, adding, " . . . and, of course, Emily is the little girl."

Anna took Rachel by the arm, guiding her toward the back of the house. "It must be fun having a girl to fix up in braids and bows and all. Jacob and I always wanted one, but we got all boys instead. I told Jacob it was his fault. The man determines the gender, you know. But I wouldn't part with any of my boys for love nor money."

Rachel saw John and David head off with Joseph and Peter while Abraham and Isaac went a different way. Jacob followed close behind Anna and Rachel, with his mother holding to his arm. He still had not said a word since they'd arrived.

When they reached the great room, Rachel gasped. She had thought it was beautiful when she looked through the windows, but it was far more so from the inside. It was the long room she had wondered about. Half of the room had an oak floor with a beautiful banquet table. The other half was carpeted. It had a huge fireplace along one wall and a big screen television above the fireplace had a football game playing on it. There was a coffee table loaded with bowls of candy. But what was most incredible was the breathtaking view of the lake and the valley.

The floor was littered with wrapping paper, but Anna didn't seem at all ruffled about the mess. In the middle of the floor, James was teaching Emily how to run the toy train that ran on tracks snaking through the room.

Anna led Rachel to a comfortable chair, and Jacob did the same with his mother. Anna patted Rachel's arm. "Now, you make yourself at home while Jacob and I put dinner on. If you don't like football, feel free to change the channel, or there are movies in the cupboard next to the television. You are also welcome to any of the candy if it won't ruin your appetite for dinner."

Anna and Jacob disappeared into the kitchen. As Emily reached for the candy bowl, Rachel told her that she couldn't have any until later.

Rachel was drawn to the big window. The white hillside and the lake beyond looked like something from a postcard.

She felt ashamed of herself for wanting to hate Anna. She understood now why Jacob had fallen in love with her. Besides the shame, Rachel felt a deeper sadness. She wondered if it was because she could see how Jacob's eyes sparkled when he looked at Anna, the way they used to when he looked at her. There was no sparkle for herself now.

Jacob brought in plates loaded with steaming turkey and ham. There were bowls of mashed potatoes, fruit salad, and every imaginable food. It wasn't long before Anna stepped into the room with a giant metal triangle and rang it loudly as she shouted at the top of her lungs. "Come and get it, or go hungry!"

People scurried from every direction. Jacob kindly led his mother to the table. Anna positioned herself and Jacob across from Rachel and Mother Davis. Once they were all settled, all of the adults and Jacob's sons folded their arms and bowed their heads. John and David followed suit, but Emily was unsure. James tapped her. "You need to fold your arms and bow your head."

Emily didn't understand why, but she did it anyway, and Rachel vowed that she would start having prayer in her own home. Once everyone was ready, Jacob spoke the first words Rachel had heard from him since they had arrived. He turned to Abraham. "Abraham, would you bless for us?"

Abraham nodded. "Sure, Dad."

Abraham gave a wonderful blessing and expressed gratitude for this chance to meet their cousins, aunt, and grandmother. He prayed that they would all enjoy their day together.

As soon as the prayer ended, there was a hubbub of activity, passing plates and bowls of food. It reminded Rachel of growing up with her eight brothers and sisters. Most of the time, her own mother had invited Jacob to join them. He had been so much a part of her family.

While they ate, Jacob was quiet, but Anna was happy and talkative. Rachel thought this was an excellent opportunity to learn more about them. She decided to see if she could get the conversation turned in that direction, so she asked Anna how she and Jacob had met.

Anna answered happily. "I can't believe he hasn't told you about it already. But you know how men are.

"I first saw Jacob at church right after he enrolled at the university," she said. "I thought he was incredibly handsome. We ended up in the same math class together the next semester. Jacob was working at a small computer software company and going to school. He was studying computer science and I was studying him."

Anna laughed, and most of those at the table did as well. Jacob grinned in embarrassment but said nothing. Anna continued. "In fact, I studied him so much, I forgot to do my math. That was okay, though. I got him to tutor me. After that first day of class, I called my mother and told her I had met the best-looking guy in the world. But when she asked me his name, I couldn't even remember."

Everyone laughed again, and Anna continued. "It took me a while to convince him to ask me out. I would have married him the first month we met, but it took a lot longer to talk him into it. He had a hard time trusting people."

Jacob glanced at Rachel and then back down at his plate of food. Rachel bit her lip to keep it from quivering.

Anna didn't seem to notice and continued on. "My mother liked Jacob right from the beginning, but Daddy didn't. He was concerned about me marrying someone who said he didn't have any family. My father told me he didn't want me to marry Jacob. I said that was fine because he wasn't the one marrying him—I was.

"Father had lots of money and told me he would disinherit me if I did. I told Father he could keep his money. Because of Father's attitude, Jacob was unsure about it, but I told him I'd elope with him if I needed to.

Mother prevailed with Daddy, and we had a lovely family wedding after all. After the wedding, Daddy said he'd help us through school, but Jacob refused. That annoyed my father even more."

For the first time, Jacob interjected. "I didn't want to take money from someone who hated me. Besides, I wanted us to be successful on our own and not have everybody say I got my money from my father-in-law."

Anna grinned. "I agreed with Jacob, and so I got a job as a checker at a grocery store while he continued to work for the software company and finish his degree in computer science. Daddy was even more annoyed that I worked at such a job. I told him that I would dig ditches as long as I could be with Jacob."

Rachel's eyes started to fill with tears, and she glanced at Jacob, but he wouldn't look up. Anna didn't seem to sense the emotions her story was causing and kept right on. "When Abraham was born, Jacob insisted I not work outside of our home. Even though I wanted to be home with my son, I told Jacob I was willing to go back to the store. But Jacob said that if he had wanted a babysitter to raise his son, he would have married the babysitter."

Anna laughed loudly again, and most of the table joined her. Rachel tried to smile. The contrast of Anna being willing to give up everything for Jacob when she herself had chosen his brother's money instead couldn't have hurt more. Rachel could also see Jacob struggling with his feelings. Maybe the similarity yet opposition of their stories was why he had never shared it in his letters.

Anna continued with her story. "It was a rough year. Jacob did everything he could. He continued to work for the small software company, but being so new, they couldn't pay much and gave him most of his pay in future stock options. It was a gamble that they would ever be worth anything. As for me, I tried to save money any way I could."

She turned and shook a fork at Rachel. "May God strike me dead before I ever have to wash another cloth diaper in my life!"

Rachel laughed but behind the laugh, the tears felt like a dam ready to burst.

Anna laughed, too, then continued. "But we had free access to a washing machine in the apartment we lived in, so I had to do it. I really can't complain. As hard as it was for me, it was even more difficult for Jacob. We had so little money, and he struggled to feed us. My dad kept offering to help, but Jacob was proud and determined."

Rachel looked at Jacob. He was looking down, toying with the food on his plate. She could see that it had been a hard time for him and this story brought back some tough memories.

"But our fortunes all changed when he graduated," Anna continued. "The software company became successful, and the stock option he had gained through those four years of work became worth tens of millions, then hundreds of millions, and more. He was offered an executive job there, directing a portion of the software development, and he became one of their highest-paid executives. But he continued to take almost half of his pay in stock."

"What was the name of the software company?" John asked.

"Ever heard of Microsoft?" Anna said slyly.

Rachel could feel the shock sweep over her. So that was why Jacob had done so well. But he had paid a price in hard work and going without. Still, it didn't answer her other big question.

"So," Rachel asked, "how did you get into politics?"

She had directed it to Jacob, but he didn't even look up as Anna responded. "Oh, that is an interesting story. Jacob, as you know, is somewhat shy. He felt he was not too good in public situations and even worked on a minor in public relations to help him in that area. The U.S. Congress was looking at some legislation about computers, and my father had been good friends with Senator Hamblin. So Microsoft, knowing these two things, asked Jacob to visit with Senator Hamblin to present their issues. My father set up the meeting, and Jacob made a big impression on the senator. For his junior and senior years of college, Jacob became part of an advisory committee to Senator Hamblin on the changing landscape of the computer industry. He even went to Congress a few times and met with many other senators in subcommittees.

"By the time Jacob graduated, one of the members of the house of representatives was retiring, and Senator Hamblin talked Jacob into running for the office. With Microsoft and Senator Hamblin behind him, he buried the competition. At twenty-six, he was the youngest representative by far."

"Did you like being in Congress?" Again, Rachel had directed her question to Jacob, but once more he didn't look up. Anna answered for him.

"It was definitely a challenge. But Jacob met so many wonderful, powerful people. He was doing such a good job that he decided to run for another two-year term."

Jacob looked up and spoke quietly. "I wanted to run on my own merits instead of just being on the coattails of Senator Hamblin."

Anna nodded and continued telling the story. "When he finished that, Senator Hamblin was planning on retiring and encouraged Jacob to run as his replacement. Jacob was barely thirty, the age required for a senator."

Jacob looked back down, and Anna continued. "Everyone loved Jacob. He received the highest marks for integrity. Oh, there were a few big entities that didn't like him because he couldn't be bribed. They were used to being able to buy someone off."

"Why did you leave?" Rachel asked.

"Well, I . . . " Anna started to say, but then stopped. When she continued, she just said, "It was for family reasons."

Rachel saw Anna and Jacob exchange a glance that told her there was more than was being said. From what Jacob had said, Rachel figured they had come back to help his mother because she was getting older and had become blind. But even after he built this beautiful house with an apartment for her, Mother Davis had chosen to stay with Rachel. In some ways Rachel felt guilty about it, but she needed Mother Davis, and Mother Davis needed the home she was used to. Rachel couldn't help but wonder how rejected Jacob felt.

Rachel's thoughts were interrupted by Anna. "Part of the reason Jacob didn't run again was so he could get our sons out on a ranch where he could work with them."

Jacob nodded, and Anna continued to talk about their sons. When Rachel asked, Anna talked more about her own family. She had three sisters and a brother, and she said they all loved Jacob. She said her father did too . . . now. She laughed as she said, "Why, Jacob has more money than Father by ten thousand times, so Daddy can't be concerned about me marrying a poor nobody anymore."

Suddenly, Anna looked shocked. "My goodness! Where are my manners? Here I've been talking and not making sure everyone has had enough to eat."

With Jacob's help, she refilled all of the food bowls. Rachel hadn't eaten such good food in a long time. As she had listened to the story, she hadn't felt much like eating, but at Anna's kind urging, her appetite returned. Rachel refilled her plate three times and ate until she didn't think she could eat one more bite. Her children did, too. When she finished, she realized that Jacob was still toying with his first plateful.

At that moment she felt very sorry for Jacob in all that he had been through. But that was all behind him now. As she watched him, she couldn't help but wonder if there was something else that was bothering him. Did he still feel uncomfortable having her around?

After everyone was so full, "that they needed a bloat needle," as Rachel's father would say, Anna and Jacob slipped into the kitchen and brought out several varieties of pie. There was apple, pumpkin, banana cream, pecan, and many types of berry. When Rachel said she was too full for pie, Anna just slapped her on the back. "No problem, we have most of the day left."

Mother Davis took a sliver of banana cream. She smiled after she took a bite. "Oh, Anna, this pie is heavenly. You are a good cook."

Anna laughed. "You mean I know where to buy good food. I don't do pies. They're from a local restaurant. I've learned to make a few things, but when we were first married it was good that Jacob learned to like charcoal or he would have starved to death." Rachel saw Jacob smile, one of the few times he had since the meal began.

When no one could eat any more, Jacob, Anna, and their sons quickly cleared the table. Rachel saw that their boys followed the example of their father and realized that her own children did not help in the same way. Rachel offered to help, but Anna wouldn't hear of it. When all was cleared away, Anna stepped in to make an announcement.

"Okay, now, Jacob has a surprise for all of you."

The Surprise

Jacob seemed embarrassed that Anna announced it as his surprise. "Well, it's not just my surprise. I mean, it was as much Abraham's and Isaac's idea as anybody's."

"Well, are you going to tell them, or are we waiting until next Christmas?" Anna joked.

Jacob nodded, but before he could say anything, James blurted out, "We got presents for you!"

"You shouldn't have," Rachel said.

Anna put her arm around her. "Oh, it was nothing. Besides, there is a reason for it. But we can't tell you the reason before we give you the presents or it will give it away."

Jacob and Anna's boys scurried into another room and started hauling in the packages. There were four gifts each for Emily, John, and David. Emily started ripping into hers immediately, but John and David hesitated. Anna waved her hand at them. "Well, go on!"

They didn't need another invitation and were soon unwrapping theirs. Each child opened a box containing a pair of insulated coveralls, a warm coat, a pair of boots, and in the fourth, warm gloves, socks, a hat, and other miscellaneous winter items.

"All right!" James exclaimed, "Let's go snowmobiling!"

Everyone laughed, and Abraham said, "Well, there goes that surprise."

James dashed off to get his own winter gear on but was called back by his mother. "You wait until Grandma and Aunt Rachel have opened theirs."

Rachel felt hopelessly embarrassed not to have a present to give in return, but when she mentioned it, Anna just shrugged. "Well, you know what? Some people collect stamps, some people collect coins, but we like to collect friends. You and your family are all the present we could ask for." Then Anna said something strange. She glanced at Jacob, who was disappearing into the other room with their sons to retrieve the last of the gifts, and then turned back to Rachel and spoke quietly. "In more ways than you even know."

Rachel wondered what she meant but didn't have long to think about it before Jacob and his sons returned with four packages for Mother

Davis and four for Rachel. Abraham laughed. "I bet you can't guess what's in them."

As they opened their presents, Mother Davis grinned. "Oh, Jacob. You think I'm supposed to go snowmobiling? I can't even see."

Anna put her arm lovingly around her. "You don't need to see to enjoy the wind in your hair."

Mother Davis patted Anna's hand and joked, "What hair?"

When Rachel opened her presents, the tears filled her eyes. It had been such a long time since she had had a new, warm coat. The only one she owned was worn and patched.

But a memory was what brought the tears the most. The last time she had gone snowmobiling was with Jacob on the Christmas before he left. They had buzzed across fields and over hills, stopping for a flirtatious snowball fight. He'd hollered when she'd stuck some snow down his back.

They had gone back to her house for hot chocolate, and while she was sipping hers, Jacob slipped outside, held his hands in snow until they were ice-cold, then came in and stuck them on her exposed neck. She had squealed and acted mad, but he saw through it and pulled her into his arms. She could remember how much her mother had laughed. Oh, how her mother had loved Jacob. But even more, she remembered how much she did.

She struggled to find her voice to thank Anna and Jacob for the clothes.

"Oh, your coat and things were Anna's idea," Jacob said with a business-like manner.

Anna looked at Jacob and frowned but said nothing, only nodding to acknowledge Rachel's shy thank you. James impatiently prodded everyone to hurry and get dressed. Everyone started stuffing themselves into their snowsuits. Emily was so excited that she got her legs down the arms and Isaac had to help her untangle. Unable to control her emotions, the tears started flowing down Rachel's cheeks. She looked at Anna and saw she was watching her. Anna patted Rachel's arm and motioned for her to follow her into another room.

Anna closed the door behind them and turned to Rachel, smiling kindly. "I thought you might like to get on your winter gear in here, away from the commotion of the others."

Rachel nodded, accepting the tissue Anna offered. Rachel dried her tears and tried to smile. "No one has done anything kind like this for me in so long. Thank you."

Anna spoke quietly. "It's not me, dear. Don't let Jacob fool you. He may fool himself, but he doesn't fool me, and he shouldn't fool you, either. Even though he struggles with his feelings, it was his idea to make it nice and get these things for you. He and the boys had a fun time buying them yesterday." Then Anna put her hand on Rachel's shoulder and looked straight into her eyes. "He still loves you."

Rachel started crying all over again and stumbled all over her words. "He can't. I mean, he doesn't. He . . . "

Anna patted her arm and looked right into Rachel's eyes. "It's okay. At first, I was scared of you, even though I didn't know you. But over the years I have grown secure in Jacob's love. I know that what he holds in his heart for you does not diminish his love for me." She then laughed. "Besides, a man who can take all the inappropriate flirtations that the debutantes of politics throw at him and still stay faithful to his marriage is a man of the highest valor. That's what Jacob is. His love for me gives me great peace and security."

Just then, Jacob opened the door. He looked from one of them to the other. "Is everything okay?"

Anna nodded. "I was just showing Rachel a room where she could get dressed away from the commotion."

Jacob pursed his lips slightly. "You know, there is an old saying in Washington that there is nothing more dangerous than leaving two women alone in a room to talk, unless it is two women who both know you."

Anna laughed. "Yes, dear. That is why you need to go out and close the door."

Anna gently pushed Jacob out the door and shut it. When she turned back, she again smiled. "I would like to keep our discussions about Jacob confidential between just the two of us. And I would also like to get to know you much better."

Rachel didn't know what to say, so she just nodded. Anna helped Rachel get her winter clothes on. When they stepped out of the room, Jacob was waiting for them. He looked at Anna and frowned. "Anna, what about you? Aren't you going with us?"

Anna shook her head. "I got enough snow to last me a lifetime on our last trip to Vermont. You take your mother and Rachel, and I'll have some hot chocolate ready when you come back."

Jacob looked at Anna and then at Rachel. Rachel could see the uneasiness in his eyes, but he just nodded. By the time they reached the hallway leading outside, James and Emily had each taken one of Mother Davis's hands and were helping her along. As they approached the door,

Rachel could hear the roar of snowmobiles, a familiar sound from long ago.

Anna slipped her coat on and went out to help direct. She put Emily and James on one machine in front of Abraham, who put his arms around them as he reached up to the controls. Emily squealed as they headed down the hill toward the meadow. Anna helped a nervous Mother Davis to climb on behind Isaac and instructed him to go slow and easy to help her get used to it.

Anna assigned David to go with Joseph and John to go with Peter, telling them to make sure they switched off and let their cousins drive, too. Then there was just one snowmobile left, with Rachel and Jacob standing there by Anna.

Anna looked directly at Jacob. "Well, Jacob, aren't you going to get your snowmobile started so you can give Rachel a ride?"

Jacob looked at Rachel, and the expression on his face was more than just nervousness; this time it was closer to terror. Was he remembering that Christmas day so long ago? Was he afraid of a memory that was too painful to recall, or was he just afraid of her and the pain she had caused him? He spoke firmly back to Anna. "Anna, I'm not sure . . . "

Anna interrupted. "Jacob, Rachel is waiting."

Jacob glanced at Rachel once more, then nodded and reluctantly started the snow machine. Rachel hesitated, so Anna took her by the arm and gently led her to the seat behind him. Rachel stepped aboard, painfully aware that there was no place to hold onto other than to put her arms around Jacob. Anna gently urged, "Rachel, you had better hold on to Jacob or you will fall off."

Rachel grabbed hold of Jacob's coat with her gloved hands. Jacob looked questioningly one last time at Anna, and then he gunned the engine. Rachel glanced back at Anna, who smiled and waved.

So many thoughts and questions went through Rachel's mind. Was she reading more into what had just happened than was really there? A woman doesn't tell you that she knows her husband still loves you and then sends the two of you off snowmobiling together, telling you to hold on to him. What was Anna thinking? She was such a wonderful lady, and she said she trusted Jacob, but this pushed the envelope of reason.

As they came off of the hill, Jacob opened the throttle fully, making the crystalline wind whip by Rachel's cheeks as the snow machine rocked from side to side. His loose-fitting parka offered no security, and she was afraid she would fall off. She had no choice but to put her arms around him. They came upon Abraham, Emily, and James. Emily's delighted laughter filled the crisp air. When they pulled up alongside them, Emily whooped at Abraham to go faster. "Don't let them beat us!"

Abraham gunned his machine forward, challenging for a race. For a couple of hours everyone raced and chased each other. Whenever John or David sailed by at the helm of one of the machines, they would always whoop and holler, "Look out, Mom!"

In the cool air, holding tightly to Jacob, Rachel felt eighteen again, and all of the horrible experiences and heartaches of the past years disappeared into the cold Christmas air.

Jacob offered to let her drive, and she excitedly switched places. With him behind her, cautiously holding to her coat, she started inching forward. John and Peter shot by, and John yelled, "Race you, Mother!"

She turned the throttle to full power, and the machine spun snow and leaped forward. Jacob slid his arms around her to keep himself from falling off. His arms felt so good around her. In an instant the years melted away as they flew across the white landscape. Abraham sailed by with Emily, and her squeals of delight brought Rachel suddenly and forcefully out of her revelry. She wasn't eighteen anymore, and things were different. Jacob belonged to someone else, and, no matter what she wished, that was the way it was.

She slowed the machine and turned toward the house. Jacob asked her where she was heading. "I think we should go back," she replied. "I'm not feeling well."

Unable to see through her tears, she returned control of the machine back to Jacob. He drove slowly, and she held onto his coat. Her mind was a blur of questions. What was going on with Anna? Didn't she understand that this was not only unfair to Rachel but also to Jacob?

When they arrived, she thanked Jacob and walked slowly to the house. "I hope you will be all right," he called after her as he turned to join the others.

When she went into the house, Anna greeted her happily. "Did you have fun?"

Rachel nodded, but she wanted Anna to understand what she was feeling. It wasn't really right for her to spend time with Jacob, but she didn't want to hurt Anna's feelings. She had been so kind. Rachel spoke quietly and slowly but with firm determination, looking directly at Anna. "It brought back lots of fond memories of Jacob. One of the last things he and I ever did together was to go snowmobiling."

If she had expected shock and concern from Anna about the inappropriate feelings and thoughts, that was not what she got. Instead,

Anna's smile widened. "Yes, I know." Anna then turned and walked into the kitchen, leaving Rachel dumbfounded, staring after her.

Did Anna not understand the feelings Rachel and Jacob had had for each other? Couldn't she see that Jacob struggled with his feelings, too? Anna couldn't be that blind. Jacob's reluctance to take Rachel on the snow machine and his silence when she was around was obvious. Rachel decided she just had to try again to make Anna understand.

She followed Anna into the kitchen and gasped as she entered. It was so beautiful. Anna turned from the hot chocolate. "Do you like it? It's my dream kitchen."

Rachel nodded. It wasn't overdone, just big and airy with lots of work space and the very best appliances. There was a breakfast nook in an alcove with a bay window. Rachel went to it and looked out over the valley and lake. She could imagine how wonderful it would be to sit there and enjoy seeing the day dawn.

Rachel turned to find Anna watching her. Anna smiled. "Would you like a tour of the house?"

Rachel nodded, so Anna turned the hot chocolate burner to warm and took Rachel by the hand. "Follow me, then."

Anna led Rachel through a doorway by the kitchen nook into a hallway filled with lockers. Anna explained that whenever anyone came home, they came through the garage into that hallway and put their things away in the lockers. At the other end of the hallway was another door. Anna put her finger to her lips. "This is the apartment we built on for Jacob's mother. The snow machining wore her out, and she's sleeping in one of the bedrooms."

They tiptoed through the door into a smaller kitchen—one about the size of Rachel's own with its own outside door. Next to the kitchen there was a cozy little living room with three doorways—one to a bathroom, one to a bedroom, and the last, which they did not enter, was to the bedroom where Mother Davis was sleeping. There were intercoms connecting the apartment to the rest of the house.

Back in the other part of the house, the tour continued to a main floor laundry room, the parlor where Rachel had changed her clothes, and Jacob's office, which was full of computer equipment and books. The last stop on the main floor was an art studio with a bay window. The window in the center was the biggest and looked west across the lake. Standing in the center of the windows gave Rachel the feeling she was standing on the edge of a cliff, and it took her breath away.

Anna stepped up beside Rachel and squeezed her hand. "This room is my pride and joy. Jacob had it built for me."

She uncovered the canvas that was on the easel. It was a painting, only partially done, but it was of Jacob. "This is to be a present, so please keep my secret."

Rachel thought it was an interesting painting. Jacob was off to one side and not centered, like in most portraits.

"It's going to take me a long time to finish it," Anna said as she covered the painting again. "I understand you paint, too."

"I used to, years ago."

"If we set up another easel in here for you, we could visit while we paint," Anna said.

"I would enjoy that very much," Rachel replied.

Anna grinned. "But you've had your last peek at my painting until it's done. I like to keep my paintings a secret until they are completed."

Rachel relished the thought of being here in this room, painting and visiting with Anna. She felt as if the two of them had been friends forever.

The downstairs of the house boasted a game room with a ping-pong table, pool table, foosball, and air hockey. There was an exercise room and a large living room with a sliding glass door that opened onto a patio and a large backyard. There were also some large storage rooms, a couple of guest bedrooms, and a bathroom.

Anna took Rachel to the third floor, which consisted almost entirely of bedrooms. Abraham had his own room, but the other four boys shared rooms, two in each. There were two bathrooms and some extra bedrooms. The last room they walked into was the master suite. It took up one whole end of the house, with windows on two sides and a sliding glass door that opened onto a small balcony overlooking the lake.

It had its own sitting room with a big screen television. There was a jetted tub inside a beautiful bathroom, complete with a walk-in closet. Rachel had never even dreamed of such a nice bedroom. "This," Anna said, "is the place where Jacob and I can get away from everything if we need to be alone together."

Leaving the master suite behind, Anna pulled Rachel to a spiral staircase that led upward. "This was something Jacob wanted."

Rachel followed Anna up the staircase into a library. It was rectangular with walls about twelve feet tall. The bottom three feet were all book shelves, the next three feet were almost solid windows, and the top six feet were more bookshelves. It stood above the house, offering a 360-degree view. She walked around the room, looking out the windows in every direction. Her own house down the hill looked small. She could see the orchard, look down the winding lane, and see across Jensen Lake. The view from the library was the most incredible yet.

As they descended the staircase, Rachel, despite her best efforts, felt jealous. It was hard to eliminate the thought that this could have been her house if she hadn't made such a wrong choice years ago.

Having finished the tour, they walked to the large living room and looked out the big picture window. Jacob, his sons, and Rachel's children were all involved in a snowball fight in the backyard. Jacob, Abraham, Emily, and John had quickly put up a fort and were behind it throwing snowballs at Isaac, Joseph, Paul, James, and David, who were the attackers. Anna laughed. "Jacob isn't anything but a big kid in a man's body."

Anna checked the hot chocolate while Rachel stayed to watch the snowball fight. When a truce was declared, those outside built a giant snowman. James ran in for some buttons and a carrot, which Jacob helped Emily stick into the white, round face. He was laughing and smiling until he raised his eyes and saw Rachel at the window. His smile vanished, and Rachel felt the tears sting her eyes. She wished Jacob could forgive her, but she wondered if he ever would.

Soon, everyone burst into the house. Jacob and his sons put their outdoor clothes in their lockers, and her own children stacked theirs by the door to take home.

They all drank hot chocolate, ate turkey and ham sandwiches on rolls, and dug into the incredible pies. Mother Davis joined them in time to hear Emily tell of how Abraham let her drive the snow machine.

She was so excited she exclaimed, "Momma, can we get a snow machine?"

Rachel stammered, "I, uh . . . No, Emily."

Jacob swooped Emily up into his arms. "You don't need one, Emily, because you can come ride ours any time you want."

"Really?"

"Really."

"All of us?"

"All of you."

"Momma and Gran, too?"

Jacob looked over at Rachel with an unexpected smile. "Momma and Gran, too."

With full stomachs and warmed feet, they trooped into the living room to watch the sun set over the lake. Jacob stood with his arm around Anna, leaving Rachel to stand alone with her pangs of jealousy and regret.

When the sun had settled itself beyond the horizon, Jacob cooked a big batch of buttered popcorn and a batch of caramel. They had a big theater popper, and it didn't take long at all. When all was ready, they settled in to watch a movie on the big-screen television.

Rachel tried not to look over at Anna snuggled up against Jacob, but when she did glance over, Anna was watching her. When their eyes met, Anna smiled.

Halfway through the movie, Emily curled up on Jacob's lap. By the end of the show, she was sleeping soundly in his arms. Jacob carried her gently to the door. As Anna tried to work Emily's coat around her, Emily stirred. "Is the show over?"

"Yes, Emily," Rachel said. "It's time to go home."

Emily threw her arms around Anna. "Thank you, Aunt Anna. This has been the best Christmas ever."

Anna smiled and hugged her back. "You're welcome, Emily, and you come back often." She turned to Rachel. "You, too, and all of your family. You're welcome anytime."

Jacob walked with Mother Davis to the car, still carrying a drowsy Emily. He buckled Emily into her car seat, and when he shut the door, Rachel touched his arm. "Thank you, Jacob."

He smiled slightly, nodded, and turned back to the house. As Rachel turned her car down the driveway, Jacob lifted James into his arms, and Jacob, Anna, and their family waved until Rachel turned her car onto the main road, heading back to her grim life.

A Change for the Better

Rachel's children practically lived at Jacob and Anna's house after that. Emily would be beside Rachel one instant and gone the next. After a frantic search, Rachel would call Anna, and, sure enough, Emily would be there playing with James.

Since it was Christmas break, John and David were almost always up there as well. At first, Rachel was concerned that Anna would get tired of them, but the one day she tried to keep them home, Joseph called to find out where they were.

Mother Davis also liked to go up there. On the days Rachel had to work, Mother Davis asked to be dropped off there on her way. She could enjoy having family around her, and when she tired, she went into the little apartment to lie down.

Rachel found herself also gravitating to Jacob and Anna's house. She felt so comfortable there, and there was always lots of food to eat.

True to her word, Anna bought another easel and put a canvas on it for Rachel. Rachel started noticing that many of the paintings in their home were Anna's originals. She was a very gifted artist. The one that caught Rachel's eye the most was a beautiful picture of Anna and Jacob together, hand in hand. Behind them, in the distance, was the spire of a building, which Anna explained was the front of the main building at the university from which Jacob graduated. She also pointed out a small apartment building in one corner where they started their lives together. There were other events from their lives painted into the background, too. Besides the great talent it showed, Rachel knew she was drawn to it because Jacob was young, the way she remembered him at the time he had left.

Rachel decided her first painting would be a landscape and would be the view of the lake from the studio. Anna insisted Rachel have the spot in the bay window where she could see it better, adding that sometimes the light hurt her eyes, anyway.

The women spent many hours in the art room together, visiting and painting. Rachel began to feel that Anna was her best friend and that Anna felt the same way about her. They talked about many things: raising children, politics, schools, the community, and, of course, Jacob.

Rachel thought it was unusual that Anna asked questions about the time Rachel and Jacob had spent together. At first, Rachel had been reluctant to share it, concerned that it would bother Anna. But it didn't. Anna would, in turn, share funny things about Jacob.

During much of the time that Rachel was at their house, Jacob was conspicuously busy, working in his office. He took time out to play with the children but was reluctant to be around Rachel.

Anna always insisted Rachel's family stay for dinner. Anna was a good cook, but she wasn't too proud to serve something premade. Holiday candies were plentiful, and Anna insisted everyone dispose of them before she did. Rachel was sure she was going to gain ten pounds that week, while Anna could eat anything she wanted without it affecting her.

As New Year's Day approached, Anna invited Rachel and her family to spend the day with them. "In fact," Anna said, with her usual big smile, "stay overnight with us on New Year's Eve, and we'll have a giant slumber party."

Rachel felt Jacob would feel awkward if she did, and at first, she declined. But Anna wouldn't take no for an answer. "We have plenty of room. You and Jacob's mother can sleep in the two bedrooms in the apartment, the boys can all sack out in sleeping bags in the game room, and Emily can have one of the small bedrooms by us."

Rachel finally agreed. Emily, though excited for the sleepover, was upset that she couldn't sleep with the boys. "The boys always have all the fun," she complained.

Rachel had to work that day, and it was getting dark by the time she arrived home and made the trek up the hill. Rachel came in without knocking. Anna had insisted that she didn't need to. "You are family," she said. "And family doesn't need to knock."

Rachel had no sooner stepped inside the door than she could hear Emily's happy voice. "You landed on my property. You owe me two hundred dollars in rent."

Rachel entered the living room to find all of the children, except Abraham and Isaac, playing Monopoly. Emily greeted her enthusiastically. "Guess what, Momma. I'm winning!"

"You are not," James responded.

"Am so."

"I've got more money than you," James retorted.

"I've got more property," Emily said, sticking her tongue out at him.

"Emily!" Rachel exclaimed. "We will have none of that, young lady!"

"Yes, Momma," Emily said quietly.

Jacob had already picked up a whole pile of take-n-bake pizzas and cases of pop. The house already smelled of melting cheese. Rachel, hungry from working all day, felt like her stomach was turned inside out. Anna came in and saw her there. "Oh, I'm glad you made it. We were beginning to worry about you, but you're just in time. The first pizzas are coming out of the oven." She hugged Rachel as she always did. "You must be exhausted. Why don't you sit down and rest, and we'll be ready to eat in a moment."

Anna called Jacob from his office, Abraham and Isaac from the game room, and Mother Davis from the apartment. After everyone was gathered in the living room, Jacob asked, "Well, who should I call on for the prayer?"

Emily's hand immediately shot up. Jacob smiled, "Would you like to say it, Emily?" She nodded vigorously. Jacob said, "All right, then. Do you need some help?" Again she nodded. He knelt beside her and helped her through it, though Emily did a lot of it on her own. Rachel had recently started having prayer in her own home. She had planned to initiate it, but the children beat her to it, asking if they could. Rachel could remember how she had helped Emily that first time, and they hadn't missed a prayer at mealtime since then.

Now, after Emily finished the prayer, Jacob and Anna brought pizza and pop in and set it on the coffee table. Anna had laid down some blankets on the living room floor, picnic style. Rachel looked on with horror as Emily knocked over her red pop, spilling it onto the white carpet. But Anna just laughed and told her that carpets were washable, and if the stains didn't come out, the carpet could always be replaced. Then she shocked Rachel by pouring her own pop on the carpet as a demonstration.

James wanted to pour his on the carpet, too, but Abraham restrained him. Anna pulled out a carpet cleaner, and when she finished, the spots didn't show—much. Rachel smiled as Anna put the carpet cleaner away wondering, how anybody would not love her. Jacob truly deserved a wonderful lady like her. The thought made Rachel melancholy. She doubted that she would ever come close to being as good.

Jacob suggested they do their evening routine so that people could go to bed as they desired. He read from Proverbs in the Bible and then asked for a favorite story he could read from the Bible reader. Rachel noted the blank look on the faces of her children, but James was quick to respond. He wanted the story of David and Goliath. After Jacob read it, they had family prayer. James was asked to say it, which he did with very little coaching.

Joseph, Peter, and James ran to put on their pajamas, but none of Rachel's family had thought to bring any. Anna quickly rounded up some extra ones from her boys for John and David, telling them they could keep them. The boys excitedly raced to put them on.

Anna appeared with one of Jacob's shirts to fashion into a nightgown for Emily. She cut down the sleeves and pinned up the neck, and Emily was set. She was cute in it, too. Anna set off to find nightgowns for both Mother Davis and Rachel, though they both told her they could sleep in the clothes they had on. Anna wouldn't hear of it, returning with two nightgowns of her own. She was wearing a big, thick, flower-covered one when she came in. As she handed the other two over, she turned to Jacob, Abraham, and Isaac and suggested they hurry and change. They expressed their reluctance to put on pajamas "in public."

"Party poopers!" Anna exclaimed.

Rachel felt relieved, not wanting to dress in pajamas in front of the others. The other boys were soon back, and the party began. They started out with Twister. James called to flip the pointer. Anna really got into it, stretching out clear across the mat in her big gown. Jacob was reluctant but joined at Anna's insistence.

Rachel didn't think she should join in the game if Jacob did, but Anna persisted, and she finally got involved, too. More than once, Rachel felt like Jacob was trying to make a move that would take him farther from Rachel, but Anna purposefully blocked him so he couldn't. She got that same strange feeling about Anna that she'd had on Christmas Day.

They played games most of the evening, and Anna provided relish trays and candy dishes. By the time they watched the ball drop, heralding in the new year, Emily was asleep in Jacob's arms, and James was asleep in Abraham's. The boys headed off to bed with Isaac telling them he knew some of the best ghost stories they would ever hear.

As Jacob carried Emily up to her bed, Anna walked with Rachel and Mother Davis to their bedrooms to make sure they were comfortable. Rachel put on the warm, flannel nightgown and slid under the fluffy quilts. As she slipped off to sleep, she thought about how Anna seemed to be promoting the friendship between her and Jacob. She felt amazed that she and Anna had become such close friends. She could hardly believe it had been only a week. Her life was so different now, and it was all because of Anna and Jacob. She was happier than she had been in a long, long time.

* * *

By the time Rachel woke on New Year's Day, the sun was already streaming in the window. She hadn't slept that late in longer than she could remember, and it felt good. She dressed and headed down the hallway to the main part of the house. She hadn't even reached the kitchen before the smell of bacon and sausage filled the air.

When she opened the door into the kitchen, Jacob was at the counter with an apron on, leaning over a griddle laden with golden pancakes and surrounded by plates of bacon, sausage, and eggs. Emily was sitting at the table in the breakfast nook with a plate of pancakes covered with rich brown syrup. Beside that was another plate of eggs, sausage, and bacon, and in front of her were three frosty glasses—one had chocolate milk, one had white milk, and one had orange juice.

The enticing smell of the food made Rachel's stomach growl. But Emily's chatter made Rachel giggle. " . . . and I'm glad you moved into this house, Uncle Jacob. James is my best friend, and that is good because Aunt Anna says a person can't have too many friends."

Emily turned and saw her mother. "Oh, hi, Mommy. Me and Uncle Jacob are making breakfast."

Jacob smiled a pleasant smile. "A certain little person came and crawled into bed with us because she was hungry. Anna doesn't sleep well at night, so I make breakfast."

Rachel laughed. "With Emily around, I doubt I'll have many secrets left."

Jacob shook his head and grinned. "Not likely."

Jacob had stopped fleeing at the sight of Rachel, though she knew he still wouldn't seek her out. She looked over again at Emily's food. "So, why three drinks?"

Jacob took off some more pancakes and flopped them on the plate as he answered. "She couldn't make up her mind which she wanted."

Rachel laughed as Jacob brought over the plates of food. "Have a seat," he said, "and I'll get you a plate. You might as well enjoy a quiet breakfast before the thundering herd wakes up."

Rachel took a seat in a chair across from Emily so she could look out the window and across the valley. "It sure is beautiful here, Jacob."

He set her plate and utensils down. "I've always loved it, and I've always wanted to build here."

Instantly, there was an awkward silence. Rachel's mind went back to that night so many years ago, and she was sure Jacob was remembering it, too. She tried to ignore the silence by forking a pancake and some bacon onto her plate.

"What do you want to drink?" he asked. "Or would you like all three?"

She laughed, and the tension lifted. "A glass of white milk would be wonderful."

He brought over Rachel's milk and a plate and utensils for himself. He looked down at Emily. "May I sit by you, Emily?"

"Of course, Uncle Jacob."

She scooted over, and he slid in by her and forked some food onto his own plate.

"Rachel," he said quietly. "I want to apologize for how I acted toward you when I first came back. It's just that . . . " He paused as if unable to put his thoughts into words.

"Jacob," Rachel said softly, "I'm sorry about what happened all those years ago. I want you to know that if I could change one thing in my life, it would be that. But I'm glad you're back, and I'm grateful I can be friends with Anna."

Jacob didn't say anything. He just looked at her and nodded. Their conversation was awkward after that. They made some small talk, but Rachel knew he was still walling her out. She wondered if he always would. He was cordial, but she considered that might be more at Anna's request rather than any change of feelings on his part.

The atmosphere changed drastically as the boys came crashing into the kitchen. Mother Davis joined them, and a few minutes later, Anna was there. Jacob went back to the griddle as Anna wearily took a seat. She looked pale and tired. "Are you all right, Momma?" James asked.

She patted him. "Yes, dear."

She turned to Rachel. "Jacob is always so thoughtful. He almost always makes breakfast. He has since I was morning sick with Abraham."

Jacob didn't say anything but just kept the pancakes coming. When they were finished, Jacob and his sons cleaned up. Rachel asked if she could help, but Jacob declined her offer. Anna cocked her head and looked at Jacob with an exasperated expression, but he just shook his head. They had obviously been married long enough that they didn't need to talk to communicate.

James wanted to go snowmobiling after breakfast. Anna said she thought that was a good idea, but Jacob said, "I think I'll sit this one out. I've got some work to do."

Anna let out a disgusted grunt. "Not on New Year's Day, you don't. You need to take Rachel. She had a good time on Christmas." Turning to Rachel, she added, "Didn't you?"

Rachel felt that confusion again, wondering what was going on.

"Well, yes, but I . . . "

Anna turned back to Jacob, cutting her off. "See? I want you to put your work aside and take her snowmobiling. She works hard and needs a chance to have fun."

"But," Rachel protested, "I didn't bring my snow clothes."

Anna laughed. "It's a good thing you're my size."

Nothing Jacob or Rachel could do could sway Anna, not even Jacob suggesting Abraham could take Rachel. It wasn't long before she found herself roaring across the snow, holding onto Jacob and feeling both divine and uneasy at having him close.

She joined the others for the snowball fight this time, and her team took on Jacob's. She forgot herself and stuck snow down his back. He laughed, returned the favor, and then seemed embarrassed at what he had done, promptly declaring it was time for hot chocolate. He didn't look at her all the way into the house and immediately went to his office, where he remained until Anna called him to lunch. He was quiet the rest of the day.

Rachel once more tried to bluntly broach the subject with Anna as to why she promoted Rachel's friendship with Jacob, but Anna eluded her queries and changed the subject, only saying she had her reasons.

They enjoyed the rest of the day watching football, playing games, and eating. Rachel said they needed to get home early because of school the next day, though her real reason was she knew that Jacob felt uncomfortable having her there.

* * *

Jacob and Anna's sons made quite a splash at school the next day. They were tall and handsome, and everyone had heard they were the sons of a former senator. That was all Rachel heard about as she was checking at the grocery store. She never joined in the conversations, but just listened to what other people said. It was especially fun listening to the teenaged girls who came in after school. Abraham was apparently a big hit.

Normally, Mother Davis watched Emily while Rachel was at work, but Anna suggested that they both come up to her house. Rachel had told her that wouldn't be fair to her.

"Fair?" Anna laughed. "I ought to pay you to let me have Emily come over. Have you ever stayed home with a five-year-old who barely missed the school deadline? It will give James somebody to play with and help me retain my sanity."

So every day, Rachel dropped Mother Davis and Emily off at Anna's on her way to work. Her boys would get off the bus and go directly to Anna's, too, where she greeted them with a hug and warm cookies and listened to them tell about their day. When Rachel came to pick them up, Anna insisted she stay for dinner. At first, Rachel objected that it was too much trouble for Anna, but Anna laughed. "We'll just add some more water to the stew."

But nothing touched Rachel as much as what she saw and learned the day she came home from work and found Anna making a fuss over John. John had a big black eye, and Anna had given him a bag of frozen peas to hold against it. David and Joseph were sitting there talking to her.

Rachel wasn't surprised to find John had a black eye. No matter what she did, she couldn't get him to stop fighting. Often the fights weren't his fault, but she was sure some were.

"John," Rachel scolded, "what have I told you about fighting?"

"It's okay, Mom," David said.

"And it wasn't his fault, Aunt Rachel," Joseph added. "The other guy started it. He was calling John names."

"What kind of names?" Rachel asked.

David and John tried to hush Joseph, but he didn't realize it. "The guy said that John's dad was a drug man," Joseph said. "And then he started calling John a drugger."

Rachel had heard from other people that Matthew had been dealing drugs, but the fact that her children had to suffer abuse from others because of him hurt her. Worse yet, her sons were acting out violently like their father did. "So you hit him? Is that right, John?" she asked.

John just looked away, but David answered. "It ended up okay, Mom."

"You call this okay?"

"Well, no," David said slowly, "but some other kids jumped in, and four of them were beating up John when Abraham, Isaac, and their friends showed up. The kids were scared and shocked to find out that they were our cousins and promised to never call us names again."

Rachel was quiet for a moment. Then she turned and looked at Anna. "Your sons stood up for my children?"

Anna shrugged. "Well, of course. What's family for?"

Rachel couldn't help but cry, and Anna pulled her into a big hug.

* * *

Things went much better for John and David after that, and they even made some new friends—good friends—just because other children learned that Jacob was their uncle. With their cousins to watch out for them, the teasing and fighting stopped.

She had been praying so hard since she started praying again, that something would happen to help her boys at school. It seemed like it had been a long time, though it had only been about six months. Could God truly have answered her prayers? Did he just do things on his timeline? Was he testing her first? Was he just moving things into place in order to answer her prayers? She had once heard that it is through others that God usually answers our prayers. Could it be possible that Jacob, Anna, and their sons were the answer to hers? She knew Matthew callously claimed things like that were coincidences, but she felt it was more.

After the New Year's Eve time together, she had determined to teach her children more about God. She asked Anna about the Bible reader and where she could buy one. The next thing she knew, Anna presented her with a whole set as a gift. She started reading them to her children, which improved the atmosphere in her home. They had also started family prayer as part of their bedtime routine. David and John resisted a little on a few nights when they were tired, but soon it was readily accepted.

But there was one thing still left undone in her life. Anna and Jacob kept inviting her to attend church with them, but she always turned them down. She longed to go, but she didn't feel she could because the church clothes she and her children had were far too worn and inadequate. She was too embarrassed about it, and there was no money to buy more. It would have to wait.

Other than that, things were almost perfect. But then, one night in mid-January, she heard a crash. Frightened and trembling, she hurried out and turned on the light. To her horror, she found that Mother Davis had fallen.

Mother Davis

Mother Davis couldn't get up, and Rachel didn't dare move her. She called for an ambulance and then called Jacob. He came immediately. At the hospital, it soon became apparent that Mother Davis would be in the hospital for a few days. Rachel was grateful that Jacob signed himself as the one responsible for paying the bill.

It was determined that a stroke was what caused Mother Davis to fall. She was stabilized, and blood thinner was administered to clear the clots. Beyond that, there was nothing they could do. The doctors did not give the family a lot of hope that she would last long. Jacob said he wanted to leave her in the hospital to see what could be done, but she begged him to let her come home to family. Jacob reluctantly faced the reality of her situation and agreed.

They all decided that she needed to stay in the apartment that was built onto Jacob's house, and Jacob purchased a wheelchair for her. Wheelchair usage had been considered when the house was built, so the doors and the hallways were wide. The doctors felt someone should be close by to take care of her, and though Jacob said he would do that himself, Rachel pleaded for an opportunity to help. It was decided that Rachel would take the other bedroom in the apartment. Emily would stay in the bedroom closest to Jacob and Anna's room, and John and David would stay in another extra bedroom upstairs.

Rachel felt uncomfortable living in the same house as Jacob, and she knew he felt awkward, too. She couldn't understand why Anna liked having her there.

Every morning, Rachel helped Mother Davis get dressed and took care of as many of her needs as she could. When she needed help, she used the intercom to call Jacob.

He would already have breakfast well underway, and by the time she and Mother Davis entered the kitchen, most of the children would be there, eating and preparing to go to school. Emily, though she didn't need to be up, was always there in the thick of things, while James was more likely to stay in bed.

Rachel appreciated the hot breakfasts before going to work. When Matthew had been home, he had never been up before she left, let alone helped with anything.

The food was always good at Jacob and Anna's house, and there was always plenty. Rachel also appreciated the warmth. It was nice to get out of bed and put her feet onto a warm floor. Her house was old, drafty, and hard to keep heated. The old coal furnace didn't work well, and she was running low on fuel with no funds to buy more.

On the days they stayed with Jacob and Anna, Rachel turned the furnace in her house down to conserve fuel as much as possible, constantly checking to make sure the house was warm enough for the pipes not to freeze.

Mother Davis's condition deteriorated quickly. Though Jacob wanted to take her back to the hospital, the doctor said there was little they could do, and she begged to stay with her family as her life was coming to a close.

Each evening, both families ate together and spent time talking to Mother Davis. She had a hard time responding because one side of her body was partially paralyzed. She could no longer feed herself, and Rachel felt a softness for Jacob and his family as she watched them help.

At first, Mother Davis sat in a chair by the window, sleeping most of the day. But within a few days, she couldn't even do that, and everyone knew her time was drawing near. Rachel knew that Jacob had promised his mother she could live in the little, old farmhouse for as long as she wanted, but what would he do after Mother Davis died? Would he then want to sell it and expect Rachel to move? She didn't know what she would do if she had to leave. If he asked her to move, she had nowhere to go. Her paycheck didn't make ends meet as it was.

She decided to ask him about it, and one evening after dinner, she cautiously approached the subject. "Jacob, I know that you own the house I live in, and I know that you promised your mother she could live in it as long as she wanted . . . " Rachel paused, feeling as if she was begging.

Jacob seemed to sense her question. He spoke so kindly. He even smiled warmly when he spoke. "Rachel, you can live in that home for as long as you like, and there will never be a charge."

Rachel's voice quivered as she spoke. "Thank you, Jacob."

He smiled at her again. "You have been so good to my mother. You and your children are family." Then he laughed. "Besides, Anna would have me sleep in the dog house if I didn't."

She was relieved to hear him refer to her and her children as family since she knew he no longer recognized Matthew as his brother. Rachel also appreciated Anna's friendship. She had never had a girl as a best friend. Jacob had always been her best friend when they were

64

younger, and she had felt she didn't need anyone else. Then, after she married, Matthew refused to let her have any other friends.

As far as she could understand, the only reason Jacob and Anna had moved their family there was so Jacob could be near his mother, and Rachel was afraid they'd move away when Mother Davis died. It was Anna she approached about that question. Anna just laughed. "Don't you worry your pretty little head about that. As far as I'm concerned, we're home. If Jacob decides he wants to leave, he will have to go alone."

With those concerns taken care of, Rachel was able to concentrate her free time on Mother Davis and her needs. In less than a week from the time she had come home from the hospital, Mother Davis was hardly moving. Emily was especially concerned because she couldn't understand what had happened to her grandmother.

On the Saturday morning that she died, everyone gathered around her. Jacob was kneeling by one side of her bed with his family and Rachel was kneeling on the other side with hers. Mother Davis indicated she wanted to say something. Jacob leaned close. She told him she was sorry that she had not stood up for him against Matthew those many years ago, and Jacob told her it didn't matter.

She then wanted a hug from each child and stuttered out "Love you" to each one. Emily wanted to stay on the bed beside her, sensing something was wrong.

Mother Davis told Anna how much she loved her. It was the first time Rachel had seen Anna unable to respond, overcome by emotion. Mother Davis then expressed her love for Jacob and Rachel. Rachel could see the tears flowing freely down Jacob's face just as they were down her own. Mother Davis took Rachel's hand and then reached for Jacob's. He accepted both his mother's hand and Rachel's hand in his own. Mother Davis said, "J-J-Jacob, p-p-please b-b-b-be g-g-g-good to R-R-R-Rachel."

Barely able to speak, he said, "Yes, Mother, I will."

Mother Davis leaned back and closed her eyes. Her breathing slowed gradually until she stopped breathing altogether. Jacob was still holding his mother's and Rachel's hands in his when he dropped his head onto the bedside and sobbed. Rachel did the same.

After a moment, Emily went to Jacob and patted him. "What's the matter, Uncle Jacob? Is Gran sleeping?"

Jacob looked up at Rachel and self-consciously dropped her hand. He pulled Emily onto his lap. "Yes, Emmy. Gran is sleeping. She has gone to live with God."

"What if I don't want her to go?"

"None of us wants her to go, Emmy."

"Then why is she going?"

"Because God wants her to come home to him."

"That's not very nice of God."

Jacob kind of smiled. "But Gran wants to go live with God."

"Why?"

"Because when she goes to live with God, she will no longer be sick but will be able to walk, sing, dance, and be with your Grandpa, whom she loves."

"Will she come back?"

Jacob hugged her tightly. "Someday, Emmy. Someday."

* * *

The funeral preparations appeared hard for Jacob. He expressed the need to contact Matthew, though he didn't look forward to it. It took him awhile to find out where Matthew was. They hadn't spoken very long before Jacob angrily said into the phone, "If you want to come we won't keep you away . . . And I suppose you could have done better? You never saw fit to do anything for her but take her money!"

When he hung up, he angrily declared, "Matthew had the gall to say we would not allow him to come because of the restraining order. He also said Mother died because I didn't take care of her. He said I killed her so I can take care of her funeral costs. All he cares about, as usual, is the money." Jacob then stormed out of the kitchen.

Rachel had told Anna about her life with Matthew, but she wasn't sure Anna could really comprehend what Matthew was like. After Jacob left, Anna just shook her head. "I can hardly imagine you being married to a man like that."

At dinner that evening, everyone was subdued—everyone except James and Emily. Emily wanted to know what it was like living with God and what Grandpa was like. She had many questions. Rachel felt she hardly had the strength to talk and didn't know what to say to Emily, but Jacob seemed to know how to answer her and was kind and patient.

After dinner, Jacob asked Rachel if she would mind helping him plan the funeral. She appreciated his willingness to include her. Jacob said he wanted the church choir to sing. He also thought his own family could do a song and wondered if Rachel's family might join them. Anna offered to play the piano for it.

Of course, they wanted Camilla Jensen, Mother Davis's dear friend, to speak. Jacob debated whether to share a few things himself until Rachel assured him, "She would want you to speak at her funeral, Jacob."

When he asked her to join his family at the viewing and at the church, she suddenly realized she couldn't get out of going to church now, even if her clothes were old and worn.

After Jacob had called everyone on the program to ask them to take part, he smiled slightly. "I don't think we'll have to worry about it being a short funeral with Camilla speaking."

Jacob asked Anna to accompany Rachel and him to the funeral parlor to pick out the casket and make the necessary arrangements.

Anna shook her head. "I think it should just be you and Rachel."

"But Anna," he complained, "it probably isn't appropriate . . ."

"That's silly," she interrupted. "It will give you a good chance to visit."

No objection could change her mind, so Rachel soon found herself riding along beside Jacob in uncomfortable silence. After a few miles, Rachel thought of something she wanted to say. "Jacob, I want to thank you for the flowers that you sent for my parents' funeral. You'll never know how much they meant to me."

"I'm glad you liked them. I would have liked to come myself, but I didn't think I would be welcome."

"You would have always been welcomed by my family, Jacob. We all loved you."

"We?" he asked, turning to look at her.

She flinched at his accusation, but she didn't back down. "Yes, we."

He shrugged. "Even if you felt I was welcome, I'm sure Matthew didn't. He was part of your family, and I was not."

She refused to be deterred. "My family never considered Matthew part of the family, Jacob. But my family has always considered you a brother and a friend, and they always will." Jacob didn't respond, and they finished the ride in silence. There were so many more things she wanted to tell him, but she could feel that invisible wall again.

When they arrived at the funeral parlor, it wasn't as hard as Rachel had thought it would be. It was almost a healing process to talk about what Mother Davis would want. They gave the funeral director the obituary notice, the program, and a picture. Rachel appreciated Jacob asking her opinion and then truly listening to her.

As they were riding home, Rachel felt Mother Davis would be pleased with how well she and Jacob had worked together. After some time riding in silence, Rachel found the courage to broach another subject.

"Jacob, I want you to know that after you left, I tried to find you, but no one I knew could tell me where you went."

Jacob answered tersely. "It wouldn't have mattered, anyway. Once I saw you kiss Matthew, I knew what was important to you, and it wasn't me."

Again, there was more Rachel wanted to say, but by the way Jacob answered her, she knew he didn't want to hear any more—that he would rather leave it in the past. They rode in silence all the rest of the way home.

Anna greeted them when they arrived. "So, how did it go?"

Jacob just shrugged, and Rachel could see by the way Anna raised her eyebrows that she had hoped for them to have talked more. Jacob kept to himself the rest of the evening.

Rachel insisted that she and her family go back to their house that night. Anna tried to persuade her to stay in the apartment at least one more night, but Rachel was sure Jacob would prefer her to be gone. Anna seemed to sense her reason and didn't push the issue.

When Rachel arrived home with her family, she found the house terribly cold. She had everyone bundle up in sweaters and blankets. Knowing the furnace took a long time to warm up, she tried to start a fire in the old fireplace, but the downdraft kept pushing smoke back into the house.

When Emily said, "I wish we could have stayed at Uncle Jacob and Aunt Anna's house," it was all Rachel could do not to cry. After she tucked her children into bed, she climbed into her own bed and shivered between the sheets, trying not to think about the nice warm bed she had slept in for the last while.

The next day, she spent most of her time trying to make sure that their church-going clothes were as nice as possible. She found that John's were too small for him, so she fixed them up for David. She found a pair of pants and a shirt that had belonged to Matthew and took them in for John the best she could. When she had the boys try on their clothes, she noted that they were a bit baggy, but she hoped no one would notice.

When she worked on Emily's dress, she couldn't hold back the tears. It was the only dress Emily had, and it was far too small. There was a tear in it, and even though she tried hard to patch it from underneath so it wouldn't show, there was no way she could hide it entirely. She had to rip up an old sheet to sew under it for a slip.

When she started on her own dress, her stomach turned at wearing it. It was so old she was afraid people would laugh. But she just bit her lip and did what she could. If people laughed, they laughed, but she loved Mother Davis, and she would go to the funeral one way or the other.

She dreaded seeing Matthew at the viewing and the funeral, but she was sure it would be unavoidable. He did show up at the viewing on Wednesday night, though he was really late. He smelled like something that she thought might be marijuana. She had smelled it before and knew that when she did, she could expect his attitude to be bad. But she knew that when he smelled of alcohol, it was even worse.

He was obnoxious all night and dropped snide remarks about Jacob, Rachel, and their families. People tried to ignore him, but when he said to Camilla that his mother would still be alive if Jacob and Rachel would have taken care of her, Camilla glared at him. "And just where were you whenever she needed you?"

She spoke loud, and her tone of voice made him wilt in front of her even though she was half his size. He was sullen and moody the rest of the night, but at least he was mostly silent. Anna set up the greeting line. She put Matthew first, telling the others that if he was obnoxious, it would be better to get it over with so people could leave with a pleasant experience. She positioned herself next, a distance away from Matthew, with Jacob beside her and Rachel next to him.

Jacob didn't want to have Anna next to Matthew, but she said she could handle it. And, indeed, it was a good choice. With Anna's upbeat attitude, a person couldn't pass her without getting a hug and feeling more cheerful. By the time she had finished with them, everyone felt they and Anna had been friends forever.

Rachel noticed that her own children avoided their father. Once he motioned for Emily to come give him a hug, and instead she ran to Jacob and hid behind him. Jacob pulled her up into his arms, and Matthew furiously stomped out of the room. Matthew also tried to flirt with Anna. Anna quickly put him in his place when she loudly said, "Excuse me, sir, but I am married to a wonderful man, and I expect you to respect that."

Rachel tried to avoid Matthew at all costs. She made sure she was never alone, and she kept an eye on her children. Quite a few times he tried to make inappropriate remarks to her, and she quickly retreated to be near Jacob or Anna. They both knew what she was doing and would always turn to face Matthew, and he would back off and leave her alone.

When the viewing was almost over, Matthew approached Jacob. "Jacob, I wanted to talk to you about dividing the property."

Jacob looked at him narrowly. "What property?"

"The house and farm, of course."

"The house and the farm belong to me. If you remember, you sold the farm to me, and Mother sold the house to me, though I let her continue to live in it."

Matthew was obstinate. "Surely you don't think you should have it all."

Rachel could see Jacob was having a hard time controlling his temper. "You already had it all, Matthew! You took the farm and everything else that meant anything to me, and you sold and abused everything that fell into your hands. You better not bother me or anyone else any further about it, or I will exercise the full power of the law against you for harassment!"

Matthew swore. He called Jacob names and yelled that he was a cheater and a thief and that he wouldn't attend any funeral where such a person was. With that he left the funeral parlor, cursing as he went.

The few people who were left looked on in shock. Jacob was angry and breathing hard. Emily was crying, and she ran to Jacob and curled up in his arms. John and David had moved over behind Abraham and Isaac. Rachel's heart was pounding with fear and anger. Anna seemed to sense her feelings and put her arm around her. "You sure have your crown in heaven for putting up with a man like that for as long as you did. I can hardly believe he and Jacob are brothers."

As they said goodbye to the last few people and were gathering up their things, James tugged on Jacob's suit coat. "Daddy, who was that mean man?"

Jacob looked as if he didn't know quite what to say. He looked at Rachel and Anna for help, but they couldn't offer any. Finally, Jacob leaned down and took his little son into his arms. "That man used to be my brother."

"He used to be?" James questioned.

"Well, when I was younger, he took everything from me, and then he didn't want me as a brother anymore."

As Jacob did his best to explain such a hard thing to a five-year-old, Rachel could feel tears burning her eyes as she thought of what mattered most to Jacob. Anna seemed to sense her feelings, and she pulled Rachel into her arms. The emotions of the whole night and the relief of having Matthew gone overwhelmed Rachel, and she sobbed in Anna's arms.

Anna insisted that Rachel and her family come stay with them for the night. Even Jacob felt it would be better. Rachel didn't object, having a hard time thinking about going home to a cold house and having the fear of Matthew filling her heart. As she changed into the nightgown that Anna loaned her, she realized she hadn't thought about how old her dress was through the whole night. Her thoughts and emotions had been so caught up in the events around her. Everyone had been so kind, hugging her and offering comfort. If they had noticed her clothes or the clothes of her children, no one had let on.

That night, as she slept, she dreamed that Matthew had come back for her. She kept telling him no, she would not go with him, but he became violent. She woke up sweating, with her heart pounding. It took her a long time to go back to sleep, and again she dreamed the same thing. She couldn't sleep again after that. She just lay there in the silence, deep in her own thoughts, feeling regret for those years that she stayed with him.

It was a relief when the sun started shining in her window, and she knew Jacob would be making breakfast. She felt she just needed to be in the presence of a friendly adult. She walked out to the kitchen in her nightgown. Jacob, busily preparing pancakes, looked up at her as she entered. "Did you sleep well?"

Rachel shook her head. Jacob seemed concerned. "Was something wrong with your room?"

"The room is wonderful, Jacob. I just dreamed that Matthew came back for me, and I was so frightened that I couldn't sleep."

Jacob stopped his work momentarily. "Rachel, I promise that I will do everything in my power to keep you and your children safe from Matthew as long as that is *your* decision."

Rachel smiled weakly. "Thank you, Jacob." His words were a reminder that her problems with Matthew were because of her decision. She realized that her decision not only affected her, but it had also affected her children in desperate ways, and it could for generations. It was hard to believe that a foolish decision made when she was young could hurt so many people.

Emily was the next to wander sleepily into the kitchen. She was always one of the first ones up. She climbed into her mother's lap and laid her head against her. Rachel smelled the wonderful smell of baby shampoo in her hair. Jacob had bathed her the night before. He always bathed James, and Emily insisted that it be her Uncle Jacob who bathed her, too, partially because he always gave her a lot more water to play in than Rachel did. Rachel had laughed the first time they had stayed over, and Emily had wanted Jacob to bathe her. He had never bathed a little girl before, and he had looked at Anna for help, only to have her shrug and say, "Don't get too wet."

After Jacob had about a dozen pancakes and eggs cooked, he announced over the intercom that breakfast was ready and that they would need to get to the church soon. The boys started wandering into the kitchen a few at a time. Anna was last and looked tired, as she always did in the morning. Jacob was efficient, and it wasn't long before everyone was fed.

71

Soon they were all dressed and on their way to the church. They arrived early so they could practice the song. Anna had picked out one that had a verse about mothers and another verse about grandmothers. She suggested Jacob and Rachel sing the one about mothers, and the children sing the other. It was beautiful.

At the funeral, Jacob did a masterful job of sharing his mother's life sketch and telling some stories about her. He had asked Rachel to speak, but she had declined, feeling she would not be able to control her emotions. Jacob asked her for some stories, which he shared in her behalf. There were a few times that he had to stop and bring his emotions under control.

Camilla did an excellent job as well, and as Jacob had said, she made the meeting fairly long. As their two families trooped to the front to sing, she felt a warmth of love for all of them flow over her. Her sons were much more timid, but Jacob and Anna's sons sang out well, and so did Emily. As Rachel sang with Jacob, she felt a closeness to him that she hadn't felt in a long time.

Even though she shed lots of tears, she did feel the funeral was a wonderful service and a great tribute to Mother Davis, mostly due to the fact that Jacob was there and Matthew wasn't. She only felt conscious of their inadequate clothing once, and that was when Emily climbed into Jacob's lap and curled up in his arms. He had smoothed out her dress, and Rachel saw him look at it. He had turned and looked at her sons and then at her. When their eyes met, she looked away in embarrassment. Even though he didn't say anything, she was sure he couldn't think highly of her.

Emily

Rachel felt a void in her life once Mother Davis was gone. She was especially grateful for Jacob and Anna then. Jacob suggested that, since she was already dropping Emily off at their house before work every morning, her whole family might as well come up for breakfast, enabling the children to catch the bus together. Rachel gratefully accepted, realizing that, with her cold house, it would also give her children a chance to warm up.

The cold in her house was really wearing her down. She tried to make the dwindling coal supply stretch by gathering wood along the river on her way home from work. She had applied for assistance at the family welfare office, but the process took a month. In less than a week after the funeral, the coal was gone, forcing Rachel to burn every stick she could find. It still didn't keep the house warm.

Then Emily came down with a fever, her temperature soaring up to 104 degrees. Rachel desperately hunted all through her house for some children's aspirin or something that would help bring the temperature down, but she found nothing. She woke John to have him watch over Emily while she went to town to buy some. But the starter on her car only turned over a few times and then quit. She laid her head on the steering wheel and cried. She was embarrassed to ask for help, but she knew Emily's life could depend on it.

It was just after midnight when she called Jacob. He groggily answered the phone, and when she explained her situation, he said he'd be right over. True to his word, within ten minutes she saw the lights of his car coming up the road to her house. She paced nervously until she heard the knock at the door.

There stood Jacob, a coat over his pajamas—he hadn't even taken the time to get dressed. He stepped into the house, and she shut the door behind him. He turned to her in shock, saying, "Rachel, it's absolutely freezing in here."

"It's just the furnace and . . . " Suddenly it was all too much, and she started to cry again.

Jacob strode over to the couch where Emily was. He felt her forehead. He turned again to face Rachel and was clearly upset. "She is burning up! She doesn't just need aspirin—she needs a hospital!"

He wrapped the blankets around Emily and picked her up. "You get your boys. We'll take them to my house where they'll be warm. We're taking Emily to the hospital!"

Rachel bawled as she spoke. "I don't want to be any trouble." Jacob turned back to her, Emily still in his arms. "Trouble! The only trouble you will be is if I have to carry you to the car, too!" Rachel wasn't hurt by his sternness; she knew it was out of his goodness and his concern for Emily.

John and David bundled up and hurried to Jacob's idling car. Rachel slid into the passenger seat as Jacob slipped Emily in between them. He drove to his house and ushered the boys inside, urging them to hurry to their beds. Then they were on their way to the hospital. He didn't say anything, and Rachel could tell he was upset. She swallowed her tears so she could speak. "Thank you, Jacob." Silence. She hated it when he was upset with her. She always had.

When they got to the hospital, Jacob carried Emily in, and Rachel started the admittance process. When the clerk punched Emily's info into the computer, everything ground to a halt. Rachel was sure it was because she still owed money on the last bill. The clerk asked Rachel about insurance, and she said she had none. Jacob looked at her, but Rachel avoided his eyes. When she was asked how she would pay for it, she hesitated. Jacob stepped over, obviously impatient with the delay. "I am the person responsible for payment."

"Are you her father?" the clerk asked.

"I'm her uncle."

"And your name?"

Jacob told the woman his name, and suddenly everything changed. Almost instantly they were ushered back to see a doctor, who determined that Emily had some kind of infection. An IV antibiotic was ordered even before the lab tests came back. She was also given some Motrin to bring her temperature down, and the nurses applied some cold packs.

Rachel hated seeing them poke the needle into her little daughter. Emily screamed as Jacob held her, and Rachel held her hand. The IV was started, and before long Emily's temperature was down to just over 102 degrees, and she slowly drifted off to sleep.

The doctor returned with the lab results. Apparently, Emily had a kidney infection, and her white count was over eighteen thousand. The doctor was concerned. "You should have brought her in much sooner," he scolded before exiting the room.

Jacob turned to Rachel and spoke tersely. "Why did you wait so long to call me? Why didn't you . . . "

Rachel dropped into the chair, started to sob, and yelled back at Jacob. "Don't you think I love her as much as you do? I was doing everything I could!"

She laid her head on Emily's hospital bed and sobbed. After a short time she felt a hand on her shoulder, and she looked up into Jacob's face. He smiled kindly at her and spoke softly. "We'll get her better, Rachel."

Rachel leaned against his waist and continued to cry softly. After she was finally able to calm her tears, she looked up. "Thank you, Jacob."

Jacob just nodded and spoke softly. "Rachel, why didn't you buy some insurance with some of the money from the house sale?"

"Jacob, the money is gone. It's been gone for a long time."

"Gone?"

"Yes, gone."

"But I paid double what the house was worth to make sure you and Mother would have plenty to live on."

Rachel looked away, unable to face him. "We used some for hospital expenses when Emily was born. We used quite a bit to try to stop the degeneration of Mother Davis's eyes. But most of it Matthew persuaded Mother Davis to give to him."

Jacob was quiet, but she could see him bristle. Then his face instantly took on an expression of realization. He looked right into her eyes. "Your house is cold because you are out of coal, aren't you?"

Rachel nodded.

Jacob's spoke tersely again. "Why didn't you tell me so I could help?"

Rachel didn't even look up as she answered. "I didn't want to ask for help from someone who hates me."

She didn't mean to use the same words he had used against his father-in-law—or did she? She wasn't sure. She was really mad at Jacob. She was angry that he had yelled at her, and perhaps she was upset that he had money when she was struggling so hard.

When he didn't answer, she looked up at him. He was looking away from her, tears rolling down his cheeks, and she knew what she said had hurt him. When he did look back at her, his eyes were soft and so was his voice. "Rachel, I don't hate you. It's just that . . . "

He didn't finish his sentence. He just averted his eyes from her, walked around to the other side of Emily's bed, and dropped into a chair. He sat silently for a long time. Though tired, Rachel hardly dared sleep for fear Emily's temperature might rise again. When Jacob assured her that he would keep watch, she finally laid her head down on the bed next to Emily and drifted into an uncomfortable sleep. Every once in a while, a noise would wake her, and she would look to find Jacob taking Emily's temperature or a nurse checking her vital signs. At one point, Jacob went out to request another dose of Motrin because Emily's temperature was rising again.

When sunlight started to glow in the window of the hospital room, Rachel tried to wipe the sleep from her eyes. Jacob said he had some things he needed to do. He asked her if he could have her house key so he could set up electric heaters to keep the pipes from freezing.

Rachel thought about what electric heaters would do to her electricity bill. Jacob seemed to read her thoughts. "Don't worry, I plan to pay the extra cost of the electricity." She handed over the key, and he left, his pajamas still showing beneath his dress coat.

When it was late enough that she knew someone would be at the grocery store, she called to tell them she couldn't come into work. Her boss was tough but fair, and though he didn't appreciate having to get someone to cover for her, he understood.

A half hour or so later, a big tray of food arrived laden with hash browns, pancakes, eggs, bacon, sausage, milk, and juice. Assuming it was for Emily, Rachel started to wake her, but the young woman with the tray stopped her. "We'll get her breakfast later when she wakes up. This was ordered for you by a Mr. Jacob Davis."

She took the tray and found a note on it. She read: "Rachel, I'm sorry I yelled at you. I know you love Emily. I do, too. I hope you enjoy your breakfast. Don't worry about your children. We'll take care of them. You stay with Emily, and I'll be back when I can."

Jacob's kindness always amazed her. The food smelled good, and she devoured it. When the attendant arrived to take away the tray, she was carrying a basket of fruit and sweet rolls. "Mr. Davis ordered these to make sure you had plenty for all day."

The food was a comfort and eased her concerns about Emily. About midmorning, a big bouquet of flowers and teddy bears arrived for Emily, and Rachel didn't even have to guess that they were from Jacob, too. Emily slept off and on all morning. She ate only a little breakfast, but she was excited about the teddy bears, falling back to sleep with them curled up in her arms.

At lunchtime, Jacob came back, dressed in regular clothes and carrying a big tray of food from the cafeteria—four huge hamburgers, two plates of fries, and two large chocolate milkshakes. "Are you hungry? I thought we might have lunch together. I hope you don't mind that I chose it, and I hope you still like chocolate milkshakes."

Rachel nodded. "That sounds so good. I haven't had a chocolate milkshake since you and I shared one together."

He flinched at the mention of them together but said nothing about it. He pulled the hospital tray table in front of Rachel and scooted his chair around to face her.

"Oh, by the way," Jacob said, pulling the key from his pocket, "Here's your key. I hope you don't mind, but I made a copy so I can help take care of your house."

Rachel told him she was glad he had one and thought it would be nice if he and Anna always had a copy in case she locked herself out.

Rachel wasn't all that hungry after all of the fruit and sweet rolls, but the food was hot and good.

"Jacob," Rachel said, as they started eating, "thank you for the food this morning and all that you have done for my family and me."

Jacob smiled slightly. "You're welcome."

"Jacob?"

"Yes."

"I'm sorry for yelling at you this morning and for what I said. No one has been kinder to me than you and Anna have been."

Jacob looked right into her eyes. "Rachel, if anyone has a need to apologize, it's me. I know you love Emily, and I was so callous about your feelings. I was just so worried about her, and there were a lot of things I didn't understand about your situation. I'm sorry."

"Jacob, Matthew at his best isn't as good as you are when you're upset."

Perhaps it would have been better if she hadn't mentioned Matthew. Jacob was quiet for a long time. They took turns looking at each other and looking away until the moment when Jacob looked at her and didn't avert his eyes. Instead, he smiled and spoke. "It's been a long time since we shared a hamburger and milkshake together, hasn't it?"

Rachel nodded. "Way too long."

He got up, checked on Emily's temperature, and then paced a bit, as if he had something he wanted to say but didn't know how to say it. Rachel waited, and finally he spoke.

"Rachel, I want you to know I don't hate you. It's just that . . . " His voice trailed off as if he were trying to put the words together, but finally he continued. "It's just that when I'm around you, it brings back memories I would rather forget."

Rachel felt mildly hopeful. This was the first time that he had been able to express any feelings about that night. She hoped that maybe, if they could talk, he could learn to forgive her.

"Jacob, I will probably never be able to get over how horrible I feel about what I did to you. I didn't do it because I didn't love you. I did it because I was stupid. But if anything, I have learned something about myself, and I promise that I will never intentionally hurt you ever again. I know that things can't ever be the way they were. You are married and have a family. But I hope we can be friends again."

"Well, I presume we are that," Jacob laughed. "Anna wouldn't let it be otherwise. I've never seen her grow to love someone so quickly and so deeply as she has done with you."

Rachel smiled. "I feel the same way about her."

Jacob came back and sat down across from her again. "Anna says I shouldn't have any negative feelings about what happened. She says I should be grateful to you for what you did because otherwise, she and I wouldn't have met. I suppose she's right. Anna always has a way of taking even the most horrible experience and putting a positive spin on it."

"Anna is a very special lady."

Jacob nodded. "Yes, she is, and I love her with all my heart. There's nothing I wouldn't do for her."

Jacob was quiet for a moment. When he did speak, his voice was quiet and soft. "Rachel, Anna has asked me to try to get beyond my feelings about what happened those many years ago. I know that every time you've tried to share with me things that have happened to you since then, I have been less than cordial. I would like you to tell me everything."

"Everything?"

"Well, everything you'd care to."

Rachel took a deep breath. "Where do I start?"

"Why don't you start after I left?"

"Let me start even before that."

She summoned her courage and began to speak. "I must confess that when you got jealous, I felt so powerful. But when you came into the room that night, I knew I had pushed it too far, and I wanted to run after you. But I was too embarrassed. I planned to apologize when you came back the next day, but you never did."

She went on to tell him how she had tried to find him. She told him how angry that had made Matthew, how scared she became of him, how he came and forced her to marry him, and how horrible her wedding night was.

She talked about how Matthew started spending nights with other women, of the first time he beat her, and of how horrible it was from there. She could see Jacob's expression of controlled anger as she shared about the abuse.

She told how Matthew had beaten her when she had mentioned Jacob's name and how she and Mother Davis were not allowed to ever talk about him. Jacob was especially appalled that Matthew beat her each time she told him she was pregnant. Jacob said very little while she talked except to ask questions now and then.

When she talked about her parents' funeral, she could see the tears forming in his eyes. She talked about how Marie had shown her the flowers he had sent and had kept them for her.

He smiled. "I always liked Marie. What did you do with the flowers?"

"After I divorced Matthew, Marie sent them back, and I planted them in my backyard. They mean a lot to me. Knowing you knew about my parents was one of the things that gave me the courage to divorce Matthew."

She continued her story, telling how Matthew stole her inheritance and how that steeled her resolve to divorce him. When she told Jacob how Matthew had been afraid she might file charges against him and had sold the farm and taken the money so she wouldn't get any, Jacob could control his anger no longer.

"He always got everything that was worth anything at all!"

"Not everything, Jacob."

"Oh, what didn't he get?"

"He didn't get the children, nor could he ever destroy my feelings for you, no matter how hard he tried."

She didn't know if saying that was appropriate, given the situation they now found themselves in, but it was still the truth, and she felt he needed to know. Neither of them said anything for a short time. However, the silence was uncomfortable, so she decided to continue.

She told him about how, when things would get tough, she would go up on the hill, and dream that he might come back. She finished, "It might not have been right, especially since I was married, but I hoped that, someday, even if you were married and things couldn't be the same, that I could tell you how sorry I was, and that we could be friends again. I never dreamed I would get such a good friend as Anna, too."

Jacob smiled. "Anna is wonderful."

Rachel looked at her watch and realized that she had been telling her story for hours, with only an occasional break to check on Emily.

Rachel hoped that Jacob would share his thoughts and feelings, too. She decided to try to get him to. "Jacob, tell me about your life."

Jacob shrugged. "I don't know what there is to tell besides what Anna told you."

"What happened between the time you left and when you met Anna? What were your feelings; what were your thoughts? Everything."

"I'm not sure I want to think about my feelings. I was too numb with pain. I simply went home, packed up what little I owned, looked through the list of universities that had offered me a scholarship, and found the one that was farthest away. I went to the bus station and used what little money I had to buy the ticket. By late that night, I was on a bus heading west. When I got there a couple of days later, I was hungry, tired, and had no money, so I slept in the bus terminal. A kindly old lady saw me and asked if I needed a place to stay. She was good to me and fed me. I stayed with her until Anna and I were married. I had done a little computer programming in high school and found a job doing that. I started school, and, well, the rest you pretty much know."

Jacob didn't seem too inclined to say much more, but Rachel felt she still knew so little. Anna had told her a lot during their painting sessions together, but she wanted to know more of his feelings. She fished for ways to get him to open up. "So who was this lady?"

"Her name was Ina Ashton. She was an old maid, and some people thought she was grouchy, but in reality, she was a wonderful lady with a big heart. She had once been in love and almost married, but he left her for another woman, and she never even tried dating again. I loved her as if she were my own mother."

Jacob's voice tapered off. Rachel tried to encourage him further. "I would love to meet her someday."

Jacob got up and leaned on the counter, facing away from Rachel. "She died only a few years after Anna and I were married. She was the only family I had at our wedding." Rachel, remembering her own wedding night and how alone and frightened she had been, felt sorry for Jacob. He had been alone, too.

He was quiet, and she could sense his wall going up again. She didn't want it to close on her. "Jacob, please tell me more about Anna."

Jacob turned, and even though he had tears in his eyes, he laughed. "Anna. Where do I even start?" He paused a minute and then his smile turned into a grin. "If I'm going to talk about Anna, I'd better get us some food first."

"I still have a hamburger and half the fries."

He shook his head. "They're cold. I'll get us something hot. What would you like?"

Rachel shrugged. "Anything is good."

"Okay, but don't blame me if you don't like what I get."

Rachel watched him leave. She didn't feel she deserved his kindness, but she was grateful for it. He returned with a big pan of lasagna, some garlic bread, two plates, and two more chocolate milkshakes. The aroma filled the air as he held it all up. "Garfield, move over for Rachel."

Rachel laughed. "You still remember!"

Jacob laughed, too. "Remember? Hey, you used to be the lasagna queen. Of course, nobody can make lasagna like your mother, but we'll pretend."

Rachel remembered how many times her mother would say in her foreign accent, "Rachel, why don't you eenvite Jacoob oafer foyr deenner. Ee ees such a goot boy." Jacob had probably eaten at Rachel's house more than he'd eaten at his own.

Emily's voice broke into Rachel's memories. She was happy to see Jacob and chatted while the nurse came in to take blood for another white count test. Emily's food tray arrived, bearing a hoagie sandwich with fruit and milk. She frowned when she saw it in comparison to the lasagna. There was plenty of lasagna, so Jacob slipped out and came back with an extra plate and silverware.

Jacob gave Emily his milkshake, too. The nurse smiled and said cold things like that would help keep Emily's temperature down.

"I'll get you whatever you want," Jacob told Emily. "It's just good to see you eat."

By the time Emily was getting to the bottom of the milkshake, she was getting full and sleepy. As her little eyes drooped, Jacob offered to watch over her and let Rachel take a break.

"Jacob, that might be nice later, but I would like to hear about Anna first," Rachel said.

Jacob's whole demeanor became pleasant and cheerful as he talked about Anna. "My first semester, I just kind of holed up, programming and studying. I went to church, and Anna's family was always there. I saw them from a distance, but I never talked to anyone because I struggled to feel like I belonged, always coming alone and sitting by myself. Sometimes I glanced at Anna, and I thought she was possibly watching me too.

"Meanwhile, at the university, I sat in the back of my classes and hardly spoke to anyone. I continued to live with Ina, insisting on paying rent even though she objected, saying I was the son she never had. I told her I wasn't a freeloader, and besides, I knew she could use it.

"When my second semester rolled around, I came into a math class and, as usual, I took a seat in the back corner of the room. A girl walked in just ahead of Anna, and both of them headed for the seat next to me. The other girl got there first and asked me if the seat was taken. I said no. Anna was not to be outdone and said, 'Forget the seat. You are the best-looking guy I've ever met. Are *you* taken?'

"I was so dumbfounded, I mumbled out something, and she said, 'I hope when that is translated into English that it means no.' She then went and got a chair and put it on the other side of me, past the end of the row."

Jacob laughed, "And the other girl didn't ever try to sit by me again."

Rachel laughed, too. She could just see Anna doing that.

"But I was so afraid of arelationship," Jacob said, "that I hardly talked to Anna. She kept saying really loud in class, 'So, is tonight the night you wanted to ask me to go out, Jacob Davis?' I was always embarrassed and blushed and mumbled something about having to work programming that evening.

"She finally called my boss and requested an evening off for me, and then showed up at my door. When she asked me if I was going to go out with her that night, and I told her I was supposed to program. She said, 'Not anymore. I talked to your boss, and he said you could have the night off. So, are you going to go with me or do you have another excuse up your sleeve to reject me?'

"Ina stood beside me, grinning at this brazen girl. She told Anna that she wanted to talk to me for a minute, and she took me into another room to scold me. 'Jacob,' she said, 'you can live in the past all of your life, filling your days with regrets for what you can't change, like I did, or you can seize the opportunities that come your way.' She then laughed and said, 'This girl looks like a gem if ever I saw one.' Ina was always a good judge of character."

Jacob became quiet again, so Rachel prompted him once more. "So what was your first date like?"

Jacob thought for a moment. "It was like . . . " He paused momentarily and then continued. "It was like the dawning of a new day, like finding new life within myself. She had it all planned. We went dancing at the college then went for a hamburger. She was the life of the party everywhere she went. Everyone loved her. She was without a doubt the most popular girl on campus."

Jacob sighed. "I don't know why she chose me, but I'm glad she did. I can't imagine what my life would be like without her. I would probably still be some programming hermit."

He smiled and continued. "After that, we went out a few times each week, and I began to feel alive again. We dated the whole semester and on into the summer. She kept asking me when I was going to propose. I wanted to, but I knew that her father didn't approve of me. He even threatened to disinherit her if she married me. But she insisted that she loved me and would live in a hut with a leaky roof if she could just be with me. She was willing to give up everything."

Jacob stopped, and tears started rolling down his face as the memory came to him. Rachel could feel her own tears stinging her eyes as she thought about the contrast with her own selfishness.

He was quiet and seemed inclined to say no more. As bad as it hurt to hear it, Rachel wanted him to continue. "So, Jacob, what did you do to propose to her?"

"Well, actually, I had made the decision that I couldn't ask Anna to give up everything for me, so I told her it would probably be best if we broke off our relationship. Anna doesn't give up easily. She knew I loved her, and she saw through me as she always did. Her mother also liked me, and they worked out a plan together. They rented a room at a local hotel and decorated it like a jail cell. They set up a candlelight dinner and asked her roommates to kidnap me and take me to her there. She was dressed like a jailer, and she declared that I was her prisoner until I proposed."

Jacob laughed at the thought. "She finally did convince me that she would rather have me than all the money her father had, and her mother said not to worry—the rest of the family supported Anna's decision, and he would, too, soon enough. So I did propose."

Rachel could envision the whole thing. Anna was a lot of fun, and she definitely knew what she wanted.

"I didn't have much money for a ring," Jacob said. "Anna said it didn't matter, and to her it probably didn't—fancy things have never meant that much to her. But I wanted to give her the best I could afford to show how much she meant to me. I saved what I could, and we went shopping together and bought her a pretty diamond and sapphire ring. Over the years, as I've had more money, I've tried to get her nicer ones, but she usually only wears them once—probably to appease me—and then puts them away and just wears her original ring. I see her polish it and take care of it, though it isn't monetarily worth a hundredth what the other jewelry is. It's the meaning behind things that matters to Anna, and nothing has more meaning than that simple ring because it was the best I could afford and it expressed my love.

"Those next few years were hard ones for us. We were so poor, and I was struggling to go to school and work, even with Anna helping in every way she could. But you know what? In some ways, those were some of our happiest days because they drew us closer. I felt I could do anything with her by my side and, it seems that everything good that has happened to me since then has been because of her. I think the people of Washington voted for me because they loved her, and I was just lucky enough to be her husband. I kept thinking my opponents would dig up dirt on my family, but they never even attempted to. Anna was always able to redirect the attention to her family, and everyone loved them."

"What is her family like?" Rachel asked.

"Well, Anna's three sisters and her mother are just like her. They look like her, act like her, and talk like her. You know how everyone always gets a big hug from Anna when they come over to our house? Well, multiply that times five when she is with them. Her father and brother are much more reserved."

Jacob talked quite a while about Anna's family. He really loved them, especially Anna's mother. She and Anna had both really been there for him when Ina died.

"Anna's very close to her family," Jacob said. "That's why I was surprised when she insisted we move back here so I could be close to Mother in her old age."

"Jacob," Rachel said, "I have a real tough question."

"Fire away," Jacob replied.

"Why does Anna promote friendship between you and me? It seems strange for her to do that when she knows you and I once talked about marriage."

Jacob shrugged. "I've asked myself that a thousand times. Sometimes Anna is hard to figure out, and when I ask her, she only says she hopes I can get over the pain I feel from what happened. Still, I often feel there is more to it."

Suddenly, Jacob became very emotional and said, "I love her so much. I just don't know what I'd do without her."

Jacob wouldn't talk about Anna or anything in his life anymore, even with prompting. He said he was tired and would rather not.

He again suggested that Rachel take a break while he watched over Emily.

Rachel nodded. "I wouldn't mind going home, taking a shower, and getting some fresh clothes."

"If you want to take a shower, you may have to do it at our house," Jacob said.

"Why?"

"Your house might be a bit torn up."

Rachel gasped. "What?"

"Well, today, when I went in to set the heaters to keep the house from freezing, I checked on the furnace. Why, that furnace is so old that you're probably spewing out more greenhouse gas than the whole country of Tibet. I decided the house needs a new propane furnace."

Rachel could hardly speak. "But I can't afford a . . . "

Jacob interrupted her. "Who said you are going to pay for it? It's my house, isn't it? And, by the way, while I'm at it, I'm also having new doors and windows put in, along with more insulation. I'm having them take off the old siding and insulate both inside and outside. The chimney also needs to be repaired so the new wood stove can be used for backup heat. It's a wonder you haven't burned the place down. I've told the contractor to do what needs to be done to make the house warm and safe, and I will pay for it along with the propane to heat it."

Rachel stood there dumbfounded. When she finally spoke, her voice was hoarse and squeaky. "Thank you, Jacob," was all she could say.

"Oh, don't thank me. It's just good business. You can't buy something like a house and not expect to keep it up, or it will lose its value. I've heard that a house that is not kept warm tends to deteriorate forty percent faster."

Rachel smiled. "And I remember somebody who, when we were younger, used to say that 72.4 percent of all statistics are made up on the spot."

Jacob grinned. "I thought it was 74.2."

Rachel laughed as Jacob continued. "Anyway, the point is, they were supposed to start today. It will take them at least three to four weeks full time. You will probably need to pack a few things and stay with us while the work is being done. I hope you don't mind."

"Of course we don't mind, but I hate to be any trouble."

"Oh, it's no trouble. You can use the apartment. Your boys have the room they've been using, and Emily can either stay with you in the apartment or in the room next to mine and Anna's." He then reached into his pocket. "Here's a key to the apartment. It will also work on the other doors of our house."

Rachel looked down with disbelief at the key he put in her hand. Yet knowing Jacob, she wondered why she was so shocked. This kind of thing was very much like him. It was just that no one else had ever done things like that for her. At a loss for words, she again just said, "Thank you."

He shrugged. "Like I said, don't thank me. I'm just protecting my investment."

Rachel knew Anna was right. Jacob was only fooling himself about his feelings. Rachel knew he was doing it mainly because he cared for her and her family.

She turned to go, and Jacob called her back. "Oh, I forgot. You will need the keys to my car. Remember, yours wouldn't start. Feel free to use it for whatever you need."

Rachel again thanked him, but he just shrugged. "I won't need it. I'll be here with Emmy."

It took Rachel a while to find the car in the parking lot, and when she climbed inside, she remembered how beautiful it was. Now that she was supposed to drive it, her hands shook with anticipation and trepidation. What if she wrecked it? She eased it out of the parking lot and started down the road. It was a wonderful feeling to drive such a beautiful machine, one that didn't backfire and smoke like her old station wagon did.

When she arrived at her house, she found it partially surrounded by scaffolding, with much of the siding already torn off. In the twilight, she couldn't tell how much had been done, but she marveled. When Jacob decided to do something, he didn't let grass grow under his feet.

Inside, she found that the furniture was covered with dust covers. She trailed through the mess to the basement stairs and turned on the light. She gasped. The old coal furnace was almost entirely dismantled, and the basement was a scene of major chaos. She was glad that she had another place to live. She could feel the excitement building within her as she anticipated having a warm house.

She gathered up what clothes she felt she and her children would need, along with Emily's teddy bear. She decided not to take it to the hospital because Emily had cuddled up with the new ones Jacob had given her, but Emily might like it when she came home.

With Jacob helping her, the trepidation she felt regarding Emily's recovery faded from her mind. Of course Emily would get better; Jacob would see to that. She had so much confidence in him. Obviously he wasn't a miracle worker, and Emily was in God's hands, but Jacob had already made the lives of Rachel's family's so much better.

She arrived at Jacob and Anna's house with a load of personal belongings. James met her at the door with Isaac close behind. Anna swept Rachel into a hug, as usual. Anna shooed the boys out to unload the car while she led Rachel into the family room. "How's Emmy doing?"

"Right now we are still fighting a high fever. The doctor says we must keep a close eye on her to keep her temperature down until the antibiotic has a chance to start winning against the infection."

Anna nodded. "Jacob was worried this morning. He was also concerned that you had been living in a cold house. He said it's his fault that Emmy got sick because you and your family were cold."

"It's not his fault," Rachel said. "Your family has already done so much for us."

"Like I told you, he still cares for you very much, even if he won't admit it."

"Doesn't that bother you, Anna?"

Anna shook her head. "No. I want him to."

"Why?"

"I have my reasons. When the time is right, we'll talk."

Anna changed the subject by telling her to spend what time she wanted to at the hospital. "Isaac, Abraham, and I can take care of things here. Jacob said he'll come home each morning and help get everyone off to school."

Rachel thanked her. The boys came in with armloads from the car. Rachel urged John and David to take their own things to their room, and she directed the other boys to take the rest to the apartment.

Rachel made one more trip back to her house to let David and John get anything else they wanted. Once that carload was carried in, Anna asked Rachel if she had eaten.

Rachel nodded. "Jacob bought dinner for us at the hospital."

"Good for him. You make sure he takes good care of you. Is there anything else you need?"

"I would like to shower before I head back to the hospital."

"Are you sure you don't want to get a good night's sleep here? I'm sure Jacob can handle things there."

"I'd like to be with Emily, at least until her fever breaks."

Rachel showered and dressed. She had to sponge her clothes because of the dust from the construction on her house.

Feeling refreshed, she stepped back into the family room just as Anna called everyone for scripture study and family prayer. Rachel joined them before she left. Abraham read from the scriptures and then read a scripture story in his father's absence. Isaac offered the family prayer, and he prayed for Emily. As Rachel left, everyone told her to tell Emily hello. "When you feel she's up to it, we'll all come to visit," Anna added.

As she drove along, Rachel thought about how nice it was to have family again. She knew her own brothers and sisters still loved her, but

Matthew's obnoxiousness had alienated them from her. She considered reaching out to them again.

When she neared the hospital room, she heard both Emily's and Jacob's voices. Jacob was telling her stories about when he and Rachel were younger. Rachel paused at the door to listen to him talk about the tree house they had built together and how much fun they had playing in it.

Emily was very animated about it, especially for as sick as she was. "I've always wanted a tree house!"

"Well, Emily," Jacob said, "I think the one your mother and I made is still there. So I'll tell you what. Let's get you better, and maybe this spring we'll go out there. What do you say?"

Rachel stepped into the room and could see Emily nodding enthusiastically. Emily saw her mother and called to her. "Oh, Momma. Uncle Jacob has been telling me about when you were little, and he said we could visit the tree house and everything!"

Rachel smiled. "That sounds like fun."

"Have they started work on the house yet?" Jacob asked.

Rachel told him all about the scaffolding, the furnace, and the changes that had already been made.

Jacob was happy to hear the news. "Getting someone on the job is often the hardest part." He thought for a moment and asked, "By the way, Rachel, while we're at it, would you like any new carpeting or anything?"

"But Jacob, you are already doing so much."

"Carpeting and new paint and such things help a house retain its value."

Rachel felt embarrassed about how kind he was, thanked him, and then tried to change the subject. "So, any more news on Emily's condition?"

"Well," Jacob said, the concern telling in his voice, "the doctor says that her white count is extremely high and dangerous, and it's continuing to climb. But the rise is slowing, which is a positive sign. He says the only thing we can do is to continue to do what we're doing."

They decided they would take turns monitoring Emily so the other could sleep. Jacob said he'd take the first watch.

"But, Jacob, you hardly slept at all last night."

"That's okay. Worrying would keep me awake anyway."

"Jacob, I love her, too."

Jacob looked sheepish. "I know, Rachel. I'm sorry. It's just . . . "

Rachel patted his arm. "You don't need to apologize for caring, but you do need some rest."

Jacob reluctantly agreed, but only after she promised to wake him halfway through the night so she could also get some rest. He lay back in the easy chair and soon fell into an apparently restless sleep since he continually shifted in the chair.

As he slept, Rachel looked intently at him. It had been so long since she had been able to. He would always turn away if she tried. But now, asleep, he couldn't turn away. His brown hair fell softly over his forehead. He still had the gentleness in his face that she had always loved, though he now had small age lines around his eyes. Even as he slept, his mouth twisted up in a slight smile. She thought about how the goodness of Jacob's life showed in his face, and how it contrasted so much with the bitterness and selfishness that were etched so deeply into Matthew's countenance.

She became so involved looking at him that she almost forgot to feel Emily's forehead for any temperature rise. When Emily's temperature started to increase, Rachel informed a nurse. The medicine would take the fever down for a while, but then it would start to climb again before it was time for another dose.

At about two o' clock in the morning, Jacob woke up. When he was alert enough to identify his surroundings, he scolded Rachel slightly for not waking him sooner so she could sleep. She scolded him back. "You needed the sleep, and I was fine."

It felt good to curl up in the recliner, though she, too, had to shift to get comfortable. Once, when she sleepily opened her eyes, she had seen Jacob looking at her. He quickly looked away and pretended he hadn't been watching her.

At three o' clock in the morning, a lot of commotion in the room woke her. The medicines weren't staving off Emily's temperature. The nurses applied cold cloths to her and sponged her with cool water. It was somewhat shocking to her hot body, and she was frightened, so Jacob was holding her on his lap to console her. Before they could get the fever turned around, it peaked at 105 degrees. Jacob tried to stay calm, but Rachel could see the frightened look in his eyes. Eventually, Emily's temperature was brought back to 102 degrees and the nurses went back to their other duties. But the experience frightened Jacob enough that he was fanatical about checking Emily's temperature at least every 15 minutes.

After all the noise and concern for Emily, Rachel could no longer sleep. Emily slipped back off to sleep, and though Rachel suggested Jacob also try to get some rest, he absolutely refused. Her heart was touched by the concern he showed for Emily.

Rachel thought of Jacob sharing the story of their tree house. "Jacob, what did you tell Emmy about when we were young?"

"Oh, you know," Jacob said with a sly smile, "things like how I used to have to pull your pigtails in school because you wouldn't quit flirting with me."

Rachel laughed. "Who flirted with who, Buddy?"

Jacob laughed, too. He looked at her, and his eyes sparkled. "Do you remember that time when you were about five—you got mad at me and told me you could whip me."

Rachel nodded and felt her cheeks get warm. She remembered it well, but Jacob went on and told the story as if it were the first for each of them. When he told about how he had finally got her pinned down, and she reached up and kissed him, she smiled. He had jumped up, gagging and wiping his face, and then she tackled him. Rachel's father had told that story often through the years.

They continued quietly reminiscing. One of them would no sooner finish a story than the other would start off, "Do you remember the time . . . " and launch into another. Each time the other would add details. They laughed and told stories the rest of the morning.

After one story, when no one said anything, Rachel looked longingly at Jacob. "Sometimes, Jacob, I wish I could go back to those happy times with you, if only for a day or two."

Jacob was quiet for a short time, and Rachel was concerned that she shouldn't have said it. But when he did speak, his voice was soft and betrayed a similar longing. "Sometimes I do, too, Rachel. Sometimes I do, too."

Jacob stepped to the bed to check Emily's temperature. When he pulled the beeping thermometer from under her arm, an expression of excitement crossed his face. "I think her temperature is dropping. That could mean her fever has broken." The thermometer read just over one-hundred degrees.

By six o'clock it was approaching the normal range, and everyone was elated. Emily woke up and seemed more alert, though her energy was gone. Jacob could hardly wait to tell everyone. He said he needed to help his family get breakfast, get the children off to school, and run some errands. He gave Emily a big hug and was soon on his way.

He had hardly left before a large breakfast tray arrived for Rachel, just as it had the morning before. Emily's breakfast also came, but she wanted to trade her French toast for Rachel's bacon. Rachel was just happy to see Emily eat well. They had just finished when another food basket and another teddy bear arrived.

The nurses drew some blood right after breakfast to check Emily's white count. By mid-morning the doctor came in with the report: Emily's white count was approaching the safe zone, and her temperature was almost normal. The doctor said she and her teddy bears would probably be able to go home by the end of the day.

Jacob arrived back in the hospital just after noon carrying a tray loaded with hamburgers, fries, and three chocolate milkshakes. Emily was sitting up and more than delighted at the prospect of working her way through her share. She was getting back to her old self—happy and talkative. Jacob gave her a big hug as she said, "I love you, Uncle Jacob."

His voice choked as he replied. "I love you too, Emily."

Emily filled the silence as they ate. She talked about how she hated needles and was glad to be getting better and would be happy to go home.

"Well, you actually won't be going to your house, Emily," Jacob said. "There are some men working on your house to make it warmer and better, so you will have to stay at our house for a few weeks."

Emily squealed with delight. "I wish we could just live with you forever."

Rachel thought about how Emily really didn't even know Matthew as her father. Jacob was the closest father figure she'd ever had.

Not long after lunch, Jacob said he had some more things he needed to do but would be back for dinner. The time crawled by while he was gone. Rachel enjoyed his company and had to keep reminding herself that he was married. There were times she almost fell back into her thoughts and feelings of long ago, and she didn't want something inappropriate to slip out.

At dinnertime, Jacob returned. He brought in three small pizzas, some cans of pop, three more chocolate milkshakes, and a bundle of flowers. Instead of giving the flowers to Emily, he gave them to Rachel as he spoke in a quiet voice. "Um, we—that is, Anna and I thought you could use something to brighten your day, too." The flowers were beautiful, and Rachel could hardly speak. She just managed a "thank you."

Jacob averted attention from them by speaking to Emily. "I brought three kinds of pizza. I thought for sure there would be one you'd like best."

He opened the boxes. Emily chose the ham with pineapple, but she took off all of the pineapple pieces and gave them to Jacob. They all laughed and talked as they ate. Emily was especially boisterous. She talked about all of the things she liked to eat. She was so happy and full of life that it raised Rachel's spirits considerably.

After dinner, Anna brought the rest of the family to visit. They only stayed about half an hour, and then Anna insisted they let Emily rest. Rachel got the feeling, however, that she wanted to let her and Jacob have as much time to talk as possible. After everyone was gone, Emily asked Jacob to tell her some more stories about when he and Rachel were young.

Jacob looked at Rachel even though he spoke to Emily. "Why don't you ask your mother?"

"Because Momma doesn't tell stories."

Rachel admitted it was true. "When Matthew refused to let us talk about you, I couldn't share stories of my past. You were so much a part of what I was that there was nothing left to tell."

Jacob still wouldn't tell Emily a story. Instead, he urged Rachel to. Rachel told Emily about how she and Jacob used to go horseback riding together. Jacob just sat and listened, only adding a few details here and there. Emily ate it up. Time passed quickly, and by the time the doctor came in at eight o' clock to tell them he had signed the release papers, Rachel had determined that she was going to share lots of stories with all of her children. Matthew may have crushed much of the joy out of her life, but sharing her memories recovered the happiness of her youth and brought peace to her heart.

Once the doctor told Emily she could leave, she could hardly get away from there fast enough. A nurse came in and removed the IV, and then Jacob held Emily on his lap while Rachel helped her dress in her regular clothes. The nurse asked Emily if she would like to ride in a wheelchair or if she would prefer to have someone carry her. Emily thought a wheelchair would be fun, so the nurse slipped out to get one. Meanwhile, Jacob went ahead to pull the car nearer so Emily wouldn't have to be in the cold very long.

Emily enjoyed the wheelchair ride with her bears, and by the time they got to the door, Jacob had the car idling at the curb. He lifted Emily gently into it as she waved goodbye to the nurse. Soon they were on their way. All the way home she chattered about how she was going to show everyone her new teddy bears. Rachel was just happy that Emily was getting well.

A New Job and a New Life

Jacob called ahead, and by the time they pulled up to the house, everyone was at the door waiting. They rushed out with James in the lead. Everyone was excited to see Emily even though they had just visited her. She was definitely happy to be back. Abraham lifted her out of the car and carried her into the house while Anna hugged Rachel and walked with her. Jacob followed behind.

They had no sooner stepped into the house than James jumped up and down excitedly. "Can we give them the presents now? Can we? Can we?"

Anna grinned at Rachel. "A person can never keep any secrets with a five-year-old around. I suppose we might as well go ahead."

Anna nodded to Jacob, who took Emily from Abraham's arms. He carried her into the family room with everyone following him. He sat down and put Emily on his lap. "Guess what, Emily? You remember how you came over to our house for Christmas? Well, Santa missed getting some presents to your house since you were gone."

"Really?"

"Yes, really. And you know what? I ran into him in town, and he asked if I would deliver them."

Emily was excited. "Where are they?"

Jacob turned to James. "James, do you happen to remember where we put them?"

James dashed into the parlor and came back with an armful of packages. He went for another trip, and his brothers joined him. Soon there were lots of packages, all for John and David.

Emily looked disappointed, but Rachel was smiling inside as she watched Jacob. She knew he was acting. He stroked his chin. "Now, I could have sworn I saw some that had Emily's name on them. They must have been put . . . "

He paused, making Emily squirm with anticipation. Finally, he turned to James. "James, I think I remember seeing something in my office."

James and the other boys darted off and soon returned with more packages. This time, as they separated them, there were packages for Emily, too.

As Emily, John, and David started opening their presents, Rachel turned to Anna. "Oh, Anna, you shouldn't have."

Anna smiled and nodded toward Jacob. "Tell it to Santa."

Rachel looked at Jacob. Jacob shrugged. "Santa figured you might have a hard time getting things out of your house, with the construction and all, and felt you could use a few things."

Rachel glanced at Anna, and by the way only one side of Anna's mouth went up, Rachel knew that Jacob was just making excuses. She watched as her sons opened up packages containing nice church clothes, Levi's and polo shirts for school, new shoes and socks, and some new pajamas.

Emily opened a package of new play clothes and pajamas. But when she unwrapped three new dresses, she was wild with excitement and wanted to try them on immediately. Jacob suggested she open the other packages first, and they contained slips, tights, socks, and everything else she would need to wear with her dresses.

Emily scampered off to try on her clothes. She came out modeling the first dress without a slip on, and when she left to put on another one, Rachel followed to make sure she was more appropriately attired. After Emily had modeled all three dresses, Jacob picked her up. "Well, let's see. Did everyone in your family get something?"

Emily shook her head. "Momma didn't get anything."

Jacob feigned a shocked expression. "You know, you're right. You don't think Santa would forget your mother, do you?"

"No."

"I don't think so, either."

"Oh, Jacob," Rachel protested, "I don't think . . . "

Jacob looked right at Rachel but spoke as if he were talking to Emily. "Of course he wouldn't. But where could I have put her presents?" He again stroked his chin. Emily nodded encouragement. "You know, I think I might have forgotten to unload them from my car."

In an instant, James was out the door, then back for the keys, and then off again with the other boys close behind. They returned triumphantly with more packages.

Rachel started to protest. "Oh, Jacob, I . . . "

Jacob stopped her. "We were really hoping . . ." He paused "I mean, Santa was really hoping you and your family might join us at church."

She remembered that Jacob had noticed their clothing at Mother Davis's funeral, and she realized that he knew why she hadn't brought her family to church. She also knew Jacob wasn't trying to embarrass her; he just wanted her and her family to feel comfortable joining them on Sundays. So she just swallowed her pride and unwrapped new shoes, slips, nylons, and three dresses. Two of them matched two of Emily's, which caused great excitement on Emily's part. But the third one took Rachel's breath away. It was a beautiful red dress with white sleeves. All the borders and sleeves were lined with lace.

It wasn't just the beauty of it that made her heart pound but also the memory that it conjured. It looked almost identical to the dress she had worn many times to the formal dances she had attended with Jacob. The first time they went to one, she had been a sophomore, and he had been a junior. Her mother had worked many hours to make the dress, and Rachel remembered how beautiful she felt and how Jacob's eyes had sparkled when he saw her descending the staircase.

As she looked at this dress now, so many questions went through her mind. Did Jacob remember that other dress? Was he thinking of it when he bought this one, or was it just a coincidence?

Her emotions must have shown on her face because Anna touched her arm. "Rachel, are you okay?" Rachel just nodded, unable to speak.

When Emily asked her to try on a matching dress, Rachel didn't feel she could, but she thought she should at least reply to Jacob's request about church. "I'll put it on on Sunday when we all go to church together."

Jacob was pleased, but he did suggest that she at least try one on for size. "You know, Santa did say we could exchange them if they don't fit."

She knew he was right. She would hate to be getting ready for church and find the dresses were the wrong size. She took her new clothes to her room to change while David and John went to try on some of theirs. She looked at the beautiful red and white dress but could not bring herself to put it on. Instead, she chose the dress that matched the one Emily was currently wearing. It fit almost perfectly. It might have been a bit snug, but that would be good motivation to lose a little weight.

Everyone was waiting for her when she returned. Everyone smiled and clapped, and Emily said, "Momma, you're pretty!"

Rachel looked at Anna and Jacob, and they both smiled. Jacob's eyes showed his pleasure at seeing her dressed nicely, though he wouldn't look at her too long. Instead, he said he would be in his office and that he would like a word with her when she had time. As he started to leave, she stopped him. "Uh, Jacob?"

He turned to look at her, and she said, "Thank you."

"Oh, don't thank me. It was Anna's idea."

The disgusted look on Anna's face spoke volumes. Anna obviously felt Jacob was in denial again, but Rachel thanked her anyway. Anna just nodded and motioned toward the apartment.

Rachel knew Anna wanted to visit alone. Jacob and Anna's boys helped Rachel's children carry the rest of their new clothes to their rooms. Rachel almost laughed as James scooped Emily's fluffy slips into his arm. Emily had chosen to sleep in the room by Anna and Jacob since she had slept there before.

Anna followed Rachel to her apartment. When they got to Rachel's room, Anna closed the door and turned to face her. "You don't need to believe for one minute that it was my idea to buy you all of those clothes because it was Jacob's. He suggested it, and when I told him to go for it, he suddenly decided it was my idea."

"When did he decide to do it?"

"Well, when we came home from the funeral, I could see that something was bothering him, and I asked him what it was. He mentioned that your clothes, though neat and clean, were clearly old and worn. He wondered if that was why you didn't want to go to church with us. He wondered if he should buy you some. When I suggested he go ahead, he resisted. He thought it might be insulting and thought that if you truly needed new clothes, you had plenty of money from the sale of the house to buy some.

"Then, when he came home from the hospital and informed me that his brother had taken most of the money from the sale of the house, he determined to do something to help out. He hoped that if you some nice clothes that you might join us for church. He came up with the Santa Claus thing as a cover, hoping not to insult you. When I said I agreed that it was a good idea, he suddenly made it out as if I had thought of it."

"So did you buy them or did he?"

"Oh, he bought them. I had to keep James home so he would think Jacob truly had run into Santa Claus. He is a typical man, though. He had no idea what sizes. I have to admit, I sneaked into your room and into your sons' room to look at the tags on your clothes."

"That was so nice of both of you."

"Well, you're more than welcome. But don't go believing that Jacob doesn't still care for you like he has convinced himself."

"But, Anna, doesn't it upset you that he wants to do things like that for my children and me?"

"No."

"But most women would be upset."

"I'm not most women. And I have my reasons. Sometime we'll talk, but not now."

Rachel felt frustrated. She loved Anna very much, and they had become very close friends. But she couldn't think of a single reason for Anna's behavior, and it was beginning to bother her. Was it just because she was family? Even that didn't make sense.

Anna wasn't about to discuss it further, and Rachel knew it. In fact, Anna changed the subject totally. "Don't forget that Jacob has something he wants to discuss with you in his office."

"What is it?"

"It's really not my right to say. But you probably don't want to keep him waiting."

A million things went through Rachel's mind as she walked the short distance to Jacob's office. His office, which was near the front of the house, was a beautiful room. It had glass double doors and a shiny hardwood floor. The walls were lined with floor-to-ceiling bookshelves, with pullout writing shelves extending along most of the wall. On one wall there were three built-in filing cabinets, and on the farthest wall there was a desk. Another desk was set so Jacob could sit behind it and see the door. Each desk had a computer monitor on it. There was lots of other computer equipment all around the room, much of which Rachel didn't recognize.

Jacob was busy typing with his back to the door when she arrived. She timidly knocked, and he motioned her in, pointing to a seat. "I'll be with you in just a minute. Give me just a second to get to a stopping place."

A moment later, he pushed the keyboard back under the desk, turned, and smiled pleasantly. "Thank you for coming." He seemed very businesslike, somewhat like when he had come to her house that first day, except much more pleasant.

He came around to the front of the desk and sat on the edge of it facing her. "Rachel, my personal secretary, Edna, who is at the company headquarters in Washington, will be retiring soon. I've contemplated hiring another secretary there to work for me, but after giving it some thought, I came to the conclusion that it might be better to have a secretary here in Middlefork instead."

Rachel's heart started to pound. Could he possibly be considering offering her a job? She would love to have something better than working as a checker at the grocery store.

Jacob folded his arms together in front of him. "I've also wanted to have someone who could be available to help Anna whenever she wanted. The job would require a lot of confidentiality, good ethics, and trust. Plus, the person would need to be Anna's friend."

Rachel wondered if her excitement was showing on her face. She was trying to control it, but she could feel her breathing intensifying and sweat beading on her forehead as he continued.

"I considered posting an ad for the job, but after careful consideration, I would like to offer it to you first. I know how much Anna loves you, and, well, I know what kind of woman you are and that you could be trusted with the confidentiality that I need."

Jacob arose and walked back and forth in front of her, as he continued. "The first things you would naturally be wanting to know are the wages and what your responsibilities would be."

When Jacob told her the salary, Rachel almost choked. It was nearly four times her current wage, which was just above minimum. Her mind reeled at the amount of money Jacob was suggesting. Her thoughts wandered to how she could use the money, and she found herself struggling to concentrate on his words.

"You will, of course, have some training, and after you have satisfactorily completed it, you will receive a twenty-five percent increase in your wage. There is also insurance and a matching retirement fund in stock up to five percent of your salary. Because you would be expected to maintain a certain image consistent with the secretary of a former U.S. Senator and a Microsoft executive, you would need to dress appropriately and would, therefore, be given an initial clothing budget. And since you would need to run errands for myself and Anna, you would also be given a car and the fuel for that car. In addition, if you wanted to take educational classes of any kind, your tuition and expenses would be paid.

"You might need to be on call for things Anna would need. Also, since a lot of your work would be done in your home, you would either need to remodel a room to become a home office or add on a room. The remodel or addition would be paid for.

"You would be provided a laptop computer, and a desktop, the laptop for business use, the desktop for personal. You would have a network tied to ours that would connect you to the Internet. The laptop would be utilized when you needed to be out of your house for assigned work."

Jacob went on talking for a while about the responsibilities and the fact she would have to sign a nondisclosure agreement. He seemed so businesslike that it almost made Rachel laugh. She had never seen him quite like this. He acted and spoke so formally. When he finally finished, he stopped his pacing and sat down on the edge of the desk in front of her.

"You are welcome to take some time to think about it, but I would need to know within a week. Do you have any questions?"

Rachel just grinned. "When do I start?"

"Does that mean you're interested?"

"I'm more than interested. I would like the job."

"You don't want some time to think about it?"

Rachel shook her head. "I'd love to work for you and Anna."

"Okay. I'll get the paperwork ready tomorrow. How long will you need to give your current employer for notification?"

Rachel hadn't even thought about that. She had quit looking for another job long ago. With nothing more than a high school diploma, she had few options available. She had been stuck in her job for so long that changing jobs was foreign to her. She told Jacob she would probably have to give a two-week notice but that she would like to start on her off days.

Jacob nodded. "Okay. Would you like to remodel a room in your house or add on a home office?"

"I would like to add on," Rachel replied.

Again, Jacob nodded. "All right. I would like to get it done while the men are working on the other things in the house. I need your house to be such that you will feel comfortable if I need someone to meet with you. I will still need you to come to my office at least once each day to discuss any assignments."

Rachel smiled. "Okay."

Jacob spoke again, very matter-of-factly. "In addition, I want you to understand that your first responsibility is to Anna. Anything Anna requests of you are highest priority, and what I need will come second. Let me know the first day you are available, and we will work on the details."

Jacob informed her that he was a tough boss—he expected perfection, and she should not be offended if he asked her to redo something, even if it was multiple times. He said she would, of course, be paid for all of it, but she would also get better at knowing what he wanted done.

When Jacob said he was finished and suggested she get some rest, Rachel could hardly resist hugging him. She was so excited and nervous at the same time. The thought of earning that much made her dizzy with excitement. She wondered whether she could perform her tasks at the level Jacob wanted. She was more than willing to learn, but she was aware that her computer and secretarial skills were rusty and limited. She knew there were others with better skills and wondered if Anna had had a hand in this. Or was it because they lived so close and this would make it more convenient, as he had implied?

She just had to talk to Anna. She found her in the kitchen working on some brownies. She grabbed Anna's arm. "Did you know Jacob was going to offer me a job?"

Anna nodded. "I will admit that I had a big hand in this. Jacob wanted someone who could help me and also do some work for him. Really, who would be better?"

Rachel hugged her. "Oh, Anna, thank you! I will do my best to do a good job."

"I know you will. We will have lots of fun together. Just realize that Jacob is a bit of a perfectionist so be patient with him."

"I will."

Anna took her oven mitts off and put an arm around Rachel. "Your first assignment with me is going to be fun. We will go car shopping for you, and then you have to go out to lunch with me."

"How much time do I count off for lunch?"

"You don't. Going to lunch with me is part of your assignment."

"But where I work now I have to count an hour off for lunch, even if I don't get a full hour."

"Not with me. If I give you the assignment to go to lunch with me, then it is part of your job. And don't worry, Jacob will pay for your lunch, too. It's not like he can't afford it, and we're going to enjoy each other's company."

Rachel and Anna talked for a long time. They didn't quit until they heard Jacob summoning everyone for the evening routine. When they entered the family room, Emily was already dressed in her new pajamas and showing them off to everyone.

Rachel enjoyed listening to Jacob read from the Bible, and when he finished, he pulled Emily and James onto his lap and read a Bible story. Afterward, they all knelt in prayer. It was Joseph's turn to pray, and he expressed gratitude that Emily was getting better. Rachel had to choke back tears knowing how much all of Jacob and Anna's family cared for her and her children.

When Rachel was finally ready for bed, she knelt and offered her own prayer of gratitude for their love and for this new opportunity. After she climbed beneath the fluffy blankets, she found it impossible to sleep. Her mind and heart were too full of excitement and gratitude as she considered what lay ahead of her.

Work, Church, Family, and Friends

The grocery store owner was sorry to see Rachel leave. He even offered to raise her wage a dollar an hour if she stayed. Rachel was barely able to keep a straight face, knowing she would be making far more than that. She just told him it was an opportunity she couldn't pass up.

He grudgingly told her that he would start working her out of the schedule. She had to work the next day, which was Thursday. Her car still wouldn't start, and Jacob felt no reason to waste time on it. He suggested she use his. She felt self-conscious going to work at the grocery store in his beautiful car, and she parked it at the far edge of the lot, making sure no one was looking before she got out. She did the same in reverse when it was time to go home.

When she arrived home from work, Jacob had all the paperwork ready for her to fill out, including the forms for two credit cards. One was for her to use for anything related to business, and the other was to be used for anything he or Anna asked her to buy for the family.

Friday was her first day off work. Anna asked Jacob to keep an eye on Emily and James while she and Rachel went shopping for a car. They looked at cars all morning. Rachel had never had a new car before and would have been happy with anything that worked, but Anna wanted it to be perfect. Jacob had mentioned that it would be nice if it were an American-made car since it would maintain his senatorial image. After they had looked at just about everything, Anna suggested a Cadillac Seville. It wouldn't be over the top, but would be comfortable. Rachel could hardly imagine herself driving one, but it wasn't long before she found herself preparing for a test drive. As the dealer handed her the keys, her hands trembled.

She climbed in, and Anna slid into the passenger seat beside her. Rachel reached up to adjust the mirror, and a voice said, "OnStar, may I help you?"

Rachel jumped and looked around, and Anna laughed as the voice said, "This is OnStar. How may I be of service?"

Anna responded. "We're sorry. We accidentally hit the button when we adjusted the mirror."

"What in the world is OnStar?" Rachel gasped.

"It is a service people use when they get into trouble or get lost or anything. You just hit the button and tell them. They can track your car by satellite, and they will send help to you—police, ambulance, tow truck, whatever. That is part of the reason I think you should have this car. Not all cars have it."

If Rachel was trembling before, she was really trembling after the OnStar voice frightened her. She finally started the car, and they pulled out of the lot. They rolled along so smoothly that it hardly felt like they were moving at all. Anna tapped the dashboard. "She's a beauty, but we ought to see what she's got, don't you think?" Rachel nodded, and Anna said, "Let's find a country road where you can open her up."

They had no sooner turned into the open country than Anna said, "Let's gun it!"

Rachel hit the gas pedal, and the car leaped forward, leaving her heart in the back seat. They went from thirty to seventy-five miles per hour in just a few seconds. Anna suggested she take it higher, but Rachel was too nervous. They drove for a while, and when they turned back toward the car dealership, Anna started asking her about all the options she wanted in a car.

Rachel thought they were looking to buy that particular one, but Anna said otherwise. "This is just the model. When you buy a new car, you order the color you want, the accessories you want—everything."

When they returned, the car dealer was pleased to know they liked it. They sat at a computer and went over colors and options. Rachel preferred the dark blue. Anna insisted it should have everything: the best sound system, a CD player, a cell phone and iPod interface, and many more amenities. Anna also insisted it have OnStar, even though Rachel wasn't sure what she thought of that.

The dealer checked the availability and said he could have one in by the following Wednesday.

When they finished, Anna turned to Rachel. "Where do you want to eat?"

Rachel shrugged. "Since the day I married Matthew, I have seldom eaten out, and then only at cheap places with my children."

"Well, then," Anna said, "let's do it up right."

They settled on a nice steak and seafood restaurant. When Rachel looked at the prices on the menu and realized any one of the meals would be far more than a full day's wage at her other job, she couldn't bring herself to order. So Anna took the initiative and ordered them steak and all-you-can-eat shrimp and salad bar, and orange juice. It was so good that Rachel ate until she thought she would be sick. When she thought she couldn't eat another bite, she found out the meal came with her choice of cherry cheesecake or a chocolate eclair. She had never eaten an eclair before, so she chose that. When she bit into it, and the cream filling filled her mouth, she was sure she had never tasted anything so good in her entire life. She took half of it home so her children could try it.

Anna spent the afternoon helping Rachel buy a cell phone and doing other shopping. Rachel needed a business wardrobe, and it was fun shopping for clothes that were not purchased at a second-hand store.

When they returned home, they found that Jacob had already started spaghetti for dinner. Rachel couldn't eat another bite after the amount of lunch she had, but she stayed at the table to enjoy the family time.

On Saturday, Jacob asked John and David if they wanted to go with him and his sons to do some work. They were happy to do so. He wanted to get some wood from the groves of trees on the other side of Jensen Lake—a load for his house, a load for Camilla, and a load for Rachel to use when her family moved back home.

They left with a chainsaw in the big pickup Jacob sometimes drove. Rachel saw them come with a load of wood early in the day, but she didn't see them again until dinner time. When they returned, John and David excitedly burst through the door and announced that Jacob had taken all of the boys out for hamburgers for lunch. They had been able to order anything they wanted, and Rachel could just imagine how much they had eaten. She knew what a treat it had been for them.

After family routine that night, all Rachel could think about was going to church the next day. When she woke the next morning, her stomach was in a big knot. What would people there think of her after all of these years?

After breakfast, everyone scurried about getting ready. Church was at nine o'clock and getting there took them to the last minute. Anna insisted on doing Emily's hair. When she finished, Rachel thought Emily looked like a little princess, and Emily clearly agreed as she spun around in her dress.

Even as Rachel chose the dress that matched Emily's, she looked at her beautiful red and white dress. It hung where she could see it, but she wondered if she could ever bring herself to wear it. Even if she couldn't, she would enjoy looking at it and remembering the wonderful memories it brought to her.

The biggest vehicle that Jacob and Anna had was a seven-passenger van, so they had to take a car, too. Emily wanted to ride with James, so Anna said she would ride with Rachel in Jacob's car.

When they reached the church, they all went in together, and people greeted Rachel as if she had never left. John and David were especially nervous, but their cousins helped them feel at ease. Anna chose seating for them on two side pews. Rachel had thought she would sit in a different pew than Anna and Jacob, but Anna seated Rachel on one side of Jacob and then took a seat on his other side.

Rachel had always sat by Jacob when they were younger, but now it felt strange. Rachel could tell Jacob felt awkward as well, so she scooted over to let James and Emily climb up between them. That didn't last long. Anna motioned for James to come down by her, and where James went, so did Emily. Needing the room for the two children, Anna had Jacob scoot over, again putting him right by Rachel.

The need to understand Anna and why she did these kinds of things nagged at Rachel once more, but she knew it would do no good to ask.

When it came time for the choir to sing, Rachel noted that Jacob, Anna, and their sons made up half of the choir. Watching them sing gave her a desire to join, too, even though she felt inadequate because of things Matthew had said to her.

When the congregational meeting was over, they moved to Sunday School and other classes. She was glad there was someone for each of her children. She watched as James grabbed Emily's hand and pulled her toward his class. Anna put her arm around Rachel, and they walked together to the adult class. Church lasted three hours, and what an enjoyable three hours it was. It felt so much like coming home. Many people hugged her, and most of the women told her how cute it was to see her and Emily dressed alike.

When church was over, Emily came running with James following behind. Rachel had to tell Emily to walk reverently in church, but nothing could quell her exuberance. She had a picture of Noah with a rainbow that she had colored in crayon, and she had to tell her mother all about it.

She made everyone laugh when she asked, "Momma, did you and Uncle Jacob know Noah when you were little?"

Lunch was also a special treat. It wasn't anything fancy, but Jacob and Anna worked together making homemade macaroni and cheese. It was creamy, filled with big chunks of cheese, and served with plates of apples, oranges, and other fruits. It was absolutely delicious. Emily ate until Rachel thought she would pop.

Before scripture time, Jacob pulled out his guitar for a sing-along. Rachel remembered how Jacob had sometimes played the guitar for her when they went on picnics, and he had played a lot for her family. Anna played a few songs on the piano, and they sang to them, too. When she finished, she turned to Rachel. "Jacob says you play the piano."

Emily, who was on Jacob's lap, looked shocked. "Momma, do you really?"

Rachel felt her face grow warm. "Well, I haven't since I got married."

Anna smiled at her. "There is nothing I would enjoy more than playing a duet with you."

"I don't think I can. I was mostly self-taught, and I was never all that good."

Anna smiled that half-smile she did when she disagreed with something. "That's not what I hear. Besides, our piano is yours. Feel free to use it all you want."

"Maybe I can practice when others aren't around," Rachel said.

They finished up the evening with a few more songs and then read scriptures and said prayers. As she went to bed, Rachel felt more at peace than she had in years. She had never enjoyed a Sunday so much. She realized it was like Sundays she'd had growing up, which had usually included Jacob.

Tuesday was Rachel's last day at work, and she was glad because she would have her new car on Wednesday, and she knew she would really feel awkward driving it to work at the grocery store.

Wednesday was Valentine's Day, and when she came into the kitchen that morning, things were different. Jacob had cooked waffles, eggs, hashbrowns, bacon, and sausage. It was obviously a holiday meal. But what immediately caught Rachel's eye was that all of the plates were turned upside down. She reached for hers, and Jacob kindly scolded her. "Hey, no peeking until breakfast time."

When Emily wandered in, her eyes widened in surprise. "What's wrong with the table?'

James had come in right behind her and was quick to answer. "Oh, that's how Daddy always does Valentine's. We call it Upside-Down-Plate Day because he always puts our surprises under our plates."

Emily wanted to turn hers over, but James told her that she couldn't until everyone came for breakfast. "If you want to hurry things along," Jacob suggested to her, "you can call everyone."

Emily dashed off with James right behind her. Pretty soon, the rest of the family gathered in the kitchen. Anna was last, looking tired as she always did in the morning. Jacob greeted her with a happy kiss. They had no sooner finished the blessing on the food than everyone flipped their plates over. Anna hardly needed to flip hers. She had so much stuff under it that the was little secret what was there.

The children and Rachel each found a bag of M&M's, some candy bars, and a box of message hearts under their plates. Anna had all of those plus a big box of chocolates, a card, and a beautiful necklace. Anna secretly let Rachel read the card. Rachel, for the first time in a long time, felt the slightest twinge of jealousy.

After breakfast, Emily and James were off to play while the other children prepared for school. Rachel helped Jacob clean up the kitchen, and just before the bus came, they had family prayer. Jacob told Rachel he had some work for her as soon as she was available. Anna seemed at least as excited about the new car as Rachel was and told Jacob that the car would come first. When they called the car dealer, however, he said it probably wouldn't be in until about noon. He promised he would call the minute it arrived.

"All right, Jacob," Anna said, "you can have Rachel work with you. But when the car is in, we all need to go to lunch and get it."

Rachel, dressed in a new blue business suit, met Jacob at his office. He suggested that they go down to her house and talk to the contractor about the new office that would be added on to it. It was almost noon before they finished there. Jacob's cell phone rang, and after he hung up, he turned to Rachel with a grin. "We'd better hightail it back home. Anna is anxious to get your car."

They hurried back to find Anna waiting with coats on Emily and James, and they all quickly loaded into Jacob's car. When they pulled into the car lot, Rachel could see the big delivery truck with the sleek, shiny car still on it. Jacob took James and Emily each by a hand and walked over to watch the unloading process. By the time the car was off of the truck, the dealer was standing beside them with the title and the keys. If she thought she was trembling when she drove the test car, she was much more nervous now. Jacob seemed to know her thoughts and reassured her. "Don't worry, it's totally insured."

After lunch, they went home. Anna and Rachel painted for a couple of hours, visiting as they did. Anna began to feel tired and went to take a nap while Rachel went to do transcribing for Jacob. He gave her a tape recorder with headphones and set up one of his computers for her to work on. He told her that her laptop was ordered and that her other computer would be ordered when her house was completed.

Rachel found the transcribing to be slow and laborious since her typing skills were rusty. It took her until three-thirty, when the children came home, just to get the letter in rough draft. Jacob suggested they take a break and have a snack with the children.

Anna woke up and joined them. The children rushed into the house, clamoring for a ride in the new car. The noise woke Emily from her nap, and Emily woke James. Everyone rushed out to the driveway with James and Emily leading the way. Everyone oohed and aahed as they climbed into the beautiful new car. Abraham asked Jacob if he could drive it, but Jacob said he would have to ask Rachel.

She said he could, and with Jacob warning him to stay under the speed limit, he was off with the older boys. Peter, James, and Emily felt left out, but Abraham assured them he would be more than happy to take them on another trip. While they were gone, the rest of the family trooped into the kitchen and pulled out some cookies and milk. Peter talked about his Valentine's Day party, and Emily and James told him about getting the new car.

Soon the others were back, and Abraham left with a new group. When he returned, Anna turned to Jacob. "Jacob, you haven't ridden in it yet. Why don't you and Rachel go for a ride?"

Jacob shook his head, and Rachel caught sight of the glance he gave Anna. "I've got a lot to do."

Anna just laughed. "All work and no play makes for a boring day."

Jacob took a deep breath and spoke somewhat under his breath. "Anna, it isn't really appropriate for me to . . . "

"My heavens, Jacob! Lighten up a little and go have some fun."

The confusion Rachel felt sprung up again.

Jacob finally agreed but turned to Emily. "Would you and James like to go with us?"

Anna let out a disgusted grunt, but Rachel had to admit she felt more comfortable having the children along. She offered Jacob the keys, but he insisted she drive.

It felt good to be gliding down the road in a sleek automobile. In some ways, she could have almost felt like it was just her and Jacob like it had been years ago except for the happy chatter coming from Emily and James in the backseat.

When they got back, Jacob quietly slipped off to work in his office, and Rachel went to the kitchen to help Anna prepare dinner. Before long, dinner was over, they were singing songs, reading scriptures, saying prayers, and going to bed.

* * *

The days started to go by quickly. The contractor said that the addition on the house would push the completion date back a little. He estimated completion around the first of April. Rachel didn't mind. It was nice to share time with other adults. She always enjoyed the breakfast Jacob made each morning. She had offered to get up early and let him sleep a little longer, but he declined her offer.

Sometimes Rachel felt guilty. She felt she was enjoying life too much. She spent an hour a day painting with Anna, and then she practiced the piano because Anna wanted them to have some duets ready by Christmas. Rachel found she enjoyed that a lot.

She felt guilty being paid for those kinds of things, but Jacob insisted because Anna wanted her to. He even suggested that she might need to record more than forty hours per week. That was because her laptop computer had arrived from company headquarters, and with it, she had been doing transcription work in her apartment at night after everyone else was in bed. Jacob realized she was doing this and wanted her to be paid for it.

She begged him not to press her to count any more hours than she already did, feeling she wasn't doing enough already. "Besides," she said, "going to lunch, painting, and those things really aren't work."

She was also getting more and more comfortable with the work he wanted. She learned, however, that he could be demanding, though he was never unkind. One day she had retyped a letter six times before he was satisfied. By then her frustration was reaching atomic levels, and when she went to print it, she accidentally deleted it instead.

She threw her paper and pencil on the floor and stomped on them, only to find Jacob grinning at her. She was embarrassed, but her embarrassment just made him smile more. "You know, Rachel," he chuckled, "I haven't seen that much fire in you since we were younger."

At first she was mad that he would laugh at her, but as she was lying in her bed that night, she thought about what he had said. When she had been younger, she had been full of "fire." She thought of how, when they were small, she had often tried to tackle Jacob, though he could always best her.

As they had become teenagers, her feistiness had come out at times against any other girl that dared flirt with him. But what had happened to that fire? She realized Matthew had crushed much of it out of her as he had done so many things. She also realized that the display of emotion she had shown in Jacob's office was only an outward sign of what she was feeling inside. She was feeling more and more confident, more and more free, and happier than she had felt in a long time. She was, in all reality, feeling her spirit coming back.

Family, Memories, and an Old Tree House

It was nearly April, and the work on Rachel's house was nearly finished. She and Anna had picked out paint, wallpaper, and all sorts of things. Jacob also insisted on new carpet, saying the old carpet would be worthless after the construction work was done.

The two families had grown close. Jacob worked with the boys most Saturdays, often doing service for other people. He especially took care of Camilla. Rachel knew her own sons enjoyed those times, especially eating lunch out somewhere. James started going along, and Emily felt left out and begged to go, too. Jacob started taking her, though Rachel knew it slowed them down because he had to assign one of the older boys to keep an eye on her.

Jacob told Rachel that his phone line had worldwide unlimited long distance, and he encouraged her to use it to visit with her family. She was happy to reconnect with her brothers and sisters now that Matthew was out of her life, and she found that Sunday was an especially good day to call. Jacob asked her to let him know how everyone was doing, so when they took a break from work during the week, she would tell him what she found out. In return, her siblings wanted to hear about Jacob. He had been such an integral part of their family.

Rachel always enjoyed church. Her family joined the choir, and she liked feeling that she was contributing in some small way. She also liked the way Jacob and Anna's family honored the Sabbath. They didn't play lots of boisterous games or watch television. Instead, they read good books and magazines, and they played friendly games like checkers. They would also use part of the day to touch base with Anna's family, write letters, or visit friends.

Rachel liked to listen to Anna tell stories about her family. Her sisters sounded so much like her. It seemed that, as they were growing up, they were always playing some kind of prank. The pranks were never mean, but they were funny.

Most of Rachel's calling time was spent talking with Marie. Marie was just younger than Rachel and had been her closest friend besides Jacob.

Unfortunately, that had changed for two reasons when she had married Matthew. With the exception of their mother, Marie had been the most adamant against Matthew. Marie loved Jacob as a brother more than any of Rachel's other siblings. When Jacob had gone away, and Rachel had married Matthew, Marie was so angry that she wouldn't speak to Rachel. Matthew didn't like Marie because he knew how she felt, so he forbade Rachel from having contact with her. Later, when Marie married, she asked Rachel to be her matron of honor.

Rachel had been pleased and excited, but Matthew refused to let her even go to the wedding. They had had a big fight about it, and he beat her. At first, Marie had thought Rachel didn't want to come, but when she found out what had happened, she was furious.

Marie was the most like Rachel, at least like Rachel used to be. She was vivacious and had a short fuse. Marie confronted Matthew and told him what she thought of him, but it just made him angrier. He had beaten Rachel again for that, and then he had done everything he could to drive a wedge between her and Marie.

Rachel had learned that, at times, Marie had tried to reach out to her. She found out about letters and birthday cards that Marie had sent, but Rachel had never received. When Rachel did respond, Marie was sure Matthew had intercepted them and destroyed them. Marie was not one to be pushed around, however. She eventually started sending letters and cards to the grocery store where Rachel worked. Rachel would read them and respond with a letter of her own.

The letters and cards hadn't come very often, maybe three or four times in a year, but Rachel always looked forward to them. Matthew acted like he suspected Rachel still had some contact with Marie. But Rachel destroyed the letters and cards from Marie after reading them so Mathew wouldn't have any evidence.

Rachel appreciated Marie showing her the flowers from Jacob at their parents' funeral, and for taking the tag to protect her from Matthew's anger. Marie had encouraged Rachel to divorce Matthew more than once, and it added a measure of strength she needed. After the divorce, the letters between the two of them increased. She would get about one each month. But after Rachel started working for Jacob, she not only started calling Marie, but they e-mailed each other.

They shared pictures of their children, recipes, fun stories, and jokes. Their friendship wasn't what it had been when they were young, but it was starting to grow again. Then came the day that Marie e-mailed Rachel and said she had some exciting news to share on Sunday when they talked.

Rachel could hardly wait until Sunday evening to call. She wondered if Marie was expecting again. Marie and Jason already had six children, their youngest still a baby, but Rachel couldn't imagine what other exciting news Marie wouldn't put in an e-mail.

Rachel's call finally rang through and Jason answered. He laughed when he realized who it was. "Boy, does Marie have some big news for you." Rachel liked Jason—at least what she knew of him. She had only met him at her parents' funeral and talked briefly with him on the phone. His comment just heightened her curiosity.

When Marie came on the phone, she chitchatted about everything until, finally, Rachel could stand it no longer. "Marie, what's the big news?"

Marie laughed. "Okay! Okay! Jason's job is transferring us up there."

Rachel could hardly believe it. Jason worked for a pizza company and had requested a transfer back home to Minnesota, but they hadn't had much hope it would come through. Rachel was so excited. Almost all of her family had moved far away, and the thought of Marie coming back home was a dream come true.

"When would the transfer be?"

"They want him there by the first part of June. We've already put our house on the market. We're hoping to be there about June first or second. And that brings me to a question I wanted to ask you. Do you know if the old family home is available for rent?"

"I know no one is living in it, but I don't know who owns it or if the owner would rent it.

"Will you check?"

"Sure," Rachel replied.

They talked for a long time about how nice it would be to see each other again and let their children get better acquainted. When Rachel hung up, she wandered out of the apartment, where she always went to do her Sunday calling. She realized she was smiling as she entered the kitchen because Jacob said, "That must have been a fun call."

Rachel told him about it and then asked. "Would you mind if I took a little time off Monday morning to go to the county office and see who purchased my parents' farm?"

Jacob looked at her with what Rachel thought was a sly grin. "You know, you could do that, or you could just ask me."

Rachel was shocked. "You know who bought it?"

Jacob didn't answer but raised his eyebrows. Suddenly, Rachel understood, and she gasped. "You bought it?"

Jacob nodded. Rachel could hardly believe what she was hearing. "Have you owned it ever since my parents died?"

Again Jacob nodded. It was just incredible to Rachel. Again there was that strange déjà vu feeling of knowing, in some ways, Jacob had been so close, and she hadn't known it. "Jacob, why didn't you tell me?"

Jacob shrugged. "You never asked."

"Oh, and what else have you not told me because I haven't asked?"

"I don't know. Ask, and I'll tell you."

"If I don't know, how can I ask?"

"If you don't ask, how can I know that you don't know?"

Rachel let out an exasperated gasp. "Oh, for heaven sakes, Jacob, you can be so male sometimes!"

Jacob just grinned. Another question crossed Rachel's mind. "Jacob, why did you buy it?"

"It connects to my parents' farm."

"You bought it before you bought your parents' farm. And you know that my parents' land isn't the best ground around."

Jacob spoke quietly as he answered. "There were a lot of good memories there."

"Then why don't you ever go over there anymore?"

Jacob looked away and answered even more quietly. "There are also some bad ones."

Rachel felt the pain again. How could one foolish mistake color so much of a person's life? All she could say was, "I'm sorry, Jacob."

Jacob stood there quietly for a moment. When he looked up, there was sadness showing in his face, but also determination. "Rachel, I think it would be great if Marie's family rented the old home. I haven't seen her in all these years, and it would be nice to do something with the old place. It will probably need some repair, so I'll get right on it so it will be done before they come. Maybe we could go out there tomorrow. After all, when Emily was in the hospital, I promised her that I would take her to see our tree house."

Rachel could hear the pain in his voice, but he spoke with a doggedness that gave her hope that he wanted to face his feelings. She needed to call Marie back, so she asked Jacob about the price for rent.

"Oh, I don't know. You work that out with Marie; whatever you think would be fair." Jacob paused a moment and then continued. "In fact . . . "

He again paused, and his eyes brightened. "I have been considering doing something to honor your parents. What if we created a scholarship fund that could be used for all of their descendants and call it the Robert and Ruth Henderson Family Scholarship Fund. We could make it so the interest from the fund could be used to pay up to half of the children's college tuitions. I'll donate one-hundred-thousand dollars into it to get it started, and Marie's family could pay their rent into it."

Jacob's generosity was always great and was a large part of what she admired in him. She could sense a softness in his voice when he talked of her parents, and she liked that. "You really loved them, didn't you?" she asked.

Jacob's voice trembled as he spoke. "They were like parents to me. Sometimes I think they raised me and loved me more than my own parents did."

Jacob then excused himself, saying there was something he needed to do, but Rachel knew he just didn't want to cry in front of her. She knew he had never healed from the loss of her parents. She wished he could have come to the funeral; it would have helped him.

The happiness she felt with Marie coming was now tempered by the sympathy she felt for Jacob, but she knew she should call Marie. Marie was shocked but excited to hear that Jacob owned the old farm and would let them rent the house. When Rachel explained about the rent and the scholarship fund, Marie was quiet. Rachel knew Marie understood how Jacob felt about their parents.

The next morning, shortly after the older children were off to school, Anna, Jacob, Rachel, Emily, and James climbed into Jacob's car to drive over to the Henderson farm. Rachel couldn't understand the apprehension that filled her heart. Why was she so nervous? Was it because she was concerned about what shape her parents' home would be in? When they pulled into the yard, she suddenly realized that it was concern about being there with Jacob. He hadn't been back since that fateful night. The trepidation nearly strangled her.

What she saw as she stepped from the car saddened her. Some of the siding was hanging, what little paint that was left was chipped and peeling, and the windows had been broken out. Rachel watched Jacob slowly get out and scan the scene around him. She expected him to turn and look at her, but she could tell he was averting his eyes from her on purpose. Rachel realized Anna was watching him as well. Anna did turn to Rachel, and when their eyes met, she could see the look of concern on Anna's face.

They walked together to the house. Jacob pulled keys from his pocket, unlocked the door, and stepped inside. The others followed. Again, Rachel's heart sank. The house was filthy, and there were signs of mice and birds. With the broken windows, anything could get in.

"Well," Jacob said in a voice that sounded like he was trying to hide his pain, "it will need a lot of work. But the structure seems sound."

Emily and James raced around the house until Anna called to them and suggested they should wait outside where it was cleaner. Jacob, Anna, and Rachel walked through the house with few words passing between them.

As they stepped through the doorway into the family room, the doorway which Jacob had entered to see her and Matthew that horrible night, he didn't need to speak for Rachel to know his thoughts. She thought about how it had been in that room that Jacob had pinned on her first corsage. It had been in that room that she had snuggled next to him near the fireplace to watch Christmas lights twinkling on the tree in the corner. It had been in that room that he had given her a promise ring, a ring that Matthew later destroyed.

She thought about the ring. That had been the only time Jacob had ever kissed her. He viewed a kiss as a very special promise between two people, just as he did the ring. She should have realized how he would feel when she let Matthew kiss her. To Jacob, in that instant, she had broken her promise along with every bond between them.

Rachel's thoughts panned through many beautiful memories that had occurred with Jacob in that room, but when she turned to look at him, she could see by the expression on his face that there was only one searing memory that burned in his mind.

Jacob didn't say anything, but turned and walked out the front door, just as he had on that horrible night. But this time, she went after him. By the time he stepped onto the front porch, she had caught up to him. She touched his arm, stopping him as she spoke. "Jacob?"

He turned farther from her. "I've seen enough. I know what needs to be done."

Rachel could hardly talk for the pain in her heart. "Jacob, please! I'm sorry!"

"Sorry about what? I was the one who let the house deteriorate so much."

Rachel knew Jacob's pain had nothing to do with the house deteriorating. It was just a cover. She knew the pain he still felt would not let him face his true feelings, and he would not talk about it. He called to Emily and James, saying that he was going to the tree house, and they were instantly by his side. He pulled his arm from Rachel and walked deliberately across the yard, the children scampering to keep up.

It was then that Rachel realized Anna was standing just behind her. Anna had long before asked Rachel about what had happened between her and Jacob. Rachel had held nothing back and shared everything with her. Anna was very understanding, but when Anna touched her arm, and Rachel turned to look at her, the concern in Anna's eyes indicated a new understanding of how deeply Rachel had hurt him.

Rachel could see tears on Anna's cheeks and realized she had tears rolling down her own face, too. Anna swept Rachel into a big hug, and Rachel couldn't hold her feelings in any longer and sobbed on Anna's shoulder. She could feel Anna's tears against the side of her face as well. They cried for some time and then Anna pulled back and looked her in the face. "Sometimes, for a wound to heal and the pain to go away, it has to be opened up so the thing causing it to fester can be cleansed out of it."

Rachel leaned against Anna again as Anna held her tightly. She hoped someday she could understand why Anna wanted the rift Jacob felt with Rachel to heal, but for now, Rachel was just grateful for a friend who would cry with her when she hurt.

After Rachel had cried for some time, she started to feel better. She wiped away her tears, and Anna said she thought that they should go out to the tree house. Anna slipped her arm through Rachel's, and they walked together across the yard. When they reached the old oak tree where the tree house was, Rachel was pleased to see that even though the corners of the playhouse hung down, the old tree stood tall and strong, bigger than it was before. Jacob was standing in the tree, inspecting it. James and Emily stood below, asking if they could come up.

Jacob shook his head. "The tree house has rotted. But we'll fix it and make it usable again."

A much happier spirit emanated from Jacob as he slid out of the tree, and he even wore a slight smile. "The tree is stronger than ever. We can rebuild the old tree house better than before." Rachel was just relieved to see him smile.

The old tree house had lots of good memories. They had used it even when they were in their late teens. Rachel could remember the last girls'-choice dance that she had asked Jacob to. They had shared a candlelight dinner together in the tree house. Her mother had cooked the meal, and Marie had been the waitress.

Jacob had built the tree house with Rachel's parents' approval when he was about nine or ten. It belonged to him and Rachel, and no one could go in it without their permission. They had had group parties there a couple of times, but she had never invited another boy to be alone with her in it, and he had never invited another girl.

"Jacob," Anna said, "how about we make some fun family memories rebuilding it? Why don't you get the wood and things we need, and when the children get home from school, we'll all come over here and have a picnic. While you and the boys work on the tree house, we women will begin to clean the farmhouse."

Jacob agreed, and they drove back to Jacob and Anna's house. Jacob left immediately, not even waiting for lunch. He said he planned to talk to the contractor about the Henderson home on his way to town. Rachel and Anna fixed lunch for themselves, James, and Emily. Then, after settling Emily and James in bed for a nap, they prepared a picnic.

By the time the children stepped off the bus, Jacob had returned, and the picnic was ready. They woke Emily and James, and everyone climbed into Jacob's big pickup and the van. There was a lot of excitement about what they planned to do.

When they pulled in at the Henderson farm, Anna insisted that they had to get some pictures before they took down the old tree house. She had brought a camera and had everyone line up in front. She took a picture, and then Jacob said he wanted one with her in it. She said they could get one after she got one of just him and Rachel. He balked at that, but Anna said it was for old times, and she wouldn't give up the camera until he agreed.

Jacob reluctantly posed with Rachel, and Anna snapped a couple of pictures. Then she told Jacob to smile more and stand a little closer to Rachel. He reluctantly did so. His hesitation made Rachel feel awkward, too. Afterward, Anna gave him the camera and said she would like one with her and Rachel. They put an arm around each other, and Rachel thought about how strange it was that she felt so good having the woman who was Jacob's wife as a friend when, for so many years, she had wanted that title for herself.

After the pictures were taken, Anna told the children that the girls would sweep the house while the boys worked on the tree house. Emily immediately complained and begged to stay with Jacob. He said he'd watch over her, so Anna and Rachel went to clean the house. Soon the sound of pounding could be heard as Rachel swept and Anna dusted. When they entered the family room again, Anna turned to Rachel. "I assume that this is the room where Jacob saw you with Matthew that night."

Rachel nodded. Anna was more solemn than Rachel had ever seen her. As Anna dusted, she spoke quietly. "I've never seen Jacob like that before. I guess I didn't realize the depth of his pain, nor the depth of his love for you."

Rachel stopped sweeping and looked at Anna to see if she was upset, but all she saw in her face was compassion as she continued. "I thought once he came back here and renewed his friendship with you, the pain would go away, but I see it is going to be a bigger task than I thought."

"You are trying to remove the pain Jacob has about me?"

"Of course. If a person truly loves another, they don't want that person to hurt for any reason."

So that's it, Rachel said to herself. Anna wanted Rachel to be friends with Jacob so he wouldn't hurt anymore. That is why she kept promoting the friendship between the two of them.

Rachel realized that if she were in Anna's place, she would not want the pain that created a chasm between her husband and someone he formerly loved to be taken away. But could that be genuine and complete love if she didn't? She marveled at the goodness of Anna's heart.

Anna went to the window, apparently to make sure that Jacob wasn't near. Then she returned to her dusting as she spoke. "Rachel, sometimes the process of healing not only opens old wounds but creates new ones. Usually, the new ones end up being to those who love that person. If you truly love someone and want them to heal, you must be willing to risk hurting, too."

"Do you mean me?"

"I mean both of us. I admit I misjudged his pain and his love, but I also underestimated my ability to help him. This is going to take both of us. Are you willing to be patient and not get angry if he is somewhat hurtful?"

Rachel nodded. "I would do anything for you."

Anna smiled. "It isn't just for me. It's for Jacob and . . . " She paused for a moment and looked deeply into Rachel's eyes. "And it's for you. You are hurting, too, and you need to heal as well."

Rachel knew Anna was right. She hurt, and she would hurt as long as Jacob did. But it was what Anna said next that she didn't understand. "It is also for our children, both yours and mine."

Anna didn't say more, but as they continued to work, Rachel wondered if the pain in their hearts was affecting their children. She didn't think so, but maybe Anna knew more than she did.

Anna was quiet for some time and then spoke out loud, as if deep in thought and actually speaking to herself. "Sometimes, the only way to overcome a bad memory is to replace it with a good one. If only there were some way we could give Jacob another good memory in this room."

As they continued to clean, Anna asked about some of the memories Rachel and Jacob shared there. Rachel talked about them, reminiscing as she did. As the sun began to set, they decided they had better have the picnic because there was no power for lights. They went outside and found that the Jacob and the boys had torn down the other playhouse and had laid the framework for the floor in the new one. It was going to be a much nicer tree house. Jacob had scrounged boards when they were young, but now everything would be the very best.

Anna and Rachel laid out some quilts to sit on and called everyone to eat. They had sliced roast beef, chicken, turkey, and ham to go on hoagie buns. There were carrot sticks, fruit, and juice to go with the sandwiches. For dessert, there were cookies and brownies with milk to drink. Everyone talked excitedly about the tree house. Jacob told the children stories of the old one and didn't seem a bit bothered by the memories.

They were busy the rest of the week, so they decided they would continue building on Saturday. When Saturday came, breakfast was barely over before they had packed up the picnic lunch and driven over. It was a beautiful day in early April, but it was still chilly. When they arrived at the Henderson farm, they saw scaffolding surrounding the house. That left a lump in Rachel's throat because she knew that meant her house was almost done, and she would be moving out of Jacob and Anna's.

Finally, at about dinner time, the tree house was done. Everyone ceremoniously came down to look at it from below. Rachel had to admit that it was much nicer, though she knew she'd miss the old one that Jacob had built just for them.

Jacob seemed pleased with their work. He turned to Anna. "Anna, come up and see the inside."

Anna shook her head. "No, Jacob."

Jacob was taken aback. "But, Anna, why not?"

Anna asked Abraham to take the children over by the pickup and figure out what pizza they would like to order. After the children were away, she turned to Jacob.

"Jacob, the reason I won't go up there with you is because, as I understand it, there was a promise made about the old tree house."

"What are you talking about?"

"When the original tree house was built, I do believe you made a promise to never invite up another girl without Rachel's permission."

Jacob looked at Rachel and then back at Anna. "Any promise I made became null and void with certain events that happened years ago."

Anna was adamant. "Perhaps a promise was broken years ago, but I don't think Rachel has ever asked another guy up there." Anna then turned to Rachel and asked, "Have you?"

118

Rachel shook her head. "No, but I understand. It's all right."

"No, it's not. You each made promises, and there are a lot of good memories here that I don't want left behind."

Jacob was visibly upset. "But the promise she broke was . . . "

Rachel felt she was going to cry, even as Anna interrupted him to keep him from saying more. "Jacob, I understand how you feel. But one bad memory shouldn't destroy all of the good ones. It was so long ago, and can't you see that Rachel hurts, too?" Anna then kissed him. "Please. I'd feel better if you'd take a moment alone with Rachel and think of all of the good times you had here." Jacob didn't say anything, so Anna continued. "You invite Rachel up, and then perhaps we can all come up when the pizza gets here."

"I'm not sure it's appropriate for me to be alone with . . . "

Anna sighed disgustedly. "Oh, for heaven's sake, Jacob! We are all family now. What could be more appropriate than that?"

There was no changing Anna's mind, so Jacob slowly nodded and walked over to Rachel. "Rachel, I would . . . " He paused and looked back at Anna, who nodded encouragement. He turned again to Rachel, and when he spoke, his voice trembled with emotion. "I would be honored if you would join me in the tree house."

Rachel nodded, and they walked to the ladder. Jacob went up first and was waiting to help her as she climbed the last step. He reached out his hand and pulled her in, just as he always had in years past.

They stood quietly side by side, leaning on the sill of one of the windows looking out at the vista that lay before them. The silence felt uncomfortable to Rachel, and she finally spoke. "I'm sorry, Jacob. It's okay if you want to invite Anna or anyone else up."

Jacob shook his head. "No, it's not. Anna's right. I did make a promise about this tree house, and I should keep it."

"But I broke my promise to you about the promise ring. I didn't love Matthew, and I should never have pretended to."

Jacob remained silent, so Rachel decided she needed to say more. "Jacob."

She waited until he turned and looked at her before she continued. "I want you to know I will never break a promise to you ever again."

Jacob gave a weak smile, shrugged, and then changed the subject. "Perhaps we should see if Anna feels we can invite everyone else up now."

Saying what she had said had taken a lot of courage, and Jacob's dismissal of it hurt a lot. Anna was right; if there was ever to be healing, there was going to be hurt.

They descended the ladder and went over to the pickup where the others were waiting for the pizza to be delivered. Jacob took Anna in his arms. "You will come up when the pizza gets here, won't you?"

Anna looked at Rachel. "Anna," Rachel said, "I'd love it if you would join us in the tree house."

Anna smiled. "I'd be glad to."

Rachel felt slightly strange about those events. Rachel truly had broken her promise to Jacob. She couldn't expect him to keep one in return, especially one so simple in comparison. And yet, Anna wanted him to. Anna wanted him to get over the pain of so many years ago, but would this help or make it worse? Rachel was afraid that it might make Jacob despise every memory of the time he and she spent together.

But when the pizza arrived, and everyone climbed into the tree house, Jacob was cheerful. He ate and laughed with everyone else, and he told more stories about the old tree house. He even told about the girl's choice dinner they had there, and how funny it was watching Rachel climb up and down the ladder in her beautiful dress.

He looked at her and smiled. Rachel looked at Anna, and she was smiling approvingly. Rachel was relieved to think that she finally knew why Anna had always promoted her and Jacob's friendship, and Rachel was glad that, in some ways, the tree house still belonged to the two of them.

Back Home and Preserved Memories

The next week, the contractor informed them that Rachel's house was ready. Rachel and Jacob went with the contractor to do the walk-through. The first thing that Rachel noticed was how warm the house was. When she commented on it, the contractor spoke proudly. "With the additional insulation and the new furnace, this is one of the best little houses around."

He then showed her all of the ins and outs of the furnace, down to the new ducts. In addition, he showed her the new fireplace insert. "This," he bragged, "is the most efficient woodstove a person can buy. Why, a log or two will heat the whole house."

"Enjoy having a warm fire," Jacob said. "The boys and I have filled the woodshed to overflowing, and we can get more wood if you need it."

The house was still dusty. Jacob suggested they have a cleaning crew come in, but Rachel said she would like to clean it herself. Anna insisted on helping, too. In fact, as soon as the walk-through was completed, Anna was there. James and Emily came along so Jacob could work in his office unencumbered. Anna and Rachel dusted, swept, vacuumed, and arranged the furniture the way it was supposed to be, and Emily and James even helped.

Rachel liked how the house looked, but her old furniture did look funny in there. The new paint, wallpaper, and carpet made it seem like a whole new house. Rachel loved her new office most of all. It projected out from the house and had windows on three sides and glass doors into the living room on the other. It was bright and airy, had lots of bookshelves, and sported two built-in desks. From there she could see the driveway, the meadow, and Jacob and Anna's house.

The only sad part was knowing that she would be working more there and less in Jacob's office. Even though he didn't say much as he worked, she enjoyed his friendship.

Anna and Rachel worked all morning cleaning the main floor of the house. By lunchtime, that part was about done. As they finished the lower level, Anna asked if there were family pictures or anything else Rachel wanted to hang on the walls.

Rachel shook her head. "Matthew destroyed all of my pictures from before we were married, and he felt having family photos taken was a waste of money."

"Well, then," Anna said, "I think it's time we had some done. One of your next assignments for me is to set up portrait sittings for both of our families." Anna paused momentarily then continues. "With that said, I understand that Jacob preserved quite a few pictures and other memorabilia from his youth. Maybe some of them would be copies of what you lost."

Rachel gasped. "But how could he have taken them with him when he went off to college?"

"When Jacob decided to leave," Anna said, "he was sure Matthew would destroy everything that meant anything to him, so he packed it all up into a couple of big trunks and took them over to Camilla's for safekeeping. As far as I know, the trunks are still there."

Rachel felt an excited shiver run down her spine. Could cherished mementos from her time with Jacob still exist? She knew that their mothers had often shared pictures, programs, and other keepsakes. She especially hoped there might be pictures of their proms together. Those were the pictures that meant the most to her. But she wondered if Jacob, as upset as he was, might have destroyed them himself. That thought made her heart ache. She dared not get her hopes up too high about what might be in those trunks.

Anna suggested that if Jacob gave his permission for them to look through the trunks, they could go to Camilla's after lunch. Despite Rachel's fears that all traces of her life with Jacob might have been eliminated by him, Rachel could hardly contain her excitement.

When they left Rachel's house and arrived back at Jacob and Anna's, Anna asked Jacob if he minded if they went and got the trunks. He paused briefly then spoke quietly. "I suppose it is time they were opened again."

"Would you like to go with us?" Anna asked.

Jacob shook his head. "I would rather not. But maybe you ought to wait until Abraham or Isaac can help because the trunks are quite heavy."

Anna turned, looked at Rachel, and apparently sensed her anxiousness because she turned back to Jacob and said, "I think the two of us can handle it."

Rachel quickly called Camilla, and Camilla said she would be glad to have them come. Rachel's stomach was in such a knot that she couldn't eat anything. They soon had the children fed and in bed, and they were on their way. Camilla greeted them cheerfully after their first knock, and, as usual, insisted they sit down for a bite to eat and a visit. Rachel could feel both her anticipation and her trepidation rising. Finally, Camilla led them to the little attic stairway. She told them she couldn't manage the stairs, but there was a light switch at the top.

Rachel stumbled her way up the stairs and felt around for the switch. She finally found it, and a dim bulb lit the attic with more shadows than light. Dust and cobwebs covered everything. Old furniture and paintings filled the room, along with enough antiques to start an antique mall. But in one corner, tucked far back under the eaves, were two trunks. Rachel knew they had to be the ones.

With Anna behind her, Rachel walked across the attic, the floor squeaking and groaning beneath their weight. Rachel knelt by the first trunk and brushed away the dust, wiping it on her pants. She started to wipe off some more, and Anna held out a handkerchief. Rachel wiped away the rest of the dust and then unhooked the latches on each end. With her hands trembling, she opened the lid.

The items inside were disorganized and thrown in randomly, all except one. Right on top was the picture of Jacob and Rachel from their last prom together. Jacob was wearing a dark suit, and Rachel was wearing her red and white dress. The smiles on their faces and the brightness of their eyes greeted Rachel from years past. From the way the picture was laid on top of the disheveled heap, it was obvious that Jacob had looked at it last before storing it all away.

"The last thing he did before he locked these away was to look at the picture of us." The thought of him locking up the pain of her betrayal of his love and trust in her overwhelmed her, and she sobbed. Anna knelt beside her on the dusty floor and pulled her into her arms.

After Rachel had cried for some time, and the tears finally started slowing, she put the picture back and closed the trunk. She and Anna carefully dragged the trunk to the stairs. They slowly slid it down to where Camilla was waiting. She shook her old gray head. "I'd almost forgotten those were up there."

They moved the other trunk down the stairs the same way. Camilla gave them a damp towel to thoroughly wipe them off. Once they were clean, Rachel opened them, and the three of them glanced briefly through the material because Camilla was curious about their contents. What excited Rachel the most were the many pictures. Among them was a picture from each prom. Jacob and Rachel had been so devoted to each other that they never had never gone to one with anyone else. Some pictures were of Jacob with her family. Most of the pictures had Rachel in them, too.

After they had looked at a few things, they closed the trunks and packed them into the car. When they arrived back at Jacob and Anna's house, Jacob came out to help carry them in. Anna suggested they put them in the art studio, and Jacob nodded. He never said a word as he helped, and Rachel wished she could know what he was thinking.

Anna explained to Jacob how Matthew had destroyed all of Rachel's memorabilia and asked if Rachel could copy his pictures. Jacob just shrugged. "That would be okay, but I think she ought to scan them when she does. Then it would be easier to make copies."

As they started to open the trunks again, Jacob turned to go back to work. Anna grabbed his hand. "Don't you want to stay and go through them?"

Jacob didn't say anything; he just looked down and shrugged again. Anna pulled him close. "Come on, honey. I'm excited to see things from when you grew up, but it would mean a whole lot more if you could tell me about them."

Jacob nodded, and they all sat down together. When they opened the first trunk and Jacob saw the picture of himself and Rachel, he looked away. Anna tried to help. "You two were definitely the most handsome couple I have ever seen."

Jacob turned to Anna and tried in vain to force a smile. They spent the afternoon looking through the items there. Jacob didn't say anything unless he was prompted, and even then he said very little. He did smile slightly at a small cardboard sword and a picture of himself with a pirate eyepatch. Rachel was wearing a cardboard crown as his captured princess.

He picked them up and chuckled slightly. Anna touched his arm. "Tell me about it, honey."

Jacob spoke briefly about that day and how he had decided he would be a pirate. As soon as he mentioned pretending Rachel was his captured princess bride, he became quiet once more. It seemed to continue that way for the rest of the afternoon. He would start to share a story only to have something touch him in a way that made him withdraw again.

They hadn't finished going through even one of the trunks before the children came bustling into the house, and Anna reluctantly closed the trunk. Rachel looked at Jacob, and she wondered if he was sad to close the trunk or relieved. She knew she felt a mix of happiness for wonderful times she and Jacob had shared mingled with a pall of regret for the ensuing years.

Jacob went back to work, and Rachel helped Anna serve fruit and cookies to the children while they listened to the children tell about their day. As the children talked, Anna handed Rachel a plate of cookies and a glass of milk. "I'll bet Jacob could use a break."

Rachel knew what Anna meant. She wanted her to go talk to him. Rachel nodded, and taking the cookies and milk, she walked with great apprehension to his office. She knocked on the glass doors, and he beckoned her in. When she entered, he looked up and half smiled as she held up the plate of cookies and the glass of milk.

He thanked her as she set them down. She turned to leave and then paused, knowing what Anna expected. She took a deep breath turned back. "Jacob, thank you for letting me have copies of the pictures."

He picked up a cookie and nodded. "You're welcome."

"Jacob, I know it's hard for you to go back through those memories, but it truly was the happiest time of my life."

"It was a happy time for me, too, Rachel."

"Can't you forget that bad memory and just remember the many good ones we shared?"

Jacob leaned back in his chair and looked at her. "You know, Rachel, I've tried for almost twenty years to forget it. But it seems that little things trigger that memory no matter how hard I try."

"Maybe," Rachel said, "when I get all of the pictures scanned, you can look through them, and that might help. The years that you were gone were so horrible for me, I hope to replace those memories with the good ones from when we were younger."

Jacob took a sip of milk and then spoke thoughtfully. "I guess my life these past years has been better than yours has, at least after I met Anna. Rachel, I hope you know that I never wished anything bad to happen to you, no matter how I felt."

"I know, Jacob. You're not that kind of person. And I'm so grateful you had the foresight to preserve those things, or Matthew would have destroyed them as he did mine."

They continued to talk for a while. As it grew closer to dinner time, Rachel went to help Anna. As she entered the kitchen, Anna looked up questioningly, and Rachel smiled. "We had a nice talk."

Anna smiled and nodded. They visited pleasantly while they worked on dinner. Rachel thought about how sad she was going to be after she moved back to her own house when she wouldn't share this time with Anna. Either Anna sensed her thoughts or had similar ones of her own because she finished turning the steaks on the griddle and then turned around to speak. "By the way, Rachel, I don't see any reason for both of our families to cook dinner every night. Since you will be over here working for Jacob, I would really like you to help me make dinner and have your family eat with us every evening. Then we can work together."

"That would be wonderful. But I probably should help pay for some of the food."

Anna just laughed. "It's not like we can't afford it."

Rachel smiled. She had learned a lot about how much money Jacob really had, and yet she had never seen anyone who less arrogant. Jacob had huge stocks in Microsoft and had invested in many Internet startups, making fortunes in many of them. He had big stakes in Google, Ebay, Paypal, Facebook, Twitter, and others. He was literally worth billions.

At dinner that night, Jacob said he had some important issues to discuss. "John and David," he said, "if it's all right with your mother, I would like to hire you to work for me. I want to run cattle on the land I own, and you could join my sons and me in repairing the fences on Saturdays. I'd write the paychecks to your mother so she could oversee the use of the money."

Rachel smiled. "I'd be happy to have them work for you. I'll let them spend some, but I'll put the rest away for college."

John and David were excited. They had never had a paying job before, and besides, they always enjoyed eating out at lunchtime.

"Well, then," Jacob said, "it's all settled. Be at our house at seven o'clock a.m. a week from this Saturday. I'll feed you breakfast, and we'll work until 5:00, with a break for lunch."

Rachel really liked to have her boys work with Jacob and his sons. They might come home tired, but they were always happy. She also realized that they emulated Jacob's goodness more and more and their father's selfishness less and less. Jacob did things like that for her family without even realizing it. Her thoughts were interrupted when she realized that Jacob was speaking to her. "Rachel, do you use the old barn or shop for anything?"

Rachel shook her head. "There might be a bunch of junk in them, but nothing really important."

"How would you feel if I had them repaired and used them? I would pay you some rent."

Rachel was aghast at that. "Jacob, you own them. Why would you pay me rent?"

"Well, I am letting you use the place, so it really is yours right now."

Rachel shook her head. "I've never heard of such a thing. I'd be more than happy to have them looking nicer and have you use them, but don't you dare try to pay me one red cent. You already do more for me than I can ever repay."

"We've never asked you to repay us. And we enjoy having your family around. Since it is by your house, I would feel better paying something for . . . "

Rachel didn't even let him finish. "So help me, Jacob! I almost whipped you once—don't make me try it again!"

The words came out before Rachel even thought about what she was saying, and she gasped and covered her mouth in surprise. Everyone turned and stared at her. Rachel could feel her face getting warm. "I'm sorry. I . . . I wasn't thinking, and the words just came out without . . . "

Jacob's laugh stopped her cold. He laughed loudly, like she hadn't heard him do since they were young. His laugh was contagious, and the others joined in. Jacob laughed until tears rolled down his face. Even Rachel felt to smile through her embarrassment. Finally, everyone started to calm down.

"Uncle Jacob, what was so funny?" Emily asked.

Jacob spoke through his subdued chuckling. "I haven't heard that phrase out of your mother in years. She used to say that to me all the time when she got mad or annoyed with me."

He laughed all over again, and the others joined in once more. This time, even Rachel smiled. It felt good to hear Jacob's laughter, even if she was still embarrassed.

When everyone started to calm down, John asked, "Uncle Jacob, what are you going to use the barn and shop for?"

"Well," Jacob said, "You can't run a cattle ranch without horses and equipment."

"We're going to have horses?" Emily asked excitedly.

"Yes. In fact, that is why we can't start work this Saturday. We, meaning anyone who wants to, are all going to go look at some horses to buy."

Emily turned to her mother. "Oh, Momma, can I go? Can I, please?"

Before Rachel had a chance to speak, Jacob did. "You know, Rachel, I told Anna I was going to buy one horse specifically for her, and she said only if you shared it with her and helped pick it out."

Anna nodded. "I've never been horse riding before, and besides, I thought it would be more fun if we shared it."

Rachel felt an excitement spreading through her. She loved horses and always had. She and Jacob had ridden together a lot, but she hadn't even been near a horse since she had married because Matthew wouldn't allow it. He knew it reminded her of her time with Jacob. She was so excited she couldn't even speak, so she nodded.

"Good," Anna said. "Saturday, all of us will go horse shopping."

Rachel smiled to herself. That sounded funny. It sounded like they would go to the local department store and pick one out. She noticed Jacob smiling, too.

Anna continued, "Jacob says we have to go clear over to Clarkston, which is about an hour and a half away, so we will all make a day of it. Rachel, maybe you can help me pack a lunch, and we'll picnic at the big park that Jacob says is there."

"Can I ride in your pickup with you, Uncle Jacob?" Emily asked.

"Actually," Anna replied, "we won't be taking the pickup this time since we won't bring the horses back until the barn is ready. I've decided we are going to buy a twelve passenger van so we can all fit. I'm tired of not being able to visit with everyone when we travel."

The next day, Rachel could hardly work for the excitement of the pictures and the horses, but she had so much to do. She scanned some photos from Jacob's trunk and printed them on his color printer. They turned out well. Anna took some of the pictures to town to have them framed while Rachel started cleaning the upstairs of her own house.

Even though it was still April, it was a warm day, so Rachel shut off the heater off and opened up the windows to air out her house. She felt funny calling it her home. It actually belonged to Jacob, and to his family before that, but that's what everyone else called it.

She had just finished making up the last bed when she heard Anna calling from downstairs. Before she could make her way down, Emily came bounding up. "Momma, come see the pictures Aunt Anna fixed up."

Anna and James were still carrying pictures into the house and stacking them on the coffee table when Rachel came down. Anna also had a big bag of picture hangers. It was hard for Rachel to put nails into the newly painted walls, but as the pictures started gracing them, it felt more like home. In fact, Rachel thought, it felt more like a home than it ever had before.

She saved her favorite picture for the main entry. It had been taken just before her brother, Richard, had gone to basic training. He was the oldest, and it was the last time the family was all together. Like so many of her family pictures, it had Jacob in it. Rachel's parents just considered him part of the family. They were so sure she would marry him that they had asked him to join them in at least one of the family pictures every time one was taken. She thought about how disappointed they must have been in her. As she leveled the picture, she suddenly realized Anna was watching her.

"You truly had a wonderful family," Anna said. "Jacob talks a lot about your family and how much he loves them."

Rachel nodded. "They all love him, too."

"I'm so happy that he can be part of your family again," Anna said. "And do you know what else I think? If you don't mind, we ought to have a housewarming dinner and eat down here tonight so we can show everyone your house."

Rachel nodded. "That's a great idea! But I better go shopping so I have something to cook."

"What food do you need?"

"Probably everything. I haven't had time to restock anything."

"Really?"

Anna had a sly look on her face, glancing at the kitchen and then back at Rachel. Rachel gasped. "You didn't!"

"No, I didn't. But perhaps you should look."

Rachel walked into her kitchen for the first time that day and immediately saw that there was a new fridge. She turned around and saw a new stove and a new microwave. In fact, every appliance was new. There was even a small television and radio system mounted in the kitchen so she could use them while she worked. She knew none of those things had been there when they had cleaned the kitchen the day before. She opened the fridge. It was full of eggs, milk, butter, cheese, and every other thing a person could want. She opened the freezer in the bottom of the fridge and found it full of meat, cheese, and frozen juice.

She looked in the cupboards and found them full of flour, salt, sugar, spices, and lots of baking item. She was shocked and stood with her mouth open. "But when did . . . ? How did . . . ?"

Anna seemed amused at Rachel's bewilderment. "I didn't know about it either until I walked in here today. The only one who has a key besides you is Jacob. He must have done the food shopping himself last night when he went to town and had them delivered while we were at Camilla's. By the way, if you check your laundry room, you'll find a new washer and dryer, too. Now, do you still want to try to tell me that deep down he doesn't care for you?"

Rachel could feel tears rolling softly down her cheek. She was already feeling so unworthy of all he had done for her, and here he had done more. But she felt more confused than ever about Anna. "But, Anna, why doesn't that bother you?"

Anna smiled. "He tries to pretend it isn't so and even convinces himself that is the case. Perhaps, under the circumstances, that is what he needs to do. But if he didn't, it would make what I am trying to do impossible."

"And what is that?"

"All in good time. All in good time."

Rachel felt so exasperated. She had thought Anna was just trying to help Jacob get over his pain, but this seemed like more than that. However, she knew that asking more questions would only illicit a similarly vague response.

It was lunchtime, so they fed James and Emily and put them to bed for naps. Anna was feeling tired, too, so Rachel suggested she use a bed upstairs. Anna thanked her and did just that.

Rachel set about making cookies. When the cookies were in the oven, she debated what she would cook for dinner. She opened the fridge, and the first thing she saw was cottage cheese. She wondered to herself if maybe . . . . She went to the cupboards, and in one of them she found what she had guessed: lasagna noodles and spaghetti sauce. With no one to hear her, she laughed out loud as she shook her head. "Jacob, you . . . " She never even finished her sentence. She couldn't think of a word to describe how she felt.

She felt so happy. She had an almost new house, a wonderful job, good friends, and family. Yes, she truly had family. The only thing that could have been better was if she could have been Jacob's wife. But then, she considered, if she were, she would never have known Anna. No, she decided, life was about as good as it could be.

She turned on the radio to the oldies station while she worked. They often played songs she and Jacob had danced to, and they brought back such good memories.

Anna got up about the time the bus was due and called Jacob, asking him to bring the children and come down for some cookies. Rachel had finished preparing the lasagna and had started some homemade bread to go with it.

Jacob and the children could be heard long before they burst into the house. When John and David stepped into the remodeled kitchen, the shock was written all over their faces. Rachel smiled at them. "Do you like the house?"

Both of them nodded vigorously. They had a good time visiting and listening to the children talk about their day as they ate the warm cookies. Anna told them not to eat too much and pointed at the lasagnas Rachel had sitting on the counter.

After the snack, everyone wanted to look around the house. Emily, John, and David led the way. Rachel hung back with Jacob. She wanted to see how he reacted to the pictures she had hung up. She hadn't felt it was appropriate to hang any of just the two of them except when they were very young, but she had hung many of him with her family. She had purposely obliterated any signs of Matthew. He was a painful memory she would rather forget. She hadn't destroyed them, as Matthew had done with her things, but she had locked them away. She realized, like it or not, that he was also part of her children's lives.

Jacob paused and looked at each picture. Each time he did, he smiled as if his mind were drifting back in time. When the tour was over, Rachel watched Jacob wander over and look again at the picture she had hung in the foyer. He stood there for a long time. She walked over and stood beside him. He looked at her and then back at the picture. "You had such a wonderful family, Rachel. My family had so many problems. I often wished your family could have been my own."

"It really was, Jacob. We all felt you were part of our family."

"They were always so good to me," Jacob said.

"They were all upset at how I treated you." Rachel paused, a tightness filling her chest. She spoke quietly, as if to herself. "But no one was more upset at me than I was at myself."

Jacob looked at her and spoke kindly. "Well, it's good to be renewing that friendship again."

She nodded and then remembered something else. "Jacob, thank you for all the nice things you've done for me. I've never had any new appliances before."

He smiled. "I'm glad you like them. I had them put the old ones out in the barn in case there was some sentimental value to them. I also told the owner of the furniture store that I would have you and Anna come in to pick out new furniture for you. I thought I could do okay on appliances, but I didn't think I should be the one to decide on your furniture. I told him to put whatever you wanted on my account."

"Oh, Jacob, you don't need to do that. You've done so much for me already."

"It's essential for business meetings that you have an appropriate place."

Rachel knew that was a bunch of baloney and barely managed to hold her smile as Jacob sounded so businesslike.

"You know," Rachel said with a grin, "it was nice to come and find the kitchen all stocked up. I had to laugh when I found cottage cheese in the fridge and lasagna noodles and spaghetti sauce in the cupboard. I knew immediately what we were having for dinner."

Jacob chuckled. "It wouldn't be your kitchen without some lasagna, Rachel."

It wasn't very long before it was time to put the lasagnas and bread into bake. Anna and Jacob joined Rachel in the kitchen, and the aroma of the food soon drew in the children. When it was time for the blessing, Rachel looked at Jacob to call on someone. He must have realized what she thought.

"It's your home," he reminded her.

She didn't know why that seemed strange to her. It had always been her father who called on someone, and she just assumed it was a man's place. Rachel appreciated that Jacob recognized her as head of her own home, and she called on David.

As they finished eating, Rachel told her children that after dinner, they would go to Jacob and Anna's house to move all of their things down. "Oh, Momma," Emily said, "do we have to? I want to live with Aunt Anna and Uncle Jacob forever."

Jacob smiled and hugged her. "Emily, you are welcome in our home anytime. And maybe you can talk your mother into letting your whole family stay over at our house sometimes, especially on holidays."

Emily looked at her mother questioningly, and Rachel nodded. Rachel knew she, too, would look forward to those days. They finalized plans for the next day and then went to move Rachel's family's things to her house. Rachel saw the new, bigger van.

After Jacob, Anna, and their family left, Rachel gathered her children around her to read scriptures and have prayers. They sang some songs, and it seemed natural to do all of it after the time they had spent with Jacob's family, but at least to Rachel, it seemed lonesome. She could sense her children felt the same way. And it didn't feel the same with her directing it instead of Jacob.

As Rachel slipped into her own bed for the first time in almost three months, her house was warm and comfortable, and she felt more at peace there than she ever had. And it was nice to know that Jacob and Anna weren't far away.

Horses

Rachel woke her children by six o'clock, but it was still after seven o'clock before they arrived at Jacob and Anna's house. They had an excellent breakfast together, packed the lunch into the new van, and were on their way.

As they drove to Clarkston, they all sang together. Rachel looked at her own children, singing along with the rest, and thought of how that would not have been the case only a few months earlier. She could remember singing as she traveled with her own brothers and sisters. Jacob had often been with them and could harmonize well.

She thought about when he had bought the old guitar and taught himself to play. Soon he was accompanying her family. Her parents and siblings had expressed more than once about the hole they felt in the family and in their hearts when Jacob left.

For her, it had been much more than a hole, especially when her life was in such turmoil with Matthew. When John had been small, she had tried to sing in the car when the family traveled, but Matthew had told her to stop "caterwauling." It had humiliated her and hurt her feelings, and she had never tried again. Even now, she still found herself singing timidly, even in the church choir.

She was sitting on the front bench seat so she could visit with both Anna and Jacob as they drove along. They had just finished a rendition of "She'll Be Coming Round the Mountain" when Jacob said, "Rachel, I wish you'd sing a little louder. I can barely hear you."

"Do you think I sing all right?"

"Oh, Rachel, you have a beautiful voice. I told Anna that I learned to play the guitar so I could listen to you sing. But now you sing so quietly I can hardly hear you at all."

Rachel started to cry, her whole body shaking. She felt as if an enormous tension was releasing from her, and she couldn't control it. Emily, who was sitting by her, asked, "Momma, are you all right?"

Jacob glanced back at her. "Rachel, I didn't mean to hurt your feelings."

By this time, everyone in the van had gone silent, and Rachel felt stupid, but she still couldn't control herself. She just waved her hand and shook her head to help Jacob understand he hadn't been the cause.

Finally, when she was able to settle her emotions so she could speak, she explained what Matthew had said to her.

Everyone listened quietly, and Rachel could see Jacob bristle as he so often did when she talked about Matthew's mistreatment of her. When she finished, he shook his head.

"Rachel, it's not true. You have a beautiful voice. You have no idea how nice it is to hear you sing again."

Everyone was still quiet, and Rachel was afraid she had ruined the day for everyone, but Anna, as usual, came to the rescue and started off with a powerful rendition of "When the Saints Come Marching In." By the time they finished that song, Rachel was feeling better and singing a little louder. Anna asked what she wanted to sing. She chose "The Battle Hymn of the Republic" because she always liked to hear Jacob's baritone voice on the bass part.

By the time they reached Clarkston, Rachel felt exhausted, yet her heart burned with a sense of renewal. She felt as though she had just finished a terrible ordeal. She tried to make sense of her feelings, but all she could figure out was that she had released from her heart a feeling of pain and inadequacy that had tortured her for years. She wondered if Jacob would ever know what his kind compliment had done for her.

When they arrived at the horse ranch, everyone piled out. The ranch foreman, Jack, came to greet them. He shook hands with Jacob and then listened as everyone was introduced. Emily was intrigued by his cowboy hat and asked him about it. He smiled and put it on her head. It slid down over her face, so he tilted it way back for her.

"Why," he drawled, "I'd swear it was made just for you."

Emily beamed as everyone laughed. Anna pulled out her camera and had to get a picture of everyone, especially one of Emily with Jack.

Jack then led them to the horses. "We brought in a few dozen of our very best for you to choose from," he said.

"Honey, you and Rachel choose first," Jacob said.

As Jack started telling the characteristics of each horse, he always mentioned if it was a mare or a gelding. "What's a gelding?" Anna asked.

"Well," Jack hemmed and hawed, scratching his ear. "A gelding is a . . . Well, it's a . . . "

Jacob came to his rescue. "A gelding is a male horse that has been neutered to make it gentler."

Jack nodded, very much relieved. "Very well put."

"I think I'd like a mare," Anna said, "so someday she could have a baby." She looked at Rachel apparently to see what she thought, and Rachel nodded her agreement.

"Look, Rachel," Jacob said, pointing out one particular mare. "She looks like Star Bright."

The horse was a beautiful dark brown, almost black, with a white star on her forehead and four white stocking feet. Rachel couldn't help but smile. Star Bright had been her favorite of her dad's horses.

"That one," Jack said, "is a beauty. She's gentle as a lamb, and friendly, too."

He walked into the barn and came out with a carrot. He walked to the fence and clicked his tongue. "Here, girl. Here, Star."

The horses crowded around, but he singled out Star to give the carrot to. He stroked her head as she munched on it. She nuzzled him for some more, and at that moment, Rachel realized she had been staring at the horse as if in a trance, unmoving, with Jacob and Anna watching her. She stammered in embarrassment.

"Oh, uh, yeah, she's a beauty."

Jack smiled. "Would you like a closer look?"

Jacob nodded, grinning as he looked at Rachel. Jack called to another ranch hand, who came with a rope. Soon Star was standing in the yard, and everyone was petting her. Jacob was looking her over as Jack spoke. "She's four years old and well broke. You won't find a horse with a better disposition or a smoother gait."

Jacob stepped back from checking her hooves and teeth and rubbing his hand up and down her legs. He looked at Anna and Rachel. "Well, Anna, Rachel, is this your horse?"

Anna laughed. "Jacob, I hardly know one end of the horse from the other. I'm going to have a hard time figuring out how to drive it if it doesn't have a gas pedal and a brake."

Jacob laughed and turned to Rachel. "Well?"

Rachel felt awkward choosing a horse and having Jacob pay for it. It was obvious she was an expensive horse. All she could do was stammer. "Well, I . . . She is beautiful. I mean . . . "

Jacob just laughed. "In other words, you like her, and she's the one you'd choose?"

Rachel just nodded, grinning stupidly, unable to talk.

Jacob patted the horse. "Do you want to keep the name Star?"

"Rachel, it's your choice," Anna said.

"I would like to call her Star Bright in memory of the other horse," Rachel replied.

Jack tied Star Bright to the hitching post so he and Jacob could look at other horses. The ranch hand brought Rachel a brush and some carrots. Rachel showed Anna and Emily how to brush Star Bright and rub

135

her down. Rachel gave her a carrot and tried to get Anna to give her one. Anna held it far out from herself, and when Star Bright reached for it, Anna squealed and drop it.

"I guess something that big makes me kind of nervous."

Emily was a little nervous, too, but she soon had the hang of putting a piece in the palm of her hand and holding her hand out flat so Star Bright could pick it up with her lips without accidentally biting her. When the carrots were gone, Star Bright nuzzled against Rachel. It felt so good being around horses again.

Jacob chose a large black gelding. He said he would name him Lightning after the horse he used to ride. He told Abraham and Isaac to each choose a horse for their own. Joseph and Peter chose one together, and John and David chose another. James felt left out, so Abraham said he'd share.

Emily asked about a horse, and Rachel said, "You can ride with Anna and me on Star Bright."

After the horses were all chosen, they had to be named. Abraham and James named their red gelding "Red." Isaac decided to follow suit and named his black gelding "Blackey." Joseph and Peter broke the pattern and called their cream-colored mare "Princess." John and David debated a long time, and with lots of input from the others, they finally named their paint horse just that: "Paint."

Jack suggested that, for one final test, they take the horses for a ride. "We don't want any unsatisfied customers."

A couple of ranch hands joined Jack in carrying out blankets, saddles, and bridles. They taught the children how to put them on their horses while Jacob showed James and Rachel taught Anna and Emily.

"I don't know why you're showing me," Anna said. "If I ever climb on the back of something that big, it'll be after somebody else has locked everything into place and guaranteed it's safe."

Anna made Rachel smile. She realized how different the two of them were. Anna was every inch a city girl, and Rachel was a country girl through and through. Rachel loved Anna and knew Anna loved her, too.

As Rachel continued to saddle Star Bright, Emily begged to help. Rachel then understood even more how much Emily was like herself. She could remember her father letting her help on the ranch and realized how much she must have been underfoot. Rachel tried to let Emily help all she could.

When the horses were saddled, Jacob asked Anna if she was ready to ride. She tried to talk her way out of it, but Jacob wanted her to so badly that she finally agreed, but only if someone led the horse around.

"I'm not about to have it run off like they do in the movies."

Jack assured her that all the horses were gentle and wouldn't run away, but she stood her ground. Finally, with a boost from Jacob, she climbed on the back of Star Bright, but only after he promised not to let go of the lead rope. Jacob led Star Bright around the yard for about five minutes, with Anna holding white-knuckled onto the saddle horn as if her life were coming to an end.

Rachel had to laugh to herself as Anna rode. She squealed at every uneven movement or turn while Jacob kept reassuring her that it was okay. Finally, Anna told him she was going to split in two with the horse between her legs, and Jacob helped her off of Star Bright.

"I brought a good book to read while everyone else rides," Anna said, and by the way she said it, Rachel knew there was no room for discussion on the matter.

Jacob reluctantly agreed. Anna retrieved her book, and Jack invited her to make use of a nice couch in the ranch house. The rest of them mounted up. Jacob lifted Emily up in front of Rachel and put James in front of himself on Lightning. The others mounted, sharing horses as needed, promising to switch places halfway through the ride so everyone could "steer."

Since most of the group had never been on horses before, Jacob gave some instructions. "Trust your horse to go the right direction. I will lead out, and Rachel will bring up the rear."

That plan soon fell apart, however. Mares are dominant in a herd, and they tried to push ahead of Lightning. Finally, Jacob and Rachel switched places, and she took the lead on Star Bright while Jacob rode at the rear.

They traveled a winding path up some hills and around to a beautiful lake. It took them about half an hour to get there.

"We'll let the horses have a break and drink some water, and then we'll start back," Jacob said.

Rachel laughed as James climbed off, awkwardly walked a few steps, and then flopped on the ground. "Man, my butt hurts."

"We don't use that word, James," Jacob said. "It's better to say 'backside.'"

"But," James complained, "it's more than just the back of it that hurts."

Rachel watched Jacob admiringly as he watered the horses. He was always so good with them. Sometimes her own father had asked Jacob to come help with the horses and cattle because he seemed to be able to do things with them that no one else could.

She went over beside him. He turned and smiled at her. "It's been a long time, hasn't it, Rachel?"

Rachel just nodded. She didn't feel a need to speak. She just enjoyed the moment of being with him again in this setting. The compliment he had paid her in the van still warmed her heart, and the memories of her experiences riding with Jacob helped wash away the pain of the last years.

When Jacob finished, they plopped on the grass side by side as the children played a game of capture-the-flag. Jacob leaned back on his elbows, looking very relaxed. "I haven't ridden since the last time with you."

"Me neither, Jacob. It's really nice to ride with you again."

Jacob looked at her and nodded his agreement, a slight smile on his face. They didn't rest very long because it was getting close to lunchtime. James complained that the break was too short because his "butt . . . um, backside, still hurt."

Jacob just said, "You'll get used to it."

When they mounted this time, James rode with Abraham, and Emily rode with Jacob. When they got back to the ranch yard, Rachel paused and didn't dismount. Everyone else did except Jacob, who needed to lift Emily down into Isaac's arms first. He had no sooner done so than Rachel turned Star Bright around, saying, "Jacob, I'll race you across the meadow."

She didn't know if he would take the bait, but as she thundered across the pasture, she was sure she could hear the sound of a horse puffing behind her. She took a quick glance and sure enough, Jacob was riding Lightning at full gallop and closing the gap between them. Lightning was a slightly taller horse and had a longer gait. That made him just faster than Star Bright. But as Jacob pulled up beside her, he slowed Lightning slightly so they stayed together.

Rachel's thoughts raced faster than the horses. In that instant, as they galloped side by side, she was a young teenager again. Old Star Bright had been faster than old Lightning, but Jacob had been a better rider and had been able to hold even with her. But now, on a faster horse, he still held back to be by her side.

As they approached the stream on the far side of the meadow, both of them instinctively reined in their horses. The horses were sweating and panting as they turned back toward the ranch yard. Rachel spoke before she even thought about what she was saying.

"Oh, Jacob. I wish this ride and this feeling could go on forever."

She had no sooner said it than she realized it was probably not appropriate to say. But Jacob only said, "Me, too, Rachel. Me, too."

They walked their horses slowly back to the ranch house, reminiscing about different rides they had gone on. When they got there, Emily was first to greet them. "Wow, Momma! That was neat! You really know how to ride!"

"Yeah," James added. "It looked like you were flying!"

Anna was there, too. "You two are awesome horse riders."

Rachel felt awkward. It was not really proper for her to challenge another woman's husband to a horse race. But Anna just seemed pleased that Rachel and Jacob had enjoyed it.

Everyone loaded in the van while Jacob went in to fill out the paperwork and pay for the horses. When he climbed in with them, he said, "We'll have some of the best horses around. I paid for their boarding until the barns are ready. Meanwhile, we better buy a six-horse trailer and some tack."

Emily turned to her mother. "Momma, what do we need to buy tacks for?"

Rachel smiled at her daughter's innocence. "Actually, this 'tack' is the word for saddles, bridles, and all of the other horse equipment."

Emily's eyes widened. "Oh. I didn't know."

"I didn't know that either, Emily," Anna said.

They went to the park by Clarkston Lake and had lunch. Afterward, Jacob started skipping rocks, and everyone except Anna joined in. Rachel found that she was still quite good at it. The older boys were, too. Peter took a little while to get a good skip but was finally quite proficient. James eventually made a couple of skips, but Emily was having no luck. She eventually got mad at the rocks and stomped them. Rachel had to laugh, seeing so much of herself in her little daughter. Jacob, was ever so patient, holding Emily's hand and helping her fling some that made little skips. That eventually satisfied her.

It was late afternoon when they finally climbed into the van and headed for home. Anna asked Rachel to take the front passenger seat. She said she wanted the bench seat by the window so she could lay her pillow against it and sleep. They hadn't been on the road long before everyone except Rachel and Jacob was asleep. They rode in silence so they wouldn't wake the others.

Rachel glanced over at Jacob and thought that he was still the most handsome man she had ever known, but, for the first time in her life, she realized that what made him that way to her was the goodness she had always seen in him.

Marie

The next month and a half went by quickly, but it went slowly, too. There was so much to do that it made the time fly, and yet, due to Rachel's anxiousness to have the horses there, the work on the barns seemed to take forever.

Jacob had started building fences with the children each Saturday. They first built one around the pasture near Rachel's house, connecting it to the barn. Rachel watched out the window off and on as she cleaned. She admired how Jacob could organize the whole group. She knew he had plenty of money to hire what he wanted done, but he seemed to like the feeling of doing a good day's work, especially working with the children. She knew how much her own children loved and admired him, and she was grateful they had such a good role model.

Rachel was grateful she didn't have to worry about money anymore, and she enjoyed her job. She would get her boys off to school and then sit down to do the transcribing and other work Jacob had for her. She also had to go through the e-mail. Jacob had two business accounts. One he let others know about, and one he didn't. She had to go through the known account, answering some and deleting spam that made its way through the filters. She forwarded any she thought he needed to know about to his private business e-mail.

Rachel was surprised at some of the e-mails Jacob received. He received marriage proposals from women he didn't even know. At first it bothered her, and she had asked Edna, Jacob's other secretary, about them. "Oh, they're just women who want money and power," Edna explained. "Try to be kind but direct. Say something like, 'Mr. Davis is happily married already, thank you.'"

Rachel liked Edna. She was a no-nonsense type of lady. Rachel called or e-mailed her anytime she had a question. Rachel knew she would miss being able to communicate with her when Edna retired in September.

One day Edna asked Rachel an interesting question. She asked, "Is there some reason Mr. Davis especially wants to help you?"

"What do you mean?" Rachel asked.

"Well, your job description is a bit strange, and since I handle his finances, I know he pays part of your wage himself. I know that you are helping Anna, but I wondered if there was a deeper reason for his hiring you."

Rachel hadn't realized Jacob was paying part of her wage himself. She had taken back her maiden name of Henderson, or that relation would have been a dead giveaway. She thought of saying she had been married to his brother, but she chose not to. Instead, she just said that they had been friends when they were young, that she was a single mother, and that she needed some help paying medical bills.

"Jacob has always been kind and generous from the time we were small," Rachel said.

"Jacob is the most loved and respected of all of the vice presidents here," Edna replied. "Each year at Christmastime, some of the bosses take a big portion of their division bonus for themselves. But Jacob makes sure that the money in his division is divided equally among everyone, including the janitorial staff. He even puts his own personal part of it back in to be divided to the other employees, feeling they need it more than he does."

"Knowing Jacob, I can believe that," Rachel replied.

"You are lucky to have him for a friend," Edna said. "But remember, as his secretary you will have all of this information, but Jacob doesn't want others to know."

In the middle of May, Jacob told Rachel that she had done well on her training and that she was going to get a five dollar per hour raise.

"But Jacob," she objected, "I feel you overpay me now."

Jacob just shrugged. "It's company procedure to give a raise once you have completed your first positive review. Besides, it's good policy to have employees feel they are well paid because they work harder."

Rachel tried to always do her best for him. She still messed up at times, but Jacob never got angry, only asking her to fix what she needed to fix. At times, she even tried too hard. Once she thought she'd be helpful, and she straightened his office. That was the only time he had really been frustrated with her because he couldn't find anything. She quickly learned that what looked like a disorganized room was his system. He knew where everything was, and he didn't like to have it changed.

At about ten o'clock each morning, after Rachel had finished her routine paperwork and e-mail, she and Emily went to Jacob and Anna's house. Emily played with James, and Rachel and Anna painted. Rachel was anxious to see Anna's painting, but she kept saying, "Not until the time is right."

After painting for a while, they usually played the piano together. Rachel had practiced almost every day, and her skill was gradually coming back. Anna loved to play duets, and at first Rachel had felt inadequate. But soon they were playing as if they were one person. Sometimes Jacob took a break from his work to listen to them. He seemed to enjoy the friendship that Anna and Rachel shared with each other almost as much as they did.

While Anna, James, and Emily took an afternoon nap, Rachel worked in Jacob's office. They didn't talk much. Jacob worked on his tasks, and she worked on her assignments. But she enjoyed his company, and he seemed to enjoy hers. Every once in a while they would take a break and visit for a minute or two, and sometimes they had online meetings with other employees in Jacob's division.

About three o' clock she headed to the kitchen to start making cookies and dinner. The cookies were ready when the children arrived home. Anna, James, and Emily got up to join the others for the after-school snack, and Jacob usually took a break to join them as well. Rachel loved the times they sat around and visited in the kitchen.

She and Anna would finish dinner, and they would all eat together at about six o' clock. Then they gathered around and sang together before she and her children headed to their own home. It was a good life, and she was so happy. She felt friendship, love, safety, and a peacefulness she hadn't had in her life during the years Jacob had been gone.

Late in May, the day came when the contractor said the barn and shop were finished. Jacob left that afternoon and came home with a fifth-wheel horse trailer that could haul all six horses. After the children got home and had a quick snack, they all headed into the farm and ranch store to pick out saddles, blankets, bridles, lead ropes, and anything else they felt they would need. Anna insisted Rachel choose Star Bright's. "If I ride her at all," she said, "it's only going to be for a short time. I'm sure you will ride her much more than I will."

It was late by the time they got home. Rachel prepared waffles for supper, and Jacob and Anna helped. All they talked about as they ate was the horses. The older children were disappointed they had to go to school the next day and wouldn't be there to bring the horses home, but the pickup, which they needed to pull the horse trailer, wasn't built for that many people anyway.

The next morning, Rachel made sure that John and David were safely on the bus. Then she and Emily were on their way to Jacob and Anna's house. Emily had made her brothers mad, bragging about going to get the horses, until Rachel insisted she be quiet about it. But after they were gone, Emily chattered on and on about how glad she was that she didn't have to go to school.

Jacob, Anna, and James were ready when Rachel and Emily arrived, and it didn't take long for all of them to be on their way. Rachel rode in the backseat with Emily and James, and they all visited happily. They made the drive to Clarkston again, singing their way there. Rachel felt better about herself and sang out more. She had even been asked to perform a solo in the church choir. In some ways, she felt she had been released from a prison—a prison of the heart. She was finding freedom from the oppression she had felt for so long.

It took them until one thirty to get the horses and get back, and it took another hour to get the horses in the corral, partly because they had to keep moving James and Emily out of the way as they tried to help. Rachel fed each of the horses a carrot to help them feel they were home, but she secretly fed Star Bright an extra one. She knew it was going to be hard not to spoil her.

Jacob said he would be over to feed them morning and night, and Rachel begged to help. He seemed reluctant, saying he wasn't sure it was appropriate, but Anna interceded and told him she thought it was a good chance for them to talk about old times.

Rachel slipped into her house to make cookies for the children, sure they would hurry down to the corrals when they got home. She was right.

***

The Saturday morning after they got the horses, both families loaded into the big van for the trip to the photo studio. Rachel had tried for almost a month to work it into everyone's schedule, but it seemed that every time she had set it up, there had been a conflict.

James complained about having to wear a suit on a Saturday, and Emily wasn't any happier about wearing a dress. But soon they were all situated in the studio, being moved here and there. They had a picture of each family separately, then one of just the children in each family. That was followed by a picture of Jacob and Anna. Anna wanted a family picture of both families together. Rachel was sure Jacob would object, but he didn't. However, he did object to a picture of just himself and Rachel. He again said that it was inappropriate, but Anna wouldn't back down. She said it was for old times, to update the ones they had from when they were younger. Jacob reluctantly agreed but refused to sit in the friendly pose he'd had with Anna, no matter how much Anna urged him to.

Everyone was relieved when it was over, and while Jacob took the children to order pizzas, Anna and Rachel looked at the pictures and chose the ones they wanted. After they finished, Anna had Rachel use the credit card she had received from Jacob for his personal things. It had taken

Rachel a while to feel comfortable using the credit cards. Matthew had one he used even when there was no money to pay for what he purchased. Rachel had been saddled with some of those debts when they divorced. But Jacob always had his accountant pay his personal one, and the company paid his business one. She never even saw the bills, so it hardly phased her to sign her name to the charge of over twelve-hundred dollars.

At church the next day, as Rachel sang her solo, both Jacob and Anna smiled at her and she felt so happy. Many people told her she did well, and Camilla told her it was nice to hear her beautiful voice again. The evening was spent, as usual, with stories and singing. She always felt renewed and invigorated as her family headed for home on Sunday nights. But this particular Sunday, they didn't head home at bedtime. It was Memorial Day the next day, so Rachel's family slept over at Jacob and Anna's.

After breakfast the following morning, they headed over to the cemetery. Jacob had purchased lots of flowers, and he had a small hand trowel and a few other garden tools. They all worked to clean the grass around the headstones for his parents and for Rachel's parents. As Jacob lovingly cleaned around her parents' headstone, he showed as much love for them as for his own parents. When he finished, he gently laid the flower bouquets there. Then he stood and put his arm around Anna, his breath coming in short gasps.

Rachel stepped forward and touched his arm. "They would be pleased to know of your love for them, Jacob, and they would be proud of you and what you've done with your life."

Rachel turned and looked at the graves, her heart hurting within her. "I'm not so sure they would be as proud of me."

"Rachel," Jacob said kindly, "they would be proud of you, too. Despite the challenges life has given you, you have been a good mother and a good woman. What you have been through might have broken someone of lesser caliber."

Rachel started crying. Again, his compliment touched her heart and tore away some of the pain of the past in ways he could never know. Anna motioned for him to put his arm around Rachel, but he shook his head, so Anna drew Rachel into her own arms.

For lunch, they had a wiener roast in the firepit behind Jacob and Anna's house. As the evening came, they spent time telling stories of those who had passed on. Jacob told stories of both his parents and Rachel's parents. Some of them Rachel hadn't even heard, such as how her mother had helped him sneak the flowers into Rachel's room the first time he asked her to a prom. As the evening drew to a close, the children went in to watch a movie, and Rachel joined them so Jacob and Anna could enjoy the sunset alone.

Tuesday, while Jacob watched Emily and James, Anna and Rachel went out for lunch and picked up the pictures. They spent the rest of the afternoon hanging pictures where Anna wanted them in her home. She hung a copy of every picture, even the one of Jacob and Rachel. They put it in the art studio since Anna said she wanted to look at it while she painted, and it wouldn't bother Jacob because he never went in there uninvited.

Rachel knew she wouldn't be able to look at it without wondering about Anna's acceptance of her and Jacob's friendship.

Rachel put up the same pictures in her own house except the one of her and Jacob. But she did put it in the drawer with her prom pictures.

That week was the last week of school for the children. There were band concerts, end of year programs, and many other events. Both families went to the events of all of the children. Again, Rachel felt like they were just one big family, and Anna acted that way as well. There were even a few people who seemed confused as to which one of them was Jacob's wife, but it never seemed to bother Anna; Jacob and Rachel, perhaps, but not Anna.

On Wednesday, the contractor called and said that Rachel's parents' home was finished. It was none too soon because Marie's family would be coming in on Saturday. Jacob said he had too much work to do and asked Anna and Rachel to do the walk-through. Rachel knew that he just didn't want to step into the house again. Anna again expressed to Rachel her desire that he could somehow replace that bad memory with a good one. But Rachel knew it would never happen if he couldn't even bring himself to enter the house.

As Anna and Rachel walked through with the contractor, Rachel felt the house looked better than it ever had. She and Anna had chosen the carpet, paints, and fixtures, and they looked good. There were new appliances and a new furnace. A cleaning crew had cleaned it. She knew it would be comfortable for Marie's family.

But there was something that bothered Rachel about herself. She could see that Jacob had made sure things were nice for Marie, and Rachel had a strange feeling in her heart. It was a slight pang of guilt and jealousy. Rachel felt that it was really silly on her part, but it reminded her of how much Marie had loved Jacob like a brother, and how much she had fought to keep Rachel from marrying Matthew. Rachel knew that, in all reality, Marie had been more loyal to Jacob than she had been herself.

That feeling came back even stronger when the big moment finally arrived. Marie's family was coming in at dinnertime on Saturday, so Anna suggested they all meet at her house and eat together. She and Rachel had spent a big part of the afternoon cooking turkey, ham, and all of the trimmings. As hard as she tried, Rachel couldn't drive the anxious feeling from her heart. And when the big U-Haul truck, with the minivan close behind, pulled into Jacob's driveway, the feeling was almost overwhelming. But nothing could prepare her for what happened next.

The vehicles had hardly rolled to a stop before Marie ran to Rachel, threw her arms around her, and hugged her. Then Marie caught sight of Jacob and did the same to him. What hit Rachel was how Jacob hugged her back. She remembered moving to hug him when he first came back and his pulling away in disdain. She knew she deserved his displeasure, and Marie, in turn, deserved his approval, but she could not eradicate the feeling of jealousy that coursed through her whole body. And to top it off, he would still never hug her.

Anna grabbed Marie and hugged her, too, and Rachel again felt some jealousy and had a miserable thought. What if Marie became Anna's friend and Anna didn't need Rachel anymore?

Marie hurried to Jason and pulled him over to meet Jacob and Anna. Jason stuck his hand out and shook Jacob's hand heartily. "I am so glad to meet you, Jacob. Marie has told me all about you, and how you are like a brother to her."

By this time the children were piling out of the van. John was proudly introducing his cousins to each other, though he hardly knew Marie's children. Marie's oldest five, three girls and two boys, ranging from two to fourteen years in age, seemed happy to be out of the van and to have some new friends.

After Marie lifted her baby, Susan, from her car seat, Jacob led them into the house. Rachel held back, feeling out of place. Anna stepped back beside her and linked her arm through Rachel's. Then she held Rachel back even more. Once Jacob had disappeared into the house with the others, Anna pulled Rachel to a stop and turned to face her. She looked directly into Rachel's eyes. "Marie may become our friend, but you are much more and always will be. You're family."

Anna always seemed to sense so many things that were never expressed, and Rachel felt much better as Anna pulled her into a big hug as she had done so many times.

Dinner was a boisterous affair. Marie had to hear all about what had happened to Jacob after he "left when he saw Rachel with Matthew." The way she said it made Rachel turn away with pain and shame, but no one else seemed to notice, and Marie didn't seem to mean anything by it.

Jacob was more willing to talk to Marie than he had first been to Rachel. He talked about the bus ride and about meeting Ina, but when he got to the part about meeting Anna, he deferred to her. Anna loved to tell their story, and Marie, Jason, and their older children were enthralled. When Anna finished, Marie turned to Jacob.

"I was so shocked to hear it was you who had bought the family farm; but boy, was I excited. And it is so kind of you to let us stay there."

"We even fixed up the old tree house," Rachel interjected, speaking for the first time during the whole meal. "Hopefully all of us can enjoy it."

"You all would be more than welcome anytime at our home," Marie said. She paused briefly then continued. "You know, I wish we could get the whole family to come back to the old place and have a family reunion."

Everyone immediately thought that was a wonderful idea. Then Anna mentioned that her own family was coming out in the middle of July and they could do it all at the same time and make it a double-family get-together. By the time the dinner had ended, beginning plans for a joint family reunion were in place. It sounded like a lot of fun, and Rachel was excited to think of seeing her siblings again, but she felt some trepidation as to how they would feel about her, especially with Jacob there. She also wondered how Anna's family would feel about her. Surely they knew of her friendship with Jacob.

The meal was soon over, and they decided they needed to hurry and get the truck unloaded. They all climbed into different cars and were off. When Marie stepped from the van and saw the old house with its improvements, she gave Jacob another big hug. "Oh, Jacob, it's wonderful."

Jacob handed Marie and Jason the keys. His reluctance to enter the house was not lost on anyone, especially Marie. She took his hand in hers and looked him in the eye. "Jacob, I hope you know we love you, and I hope you will always feel welcome in our home."

Jacob didn't say anything. He just nodded and smiled a forced smile. Marie turned and looked at Rachel, and Rachel almost felt there was an accusatory gleam in her eye. Jacob tried to change the subject by suggesting Anna and Rachel show Marie and Jason around the house while he showed the children the tree house.

Anna led Jason and Marie into the house for the tour, but Marie pulled Rachel aside privately. "Jacob still hurts about what happened, doesn't he?"

Rachel nodded. "Marie, I've done everything I can to tell him I'm sorry, but the pain is just too deep."

Marie spoke with great hope. "Well, at least he's back. That's a good start. Maybe Anna, you, and I can all help him now."

They hurried to catch up to Anna, who had led Jason into the remodeled kitchen. When Marie entered it, she gasped at how nice it was, especially with new appliances. When Rachel explained the new heating system and talked about the insulation, Marie shook her head in disbelief. "Jacob did all of this for the Henderson family?"

Anna nodded. "Jacob says that the Henderson family is, in many ways, his family."

By the time they finished looking through the house, Jacob and the children were back to help unload the truck. Jacob still refused to enter the house, working instead in the truck lifting down boxes.

To keep them out of the way, Anna took Susan, Emily, and Marie's other two small children and disappeared into the kitchen, and before the truck was unloaded, the house smelled of cookies. Rachel went to help Anna and found her rocking Susan and gooing at her. Emily and her two small cousins were sitting at the table with cookies and lemonade.

Rachel and Marie invited everyone in for a snack, but Jacob said he thought he'd just stay out there and enjoy the sunset. Marie kindly linked her arm through his. "Oh, come on, Jacob. You've got to come in to the kitchen for some cookies and lemonade."

Jacob smiled slightly and went with her. Rachel was sure if it had been the living room he would have refused. The younger children were soon off to play in the tree house while the older children went to explore, and the adults chatted about the house and Jason's transfer.

"Well," Jacob said, "when the children and I work on Saturdays, if they choose pizza, we'll come to support you."

Jason smiled. "If I'm working, just ask for me, and I'll make sure you get the best pizza you have ever eaten."

They talked a while longer and then, because it was getting dark, they figured they should get the children gathered so everyone could get some sleep. As they climbed into the cars, Rachel's thoughts were still on what Marie had said. Rachel hoped that between herself, Marie, and Anna, Jacob could truly get over the pain he still felt.

Family and Family Reunions

The days went even faster after Marie came. The children were out of school, and there was always so much to do. Summer was coming, and that meant gardening. Jacob loved gardening and bought a tiller to till up his own spot, the big flat area that had been leveled on the top of Pine Ridge. He had some loads of manure hauled in and tilled it again.

He also helped Rachel prepare her garden. Matthew had always said gardens were stupid and wouldn't invest in time-saving tools. He was always more than willing to eat the food, but he would never lift a finger to help.

Rachel had found gardening to be good therapy for the hurt she had felt during those dark years. That was the one place she missed Mother Davis the most. They had had lots of good talks while they weeded. But now Marie and Anna would sometimes come over. The three of them became close friends. Rachel's fear of being left out was gone, and instead, they would all three often go together to lunch or shopping.

Jason was good to help, too, but mostly, when she needed something, Jacob was there for her. She went out early to help take care of the horses every morning. They would have nice visits while they fed the horses and watched the sun rise.

Rachel spent mornings working in her office, afternoons with Anna and working for Jacob, and evenings making dinner for the two families. If it was a nice evening, they sometimes had a barbecue in the new picnic pavilion by the lake, and Jacob would invite Marie and Jason's family to join them.

Once a month, Jacob and Anna would go off to the city for some alone time for a couple of days while Rachel helped take care of their family. Life felt empty when they were gone. They were always tired when they returned, especially Anna, and it would be a few days before she felt like painting or playing duets again.

On Saturdays, Jacob worked with the children. Marie's sons were soon joining them, and later, one of her older daughters went along. The children enjoyed it, and it gave them a bit of spending money and a chance to eat out together. Jacob driving the twelve passenger van, with Abraham driving the smaller van, both vans full of children, became a common sight in town on Saturdays. They often went to eat pizza where Jason worked, and he joked that they alone could keep him in business.

Marie told Rachel how much she appreciated Jacob's good example to the children. Marie's children called him Uncle Jacob even though he wasn't truly their uncle. But Jacob thought of all of Rachel's siblings as his own family, so it was very natural, and he seemed to like it. Anna was Aunt Anna, and Jacob and Anna's children were considered cousins by Marie's children.

Rachel still enjoyed Sunday the most. The three families sat together at church, and soon nearly all of them were in the choir. With Marie there, Rachel had once again tried to sit on her own pew with her family, but Anna kept working it out so she and Rachel always sat on each side of Jacob.

Rachel and Marie talked about Anna and her apparent obsession to have Rachel and Jacob be good friends. Rachel told Marie that it was because Anna wanted him to heal from the pain he had over her.

"Though it is strange for a woman to do that," Marie said, "I'm grateful he married someone as wonderful as Anna, who is so kind and understanding."

The family reunion was coming quickly, and there was so much to do to prepare. Rachel, Marie, and Anna had more frequent lunch dates to finish up the planning. All of Rachel's brothers and sisters were going to be there except for Richard, who was still stationed in Europe. Every one of Anna's siblings, along with her parents, were coming.

When that Friday came, Rachel's anxious feelings concerning her brothers' and sisters' acceptance of her almost made her sick. But she needn't have worried. As each family arrived, they hugged her and were happy to see her. She, Anna, and Marie kept up a steady supply of cinnamon rolls and fruit for everyone. Jacob stayed outside to greet everyone.

When a big van pulled up, everyone gathered around to see who it was. When four beautiful blond women stepped out, Rachel knew immediately they were Anna's mother and sisters. Jacob hadn't lied when he'd said they were a lot like Anna. They had to hug everyone. Jacob and his family were hugged over and over, but so was everyone else.

To Rachel's surprise, however, before they had even met her, she overheard them asking Anna which one she was. Anna immediately brought them to meet her. As Anna's mother, Mary, threw her arms around Rachel and hugged her tightly, she said, "We've heard so much about you, and we hope you will feel we are your family, too."

All of Anna's sisters hugged her and told her how grateful they were for all she did for Anna. Rachel tried to tell them she had done little compared to what Anna had done for her, but it was as if they hardly heard.

They were still visiting with Rachel when Anna disappeared and came back with an older gentleman on one arm and a younger man on the other. She made her way through her sisters and introduced the men as her father and her brother. Anna's father slowly extended his hand, as if he were sizing her up.

"Glad to meet you, Rachel."

The way he said it, Rachel wasn't sure he meant it. He seemed as if he didn't approve of her for some reason, and that made her uncomfortable. Anna's brother wasn't much friendlier, just saying "Hello" as he shook her hand.

The rest of the day, there was always one of Anna's sisters with her. They seemed to really want to get to know her. She soon felt they were all her friends. But none of them impressed her as much as Anna's mother. She seemed to have a love for Rachel that Rachel couldn't understand, even though she could feel it.

Soon, everyone who had said they were coming had arrived at Marie's house, and the party moved to Jacob and Anna's house. Jason left and came back in a huge truck full of pizza. Jacob had paid for it and ordered it through Jason. Jason said his workers had been working all afternoon to get it ready.

It was good, too. Jacob had spared no expense, and Jason had made sure it was right. After dinner, there were lots of activities. There was a movie on the big screen television. There were games in the basement. There was fishing at the lake, led by Jason and Marie. And Jacob and Rachel took groups horseback riding. One of Anna's sisters even came riding with them. But there were things with Anna's family that made Rachel feel strange. She felt that Anna's sisters and mother were promoting her friendship with Jacob just as Anna was. She wondered if it was all in her mind. But Marie noticed it, too, and asked her about it. On the other hand, Rachel felt Anna's father and brother didn't like it.

Once, when Rachel found a brief moment alone with Marie, she asked Marie's opinion on the matter. Marie shook her head. "There is definitely something strange going on beyond healing an old wound, but what or why, I don't know."

Marie then suggested Rachel just forget about it and enjoy the reunion. And Rachel did enjoy it. She enjoyed seeing brothers, sisters, nieces, and nephews she hadn't seen in years, and some she had never met. She enjoyed their closeness, something she had felt missing in those years with Matthew.

That night, Anna's parents and siblings stayed with Jacob and Anna. Many of Rachel's family had brought campers, and some parked in the different yards. Rachel's youngest sister, Angeline, and her family stayed with Rachel. The two of them stayed up far later than they should have, just visiting.

Saturday morning, when Jacob came down to feed the horses, he already had grills loaded into his truck and was on his way to Marie and Jason's house to set them up. Rachel joined him to help feed the horses and then went in to get her own family ready.

By the time she, Angeline, and their families arrived at the Henderson home, Jacob had all the grills ready. He was a master of outdoor cooking. He had bacon on one grill, ham on one, sausage on one, hashbrowns on one, and pancakes on two more. Rachel, Jason, and Marie jumped in to help, but it still took a while to feed more than eighty.

When breakfast was over, Anna wanted to have everyone introduced. After the introductions, the children went off to play, and then Jacob asked each of the adults tell what they had done from the time he had left. Rachel felt very uncomfortable when Marie said, "Anna and Jacob, now that we're done, you tell us your story from the time Jacob saw Rachel with Matthew."

Rachel decided she needed to ask Marie to refrain from mentioning it that way because she hated to hear it, and she could tell Jacob didn't like the reminder, either.

Everyone sat almost spellbound as Jacob and Anna told their story. Anna had her mother chip in on the part about how she got Jacob to ask her to marry him. They were careful in how they described Anna's father's feelings about Jacob in the beginning, only suggesting he wasn't sure about a man who seemed to have no family. Anna's sisters told some funny stories about Jacob and Anna, too. Then Anna talked about her family. That was when Rachel first learned that Anna's father had made his money in real estate development.

It was lunchtime before they all finished. They were just putting the food on the table when a van pulled up, and everyone gasped as Richard and his whole family stepped out. Richard grinned as everyone started hugging them.

"There's no way I could miss our first family reunion back at the old place," he said between hugs. "Jacob paid for our tickets and helped keep our surprise."

Rachel could hardly believe it. Everyone was there. After lunch, before the children could go off to play, a photographer came. Rachel had scheduled this at Anna's request. They started with pictures of the whole group together. There was one of Rachel and all of her brothers and sisters, including Jacob. Then there was one of them with their spouses. Then there was one of Anna's family. Then Anna wanted the same with Rachel in it. Rachel felt a little strange and objected, but Anna insisted. Rachel noted that Anna's sisters and mother were also pushing her to join them, but Anna's father and brother just scowled.

Next came individual family photos. It took a lot of the afternoon because they had to keep rounding up the children. Anna again insisted that one be taken of Rachel's family along with hers and Jacob's. Rachel looked at Jacob each time, but he said nothing. At one point, Marie sidled up to her and said, "There is *definitely* something strange here."

Rachel was relieved when the photo session was finished. She, too, knew it was unusual, but not knowing what was going on made it more than strange; it was absolutely bizarre. But she sensed that Anna's family all knew why Anna acted as she did. Rachel wondered if Jacob knew.

When the photo session was all done, Marie told everyone about the family trust fund. Jacob didn't want them making a big deal about it, but everyone was very pleased. Before Rachel knew it, it was dinnertime, and they were all heading over to the new picnic pavilion by Jensen Lake.

There were others who joined them there. Everyone had been told to invite guests if they wished, just as long as they let Jacob know how many so he could plan the food. He'd had salads catered and set up all of the grills he used at breakfast to cook hamburgers. Camilla came, and so did many friends of Rachel's brothers and sisters, but Rachel didn't really have any other friends to invite.

When dinner was over, Jacob lit a campfire and pulled out his guitar. Rachel's family seemed to love that part best of all. They sang the old songs they had sung so many years ago. Anna's family joined in, and so did most of the children. As the sun started to set, each of Rachel's siblings, in turn, shared some memories of their parents.

Marie talked about the love she felt for them at their funeral and talked about how good it made her feel when she saw the flowers from Jacob. She told of how she had shown them to Rachel and then kept them until Rachel was divorced and could plant them.

Angeline turned to Jacob. "I was surprised you knew about the funeral, and yet I didn't see you there."

Jacob answered quietly, "I wasn't sure I'd be welcome."

Richard answered for all of them when he said, "You always were and always will be part of our family, Jacob, and we want you to feel welcome with us."

Marie spoke in a tone of disgust. "If there was anyone I didn't welcome, it was Matthew."

It was quiet for a time after that, and Rachel felt that it was her fault, though she knew none of her family still held feelings against her. Anna, as usual, was the one to come to her rescue. She suggested everyone tell their favorite memory from when they were young. They went around the circle, starting with Marie.

Marie reminded everyone of the story when Jacob and Rachel were young, and she tried to wrestle him. After he had pinned her, she kissed him to get him off and then tackled him while he was wiping his face. Rachel knew none of them had seen it, but her father had, and he loved to tell it as much as the others loved to repeat it. Rachel was afraid of what Anna and her family would think, but Anna and her sisters just laughed and laughed, especially as Marie reminded everyone that Rachel was wont to say, "I almost whipped you once, Jacob, don't make me do it again!"

Many stories were of Jacob and Rachel. When it came to Rachel's turn, she was a little nervous about saying what she wanted to say, especially with Anna's family there, but still, she knew it was her favorite memory. So she told about the night of her first prom with Jacob, and how she felt when she came down in her red dress and he pinned on her corsage.

She finished by saying, "I suppose it is my favorite memory because that night Jacob truly made me feel like a princess."

Everyone was quiet for a moment, and then Anna said, "I like that story." She then turned to Jacob. "How about you, honey? What's your favorite memory?"

"Oh, I don't know," Jacob said reluctantly. "It's hard to choose one. Maybe being in the tree house or something."

"Oh, come on, Jacob," Anna persisted. "Tell us a story about it."

"Well," Jacob started out slowly, "there was that time we ate our formal dinner in the tree house. It was spaghetti, and we ate with spoons and chopsticks."

Everyone laughed. Then Marie chimed in. She told how it had been a preference dance, so Rachel had planned it. Marie said she had been the "Italian waiter" even sporting a fake mustache, and their mother had been the cook. There was more laughter as Marie graphically described Rachel trying to climb the ladder in her formal dress. Marie was a good story teller, and Rachel found her thoughts going back to that night. When she glanced at Jacob, he had a faraway look in his eye and a slight smile on his lips.

After they had shared many stories, Angeline said, "One of my favorite memories is a very recent one. I can't tell how I felt when Rachel told me Jacob was the one who owned the old family farm." Everyone nodded in agreement.

"And how about when Rachel and Marie told us about the reunion?" Melanie, the second youngest, asked.

"I think we owe a big round of applause to Jacob, Anna, Marie, Jason, Rachel, and their families, don't you?" Richard asked.

Everyone agreed, and they clapped and cheered lowdly.

"Jacob," Richard asked, "how did you know about things back here, and that our parents had died?"

Jacob mentioned about Camilla, and then Camilla picked up from there, telling how Jacob kept in contact with her, and through her, with his own mother.

"I wish we had known," Marie said. "We would have liked to have kept in contact all of those years."

"Yeah," Richard added. "Don't every let that happen again, little brother."

Jacob smiled at the laughter that brought. Rachel wondered what Jacob really thought. Did he ever regret not being in contact with them? Did he regret any of those eighteen years as she did? It is true that he had Anna and her family. He had also become a senator and multi-billionaire, but did he ever feel that his life lacked some of what it could have had?

As the night wound down, everyone made plans to attend church the next day. Then Jacob played the song "Coming Home" on his guitar, and all who knew it joined in.

There is no place that you will ever go
In this world that will beat coming home.
Be you king or pauper, rich or poor
In your heart, home will call ever more.

And when a day turns into a year.
And the world causes your life to roam
Then one day there is something you will hear
That turns your heart to home.

When the world is getting you down,
It is then that your heart turns to home.

Where your friends will all gather 'round
And you know that you're never alone.

But home is more than a place.
It's the family and friends you have known.
It's someone that needs you that you can't replace,
In your heart when you're gone.

There is no place that you will ever go
In this world that will beat coming home.
Be you king or pauper, rich or poor,
In your heart home will call ever more.
In your heart home will call ever more.

As the song ended, the families gradually headed to their different places for the night.

* * *

The next morning, Rachel was up early. First they were all meeting at Jacob's for eggs and cold cereal before heading off to church.

Church was fun. Those who had known the Henderson family were excited to see them back. There were lots of introductions. The additional people packed the church to overflowing. Rachel felt happy being there with all of her brothers and sisters.

Church was over far too soon, and everyone headed back to the Henderson home for hoagie sandwiches. They milled around and visited, and even though most of them needed to be on their way, few left before late afternoon. When they did leave, all were sent off with extra sandwiches for their trip.

Anna's mother and oldest sister, Marilyn, each said something as they were leaving that made Rachel curious again. Anna's mother said she would gladly have Rachel as part of their family, and Marilyn said she felt Anna had chosen well in choosing Rachel. When Rachel asked Marilyn what she was chosen for, Marilyn just glossed over it. But still, Rachel knew she wasn't understanding something.

It was evening before the last car pulled out. When it did, Rachel felt exhausted. It had been a wonderful but long weekend. Marie invited them in for some lemonade, but Jacob said he thought he'd enjoy the evening outside. Rachel, Marie, and Anna looked at each other, and Rachel knew Jacob was fooling no one about his desire not to go into the house.

Anna said, "It might be nice to have the lemonade out here on the porch."

And that's what they did, catching their breath from the hectic weekend. Emily asked Jacob to play some songs, so he pulled his guitar out of the van. They sang together, ending again with "Coming Home."

. . . There is no place that you will ever go
In this world that will beat coming home.
Be you king or pauper, rich or poor,
In your heart home will call evermore.
In your heart home will call evermore.

Matthew

With July winding down, summer was rushing to a close. Jacob and Anna's family planned a vacation for August, and Anna told Rachel she wanted her family to come along, too.

"Wouldn't you prefer it to be just your family?" Rachel asked.

"Nonsense," Anna replied. "You are family, and it will be easier having another driver and help with meals and all."

"But wouldn't your children prefer more room in the van?"

Anna laughed. "Who said we'd take our van?"

And indeed, they didn't take the van. On the appointed day, Jacob pulled into his yard in a huge, bus-sized motorhome.

"It will sleep twelve quite comfortably," Anna informed her, "and it ought to be used. It just sits in an RV storage most of the year."

When Rachel stepped inside, she could hardly believe how nice it was. Emily squealed with delight to think of traveling and being able to watch television.

Jacob didn't seem to have any problem at all with Anna inviting Rachel and her family. He was clearly getting used to their two families being together. In fact, what he did say had nothing to do with her at all but about the motorhome. He simply mentioned, with a smile, that the nice part was that they wouldn't have to stop every five miles for a bathroom break.

It wasn't long before Jason and Marie had taken last minute instructions on how to take care of the horses and gardens. Anna counted to make sure everyone was onboard, and then they were on their way. Anna preferred to sit back with the children and relax; at least that's what she said. So Rachel sat up with Jacob to be the "copilot," as they called it. She thought she would need to read maps and signs, but she just had to set the GPS navigation. She had heard about them, but she had never seen one before. It amazed her. She did whatever Jacob needed her to do, but mostly they just visited. She enjoyed that part most of all.

After they had been on the road for most of a day, Jacob asked her if she would like to drive. She told him she was nervous about driving something so big. He laughed. "This from the girl who burned rubber in her father's hay trucks."

Rachel smiled at the memory of driving trucks for Jacob as he loaded hay on her father's farm. She had dumped him off more than once, but he never scolded her. At least not too much.

When they reached some open interstate, Jacob talked Rachel into taking over the controls. After they had switched seats and she eased the motorhome onto the road, she thought it felt good to be at the wheel of such a powerful machine. She truly enjoyed it and soon felt quite comfortable. Anna never drove. No amount of coaxing on Jacob's part could even get her to try, so it was always Jacob and Rachel switching off.

Rachel still didn't feel comfortable driving in the cities, but whenever they reached the open road, she was happy to take a turn. They rolled down through Iowa and into Missouri. They stayed in the nicest campgrounds that Rachel had ever seen. Anna liked lots of evening time at campgrounds, so they didn't drive more than about six or seven hours each day. On Sundays, they drove even less because they spent a big portion of the day at church. The short driving schedule was unusual for Rachel; she had always been in the mode of getting to a place as fast as possible.

The evenings—swimming in the pools, singing songs around the campfire, fishing in the lakes, and enjoying many other amenities—were definitely relaxing. Rachel made sure she always helped with the meals. At lunchtime, she took a break from her copilot position to help Anna make sandwiches. In the evening she did some cooking, but mostly she helped Jacob as he made Dutch oven potatoes, chicken, and cobbler.

The one bathroom was quite limited for so many people, so Jacob and the boys mostly used the showers and bathrooms at the campgrounds where they stayed. That left the motorhome more open for Anna, Rachel, and Emily.

Branson, Missouri was their first big stop. They went to some wonderful shows and spent a day at Silver Dollar City enjoying the rides. From there, they turned and headed through Kansas and Nebraska on their way to South Dakota and Mount Rushmore.

Emily was especially awed by Mount Rushmore and wanted to know how those men got their faces in the rock. "It's called erosion, silly," James said.

He scowled when everyone else laughed at him, but Jacob kindly said, "Someone had to help chisel them out of the rock."

Then it was Emily who made them laugh when she asked, "How did he know they were in there?"

When they finished at Mount Rushmore, everyone seemed ready to go home, and Jacob turned the motorhome back toward Minnesota. They drove longer days, and soon, just after sunset one evening, they pulled into Jacob and Anna's yard. Rachel heard Anna wake a sleepy Emily and tell her they were home. Emily yawned and said, "I want to go pet Star Bright."

Rachel told her that it was too dark, and she'd have to wait until the next day, but Rachel had to admit that she was anxious to see Star Bright, too. They only unloaded what they needed for the night, and Rachel's family stayed over at Jacob's house. But Rachel made Jacob promise to wake her in the morning to feed the horses, and he was true to his word. It felt good to get up at dawn and enjoy that time with Jacob again.

It seemed strange to get back into the swing of things. Rachel hadn't been on a vacation since she had married Matthew, and the change of pace, though good, had thrown her whole system off. But there wasn't much time to think about it. School started on Monday, in just under a week, and there was a lot to get done.

Anna and Rachel found little time for painting or the piano as they were shopping for school clothes, taking the children for eye exams, and buying school supplies.

In addition, Abraham decided to go out for the football team. He was big and strong and made the varsity cut. He hadn't been able to do too much before. He was playing linebacker, and Jacob spent many evenings throwing a football to Isaac, with Abraham trying to block or intercept.

On the first day of school, Rachel, taking Emily with her, drove Anna and James to get James settled into kindergarten. James appeared slightly timid about stepping into the classroom, but he clutched his new crayons and pencils excitedly. Emily was upset that she couldn't go, too, and pouted most of the morning about it. Rachel would have loved having her go to school with James, but her birthday wasn't for a couple months, so she was too young.

When James finally found his desk and seemed content, it was actually Anna who had a hard time. Anna's eyes were full of tears, but she tried to smile as she stepped out of the classroom. She shook her head and spoke as if to herself.

"Life goes so fast."

Rachel had seldom seen Anna that way, and she put her arm around her. Anna, to Rachel's surprise, sobbed against her. Usually it was the other way around. Rachel asked Anna if there was something she wanted to talk about, and all Anna said was, "When it's right." It reminded Rachel of what Anna said when she asked her why she wanted her and Jacob to be friends.

With the children back in school, things settled into routine. But something seemed slightly different about Anna. It was only a small thing, but sometimes when they painted, played duets, or spent time together, Rachel would see a tear on Anna's cheek. If Rachel ever mentioned it, Anna just brushed it off and changed the subject.

And Rachel noticed something else. Anna seemed to cherish her time with everyone more. Though Anna seemed more tired than usual, she refused to miss painting, playing the piano, or going to lunch. More and more, Jacob joined Rachel, Anna, and Emily as they picked up James from kindergarten, and then the five of them would eat out together.

Abraham's first football game came, and they were all there. Marie even brought her family though Jason had to work. Abraham didn't get to play much, but he did well when he did play. His team won, and his coach said Abraham was getting better all the time and would be playing more.

Jacob had been asked to speak at the community picnic on Labor Day, so Rachel had volunteered to be in charge of the ice cream cones. Jacob had Rachel read his speech, and he adjusted it a good half a dozen times. She knew he was a perfectionist, but this seemed even more particular than usual. His speech was strange for Labor Day since it was about the family being the cornerstone of the community.

Something else was odd about Jacob as well. His mind didn't seem to be on his work. More than once she had asked him a question only to have him look up and ask, "Were you talking to me?" At times, he would be a little irritable, something he had never been before. He would also drop everything to go to lunch or somewhere else with Anna. These changes in Jacob and Anna started to concern Rachel. But she didn't have much time to ponder it. She always had so much to do with her regular work, making cookies for the children's after-school snack and cooking dinner. And since Anna seemed more tired than usual, Rachel made sure she helped out even more.

When Labor Day came, Jacob gave a great speech. He said, "Any speech can be great if it's short." And he did keep it concise, speaking for only about ten minutes.

Rachel had organized the ice cream, donated by the Chamber of Commerce, by flavor. People got into the line of the flavor they wanted. She was dishing the chocolate. She was so busy, she hardly had a chance to look up and see who she was handing a cone to. That is, until she reached out with a cone and, instead of taking it, the man grabbed her wrist. She looked up into Matthew's face.

Instantly anger filled her heart. "Let go of me!"

"Oh, with your loverboy back, I'm not good enough for you anymore? I've seen the fancy car you drive and the airs you put on."

Rachel wanted to spit in his face. "Jacob has given me a good job and is kind to me. That's more than I can say for you."

Matthew's grip tightened. "And what did you give him to get the job?"

Rachel knew what Matthew was implying, and it infuriated her. "Jacob is kind without expecting anything in return, unlike you. He's a thousand times the man you'll ever be. But then, that isn't saying much is, it?"

Rachel saw the fury in Matthew's eyes. He raised his fist to strike her. Normally she would have turned her face from him, bracing for the blow, but her anger and her freedom from him had made her strong. If he was going to strike her, he was going to do it with her looking straight into his eyes. Her lack of intimidation caused him to falter, and in that instant, Jacob appeared at her side.

"What are you doing here, Matthew?"

Matthew dropped Rachel's wrist and scowled at Jacob. "Just coming to a community picnic and having a little discussion with Rachel."

"You leave Rachel alone!"

"Oh, you're afraid I might move in on your territory?"

"I'm sick and tired of you abusing her, and you have a court order to stay away."

The sheriff appeared. "Senator Davis, is there a problem?"

Jacob looked Matthew in the face. "I think Matthew was just leaving."

Matthew cursed and spat. "But only for now!" He spun on his heels and stormed away.

Jacob turned to Rachel and spoke with concern, "Rachel, are you okay?"

She nodded, but then, even though she tried to control them, tears started to run down her face. Jacob reached out and touched her arm. "Rachel, you're trembling."

She realized she truly was, and she started to gasp for breath as she turned her eyes from him. But then Jacob did something Rachel hadn't expected. He pulled her into his arms and held her close, and she just closed her eyes and sobbed against his chest. It was the first time in nineteen years she had felt his arms around her. It wasn't the way she had always dreamed it would occur, but she didn't care because he was holding her again.

Rachel heard Abraham ask his father what happened. Jacob just told him to go get Anna. But then Rachel heard Anna's voice.

"I'm here, Jacob. I saw the whole thing."

Abraham stepped in to take Rachel's place serving ice cream. The picnic had gone silent as those attending had watched the events unfold, and Rachel was embarrassed as they stared at her in Jacob's arms. But it was so comforting she didn't want him to let her go. Finally, as Rachel's tears subsided, Anna suggested that Jacob led Rachel to a chair so she could sit down. She had no sooner done so than Emily was there and very concerned. "It's okay, Momma. That mean man is gone."

Rachel hugged Emily tightly and was glad Matthew was gone. But his final words, "But only for now!" haunted her.

Matthew Again

It had been over a week since the Labor Day picnic, and the thoughts of Matthew were finally beginning to fade. The three families had again gone to see Abraham play football. He got to play quite a bit more, sacked the quarterback a couple of times, and made one interception. Everyone was proud of him, and James had to tell everybody they met that Abraham was his big brother.

That evening as Rachel was reading scriptures with her children, she thought she heard the back door rattle. She checked it and saw nothing. She went back into the family room, and they knelt in prayer. They had just stood up when she knew for sure there was a rattle at the front door.

As she approached it, the door suddenly burst open in splinters, and there stood Matthew with a crowbar in his hand. Rachel was so shocked that she stumbled backward and fell to the floor. Her heart started to pound, and she jumped to her feet to face him. "Get out of my house!"

Matthew smirked and raised the crowbar menacingly. "And who's going to make me? I'd thought you would be welcoming me home with open arms. But instead, you changed the locks on the doors."

"I'm calling the sheriff."

As Rachel reached for the phone, Matthew stepped forward and hit her, sending her sprawling across the room, but not before she smelled the alcohol on his breath. At that moment she knew she was dealing with someone dangerously out of control. She could feel the blood starting to ooze down the side of her face, and Emily started to cry as John pulled her and David close.

Matthew turned to Emily. "Shut up the bawling, you little brat!"

Rachel rose slowly to her feet. "What do you want, Matthew?"

He reached out and touched her arm, speaking with a disgustingly sweet tone in his voice. "I wouldn't mind a little kindness and affection to start with."

She slapped his hand away. "You filthy animal!"

Again he slapped her, knocking her to the floor. "You're lucky I came for money!"

Rachel again rose to her feet. "I'll get you what money I have, and then you get out!" She retrieved her purse, always keeping an eye on him. Luckily, he seemed nervous that one of the children might try to call the police and was absorbed in keeping an eye on them. Rachel rummaged through everything she could think of and came up with just over two-hundred dollars. Matthew jerked it from her hand as she offered it to him.

"That's it?" he said after counting it. "You expect me to believe you drive that fancy car and wear those fancy clothes and put on your high and all-mighty airs, and you only have two-hundred dollars?"

"I put my money in the bank where I can use it when I need it to take care of my family."

Matthew raised his hand to strike her again, and Emily yelled, "Leave Momma alone, you mean man!"

Matthew looked at Emily and then back at Rachel. "What kind of disrespectful brat are you raising?"

He marched over to the children. John and David tried to hide Emily behind them to protect her, but Matthew viciously shoved them out of the way and grabbed her.

Emily started to scream. Matthew slapped her and told her to shut up, and then he held the crowbar at her neck. John went for him, and Matthew hit him hard, sending him over the couch. Rachel rushed to John as he lay there, dazed and bleeding. Matthew yelled at him. "You're a stupid boy! You're all stupid to think you can get away from me! You will never be free of me."

Rachel looked up at him. "Matthew, leave Emily alone. Please, leave her alone. Take my car, take whatever, but don't hurt her."

Matthew smirked again. "So, 'please' is it now? It's about time I got some respect."

He pulled Emily over by the door and looked out at the beautiful blue Cadillac Seville. "It's indeed a nice car, Rachel, and I'm flattered at your offer, but it would just give the police something to track me down, and you know it."

"I don't have anything else to give you."

Matthew reached up and jerked the picture of Rachel's family from the wall, the one that had Jacob in it. He hurled it to the floor. "No. But your rich loverboy does." Matthew pulled a gun from his coat and stuck it up against Emily's head. "You call him and tell him to get down here with every bit of money he can scrounge up, or he's not going to see his precious little niece alive again."

Rachel stood and went to the phone. She considered trying to call 911, but she was afraid for Emily. She felt she would have to trust Jacob.

Her hand trembled as she dialed the number. She couldn't keep the fear from her voice as Joseph answered and she asked for Jacob. When Jacob came on the phone, her voice quivered as she spoke through her tears.

"And tell him not to be stupid enough to call the police!" Matthew demanded from behind her. "Or all of you will be dead by the time they get here!"

She nodded and relayed the message. Jacob simply said, "I'll be right there."

Rachel wanted to try to take Emily from Matthew but feared he might hurt Emily more, so she knelt beside John and pulled him close as David joined her. Rachel could feel her heart pounding so hard it was about to explode in her chest. The sweat was beading on her forehead as they waited the few minutes for Jacob to get there. Matthew spent the time gloating to her that she belonged to him, she would never be rid of him, and she better get used to the idea.

When Rachel heard Jacob's car in the driveway, she was grateful, yet afraid of what might happen next. She heard his car door slam and almost immediately, Jacob stepped through the shattered doorway into the house. He looked around the room and seemed to quickly take in what had happened. Matthew stood holding Emily with a crowbar against her throat and a gun to her head. John lay on the floor, dazed and bleeding, with Rachel and David with him. Blood was dripping down Rachel's face and onto her clothes.

Jacob quickly turned to Matthew. "I brought every bit of money I had in the house, and Anna sent her jewelry."

Matthew slid the crowbar under one arm and knelt so he could still hold Emily and take the sack Jacob offered. He quickly counted the money then looked up in disgust and anger. "Twenty-five hundred dollars and a bunch of junk jewelry are all she's worth to you?"

That angered Jacob. "Look, Matthew, that's all I had around the house!"

"Oh, you expect me to believe a rich snob like you only has that much money?!"

"I didn't become rich letting money sit around my house!"

Matthew seemed to be taking it all in and thinking. "So what do we do now? I have a bill I need to pay tonight."

Jacob's expression showed he was trying to figure a way out of the situation as he answered. "How much do you need?"

"Fifty thousand dollars."

"Anna's jewelry is probably worth thirty to forty thousand easy."

"So how am I supposed to get the money out of it?"

"I don't know," Jacob said in frustration.

"Well, you'd better think of something," Matthew snarled as he stuffed the money and jewelry into his coat and pulled the crowbar so tight against Emily's throat that she was standing on her tippy-toes, gurgling.

Rachel could hardly speak for fear. She had great trust in Jacob, but she could see him searching for a way out of this. Even his voice trembled as he spoke.

"Matthew, look, maybe we could . . . "

He paused, desperately trying to come up with something. Matthew grew impatient. "Yes?"

Suddenly a light seemed to spark in Jacob's eyes as if an idea came to him. "Maybe we could get some money out of the ATM for you."

Matthew nodded. "Great, you do that. You go get me fifty thousand dollars from the ATM." Then he scowled. "Heck, if you are getting it out, why not make it an even million. It's not like you can't afford it."

Jacob shook his head. "ATMs don't allow more than ten thousand from my account in any twenty-four-hour period."

"That is the stupidest thing I ever heard!"

"Well, it's the way it is, and it's to protect against theft."

Matthew thought for a moment. Finally, he relented. "All right, you go get it."

Jacob looked at Rachel, and she could read in his eyes that he was telling her to trust him. He turned back to Matthew.

"Why don't you just go with me? It would be easier. I could give you the money, and you'd be on your way sooner."

"Yea, and have you try your fancy judo stuff on me? Do you think I'm crazy?"

Jacob acted calm and unflustered, even though Rachel could sense his nervousness. "I'm not crazy enough to try anything against someone with a gun. I can't fight a bullet."

Matthew smirked. "You got that right." He thought for a moment, and then motioned Jacob toward the door with the gun. "All right. You've convinced me. Let's go."

"Wait a minute. You will want to let Emily go."

"Oh, I will, will I? And just why is that?"

"Because she will just slow you down when we are done, and besides, you will have me for a hostage if that's what you need."

Matthew thought for another moment and then nodded. "You are finally talking sensibly."

He let Emily go, but instead of running to Rachel, she ran to Jacob. Rachel didn't know if that was because he seemed like a strength to her or if she understood what was happening and was afraid for him. Jacob, lovingly, pushed her away from him, speaking firmly. "Emily, go to your mother."

She looked up at him, and he nodded reassuringly. She moved toward Rachel, keeping as far from Matthew as possible, keeping an eye on him. As she passed right across from him, he jumped at her and yelled "Boo!" She screamed and ran behind Rachel as Matthew laughed.

He again motioned Jacob toward the door with the gun, holding the crowbar ready in the other. He turned back to Rachel. "And don't go calling the police or Lover Boy gets it."

Rachel could hear the pain in Jacob's voice as he responded. "Would you stop with the Lover Boy stuff? She chose you, not me."

Jacob's last words bit into Rachel's heart with more force and pain than any bullet could have. She gasped from the wound it made.

Matthew turned and looked at her with an evil grin. "Don't we know it?"

Suddenly, the hatred Rachel felt for Matthew tore at her like a fire that would consume her whole soul. The pain in Jacob's voice and Matthew's mockery of him made her tremble with anger and hate. She had despised Matthew for a long time, but this was more intense than anything she had ever felt in his actions toward her. She wanted to fly at him and tear and scratch and bite. The feeling was almost overwhelming. If it had been just her life, she might have done it even if he had killed her, but fear for the safety of her children and Jacob held her back.

Jacob seemed to sense her feelings and knitted his eyebrows at her as if to tell her to be careful. Matthew let out another loud laugh, and Rachel trembled with fury.

As Jacob stepped to the door, he turned back to Rachel. "When we're gone, take your children and go to my house. You'll be safer there."

Matthew raised the crowbar threateningly. "You shut up!" He then turned back to Rachel. "You stay put in case I decide to come back for you. If I do and you're not here, that's the last you'll see of him."

Matthew then pointed the gun more fully at Jacob as if to emphasize his point. Jacob nodded his head toward his house and creased his eyebrows to tell her to do it anyway. She knew he was telling her it wouldn't help any of them to put her family in further danger.

Matthew turned and pushed Jacob out the door with the end of the crowbar. Matthew turned one more time to Rachel. "And don't try to come after us, or I will shoot you both!"

The two of them went to the car. Rachel went to the window and watched as Jacob climbed in to drive, and Matthew worked his way into the backseat, keeping the gun fixed on Jacob. The car turned and headed away. Rachel knew Jacob was putting himself in great danger in an attempt to lead Matthew away from her family. As the lights faded down the road to town, she hurried back to John. "John, are you okay?"

He nodded, so she continued. "I'm going to take you children up to Anna's. Can you get up?"

John staggered to his feet as David asked, "But what if they come back and he doesn't find us here?"

Rachel tried to stay calm and sound convincing. "It won't help for us to be in danger, too."

John was unsteady on his feet, so Rachel helped him to the car. Once everyone was in, she spun out of the driveway up to Anna's. Anna and Abraham were apparently watching because when they pulled into the driveway, the door was thrown open and the two of them hurried out of the house.

Abraham's voice quivered as he asked, "Where's Father?"

Rachel quickly told what had happened. As the children crossed the threshold into the house, Rachel turned back to her car. Anna grabbed her arm. "Where are you going?"

"I'm going after Jacob."

"But, Momma," David objected fearfully, "he said he'd kill you if you did!"

Suddenly Rachel could not stop her tears. "He'll probably kill Jacob if I don't. We can't call the police, or Matthew will kill Jacob. I've got to do what I can, no matter what Matthew does to me. I'd rather die than lose Jacob."

As she ran to the car, she called back to Anna to please take care of her children. She threw herself into her car, spun it around, and headed to town. She didn't even think of her own safety as she floored it on the open road. The car almost flew at times as she maxed out the speed it would go.

Her mind raced faster than her car. She felt a burning in her heart, a burning that whatever happened was her fault. If she had not gone with Matthew, if she had not let him kiss her, if she had not married him, none of this would have happened. She knew that if anything happened to Jacob, she could never forgive herself.

The town wasn't large, only about thirty-thousand people, and she could only think of five ATM machines. She was afraid to drive right by them for fear Matthew would see her and do something to Jacob, so she drove slowly across the intersection nearest to each one and looked down the street. She had gone past three and had seen nothing, and her heart was pounding from feeling she might be racing the clock for Jacob's life.

She drove across town to the fourth one. As she drove through the intersection and looked down the street, she thought she could see something on the sidewalk. There was no sign of Jacob's car, so she backed up and turned that way to investigate. As she drew closer, she could tell it was a person lying there. When she pulled up alongside, she knew it was Jacob, and he was lying face down in a pool of blood.

She gasped with panic as she reached for her cell phone. Then she realized she had left everything at home in her hurry. Jacob needed help, and he needed it now. As she slid her car to a stop, she choked out a prayer. "Oh, Father, please help me know what to do! Please don't let Jacob die!"

Instantly her mind was filled with a flash of memory, and she knew what to do. She reached to her mirror and was relieved to hear the clear voice. "OnStar, how may I help you?"

"There's been an accident. I need an ambulance and police to my position as fast as possible."

"Yes, Ma'am, right away."

Rachel threw her door open and ran to Jacob's side. Beside him lay the crowbar, covered with blood. Jacob's wallet and its contents were strewn across the sidewalk. She raised his head out of the blood, though she didn't dare move him much for fear of further injury. She checked and found a weak pulse. She thanked the Lord that he was still alive. The only thing she could think of from her first-aid training was to apply pressure to the wound to reduce the flow of blood, so that's what she did. And as she held her palm tight to the wound on his head, she started to sob as she prayed again, "Oh, Lord, please don't let him die! Please, please, don't let Jacob die!"

The Secret of the Last Gift

It seemed like forever before the ambulance arrived. Everything was a blur after that. The paramedics started working on Jacob and loaded him into the ambulance. The sheriff arrived and asked her questions, but all she could choke out between sobs was that it was Matthew and that he was driving Jacob's car. That was enough for the sheriff to put out an all-points bulletin for him.

Rachel wanted to ride in the ambulance with Jacob, but the paramedics needed the space. Rachel was dazed and confused, so a deputy drove her to the hospital in her car and helped her get into the emergency room.

Jacob was immediately wheeled into surgery. A nurse wanted to look at the cuts on Rachel's face, but she said she was fine. She was so worried she could think of nothing but Jacob. Finally, they persuaded her to at least take a washcloth and wash the blood from her face and hands. The thought that the blood on her hands was Jacob's wrenched her heart, and she again felt that what had happened to him was her fault.

The sheriff came and asked somebody to get her some hot chocolate to help calm her. He asked her to sip it slowly and try to tell him what happened. Though her anxiety continued, she gradually felt calmer and was able to tell the sheriff the story. When she finally finished, he stood and reassured her.

"Don't worry, Ma'am. We have extra patrols out in that area where your children are. Sooner or later we'll catch him, and when we do, we'll put him where he won't be bothering you again."

He asked her if she wanted to call Anna or if she wanted him to. She felt she could hardly face Anna and the children feeling the way she did, but she felt it would be better if it came from her. She tried to be positive and upbeat on the phone, but she knew the tremor in her voice gave her feelings away. Anna told her they knew something had happened when patrol cars started going back and forth down the road.

It was Anna who ended up reassuring Rachel. "Don't worry. I have a strong feeling Jacob will be all right. And don't worry about the children; we'll take care of them. You stay with Jacob, and I'll come in when I can."

That made Rachel feel quite a bit better. Anna always seemed to be right about everything. Rachel had no sooner finished the phone call than a newspaper reporter showed up. Rachel didn't feel in the mood to talk, but there seemed to be no way to avoid it, so she answered his questions so he would leave her alone. He especially seemed interested in the fact that Jacob had been willing to become Matthew's hostage in Emily's place.

The hours seemed to tick slowly by after that as Rachel waited for news about Jacob's condition. It was a long time before a doctor approached her. "Mrs. Davis? Your husband is out of surgery now."

She started to tell him that she wasn't Jacob's wife but stopped. She considered that, due to privacy laws, he might not tell her about Jacob if he knew.

"Your husband is lucky you found him when you did. As it is, I regret to say he still only has about a fifty-fifty chance of making it, and only that because he's healthy. But if it had been any longer, he wouldn't have had any chance at all. He's in a coma, and at this point all we can do is continue to monitor his condition. If you would like, you can see him now."

He directed her to the Intensive Care Unit, where a nurse directed her to Jacob's room. As she walked in and saw all of the tubes connected to him and the bandages around his head and face, the tears started coming again. She leaned over and softly touched his cheek. "I love you, Jacob. We all love you."

She then fell into the chair by his side and put her head on her arms on his bed and sobbed. As she did, the events of the evening played out in her mind again, and again she couldn't help but blame herself. She thought of the hurt she could sense in Jacob's voice as he'd said she had chosen Matthew over him. She also thought of the hatred she had felt when Matthew had mocked Jacob, and she realized how deep her love for Jacob truly was.

She didn't know how long she cried, but as her tears ebbed, she felt a strong feeling there was someone else in the room. She turned, and there stood Anna watching her. She felt embarrassed, embarrassed for crying at the bedside of another woman's husband. She wondered how long Anna had been watching her.

Anna smiled kindly. "You really do love him, don't you?"

Rachel stuttered, "Well . . . I . . . " She was so embarrassed she tried to change the subject. "Anna, I want to thank you for sending your jewelry to save Emily."

Anna just waved her hand. "Oh, jewelry, schmewlry. Most people who wear it are as fake as what they wear. Jacob, unfortunately, buys me expensive stuff, and then I have to wear it so he won't feel bad. I'd prefer my only jewelry was my wedding ring."

Anna kissed Jacob, and for a moment she lovingly caressed his face. She then turned and kindly touched Rachel's arm. "Rachel, I don't want you to be embarrassed about loving Jacob. I'm glad to know you do."

"Why, Anna? I can't understand why any woman would want another woman to love her husband."

"I've been waiting a long time to know if you still truly loved him," Anna said. "You've worked hard at hiding it. I know you wanted to be appropriate in what you did because he's my husband, and I appreciate that, but I really needed to know if you loved him, and how much. When you left my house tonight, willing to die to save his life, all my doubts disappeared."

Rachel felt confused. "But Anna, you still haven't answered my question. Why do you want me to love him?"

Anna pulled up a chair facing Rachel. "I think it's time we had a woman-to-woman talk, and that I laid all of my cards on the table." Anna took a deep breath and continued. "Do you know why we moved to Minnesota?"

Rachel nodded. "You moved here so he could be close to his mother since she had become blind and was growing old."

"Is that what Jacob told you?"

"Yes."

Anna slowly shook her head. "I am the one who convinced Jacob that we should move here, and it's true that I used his mother as the reason, but the real reason I persuaded him to move our family here had nothing to do with his mother."

"It didn't?"

Anna shook her head. "However, the real reason was . . . " She paused and took Rachel's hands in her own. "The real reason was you."

Rachel gasped. "But why? You didn't even know me."

"But I knew of you, and I realized you were the answer to my prayers."

"What prayers? To get over the pain I had caused him?"

Anna shook her head. "That was part of it. However, the reason is much deeper than that." She paused and seemed to be pondering how to say what she wanted to say. It was the first time Rachel had seen Anna concerned about her words. She had always seemed so confident before. Anna gripped Rachel's hands tighter. "What I'm going to tell you I am going to share with you in the strictest confidence. You've got to promise me you won't tell anyone, not even Jacob, though I think he suspects."

Rachel nodded, so Anna continued. "Rachel, I . . ."

She paused and looked over at the open door. "Hang on a minute."

Anna got up and closed the door, then came back and sat down. She again took Rachel's hands in her own. "I think the best way to help you understand is to show you something instead of telling you."

Anna let go of Rachel's hands and reached behind her head. She gave a quick tug, and then all of Anna's beautiful blond hair fell into her lap, and Anna sat in front of Rachel, totally bald.

Rachel gasped, and Anna laughed slightly. "That was the reaction I thought I'd get." Then, as Rachel felt the shock of it all, Anna continued in a serious but subdued tone as she slid her hair back into place.

"Do you know why a woman my age loses all of her hair?"

Rachel could think of only one thing, but she shook her head, hoping beyond hope that it wouldn't be that. Anna reached down and took Rachel's hands in her own as she continued.

"It's due to chemotherapy. Rachel, I have cancer, and I'm dying."

Rachel started to cry all over again. "But you can't! I don't want you to die!"

Anna seemed back to her more humorous self. "Well, to be honest, I'm not all that thrilled about it either. But I've long decided there are worse things than dying."

"Like what?"

"Like living in pain forever. Like not being loved while you are alive. I'd much rather be dead than be despised by all who know me, like your ex-husband. But the thing I think would be worst of all is not being as ready as I can be when the time comes." Anna then pulled Rachel's hands close, drawing the two women together. "And that is where you come in."

"I don't understand."

Anna let go of Rachel's hands and walked to the window, looking out as she spoke. "When I first found out I had cancer, we lived in Washington, D.C. We attacked it vigorously and thought we had it beat. But when it came back, I knew we wouldn't win again. Jacob decided it would be his last term, hoping that leaving the Senate and D.C. would somehow help me heal. He had planned for us to move back to Washington State. But I had three problems with that. The problems were Jacob's success, money, and power.

"You see, there were many women who would have loved to marry Jacob, but all for the wrong reasons. Those prima donnas all wanted Jacob for his money and the power of his position. Oh, don't get me wrong—there were surely some good women who would probably really love him. But it was impossible to tell which ones were sincere and which ones only looked at him as a possible ticket to becoming First Lady in the White House."

Anna paused and turned from the window as if letting what she was saying sink in before she continued. She looked at Rachel, smiled, and sat back down, speaking quietly, as if they were sharing a secret together.

"In addition, you and I both know that my almost-perfect husband carries a scar deep within his heart, a scar he has tried in vain to erase for many years.

"Jacob and I both prayed for a miracle, but the miracles we prayed for were different. He prayed that I would get well, but I was at peace with life and what would happen, so the miracle I prayed for was even greater. I prayed that it would be his heart that was healed instead of me, and that when I was gone, his new wife would love him for the great man he is and not try to mold him into something he was not. In addition, I wanted her to be a mother to my children, who would help them know of my love for them and raise them the same way I would. This was what I desired more than anything for the last and most important gift I could give Jacob—a healed heart and a loving wife. And my final gift to my children would be a good mother.

"Years ago when we got word of your divorce from Matthew, I felt a powerful feeling surge through me that you were the answer to my prayer, a feeling as if God were opening a door for my miracle. It was up to me to make the decision to step through it. I've watched you and waited for the time that I was sure beyond all doubt that you loved him and could love my children, too. I determined to see what kind of woman you are, and if you could have the strength to be what he needed." Anna looked away and then spoke as if to herself. "My biggest concern now is that I've waited too long."

Rachel wanted to know what Anna meant by that, but the shock of what she was hearing was already too great. The mystery of why Anna wanted her and Jacob to be friends began to unwind. Anna was not only wanting Jacob to heal from the pain he felt about Rachel being with Matthew, but she was also planning for Rachel to become his wife when she was gone. It all seemed too much, too fast, and she felt dizzy. Her emotions through the night—the fear of Matthew, the concerns of possibly losing Jacob, the sudden knowledge of Anna's cancer, and finally, the thought that all along Anna had planned for Rachel to be Jacob's wife—combined together and drained her strength, and she slumped in her chair.

Anna, as always, seemed to understand. She rose and patted Rachel's shoulder. "I've given you a lot to think about. I'm going to go get us some breakfast, and then we can talk more."

Anna was gone for only about 20 minutes, but Rachel's mind raced at high speed. She thought of how much she had wanted to be Jacob's wife, but she didn't want that at the expense of losing Anna. She realized she should have seen the signs to understand that Anna had cancer: the tiredness and long trips to the city. Had she really realized but denied it, or was she just blind? Looking at Jacob lying quietly in a coma, and with the thought of losing Anna, the tears started flowing down her face again, and that was how Anna found her when she came back.

When Anna saw her, she was stern. "Now, don't you go getting emotional on me, and don't you go being like Jacob. He tries to deny the inevitable, and that won't help at all. It's going to happen, sooner, I feel, than we might expect, and whether we like it or not. I want to make the best use of what time I have left."

Anna set a tray down, and on it were two plates. Each was loaded with three pancakes, sausage, bacon, eggs, and one container each of jam and syrup. There was also a glass of milk and a glass of orange juice for each of them. Rachel wondered if she could eat at all. It was only about five o' clock in the morning, and her stomach was still tight from the emotions of the night. But as they ate together, she found a peacefulness settle on her—a peacefulness that always seemed to permeate Anna's demeanor and, in some small way, transferred itself to Rachel.

She asked Anna how she could watch her husband being friends with another woman and not feel jealous.

Anna just shrugged. "I had four years to plan for it. At first I was jealous, mostly that others would get to live when I wouldn't. But as the determination settled on me, I knew what I needed to do, and I was able to put jealousy away. I can't say I'm perfect. Sometimes, especially in the beginning, I'd feel a twinge of jealousy when he would have fun and laugh with you. After all, I'm human. But the more I have grown to love you, the less of it I feel, and the happier I am that he and my children will have you when I'm gone.

"The reason I feel I might almost have been too late sharing this with you is because I realize that some of the single men of the community are beginning to take notice of you. You might not realize it, but I heard that the reason men had not shown any interest in you before was because Matthew made it clear around town what he would do to anyone who did. He was still trying to control your life after the divorce."

"I had heard from others about Matthew's threats," Rachel said, "but I hadn't noticed any interest from anyone."

Anna spoke quietly, looking directly at Rachel. "Rachel, with what Matthew has done, I'm sure he will be gone from your life for good. Either he will be in prison, or he will flee the country. But either way, he most likely won't be around. You may immediately find that there are men who want to date you." Anna's voice turned almost to a pleading. "Please, if you love Jacob, don't go out with them until you've given Jacob a chance to love you in return."

Rachel felt strange talking to Anna this way, but she felt that if Anna was going to be so open about her feelings, then she needed to also.

"Anna, I've never loved any other man except Jacob. The biggest mistake I made was pretending to care for another man when I didn't. I'm never going to do that again. My heart wouldn't let me."

Anna's eyes filled with tears. "Thank you, Rachel. You don't know how much that means to me. Of course, a lot depends on Jacob. If he does marry someone else, I don't want you to feel bound to any promise to me. But I strongly feel that, when I'm gone, Jacob will again find the love he has for you that is still buried deep in his heart."

"With what my life was like when I was married to Matthew, I'm not sure that I could ever consider marrying someone other than Jacob," Rachel said, "even if he did marry someone else. The biggest problem I see is that if he does marry someone else, she might not be happy about him continuing his friendship with me."

Anna nodded. "I'm banking on the fact that Jacob realizes that, too, and I don't think he would be willing to give you up."

They talked for a long time. When the light started to shine through the window, suddenly Rachel thought about something else. "Anna, what about the children?"

"Oh, don't worry about them. Part of the reason I was so long is that I had to wait until Marie could come over to take care of them. The sheriff suggested they not go to school until Matthew is captured. When Jason goes off to work, he plans to take their children to our house for Marie to watch as well. Their children might be in some danger from Matthew, too. Jason said he would also take care of the horses."

Rachel felt much better. She could hardly believe Anna had thought of everything when it had just gone clear out of her own mind.

Nurses would come in and check on Jacob now and then, but

Anna and Rachel continued to talk until nearly noon when the doctor and the sheriff came in. The sheriff seemed pleased to see both of them there and said they both needed to hear the news he had.

"Senator Davis's car was found," he said. "It was driven over a cliff. There was a body inside, and we think it is Matthew, but the person is unidentifiable because the car burned. We will have to match some dental records to make sure. It was made to look like an accident, but we don't think it was. We've been watching Matthew for some time because we were sure he has been involved in drug deals and illegal gambling, but we could never find enough evidence. We think he might have run afoul of a big drug cartel or a loan shark."

The sheriff then turned to Anna. "Mrs. Davis, we didn't find any of your jewelry in the car. Any of the cash would have been burned, but we should have found the jewelry. That's part of the reason we feel it wasn't an accident. He may have paid them what he had, but perhaps it wasn't enough."

Anna shrugged. "I'm not worried about the cash or the jewelry, but please do tell us what you learn about who was in the car."

The sheriff said he would, and then he left.

The doctor looked at Rachel in confusion. "I thought you were Mrs. Davis."

Rachel felt slightly ashamed she had let him think that. "I used to be because I was married to Jacob's brother, but I have taken back my maiden name of Henderson."

"But," Anna quickly added, "we are a close family, and anything you can tell me you can tell her."

The doctor turned his attention to Anna. "So, I take it you are Senator Davis's wife." Anna nodded.

"Well, I came in to tell you of his prognosis," the doctor said. "He seems to have stabilized, but the blow to the back of his head cracked his skull and caused major trauma. A person in his condition may never come out of the coma."

"Is there anything we can do to help?" Anna asked.

The doctor nodded. "Recent studies indicate that people in comas who hear the voices of those they love seem to recover faster. Some doctors don't like lots of family in intensive care, but in this case, I am in favor of all the visits possible."

The doctor paused a moment and then continued. "There is one other thing. There very likely could be some brain damage, and if he does come out of the coma, he may struggle to put everything together. Often, in a case like this, some memories will be clear, and others might take some time to return, if they return at all."

The doctor briefly discussed this with them and then left. Anna and Rachel talked about ways they could help Jacob. Anna suggested that Rachel read to him.

"I remember him telling me about how the two of you read books together."

Rachel smiled at the memory. Even though Jacob was a year ahead of her in school and there weren't a lot of classes they could take together, when she was a freshman, and he was a sophomore they both signed up for a literature class. They had taken turns reading the assigned books to each other while sitting in the tree house. After the class was over, they had continued doing that. They had put a beat-up old love seat up there, and Rachel could remember leaning against Jacob as he read. She liked to hear him, but she also enjoyed it when he would put his arm around her as she read. They read a lot of books that way, and it was with Jacob that she had gained her love of good stories and fine literature.

Rachel shared some of this with Anna, and they decided to try it. Rachel suggested that Anna read to him, too, but Anna didn't feel it would be as effective because Jacob had always done all of the reading in their relationship.

"I think the memory of your voice would be better," Anna said.

"But the doctor said it wasn't so much the memory, but just hearing the voice," Rachel replied.

"I might come and talk to him," Anna replied, "but I don't really read that well."

Anna asked what books Rachel felt would be best. Rachel could remember James Herriot's book *All Creatures Great and Small*, Laura Ingalls Wilder's *Little House on the Prairie*, and other classics they had enjoyed, including *Treasure Island*. They decided to start with those.

"Would you like to go home and shower and change?" Anna asked.

Rachel shook her head. "I'm concerned about John, but other than that I would like to be here when Jacob wakes up."

"I don't think you need to worry about John," Anna said. "He seemed back to normal by the time I left."

Then Anna said something that made Rachel feel almost as if Anna could read her thoughts, as she often seemed to. She took Rachel's hands and looked into her eyes.

"Rachel," Anna said, "I know why you feel you need to be here when he wakes up. But what happened is not your fault. No one blames you."

Rachel lowered her eyes, unable to face her. "If I hadn't done what I did to Jacob all those years ago, none of this would have ever happened."

Anna spoke in almost a scolding tone. "Rachel, it doesn't do you or anyone else any good for you to keep beating yourself up about it. You need to forgive yourself. Everyone else has."

"Jacob hasn't."

"I don't think Jacob feels anything against you. He's just haunted by a memory he can't erase."

"I'd still like to be here to tell him I'm sorry."

"As you wish. But you've got to promise me to get over your feelings about what happened. Your life is different now, and it will only be as good as your ability to put the past behind you."

She then patted Rachel's hand. "Besides, I'm trying to get Jacob to heal from that memory, but he can't if you can't."

That statement hit Rachel hard. Could it be that the pain each of them felt added to the pain of the other? She had never considered that before. Anna had a way of bringing things right to the point. Rachel wished she was like Anna, but instead she let her feelings rule her life too much when she should have made what she wanted from life rule her feelings.

"Anna, how can you be so calm about having cancer?" Rachel asked.

Anna, who was always upbeat, funny, and cheerful, became very serious. "You know, Rachel, most people don't have any idea when they are going to die. But I, on the other hand, am lucky because I do. It has given me a great opportunity to ponder about it. I've thought about life and realized that, when all is said and done, the only thing that truly matters is the loving relationships we build. And I am sure we will have them again after we die."

"How can you be so sure?" Rachel asked.

"God commanded us to love one another, didn't he?" Anna replied. "Why, then, would he punish us for doing as he commanded? If, after this life, he took away those relationships we treasured most, it would be the worst punishment of all. God must be just, and justice would, therefore, dictate we will again be with those we love, sharing the same relationships we enjoy here, loving one another as God commanded."

The logic and beauty of what Anna said astounded Rachel. She realized that Anna had thought a long time about this. But what Anna said raised another question in Rachel's mind. "Anna, what about relationships we don't like, such as mine with Matthew?"

Anna spoke with kindness and understanding. "Would it be just for God to allow the abuser to continue to abuse his victim? Matthew hasn't really loved you, nor have you loved him, so how could it be just to allow such a relationship to remain?"

There was one other question this brought to Rachel's mind. "Anna, if you believe that we will have the same relationships of love in the next life, doesn't it bother you that, if Jacob married me, we would both be with him there?"

Anna just laughed. "I'd rather be one of two wives to a good man than the only wife to a rotten one."

Rachel thought about Matthew versus Jacob, and what Anna said struck home with great force.

"Besides," Anna continued, laughing even more, "if I am going to share my husband with someone, I want to be the one to choose who she'll be."

Then Anna, though still smiling, became serious again and said something that brought tears to Rachel's eyes. "Rachel," she said, "I've grown to love you as a sister and a dear friend. If I am going to share my husband with someone, I want her to be you."

Tears started to flow down Rachel's face, and Anna stood and pulled Rachel into a big hug. Rachel could see tears glisten in Anna's eyes as Rachel said, "I love you too, Anna."

They talked a while longer, and then Anna decided they needed some lunch. She asked Rachel what she would like, and Rachel suggested the hamburger, fries, and milkshakes like Jacob always brought.

"One thing about it," Anna said with a laugh as she headed out the door, "I know it isn't cholesterol that will kill me, so I can eat anything I want."

They had a fun lunch together and spent most of the afternoon visiting. The thought of losing Anna was almost unbearable for Rachel, and yet Anna's view of life and death made everything less traumatic.

As it grew late in the afternoon, Anna felt she should go check on the children and help Marie. She said she would bring the children in for a visit in the evening and bring Rachel some books and a change of clothes. She was just leaving when the sheriff came. He informed them that the dental record had made a conclusive match—the person in the car had been Matthew. He said they weren't sure what to do with his body.

Rachel didn't know what to say, but Anna did. "Jacob would want his brother taken care of. We will pay the mortician for everything

181

and have him buried by his parents. Perhaps we will have a service later when Jacob is better."

Since Rachel didn't want to leave Jacob's side, Anna said she'd take care of everything. She did say she would need Rachel's help on the obituary for the paper, and Rachel agreed. As the sheriff was leaving, he turned back to Rachel. "I would usually express my condolences, but I'm not sure what is appropriate here. I am sorry for what you have been through."

Rachel thanked him for his kindness, and he left. Rachel didn't feel sadness, and she almost felt guilty for it. Matthew was the father of her children, but she felt no affinity to him for any other reason. The hatred she had felt had burned out any other kind of feeling, but now that he was gone there was an emptiness. Not an emptiness as if she had lost someone, but an emptiness as if there were no feeling there at all—not affection, hate, anger, or anything. Just an emptiness.

She told Anna that she felt guilty not feeling sad about it. Anna was kind. "No one can blame you after what you have endured."

Rachel was more concerned about the feelings of her children. "Emily never knew him since he left before she was born," she told Anna. "But he was still around when John and David were young."

Anna smiled kindly. "Children are resilient enough that they will be fine."

Anna kissed Jacob once more, lovingly caressed his face, and told him she loved him. Then she went home to help Marie.

Rachel was left with her own thoughts and feelings. She contemplated the many things that they had talked about. She was glad Anna was bringing some books back so she would have a place to bury her thoughts.

Anna wasn't gone for more than a couple of hours before she was back and had Marie and all of the children from the three families with her. She also had some pizzas. The nurse was nervous about such a big group, but Anna assured her it was the doctor's orders.

Anna said that since the sheriff had asked that the children be kept home and inside all day, they needed to get out and do something, so they had met Jason at work for a pizza party. Rachel was hungry and grateful for the last of the pizza. Anna told her to make sure she used Jacob's personal credit card for anything she needed or wanted while she was at the hospital.

Rachel asked John how he was feeling. He said he was fine and seemed annoyed at the attention. Emily wanted to know what was wrong with Jacob. "Did that mean man hurt him?"

Rachel nodded. "But that mean man is gone and won't ever be coming back to hurt anyone again."

Rachel asked Anna if she had told them about Matthew, and Anna shook her head, saying she thought that should be Rachel's prerogative. When Rachel told them about Matthew, no one seemed very upset, not even John or David.

Marie seemed to have no remorse that Matthew was gone, but she did show tenderness toward Rachel. Marie put her arm around her. "So how are *you* doing, Sis?"

"I'm okay. Just tired and concerned about Jacob."

"He will get better, won't he?" Emily asked.

"I'm sure he will, sweetie," Anna replied. "With all of us praying for him and your momma here to watch over him, how could he help but get better?"

Anna showed Rachel that they had brought her some changes of clothes and a box of books. "We have something else you will want to read, too," she said, holding up a newspaper. Rachel took it and found a picture of Jacob on the front cover along with the headline, "Former U.S. Senator in Critical Condition After Risking Life to Save Child."

Rachel read the article. It was quite well-written. It quoted her many times talking about Jacob's bravery. It quoted the doctor saying that if she hadn't arrived to help Jacob when she did and performed the first aid she had, he wouldn't be alive. It made her out to be a hero, too, even though she felt far from it.

Marie patted her. "My sister, the hero."

Rachel shook her head. "I don't feel much like one."

"Well, whether you feel you are a hero or not," Anna said, "we are all grateful to you for saving Jacob's life. But one thing you might be aware of, there might be quite a bit of press coverage from this."

Rachel didn't want that, and Anna said she'd do what she could so Rachel wasn't bothered.

After they had been there for an hour or so, they decided it was time to leave. Rachel hugged each of her children. Anna and Marie each gave her a hug as well, and so did most of the other children. As they were leaving, each of Jacob's sons patted his hand. Abraham was last, and seemed to understand the seriousness of the situation more than the others. With tears in his eyes, he held Jacob's hand in his own and said, "We love you, Dad."

Marie kissed Jacob on the cheek and held up Emily and her own small daughters so they could too. She held baby Susan next to him for a moment and let her pat him with her chubby little hands.

After the others had all gone out, Anna kissed Jacob. "You get better, honey. We all love and need you." She then put her cheek next to his and stayed there for a long time. Finally, she stood and turned to Rachel, with tears in her eyes.

"Take good care of him, and I will come to visit each day as my strength permits."

Rachel nodded and Anna hugged her one last time. Then they were gone, and it was quiet. Rachel settled into the chair, picked up *All Creatures Great and Small* from the pile of books, and began to read to Jacob.

Recovery

The days passed slowly after that. Flowers and cards started to pour in from all over the country and even other parts of the world. Rachel spent much of the time reading to Jacob, and she always looked forward to Anna's and Emily's visits. They always came in the early morning after the other children were on the bus. Rachel hardly dared venture out of the room, and Anna became her link to the outside world. Not only did she want to be there the minute Jacob woke up, but reporters and cameramen hung around outside like vultures.

Anna was much more used to them, and Rachel learned from the nurses that Anna was visiting with the reporters to deflect their intrusion. However, Rachel also learned that Anna wasn't against making Rachel and Jacob both look like heroes.

Rachel learned how to order food without leaving Jacob's room and was grateful everything else she needed was already there. If she ever took a shower, she did it quickly, not wanting to be away from Jacob when he awoke. She always tried to use the word "when" and not "if," as the doctor did. Anna said he would get better, and Rachel kept telling herself that Anna was always right.

At lunchtime, Anna would leave Emily and slip off to get James. She would bring him back so they could all eat together. Then Anna would take the two children home so they could all get a nap. Marie dropped by every afternoon after the older children were home from school. Rachel felt their old love and friendship rekindle, and she was grateful for her sister. Only once did Marie bring up the fact that she thought it was strange that Anna felt it was okay for Rachel to stay with Jacob. Rachel wanted to tell her what Anna had said, but she had promised not to. She did tell her that the two of them had talked and that she understood more. Marie didn't press her about it, and Rachel appreciated that.

In the evenings, Anna or Marie always brought any of the children who could come. Rachel liked to hear how everyone was doing. Emily always liked to tell about Abraham's football games even though she didn't understand football at all. To hear her tell it, Abraham pretty much won the games single-handedly, and that clearly embarrassed him.

It always seemed quiet and lonely at night after they left. The nurses had rolled in a second bed she could sleep in, but it wasn't very comfortable, and she spent many sleepless nights. Sometimes she had nightmares of Matthew coming and would wake from her own screams as the nurses came running in panic. She was always glad when morning came.

The days by Jacob's side turned into one week and then two. Rachel tried not to become discouraged, but she had to admit that, as she knelt by his bed each night to pray and poured out her heart to God for Jacob, Anna, and all of her family that she loved so much, tears of helplessness and discouragement always seemed to come.

But then, one afternoon, she had been reading from *The Long Winter* when suddenly Jacob spoke. She had seen no indication of anything being different. She hadn't heard or seen him move—nothing. But he spoke. Quietly, but clearly, he said, "I love to hear you read, Rachel."

She almost shouted with joy and surprise. "Jacob, you're awake!"

"Yeah. Wow, my head hurts! What happened? Did I fall off of the hay truck?"

"No, it was . . . " Rachel paused. She almost said it was Matthew, but she wondered if she wanted to tell him all of that. Apparently, he wasn't remembering.

She patted his hand. "You just had an accident."

"You'll tell your mom, won't you, so she'll know why I didn't come over for dinner?"

Rachel said she would, and then Jacob was quiet again. She tried to talk to him, but it was as if he was back in the coma. She ran out to the nurses' desk and told them the news. The doctor was immediately summoned. Rachel returned to Jacob's side and called Anna, waking her from a nap. Anna was elated and said she would be right over with James and Emily.

When the doctor came in, he wanted to hear what happened. When she told him, he tried to rouse Jacob, but Jacob lay there quietly. The doctor said that sometimes a person will come out of a coma briefly and then lapse back into it. However, he did say that if it happened once, it was much more likely to happen again. He told her that if it happened again, he wanted her to push the nurses' call button and just try to keep Jacob talking.

When Anna arrived, Rachel was disappointed to have to tell her that Jacob had lapsed back into his coma, but Anna's positive attitude raised everybody's spirits.

Rachel continued to read to Jacob over the next two days. Then late in the evening, after she finished *The Long Winter,* she asked him whether he would like to hear *Treasure Island* or *Huckleberry Finn.* She didn't expect a response, but he spoke slowly and distinctly.

"Which one do we have to do a book report on first?"

She was elated and quickly hit the nurses' button, continuing to talk to him.

"I don't know, Jacob. I think they might be due at the same time. Tell me what to write for you on the last one we read. Do you remember it?"

"You mean *The Long Winter*?"

Rachel just about choked with excitement. "I didn't know you were awake."

"Yeah, I was listening, but I couldn't seem to talk. It was like I was in a dark tunnel."

"What would you like me to write about it?"

"Well," Jacob said slowly, "an Indian came and told them the winter would be bad, so Pa Ingalls moved his family into town . . . "

The nurse slipped in, saw Jacob talking, and quickly disappeared to get the doctor. Jacob continued to talk, and Rachel kept encouraging him. He paused once and said, "Rachel, you sound slightly different."

"In what way?"

"Oh, I don't know, just different."

"Well, it's me."

"I can tell it's you. Maybe you have a cold or something. I sound different, too, so maybe it's just the echo in this room."

Rachel knew it was because they were older, but she didn't want to confuse him. He was thinking they were still in high school. The doctor wanted him to be able to sort things out slowly. Rachel was glad Jacob had his eyes bandaged or he would have seen she was older.

Jacob continued to tell her the story of the book and was in the middle of it when the doctor walked in. He seemed pleased to see Jacob talking. He listened to him for some time before he finally spoke. "Well, Mr. Davis, how are you feeling?"

Jacob was quiet for a moment and sounded confused when he spoke. "Are you speaking to me?"

The doctor patted his arm. "Yes."

"Oh. People usually call my dad Mr. Davis, not me."

Rachel tried to motion that Jacob wasn't remembering everything. The doctor immediately understood. He instead started asking questions. "So how many are there in your family?"

"Four."

"What are their names?"

"Well, there's my father, Jonathon; my mother, Martha; my brother, Matthew; and me. Of course, Rachel's family is kind of like my family, too."

"Oh, and what are their names?"

"Well, there's Rachel, of course. She's my best friend. Then there's her mother and father, Ruth and Robert, but I usually just call them Mom and Dad Henderson."

Jacob went on and named each of Rachel's brothers and sisters, but Rachel's mind and thoughts caught only on the words he said about her being his best friend. He was not remembering the episode with Matthew, nor the years that followed. How she wished she could keep that erased from his memory, but she knew she couldn't because, in order to do that he would not be able to remember Anna and his sons. Even if she could, she wouldn't erase some past events at the expense of the present she shared with Jacob, Anna, and their family.

But how would he feel about her as those memories returned? Would he have to relive that pain, or would he be able to jump past it to where things were now? Her heart nearly burst with fear at the thought of Jacob reliving that evening.

The doctor had the nurse take over visiting with Jacob to try to keep him alert. He had her ask him about his teachers and many other things. The doctor pulled Rachel aside. "He obviously doesn't remember everything yet. Can you determine at what point he thinks he is at?"

Rachel nodded. "He thinks we are back in high school."

"I think it would be best not to push him too fast. I would rather not have anyone who might confuse that memory come to visit until the recollection of them returns. I want you to just let him ask questions and answer them honestly because then his mind is probably starting to remember those particular events."

The doctor then asked Jacob if he felt he could eat something. Jacob said he did feel hungry, so a bowl of broth was ordered. The nurse was going to feed it to him since his eyes were covered, but Rachel asked to do it. As she fed him, the doctor and the nurse slipped in and out to monitor the situation. Jacob asked questions while he ate. The obvious first one was what happened. She told him it was a bad accident and she didn't want to talk about it yet, and he accepted that.

He asked about school, and she admitted to him that they were graduated. He seemed to remember his graduation and they talked about it. She tried to keep his thoughts there so he wouldn't ask more. She didn't know if he was ready for more, but she knew she wasn't ready to face what would happen when he remembered that horrible evening. She was also afraid it wouldn't be good for him to remember it, yet. But he did bluntly ask her if they were married.

She didn't know quite what to say, so she just said, "Yes, Jacob, you're married."

He smiled. "I love you, Rachel. I'm so glad we're married."

Rachel was glad he couldn't see her cry. Jacob started sounding tired, and the doctor asked Jacob if he wanted to rest. He said he did, and the doctor felt he was safely out of the coma, so they let him sleep.

Jacob slept, and Rachel struggled with her feelings. She felt she needed to talk to someone, so she slipped to the other side of the room and called Anna. She spoke quietly so she wouldn't wake Jacob. It was hard to explain to Anna what Jacob was feeling and thinking, but she felt she needed to. They talked about what the doctor had said. Then Rachel told Anna that Jacob thought he and Rachel were married, and she wondered if she needed to tell him the truth.

Anna was strong with her. "Just do what is best for Jacob, even if he doesn't remember about me and the boys, yet. Don't worry, I trust you completely."

When Jacob awoke, Rachel called the nurse. The doctor had ordered broth for him whenever he was hungry, so Rachel fed him again. His speech and actions were becoming slightly intimate, and she decided she needed to tell him the truth. When he finished the broth, she took his hand in hers. "Jacob, there's something I need to tell you."

He smiled at her from beneath the bandages. "What?"

"Jacob, it's not me you're married to."

A confused expression came across his face. He was quiet, and his voice was choked with emotion. "Then who did I marry?"

She spoke quietly, almost in a whisper. "Remember Anna?"

"Anna?" Jacob spoke her name softly. He said it again and again as if her name was far away and saying it brought it nearer. He continued to repeat it as if the train of her memory was arriving at the station of his consciousness. And then Jacob said it vigorously and gripped Rachel's hand as if it fully came to him.

"Anna. I met her in college." Jacob smiled pleasantly. "Anna is so wonderful." Then Jacob grew quiet, saying nothing for a long time. Finally, Rachel squeezed his hand. Jacob pulled his hand away. "I left to go to college because . . . " Jacob paused, and Rachel could sense the horrible pain in his voice. That was exactly what Rachel feared

189

most—that Jacob would relive that experience when the memory came back.

Jacob's voice trembled with emotion as he spoke. "I'm tired. I think I will sleep now."

She could sense his pain and knew he was trying to shut her out. She could feel the fear welling up in her, thinking she might lose him. She couldn't leave it here; she just couldn't.

She fell on her knees by his bedside and touched his arm. "Please, Jacob! Please don't go to sleep without remembering you're back and we're friends again! Please don't forget that my family and I all love you! Please don't hate me! Please!"

Jacob didn't move, didn't answer her, didn't show any indication he even heard. She dropped her head onto her arms and cried. Their friendship had come back so far. Was she going to lose all of that?

As her tears started to soak her sleeve, she felt Jacob's hand on her hair, gently stroking it. She looked up and he was smiling weakly.

"I could never hate you, Rachel. I loved you far too much."

She took his hand and held it in hers against her face. He moved it slightly to wipe the tear from her cheek. Suddenly she was overcome with emotion, and she laid her head on the bed by him and wept again while he continued to stroke her hair.

When she finally quit crying, he spoke weakly. "I'm beginning to remember things. I vaguely remember I was with Matthew and he told me to turn around. I felt a sharp pain, and that's all I remember. Tell me more."

She started by telling him about how Matthew had come and taken Emily hostage and continued through the whole story. When she finished, Jacob said Emily's name and smiled. Then he asked if she, David, and John were all right. Rachel hadn't mentioned David and John's names, so she knew his memory was returning.

They talked for hours, until late into the night. Jacob was remembering more and asking less. He did want to know how long he had been in the hospital. When she told him how long it had been, he wanted to know what had happened in those two and a half weeks. She talked about Abraham's games and how excited Emily was. She told him about the newspapers and reporters. She told him everything she could think of.

As they continued to talk, she told him that she had begged Anna to let her stay with him so she could apologize for what he had been through when he woke.

Jacob patted her. "No one is blaming you, Rachel. What Matthew has done is not your fault." Jacob cocked his head slightly.

"Rachel, have they ever caught Matthew, or do they have any idea where he is?"

Rachel didn't know how Jacob would take the news, but she couldn't hold it back. "Jacob, Matthew is dead."

"What? How?"

Rachel told him about the sheriff telling them the news and how Anna had had him buried next to their parents, assuming they would have a simple service when Jacob was well. By the time she finished Jacob was gasping slightly and she knew he behind the bandages he was crying.

"Jacob, are you all right?"

"Oh, Rachel! I didn't want this to happen to Matthew. I would have given him the money if I could have gotten it. I never wanted anything from him in life except for him to really think of me as a brother."

Jacob's grief over Matthew's death shocked Rachel, but only briefly. Jacob was so kind and caring, she should have realized how he would feel. It made her feel guilty for her lack of feeling over Matthew's passing. But no matter how she tried, she couldn't find much compassion for Matthew in her heart.

Jacob breathed short breaths, apparently trying to stifle his grief. Rachel took his hand, and he squeezed hers tight. "I'm sorry for all you've been through, Rachel," he said.

"I haven't been through any more than you have, Jacob, and much of what caused grief for both of us was my fault."

"Anna keeps telling me we need to put it behind us," he replied.

Rachel found herself nodding by habit even though Jacob couldn't see her.

Jacob tried to sit up but couldn't and lay back down. "Rachel, how is Anna doing?"

"She's doing okay." Rachel paused and then decided she should tell Jacob more. "Jacob, Anna told me about the cancer."

"What else did she tell you?"

"Lots of things?"

"Like what?"

"Jacob, I can't tell you everything."

"Did she make you promise not to?"

Rachel felt that by answering that question she would already be breaking her promise. Jacob seemed to sense that and turned toward her even though he couldn't see her.

"You don't need to answer that. I can tell the answer. She's wanting you to take her place if she . . . "

Jacob couldn't finish the sentence. His voice choked.

"Jacob, I'm sorry," she said.

"Rachel, I don't know what I'll do if I lose Anna. She's got to get better."

His pain made Rachel hurt, too. His voice was quiet as he continued. "I pray every day for a miracle."

They talked for some time about Anna, but when Jacob sounded tired, Rachel suggested that they both needed some rest.

Rachel could hardly wait to call Anna the next morning. So as not wake Jacob, she waited until he awoke and then she immediately called. Anna decided to bring the children and come over instead of sending them off to school.

The doctor came in and was pleased with how well Jacob was doing. Jacob ate his broth and a little Jell-O. The doctor said he would have to gradually work his way to more solid foods.

Jacob said he was feeling somewhat distraught about being in the darkness of the bandages, but the doctor said the light would not be good for him yet. Jacob perked up a lot when he heard Anna's voice and the voices of the children. Anna immediately hugged and kissed him, crying tears of joy. Emily wanted to be up by Jacob, so Isaac set her on the bed.

She hugged Jacob and said, "Oh, Uncle Jacob, we've missed you a lot. And lots of people keep coming to your house wanting to see you."

Jacob put his arm around her and smiled. "I've missed you, too, Emily. So, tell me, who's been coming to my house?"

"Well," Emily said, "I don't know who they are. But they have cameras, and they are bossy and ask lots of questions. But Aunt Anna tries to keep them from bugging us."

Jacob smiled at Emily's description of the reporters.

"Emily is right," Anna said. "You have a big fan club now, all over the country, and so does Rachel."

Rachel had downplayed her role in helping him, but Anna emphasized it in great detail as she recounted the stories in the news. Rachel felt Anna exaggerated a bit about Rachel's role in saving Jacob, so she figured she might also be doing so with regard to the reporters.

They all visited most of the morning. When Jacob started to get tired, Anna said she was going to take the children to a half a day of school and that she needed to go home and rest, too. Jacob seemed concerned about her, but Anna brushed it off.

"I'm fine, dear. You just worry about getting yourself well so you can come home to us."

He looked to be tiring, but seemed to enjoy the family visit above everything else and hated to have everyone leave. Anna brought the children back that evening, and Marie and Jason came with their family as well. Jacob wanted to hold baby Susan, and she gooed softly in his arms. After everyone had left, he told Rachel he was grateful to her for her kindness in staying with him. His softness when he said it touched her heart.

Jacob did try to do everything he could to get better. He followed the doctor's orders to the minutest detail. After he had been out of the coma for a couple of days, he asked about removing the bandages. The doctor had planned to leave them on for a few more days, but he agreed to take the bandages off the next day only if Jacob would wear an eye covering when family wasn't around. Anna brought Emily the next morning so they could be there when the bandages were removed. Rachel, Emily, and Anna moved close to his bed so he could see them as the bandages were snipped away.

As they dropped from his eyes, he blinked, even though the lights were turned down. After a moment, when his eyes adjusted, he looked at them and smiled. "It's so good to see you again."

Jacob couldn't look around long, or he became dizzy, so he kept the eye cover on most of the time. The next week Jacob and Rachel talked a lot, and the time passed much more quickly and pleasantly for Rachel. Anna and Marie came in every day and brought the children. Jacob was happy when the doctor said he could have any food he wanted, and he immediately ordered a hamburger, fries, and a shake.

Jacob started sitting up for a few minutes at a time, gradually working his way up to an hour. Rachel then started pushing him in a chair around the hospital. He would say, "Let's you, me, and Ivy go for a walk." Rachel felt stupid the first time when she asked him who Ivy was and he pointed at the IV he had connected to him. They couldn't walk around near the waiting room because the reporters had gotten word he was out of the coma, and their numbers, which had apparently dropped in the intervening weeks, increased again. But the reporters weren't allowed in the halls near Jacob's room.

As the next weekend neared, Jacob was walking by leaning on Rachel, and he was feeling eager to go home. He was hoping to go to Abraham's football game, but when Friday came, the doctor was not ready to let him leave. He said Jacob especially could not be out in the cool fall air for a long time.

Jacob was disappointed, but Anna came to the rescue, finding a company that could set up cameras and send the feed across the Internet so he could watch it live. They brought Rachel's laptop, and she logged in to the hospital's wireless Internet connection. Together she and Jacob watched the game. The camera was set up in the stadium right behind Anna, Marie, Jason, and all of the children so Jacob could see them, too. Abraham did a great job, and Jacob was proud of him. Abraham knocked down some passes, sacked the quarterback three times, and made one interception that he ran back twenty yards.

Sunday morning, the doctor finally decided that Jacob could go home. Rachel asked Jacob if he wanted her to call Anna, but he smiled and said, "Let's surprise them at church. If we hurry we can meet everyone there."

Jacob became fidgety and urged the nurses to hurry up the paperwork. Because Jacob's clothes had been covered with blood, Anna had brought him a new set for the eventual time he would be released. They weren't church-going clothes, but neither were Rachel's. Jacob didn't care, and Rachel realized how strong Jacob's devotion to God was. She thought about how her lack of proper clothes had kept her from church, and she made a determination it wouldn't ever happen again.

They finally finished the paperwork, and Jacob put his arm around Rachel's shoulders for support to walk out. The nurse stopped him and said hospital policy required he be wheeled to the front door. Jacob was reluctant, saying he wanted to walk out, but he finally gave in.

Rachel went to pull her car around to the hospital door. It took some time to remember where it was, and Jacob was anxiously waiting when she pulled up to the curb. She and the nurse helped him into the car, and Jacob and Rachel were on their way.

Jacob again thanked her for her kindness to him. She answered quietly, "Jacob, what I have done for you is nothing compared to what you and Anna have done for me."

Church had started by the time Rachel parked the car, so she hurried to the passenger side and helped Jacob out. He put his arm around her for support. It felt good, but she tried not to think about it too much, feeling it was improper to let her thoughts and feelings dwell on it.

The congregation was singing as they stepped into the chapel. All eyes turned to them, and the hymn almost ground to a halt. Abraham jumped up quickly, ran to his father, and steadied him from the opposite side from Rachel. Emily and James escaped from the pew before Anna could stop them and ran to Jacob, throwing their arms around his legs. He reached down and patted them, and then they all made their way to their seats as fast as possible so as not to disrupt the meeting any further.

As Jacob slid in beside Anna, he whispered, "I didn't mean to make a commotion."

Tears streamed down Anna's cheeks as she threw her arms around him and kissed him. "That's the kind of commotion we like here."

Everyone was happy to see Jacob back. He could hardly move around church without someone stopping to talk to him. Abraham and Rachel helped him wherever he went. Both Jason and Isaac offered to take her place, but Anna wouldn't let them, and Rachel felt reluctant to relinquish her position. For now, Jacob was allowing her to be closer to him than he had in a long time, and she wanted to make the most of it while it lasted.

It's All about Family

Jacob recovered steadily after that, but it still took a couple of weeks before he could work a whole day. Rachel found out that Anna hadn't exaggerated the media coverage about herself and Jacob. The media had interviewed Anna, John, David, and Emily. They had been especially interested in Emily since she was the one Jacob had intervened for. With her personality and vivid imagination, Emily had made out Jacob and Rachel to be larger than life, and the media had eaten it up.

It took weeks before the unwanted attention dissipated. By Halloween, Anna's strength was really starting to wane, and the secret of the cancer could no longer be hidden. On Halloween night, since they lived in a rural community, a "Trunk-or-Treat" was held in the church parking lot. Both children and adults came dressed in costumes and opened the trunks of their cars for the children to trick-or-treat. It was a lot of fun, but for Rachel, it was sad seeing Anna tire quickly and have to sit on the back of the van to hand out candy.

As Anna's condition worsened, it became clear to the media why Jacob had left the Senate. This brought another round of unwanted interviews. But finally, just before Thanksgiving, it all faded, and they could just enjoy being a family.

It was then, after things quieted down, that Jacob decided to have a service for Matthew. He put a paid obituary in the paper, and it said nice things about Matthew, ignoring what his life was truly like. Jacob told Rachel he didn't expect any of them to come unless they wanted to. Marie said she would refrain from going, but at the last minute, she came to support Jacob and Rachel. Rachel took her children, and Jacob and Anna took theirs.

Jacob pretty well did all of the service. He told some good memories about his brother and sang a song as he played his guitar. Rachel felt she should say something, but she couldn't bring herself to do it. The horrible experiences she had been through were so interwoven through their time together that she didn't feel she could separate any good from it.

Anna had paid for a company to put up a nice tombstone with a picture of the mountains carved in it. Many tombstones had the names of families etched in the back, but Rachel didn't want her family there, saying she didn't feel he ever truly wanted her or the children. Truly, she knew she didn't even come to the service for Matthew, but for Jacob.

There was only one other person there—a woman. Anna graciously brought her to join them. When the service was over, the woman pulled Rachel aside and told her she was one of many women Matthew had spent his nights with, and she said she came not for Matthew, but to apologize to Rachel. At first, Rachel was angry, but the woman seemed so ashamed of herself that Rachel felt sorry for her. Rachel's heart softened, and she told the woman all was forgiven. As they embraced each other, Rachel found that she felt better by letting go of the anger.

As Thanksgiving approached, Rachel and Marie's families made plans to celebrate it with Jacob and Anna's. Rachel and her family would have stayed overnight at Jacob and Anna's house, as they often did for holidays, but Anna's parents were coming in late at night and would be using the apartment.

By Thanksgiving, Anna could hardly stand, and definitely not for long enough to make dinner. Jacob planned to do it all, but Rachel said, "Please, Jacob, let me help. If not for you, then for Anna."

"That would be nice, Rachel," Jacob replied. "Anna's mother will be helping, and Anna will be there. It would be a good time for us to all be together. In fact, why don't you bring your family over for breakfast, too?"

So at seven o' clock in the morning, she and her children walked the hill to Jacob and Anna's house. Jacob nearly had breakfast ready, his usual holiday fare of bacon, eggs, ham, sausage, and lots of pancakes. Jacob and Anna's sons were already there, and as they started to eat, Anna's mother joined them.

As soon as breakfast was cleared, the children went off to spend the day together while Jacob, Rachel, and Anna's mother started preparing dinner. Rachel had been calling Anna's mother Mrs. Anderson, but she hugged Rachel just like Anna did and said, "You'll call me, Mary, won't you?"

Around mid-morning, Anna came motoring into the kitchen. Jacob had bought her an electric wheelchair. They had had the foresight to build large doorways and halls, so she had no trouble getting around. When she wheeled into the kitchen, Emily was sitting on her lap running the controls. They smashed into the walls a couple of times before Emily brought it to a stop, but Anna just laughed.

"I'm glad it will be a few years before you get your driver's license, Emily."

Emily jumped off Anna's lap and ran excitedly to her mother. "Momma, did you see me? Aunt Anna let me drive her wheelchair!"

Jacob helped Anna get situated at the table and set some breakfast in front of her while Emily scampered off to play with James. Anna had long ago admitted to Rachel that her own family knew of her hope for Rachel to marry Jacob, and at first that made Rachel uncomfortable around Mary, but Mary just treated Rachel like she was also her daughter.

Rachel had told Anna that Jacob had guessed it, too. Anna said she suspected that was the case, but they still never talked about it in front of him. He could not bring himself to face the fact that he was losing her.

Not long after Anna joined them in the kitchen, her father did, too. Jacob served him some breakfast as well. Rachel watched Anna's father's tenderness with Anna, and Rachel's feeling about him being gruff melted away. She realized that his coolness toward her was because it was so hard for him to face losing his daughter.

The situation presented a strange dilemma. Rachel knew that Anna's cancer was on everyone's mind, and yet no one wanted to talk about it. It was that way all day, even at dinner.

Anna's father told Jacob and Anna he really wanted them to come out to Washington for Christmas. Anna didn't feel she could make the flight, so Jacob suggested that they drive in the motorhome, where she could rest on the couch.

"Only if Rachel's family comes along so Rachel can help Jacob with the driving," Anna said.

All eyes turned to Rachel. She nodded. "We'd love to come with you."

Anna's father warmed up to her quite a bit after that. He even told her to call him Harold instead of Mr. Anderson.

Despite the overhanging pall of sadness, Thanksgiving was wonderful. Marie's family came over, and it was a big family gathering.

The days between Thanksgiving and Christmas flew by. There were concerts and school programs. Santa was coming to the church party, and Emily was excited to see him. James was more skeptical, and Rachel could tell he wasn't sure he still believed in Santa.

The weeks were spent mostly with Anna. Jacob hardly worked at all. With all that was happening, it seemed impossible for him to concentrate on anything except Anna. Jacob, Anna, and Rachel, along with James and Emily, ate lunch out almost every day. They also spent a lot of time shopping together. Anna loved to eat out and shop for gifts, and the fact that she was in a wheelchair didn't slow her down. Sometimes she would get Jacob to take Emily to the other side of the store so they could buy something for one of them. Sometimes Anna would suggest Rachel take Emily, and Rachel was sure Anna was buying something for her.

Anna still insisted on a little time each day for painting. Rachel was anxious to see Anna's work, but Anna still kindly refused. Anna also made sure they had time to practice their duets. She wanted to perform them at the church Christmas party. Her favorite one was "Sleigh Ride," and they practiced it a lot. Jacob often came in and listened to them. He usually brought a book to read, but Rachel noticed that most of the time he just watched them. She sensed the grief he was going through, but he held it all inside. When it was his turn to pray in the family, he prayed mostly for Anna, and could seldom contain his emotions.

When Anna, Emily, and James took a nap, Rachel headed to the kitchen and took on most of the work of making dinner. She didn't do much office work for Jacob because he couldn't bring himself to work. He often wandered aimlessly into the kitchen to help her.

Rachel learned to make macaroni and cheese for Sunday lunch the way Anna did—the way their families liked so much. Every week, Marie and Jason's family joined them for that. Now that Anna's health secret was out, Marie had realized Anna's plans for Rachel and Jacob and sometimes talked to Rachel about it.

When the night came for the Christmas party, Anna, despite being weak, played flawlessly. Rachel didn't feel as good about her own performance. She had to keep blinking back tears, and it blurred her vision and impeded her playing. But still, with all the practice, she didn't need to see the music. "Sleigh Ride" was the last piece. It was almost perfect even though Rachel could hardly see the music at all. When they finished, the whole hall erupted into boisterous applause as Anna hugged Rachel tightly.

All too soon it was Christmas Eve. Rachel and her children stayed the night at Jacob and Anna's house. Once the children were in bed, Jacob, Anna, and Rachel put out the last of the gifts and filled stockings. Anna sat in her motor chair and directed the stuffing of the stockings, which were almost as tall as Emily. Anna joked and laughed while Jacob said almost nothing. Rachel tried to be cheerful, but her heart was heavy.

Emily and James were up early the next morning and woke Jacob. He woke Rachel because he insisted that the animals had to be fed first, and she had made him promise to let her help. It was only five-thirty when she heard the knock on the apartment door. She quickly threw on her clothes, and they headed out the door after waking Abraham to make sure Emily and James didn't get into the presents.

Jacob made sure the horses had an extra helping of oats for Christmas, and Rachel slipped an extra carrot to Star Bright. When she glanced over at Jacob, he was sitting dejectedly on a bale of hay, the tears coursing down his face. She went over and sat by him, and neither spoke for some time.

When Jacob turned to her, his eyes were red, but he tried to smile through his tears. "Christmas is the season of miracles. I've tried to live my life the way I feel God would want. I've prayed and prayed for a miracle, because if I've ever needed one, it's now."

Rachel couldn't speak. She just put her hand on his arm and nodded. They finished up the chores and went back to the house. Jacob quickly worked up some bacon, sausage, and eggs while Rachel made pancakes.

Soon, breakfast was ready, and everyone was called. Jacob went upstairs and carried Anna down to her motor chair. They ate breakfast to Emily and James's happy chatter. After breakfast they went into the family room, and the children dug into their stockings while Anna happily snapped pictures. Rachel insisted on taking some with Anna in them, too. Emily said she had never seen so much candy in one place, and she apparently planned to eat it all, but Rachel made her stop for fear she would be sick.

It was Joseph's turn to be "Santa Claus" and hand out the presents. He would choose one, read whose it was, and give it to them. Then they all would wait while the person unwrapped it. Emily and James became anxious and started helping him choose the presents to try to hurry things along.

Of all the presents Rachel received that day, the ones from Anna meant more to her than all of the others. One was a picture of the two of them with an arm around each other in front of the tree house, smiling and happy. Across the bottom of the picture Anna had written, "Rachel, Always remember I love you and will forever. Your friend, Anna."

Rachel thanked her and then fled from the room to cry. Jacob and Anna followed her. When Jacob saw what it was, tears came to his eyes, too. Rachel hugged Anna, but after a moment, Anna pulled back. "Now, I didn't give you that to make you cry. I have given one to each person in our families, and they are meant to be a reminder that I will still be here with you even after I have passed on. So I want you to dry your tears and make this a happy Christmas." Rachel nodded, but no matter how positively she tried to look at it, she couldn't keep from crying.

Jacob was no better when he opened his picture. It was of him and Anna looking into each other's eyes. They were out on Pine Ridge with Jensen Lake shimmering in the background. Rachel glanced over Jacob's shoulder and saw that Anna had written on it, "To the greatest husband in the world. Jacob, I love you, and I know we'll be together again someday. Love, Anna."

Jacob set it down and walked out of the room. Anna and Rachel followed him. He was clearly embarrassed to have them find him crying, but no attempt at masculinity could ebb the tears flowing down his face. Again, Anna scolded. "I am as sure as I can be we will be together again. If I would have thought these pictures would cause such sadness, I would have given them to you later." Jacob nodded and offered a half smile.

As the children opened their pictures, their reactions varied. James and Emily didn't understand. Emily's picture was of her sitting on Anna's lap, and Anna was reading her a story. Emily ran to Anna and gave her a big hug. "Oh, Aunt Anna, I love it. Can I keep it in my room?"

The reactions of the older children, who understood, were tearful as well. Abraham and Isaac especially had a hard time. But the picture that hit Rachel the hardest was one that was in a package addressed to both herself and Jacob. It was the picture of Jacob and Rachel that Anna had taken in front of the tree house. Anna had written on it: "To Jacob and Rachel, my two best friends, together again. With all of my love, Anna."

Anna had quit hiding her feelings that she wanted Jacob to marry Rachel when she was gone, and this picture carried no pretense. The fact that it was both of theirs made that clear as well. Jacob again left the room, and Rachel did, too. Anna followed them. Rachel stopped just outside the family room to weep, and Jacob went to his office.

Anna stopped her motor chair by Rachel and gently took her hand. "Rachel, please come with me."

Rachel followed her to Jacob's office, where Jacob was leaning on his desk, sobbing openly, his back to the door. When they entered, he turned and said, "Anna, I just can't take this. I just can't lose you."

Anna, in her frank way, spoke with kind determination. "Jacob, this is not the end; it is only the beginning, and I want you to remember that."

"But how can I make it until I am with you again?"

"That is why it is important for you to have Rachel to love, and to have her to love you."

Jacob turned away from them again. "Anna, I know that's what you want. But I don't know if I can ever get over that image in my mind of her in Matthew's arms that night."

Rachel couldn't take the pain in her heart anymore. The pain of losing Anna and the pain she had caused Jacob overwhelmed her. She pulled from Anna's grasp and fled out of the office and out the front door into the freezing cold winter air. She ran across the top of Pine Ridge, the deep snow dragging at her legs until it pulled her into its freezing arms. There she crumpled into its cold embrace and wept. She wept harder than she could ever remember weeping since the night she knew Jacob was gone so many years ago.

She didn't know how long she was there, but suddenly, she felt a coat wrapped around her shoulders. She looked at it, and it was Jacob's. She turned and looked into his face as he stood there in his short sleeves.

He smiled through his own tears. "Rachel, I'm sorry. Please come back."

Rachel lowered her head and looked at the ground. "It's not your fault, Jacob. I can't blame you. I was the one who hurt both of us." She looked up into his kind face. "But does the pain never go away? Can a person never find a way to wash away the hurt from a mistake made for which she is sorry? For twenty years I have paid the price of that indiscretion and done what I could to make up for it, but it never seems to be enough, and together with the pain of losing Anna, it's just too much to bear."

"I don't know. Perhaps time will still heal such wounds."

Rachel stood, looked at him momentarily, and then again lowered her eyes. "Jacob, I understand how you feel. I don't expect you to ever love me like Anna wants, but I pray all the time that you can find some way to totally forgive me and that somehow the pain can be erased from your heart. I can't hope or ask for more than that."

Jacob smiled a genuine smile at her. "Let's just continue to let time and God work their magic." He then slipped his arm around her shoulders and gave her a slight hug. "It's Christmas; let's go home."

He dropped his arm, and they walked slowly back to the house. Anna had returned to the children and let them continue opening presents so Rachel and Jacob could have what time they needed alone.

After receiving Anna's pictures, almost everyone was more subdued. When they got to the presents Rachel had for Jacob and Anna's family, she was concerned about how they would like them. She had felt that it wouldn't do much good to buy things since they had money to buy what they wanted, so she had knitted everyone matching scarves and hats. Anna told her they were beautiful, and Rachel felt she had done a good job.

From Jacob, Rachel received a beautiful necklace. He looked

away, embarrassed, as she thanked him, but he quietly told her she was welcome.

After the presents were finished, Rachel helped Jacob prepare dinner. Anna joined them in the kitchen and said, "Just think, Rachel, it was a year ago today that I met you for the first time. Who would have known that, besides Jacob, you would become my best friend?"

Rachel thought, "What a year it had been." She remembered the past Christmas, feeling afraid to meet Anna and wanting to hate her. And, yet here Rachel was, loving Anna so much that her own heart was breaking at the thought of losing her. She thought of how she had had so little money, and now, this Christmas, things were better financially. If she could go back to being poor and have Anna be well, she would do it in an instant.

After dinner, Anna insisted they take some time to ride the snow machines even though they would be leaving the next day for Washington. Anna again insisted that Rachel ride with Jacob, but this time Rachel understood why, and the tears rolled down her face and froze on her clothes as she held onto Jacob and leaned her head against him for comfort. He didn't seem to mind and even appeared to take comfort from her presence, tears flowing down his face as well.

In the evening, Jacob left and came back with the motorhome. They spent a lot of the evening packing it. Jacob filled the water tanks and then plugged it in and turned on the heat to keep it from freezing. At five o'clock the next morning, Jacob woke Rachel to help him feed the horses, as he had promised. When they got back, they woke the children, and as soon as they were in the motorhome, Jacob carried Anna out and set her comfortably on the couch. He tried to be cheerful. "Well, honey, are you ready for a Christmas trip home?"

"Jacob, that is not my home," she kindly chided him. "It's my parents' home. My home is with you, wherever you are."

Rachel and Jacob traded off driving so they could keep moving as much as possible. They traveled long and hard for more than two days, staying only for short times in parking lots to sleep. They had to avoid some areas of snow closure, which added some distance, but finally, on Saturday evening, they pulled into Anna's parents' large driveway. They had phoned ahead and let her family know they were getting close, and all of Anna's family was there to greet them. Her father was first out the door. James and Emily ran to him, and he scooped them up. Emily had started calling him "Grandpa" because James did. Harold seemed to like it and smiled.

After he had greeted the children, he stepped into the motorhome to find Anna. She was still lying on the couch. He gently took her hand. "Hey, Punky, how are you doing?"

His gentleness and endearing word for her made Rachel smile. This man, who had seemed so gruff, was actually a big, tenderhearted softy. Anna just laid her head against him. "I'm tired, Daddy."

He lifted her into his arms. Anna was quite light, having lost a lot of weight due to illness. Jacob met him at the motorhome door and offered to take her, but Harold insisted on carrying her into the house himself. With all of Anna's family there, it was quite merry, under the circumstances. Rachel was pleased to meet Anna's sisters' husbands and their children since they hadn't been able to come to the reunion. The evening seemed like a giant family reunion of its own.

Harold ordered tons of pizza, and Rachel almost never found herself alone. Anna's sisters made her feel like she was one of them. But at one point in the evening, when she was by herself, Harold sidled up to her. "I want to thank you for helping drive Anna and her family out here."

"My family and I wanted to come, too," she replied.

He patted her arm. "I also wanted to apologize for how I acted to you at first. The thought of losing Anna has been so hard that I just . . . "

He stopped, unable to finish his sentence. With tears in her own eyes, Rachel nodded. "I understand. She and Jacob are my best friends, and the thought of losing her is unbearable."

They were both quiet for a moment. Then he took her hand in his and looked her in the eye. "I want you to know that you are always welcome in our home, and I hope you will feel you are part of our family because I know that is how Anna feels about you."

"Thank you," Rachel said.

As the evening wore on, Anna grew tired, so they decided they should get some sleep in order to make it to church on time. With all of the family home, Anna's parents' house was full, so Jacob planned for his family to use the motorhome. Harold felt Anna would be more comfortable in a regular bed, so it was decided that Jacob and Anna would stay in the house. Rachel said she was fine taking care of the children in the motorhome alone, but Anna's sister, Marilyn, asked to help so she could visit with Rachel.

As soon as Rachel and Marilyn had the children in bed, they climbed into their beds, too, but they didn't go to sleep right away. They turned out the lights, leaving only a night light glowing. Marilyn leaned up on one elbow and looked at Rachel. "Rachel, I'm glad I've gotten to know you. I feel like you are my sister. Why, you would look just like us if it wasn't that you have dark hair and we are blond."

With that, they both laughed. They knew they looked nothing alike. Rachel asked Marilyn to tell her stories about Anna.

Marilyn laughed. "Oh, Anna. She and I are probably the closest of the sisters. You may have thought it strange that Anna would encourage you to be friends with Jacob again, but Anna has always been her own person. She has the ability to look deeply at a situation and seek for the best solution, unhindered by norms, traditions, or even the usual feelings. She is unique that way.

"Anna has carefully analyzed her feelings about God and life. She's deeply religious and always has been. In fact, that was part of what drew her to Jacob. We had all seen him at church before she ever met him at school. He would come by himself, sit alone, and avoid talking to anyone, but his devotion was real, and Anna appreciated that. Anna's strength of conviction that our relationships will continue in the next life helps strengthen all of us."

Rachel's voice choked as she replied. "I love Anna so much."

In the dim light, Marilyn reached out her hand and patted Rachel's. "And she loves you. We all do. And as hard as it is losing Anna, I'm glad Jacob and his children will have you."

As Marilyn said that, Rachel felt her chest tighten, partly for the love she felt from Anna's family and partly for what she knew Marilyn was implying. "I'm not sure if Jacob will ever get over his feelings about what happened between us."

"Anna says he will," Marilyn said, "and Anna always seems to be right."

It seemed to Rachel that morning came too early, especially since she and Marilyn had talked half the night. But they had to hurry and get breakfast and get everyone ready for church before nine o'clock. Rachel had brought matching dresses for herself and Emily, and everyone liked that.

When they went to church, it was easy to see how much everyone loved Anna. After Jacob had wheeled her in, most of the congregation surrounded them. Rachel wanted to melt back into the shadows, but Anna wouldn't let her, insisting on introducing her to everyone. They all made Rachel feel like she really belonged.

When church was over, they had macaroni and cheese, a tradition Anna had gotten from her mother. Rachel watched as her children played with their cousins and Anna's siblings' children. They were accepted as if they were cousins, too.

Jacob wanted to visit the cemetery where Ina was buried and put some flowers on her grave. He asked Anna if she would like to go, and she said she would. She also wanted Rachel to go with them. Rachel felt that Jacob and Anna should have the time alone, but Anna was persistent. "You need a chance to see this part of Jacob's life."

Rachel realized Anna was right, and while Jacob was pulling around the car that Harold was loaning them, Anna took her hand and pulled her close. "I'm also hoping that putting you into this environment where Jacob came after he left home, that it can help his heart to heal."

The three of them had a wonderful afternoon together. Jacob, at Anna's insistence, took them around to all sorts of things. They visited the university Jacob graduated from. They drove past Ina's house, and Rachel learned that Ina had left it to Jacob when she died and that he still owned it. It was a cute, little older house on a quiet street, and Harold managed it as a rental. They drove to the apartment complex where Anna and Jacob started their married life together and finished by going to the cemetery.

Jacob lifted Anna into the wheelchair, and the three of them made their way over to Ina's grave. Jacob cleaned around the beautiful tombstone he had placed there. Anna pointed out the back of it to Rachel. It said "My Son," under which was written "Jacob Davis." Anna told Rachel that Ina had requested that be put on it.

Underneath that, Jacob had engraved a poem taken from the song "Rest Well My Baby" from the musical *Lilacs in the Valley* with the words changed slightly. It read:
Rest well, my mother, I love you.
God in heaven loves you, too.
And I'll be there to greet you
When dawn brings life anew.
As you dream, His angels watch over you.
Rest well, my mother, rest well.

As Jacob finished cleaning around the headstone, he gently laid the flowers there. He joined Rachel and Anna, and as he read the words carved there, tears started down his face. He put his arm around Anna and held her tightly as if willing her to never leave him. Rachel shed quiet tears of her own as she sensed the pain Jacob felt, having lost Ina and knowing he was losing Anna.

Anna looked at Rachel, her own eyes full of tears. She reached her hand out, Rachel took it, and Anna drew her close. The three of them stood in the quiet solitude of the setting sun and let the peace of the evening draw them together.

Saying Goodbye and Anna's Last Gift

Sunday evening was spent eating popcorn and visiting with Anna's family. That night, Anna's sister Cheryl said it was her turn to help Rachel. Cheryl and Rachel, too, spent half the night talking and got little sleep.

Monday was spent visiting Jacob and Anna's friends. Jacob took his family and Rachel's family to Microsoft. It was fun for Rachel to meet some of the other secretaries that she worked with through e-mail, especially Edna. Edna was older, with gray hair and glasses. She had retired but had come over for the occasion. Rachel liked her even more in person than she had over phone and e-mail.

Rachel knew the visit was really for people to get to see Anna, and she tried to step back into the shadows. But once more Anna wouldn't let her. Anna refused to say hi to anyone without also introducing Rachel. Rachel liked the people she and Jacob worked with. It was strange to say they worked with them since they did it all over the Internet, but she knew all of them in some way, and it was nice to put faces to the names.

After visiting at Microsoft, they went out to lunch. They just grabbed some fast food because they needed to hurry over to the headquarters for the United States Senator. Everyone there was happy to see them. With their whole group, it made for a lot of commotion, but no one seemed to mind. Again, Anna wanted everyone to meet Rachel, and Rachel tried to not let the awkwardness she felt get in the way. Emily clearly didn't feel awkward at all and continued to say things that made everyone laugh.

For dinner that evening all of Anna's family, and many, many friends joined them for dinner at a beautiful restaurant on the bay, probably over one-hundred people in all. The restaurant was on the top floor of a tall building, and the view of the harbor was magnificent.

The food was incredible. Rachel knew there might be events like this and had been having her children practice at home what she called "restaurant manners" just in case. Anna had set up the seating and had situated herself and Rachel on each side of Jacob. Across the table from them sat Anna's parents, with Emily beside Harold, directly across from Rachel. James sat by Emily.

Emily and James each ordered the children's fried chicken meal. When James picked up his chicken, Emily pouted.

"Momma, do I have to use restraint manners like you told me, or can I pick up my chicken and eat it like James is?"

Everyone laughed, and Rachel felt a little embarrassed, but it was Anna who answered. "Why, Emily, you eat it however you like best. In fact, I think I will order a piece of chicken to go with my dinner so I can use my fingers, too."

And that was exactly what she did. Anna's fun-loving attitude made the meal much less formal than it might have been.

The whole time they ate, Anna kept giving the waiters her camera to take pictures. When they finished the meal, they went to a lounge area, where there were windows looking out over the ocean. By that time, the sun had set, and the lights shimmered and danced on the water. There, a photographer met them and took lots of pictures. There was one with all of Harold and Mary's descendants and their in-laws. Anna insisted that Rachel and her family join them in one, and this time neither Harold nor Anna's brother seemed bothered by it.

As the photographer tried to group them together as families for one shot, Anna insisted that she and Rachel both be by Jacob, with their families gathered around them. She also had one taken of just herself and Rachel with Jacob between them.

By the time the pictures were all taken, Anna was feeling tired, and the evening was getting late. They all headed back to the Andersons' home for the night. That night, Anna's youngest sister, Arial, stayed with Rachel and the children, and they talked half the night.

Rachel really enjoyed getting to know Anna's sisters better and was grateful she had this chance. Because of the long nights, she didn't wake up until eight o' clock, and she felt lazy. But everyone happily greeted her when she entered the house, and Jacob and Mary had breakfast for her almost immediately.

That was to be their last day there. They hated to leave, but the children were already going to miss at least a day of school, and maybe more if the roads were bad. All day long, friends and relatives dropped by to see Anna. She sat in a big easy chair and greeted them. There was plenty to eat, and Anna's sisters helped entertain the children with games and videos.

Rachel tried to help with the children, but Anna wanted Rachel to stay by her to meet each person who came. By the end of the day, Rachel's head was spinning just trying to remember half of those who had stopped by. It was easy to see why Jacob said that Anna was the reason he became the man he did; everyone loved Anna and her family.

As the day was ending, after everyone but family was gone, Anna's father came over to them. He sat down on the arm of the chair by Anna and stroked her hair lovingly.

"Sweetheart, don't you think this trip is too hard for you? Your mother and I would be glad to have you stay here at home with us where we could take care of you. Jacob and the children could fly out when they wanted to . . ."

Anna stopped him and gently scolded him. "Daddy, I love you and Momma and the rest of the family, but this isn't my home anymore. My home is with Jacob. When I go, I want to be with him, not just have him be with me." And then she turned and smiled at Rachel, even as she continued to speak to her father. "And Rachel will be there to help both of us."

Harold nodded. His tough exterior melted away, and he started to sob. Anna weakly stood and told her father she wanted him to sit in the chair. She then curled up in his lap and said, "Daddy, sing to me the silly songs you used to sing when I was little."

He nodded, but it took him some time to get his emotions to a point where he could sing. Then he sang familiar songs with the words changed, such as "You are my daughter shine, my sweet, sweet daughter shine, you make me happy the whole day through . . ."

As he choked his way through the words, Anna's sisters, mother, and eventually even her brother came and joined in on some of them. Rachel cried as she watched the closeness of this family. When they finally retired to bed, Marilyn joined her again to take care of the children, but they didn't talk much. Their emotions were too near the surface.

The next morning it was hard for everyone to say goodbye. Even though breakfast was over before eight o' clock, it was almost noon before they were ready to pull out. After lots of last minute hugs and kisses, Jacob carefully lifted Anna onto the couch in the motorhome. Before Rachel could climb in, each of Anna's family members gave her hugs, including Harold, and Anna's brother, Samuel. Anna's mother was last. As she hugged her, Mary held her close for a moment.

"Take good care of Anna, Jacob, and the children for us, won't you?" she said.

Rachel promised she would. Again, though no one spoke directly of her and Jacob together, everyone implied it. As they rolled out of the driveway and turned the motorhome east, Rachel could hear some sniffling from the children. They hated to leave, and for the older children who understood, it was bringing it closer to home that Anna wasn't going to be with them for very long. Anna, as always, tried to cheer everyone up with a rendition of "Country Roads." Rachel and Jacob tried to help out, but both of them choked up.

When the song ended, Anna looked around. "Well, aren't we a sorry lot? I think we need to try that again."

It took a few more attempts, but finally, everyone cheered up considerably.

Even though they pushed hard, the trip home seemed long. Anna slept most of it, and the children watched videos. Sometimes Abraham or Isaac would ride up front with Jacob while Rachel slipped back to make up sandwiches or to take care of the children and Anna. Sometimes, while they drove, Jacob would tell Rachel stories about events that had occurred at places she had just seen. He told her a whole lot more about Ina and Anna, and Rachel enjoyed that. But often they would just travel quietly along, both of them deep in thought.

They arrived home on the evening of the fourth. The children had already missed a couple of days of school. It was late enough that Rachel's family decided to stay the night at Jacob and Anna's house. The next morning, Jacob made breakfast, and Rachel helped James get everything ready for school.

It was hard to get back into the usual routine, but it was harder to see Anna getting weaker and weaker. As February approached, Anna couldn't sit up for more than an hour at a time. She still wanted to play the piano with Rachel, but she couldn't manage more than about fifteen-minute intervals, even sitting in her electric wheelchair. Rachel scooted the bench clear over so Anna could have her wheelchair right up to the piano, and Jacob always came in to listen.

Anna also insisted on painting because she wanted to finish what she was working on. Rachel desperately wanted to see it, but Anna still kept saying, "When the time is right."

Since Anna could no longer go out for lunch, Rachel picked up James from kindergarten, brought him home, and then made lunch for all of them. They still enjoyed being together, and it was always Anna who tried to keep the conversation going when everyone else became quiet. James and Emily didn't understand what was happening, and Emily often asked when Anna would get better.

Anna wanted to make it past Valentine's Day so she could celebrate that special day with Jacob once more. As it grew closer, Anna became so weak that she could no longer sit up at all. Jacob carried her down to the couch and propped up pillows behind her. Anna's parents, sisters, and brother flew out and arrived the day before Valentine's Day.

Valentine's Day was Friday, and even though there was school, they decided to keep the children home. Jacob invited Rachel and her family to come over.

Jacob made his usual holiday breakfast and had the plates turned upside down, with candy under them. Under Anna's was a huge box of candy and Anna's wedding ring. Anna had lost so much weight that it hadn't fit, so Jacob had it resized for her. Anna had some special surprise gifts of her own. She had worked on them before she had gotten too weak. There was a DVD of her reading stories so Emily and James could play them when she was gone. She had also made a DVD of pictures of the things she had done with her family. At the end of it she narrated, in her own witty style, the story of her and Jacob's courtship and life together. It was a wonderful treasure and must have taken hours to put together.

Toward the end of the day, Anna got a bit of a cough. Jacob wanted to take her to the hospital, as he had over every little thing. It was like he felt somehow they could do something to stop the inevitable. But she begged him, as she always did, to let her stay home because that is where she wanted to be when she passed away.

Saturday, everyone knew the time was very short. They all gathered around Anna's bed, and Marie joined them. Anna reached out and weakly took Jacob's hand. "Jacob, sing for me."

Jacob fell on his knees by her bedside, sobbing. "Oh, Anna, I can't."

"Please. Sing me the song you wrote for our wedding."

"Oh, Anna. That would just be too hard."

"Please? For me?"

"But I don't have my guitar, and I . . . "

"Please, one last time. I do want you to sing it at my funeral, but please—one last time for me."

Jacob slowly nodded. Isaac retrieved the guitar, and Jacob stood and tuned it. He tried to wipe away his tears and cleared his throat, but his voice was choked with emotion as he struggled through it.

Before I knew you, my life was so dark and dreary
Before I knew you, I felt so tired and weary
Before I knew you, perhaps the sun did shine,
But it didn't shine for me
But all that changed the day that I met you.

Before I knew you, my life had no meaning

Before I knew you, I had no reason for singing
But since I found you the world is bright,
And everything's wonderful and new,
And all because I have known you

And since I found you, I feel I can do anything.
Whenever I'm weak you make me strong in everything
Whenever I am feeling doubt you give me courage to carry on
Nothing's impossible now that I have you.

And now I know you, I feel to shout hallelujah
That I have had the chance to know and love you.
And the emptiness I felt is all now gone
Because I have known you
I thank God every day that I've known you.

Life is good because I've known you.

When he finished, he fell on his knees by her bed, and sobbed, his head buried in the blankets. She weakly reached out and stroked his hair. When he finally looked up, she held out her hand, and he took it. She then turned and beckoned to Rachel. Rachel, tears streaming down her face, knelt beside Anna's bed. Anna held out her other hand, and Rachel took it. Anna pulled her hands over her chest, pulling Jacob's and Rachel's hands together. She held them firmly there, wrapped in her own.

She looked at Jacob. "As my last gift to you, Jacob, I want you to find peace and healing in your heart, and a wife who loves you as I do. And I want our children to have a good mother. Please try to find the healing and love for Rachel I have so desperately sought for you."

Jacob just nodded, unable to speak. Anna then turned to Rachel. "As my last gift to you, I want to give you the best husband in the world, and to your children, the best father."

She then looked back and forth from one to the other of them and said, "Of course, I don't mean to take away your agency, but I want you to know I would very much approve."

Both Rachel and Jacob laid their heads on the bed and sobbed. As they did, Anna let go of their hands and reached out to Marie. Marie took her hand, and Anna drew her close. She kissed her and told her she loved her and asked her to continue to help Jacob and Rachel. Marie said she would.

Anna then reached out to her own children. She took each one by the hand, drew them close, and kissed and hugged them, telling them she loved them. She did likewise to Rachel's children and to her parents and brother and sisters.

One more time, she reached her hand out and pulled Rachel close. She kissed her and told her she loved her. Finally, she reached out both arms to Jacob. He sat on her bed, kissed her, and held her for a long time.

Anna weakly and lovingly touched his face. "Jacob, I love you. I will be waiting for you when it comes time for you to join me." Jacob nodded and hugged her tighter, as if willing her to not leave him.

Anna's mother signaled for everyone else to slip out of the room, and they did. And there, in Jacob's arms, Anna quietly and peacefully left the cares of the world behind to be with God.

Healing

Word was hardly out that Anna had passed away before the flowers and cards started to pour in from all over the country and different parts of the world. Jacob asked Rachel to record who sent them so they would have it for a remembrance. She did this by taking a picture of each one and putting the pictures into a book. There were so many flowers that there was hardly room for them all. And then there were cards and letters. Some of them were from people who were very famous. There were even a notes from the President and the First Lady of the United States.

So many people came to Anna's viewing that it was far after midnight when they closed the doors, even though it was supposed to end at eight o'clock in the evening. Anna's mother and sisters hugged everyone. Jacob and Anna's sons stood respectfully in the line. Jacob asked Rachel to join them, but she wasn't sure how she would respond to people when they asked her how she was related. But Mary insisted Rachel stand right by her, and she introduced Rachel as a close friend of Anna's.

At the funeral, the church was packed with people in the foyers and standing along the walls. There were many senators and many other prominent politicians. And even though Anna had lived in Middlefork for only just over a year, the impact of her genuine friendship was great, and everyone loved her. The people of the town turned out in great numbers. What's more, almost all of Rachel's family came.

Anna had written out everything she wanted for her funeral, and it was a beautiful service, a wonderful tribute to an incredible lady. Abraham gave the family prayer before the family moved to the chapel. Anna had written a poem that expressed her feelings of life and death, and Jacob had put it to music. The choir sang it.

When one we love from us departs
And leaves an emptiness in our hearts
Our thoughts, oh God, we turn to thee
To understand what we can't see

For thou art Father of us all
And thou dost love both great and small

And it's in thee we know we'll find
That lasting peace for all mankind

The more the love, the more the loss
And we must contemplate the cost
Of loving all of our fellow man
As thou each of us did command

Yet Thou art merciful and just
And Justice tells us that Thou must
Provide a way that we may be
With those we love eternally

For why wouldst thou punish man
For doing what Thou didst command
Reason from Thee tells us not to fear
Loving relations continue there

As I sorrow, Father, for those now gone
Help me have faith to continue on
To do the work thou wouldst want of me
Until I come to join them and Thee.

Marilyn talked first and shared stories about Anna's early life. Jacob spoke next about their life together and his love for Anna. Rachel had heard him try to beg out of it, afraid he wouldn't be able to get through it, but Anna had wanted him to try. Jacob struggled through it and had to pause many times to get his emotions under control. Rachel could tell that it was one of the hardest things he had ever done. When he finished, he was supposed to sing the song he had written for Anna when they were married, and Rachel was to accompany him on the piano.

Rachel felt sorry for Jacob. He hadn't even gotten the first line out when his voice choked, and he couldn't continue. He tried to start again but couldn't. Finally, Abraham and Isaac stood up by their father, put their arms around him, and helped him complete the song. By the time they finished, Rachel couldn't see the music because of the tears in her own eyes, and she was grateful she had practiced it a lot and could play it from memory.

Next, Anna's father and mother spoke together. They, too, struggled through their talks. They shared loving stories of Anna when she was growing up and added to the ones Marilyn had told. In addition,

Mary talked about Jacob and Anna's dating and engagement and made everyone laugh at Anna's boldness and wit.

Anna had asked Rachel to speak, but Rachel said she couldn't. They compromised by having Rachel speak for a very short time and then help with musical numbers. Rachel briefly expressed her love for Anna and how much Anna had strengthened her. She talked about the song the choir sang and told of Anna's philosophy of how we would share the relations after this life that we cherish here.

Then came the final musical number. Jacob with his children, Anna's siblings with their children and spouses, Anna's parents, and Rachel's family, including her brothers and sisters and their children, all sang "Coming Home," and Rachel accompanied them. Rachel felt it was almost as if Anna was speaking when they got to the verse in which they had changed one word:

But home is more than a place.
It's the family and friends you have known.
It's someone who needs you that you can't replace.
*In your heart when **they're** gone.*

Rachel thought, in her heart, that Anna had gone home and would be there waiting for the rest of them. By the time the song was over, Rachel's heart hurt more than she could ever remember it hurting at a funeral. It hurt more than at Mother Davis's funeral or even at her parents' funeral. She knew she would miss Anna desperately.

She also thought about how it was such a contrast from the service for Matthew. Anna had truly been right when she said it would be worse to be despised.

After a short talk by the church leader, the congregation finished by singing, "God Be With You 'Til We Meet Again."

As the music continued, Rachel again felt the strength of Anna's conviction that they would be together again, and it strengthened her in return. The pallbearers were Anna and Jacob's sons, Anna's brother, and John and David.

Jacob had obtained the permits necessary to create a small cemetery on Pine Ridge. It was about a quarter mile across the ridge from his house in a beautiful grove of oak trees. He said that when spring came, he would put a fence around it and make it even more beautiful. That little cemetery was where the funeral procession went. When they reached it and the family had gathered, Jacob gave a beautiful prayer and blessing on the grave site. After they mingled for some time, they eventually returned to the church. The wonderful ladies of the congregation had made a dinner for all of them.

With most of Rachel's brothers and sisters and their families there, along with Anna's family, it was almost a repeat of the family reunion they had enjoyed in the summer. If it hadn't been for the sadness that hung over them at the loss of Anna, it would have been wonderful. As her family was leaving, Rachel's brothers and sisters all hugged both her and Jacob, and Rachel could feel their love and concern for her. They also spent time hugging and consoling the children.

However, as everyone was finishing up, she heard something that made her heart tremble. She heard Anna's father visit with Jacob and suggest he move back to Washington state where he would be around family. Rachel couldn't stand the thought of Jacob leaving, and moved a distance away from them so she wouldn't hear more.

A while later, Jacob asked her what was bothering her. She couldn't control her emotions, and her voice quivered as she spoke. "Jacob, I heard Harold talking to you. You aren't going to move away, are you?"

Jacob spoke kindly to her. "Rachel, don't worry. I will make sure your family is cared for."

His answer hit Rachel hard. It took her back to when she had blatantly acted as if she valued Matthew's money more than Jacob's friendship, and in so doing had lost him. Whether that was what he was referring to or not didn't matter; her emotions were so near the surface with the loss of Anna that she started to sob as she spoke.

"Jacob, do think that money is all I care about? Don't you feel that yours and Anna's friendship means more to me than any money ever will?"

She was so overcome with her grief and pain that she fled from the room. She found a small classroom, shut herself in it, and sobbed. She heard the door open and turned to see Jacob. She turned from him, unable to face him, but he reached out and pulled her into his arms.

As she sobbed against his chest, he spoke quietly and comfortingly to her, his own voice choked with emotion. "Rachel, I'm sorry. I didn't mean it that way at all. I promise I didn't. I actually told Anna's father that this is my home. Anna is buried here, and I will stay here."

She looked up into his kind face. "Jacob, I want you to know that I do value yours and Anna's friendship far more than money. I would rather keep you as a friend and have to work at the grocery store the rest of my life than have all of the money in the world."

He smiled at her and pulled her tight against him. "I feel the same way about you, Rachel."

He held her for quite a while. Finally, he pulled back and looked at her. "We better get back. Anna's family will have to leave soon to make it to the airport this evening, and we will want to say good-bye."

They returned to the room where the dinner had been and found that Anna's family had been searching for them. They said their last goodbyes to each other, and Anna's family all gave her hugs. Anna's mother was last. As she hugged Rachel, she again told her how grateful they were for her and how they hoped she would feel like part of their family.

After everyone else was gone, Rachel and her family climbed into Jacob's van with his family. When they arrived back at his house, he invited her and her family to stay for dinner. The ladies of the church had sent home lots of leftovers, including potato casseroles and ham. Rachel was grateful for the invitation, dreading going home and being alone with her thoughts of not having Anna.

Dinner was quiet, as was the evening scripture time. No one felt like singing. James and Emily were especially struggling because they didn't understand and wondered when Anna was coming back.

The next few weeks were hard for everyone. They each tried to carry on the best they could, but life was so different without Anna there. Rachel worked for Jacob as she always had, but he clearly struggled with his feelings. At times he would leave the office, unable to control his tears. Once or twice he snapped at her, only to quickly apologize. She felt so sorry for him. She was hurting, but she knew he was hurting even more. He was allowed a month off from work, but he tried to work anyway, to bury his thoughts and feelings into something.

In some ways, Rachel felt lost not knowing where she stood with him or what she should do. At church, she asked him if he would prefer she sat on another pew. He kindly told her he wanted her to sit by him because it was what he was accustomed to. She was glad he did because his presence helped her as well.

Another thing she was unsure of was what to do with e-mails from women proposing marriage. She started forwarding them to him because she could no longer say he was married. The night he asked her to filter them out she felt a great relief and realized in her heart she was concerned he would find someone else.

As they all tried to heal, there were a few things that happened that really touched Rachel. She took Emily with her each day to pick up James from kindergarten. They would then go to Jacob's house, and she would make lunch for all of them, including Jacob. On one particular day, about a month after Anna had died, James came in and dropped his pack in the middle of the kitchen floor instead of putting it in his locker.

Rachel asked, "James, would you put your pack in your locker?"

Suddenly James screamed at her. "You aren't my momma! You can't tell me what to do! I want my momma! I want my momma!"

He then collapsed on the kitchen floor, sobbing. Rachel started to cry, too, as she knelt on the kitchen floor and pulled him into her arms. "I want your momma too, James. I want her, too."

She held him close, and they cried together for some time. When she looked up, Jacob was standing there watching them, and she knew he had seen it all. He knelt down and wrapped his arms around both of them. Rachel leaned back against him and felt his strength and comfort. Emily came over, too, and wanted to be part of it, and Jacob pulled her into the circle. There, on the floor of the kitchen, they all grieved together.

After Rachel put Emily and James in bed for a nap that day, she cleaned the kitchen and then went to Jacob's office to see what work he wanted her to do. But Jacob wasn't there. She checked all around the house, but he was nowhere to be found. She checked the garage, and his car was still there. Suddenly, she considered where he might be. She climbed to the top of the house, to the library. She looked out across Pine Ridge, and sure enough, there he was kneeling by Anna's grave.

Rachel's heart ached for him. She checked to make sure the children were asleep, and then she put her coat on and walked briskly to join him. He looked up at her and forced a smile as she stepped up beside him. "Jacob, are you all right?"

Jacob spoke through his tears. "I don't think Anna would be very happy with me."

"Why?"

"Because I've let the joyful spirit she brought into our home die with her. I've let the music and happiness fade from our lives. She wouldn't have wanted that."

He stood and put his arm around Rachel as he continued. "I need to do better."

Jacob did try to bring back some of the happiness into his home. After dinner, he pulled out his guitar and the family tried to sing. They were all melancholy at first, but everyone did better by the time the evening ended. Each night it was hard for Rachel to leave Jacob's home because at her own home she felt sadness settle on her.

Jacob's commitment to try to do better also meant that he wanted Rachel to do the things Anna would have had her do. Rachel hadn't stepped foot inside the art room since the last time she and Anna painted together. At Jacob's insistence, Rachel decided to try to paint again. But as she walked through the door, she was immediately struck with a horrible realization.

Anna's painting was gone.

She ran from the room and rushed to Jacob's office. When she asked him, he said he didn't know anything about it. They asked the children that evening, but they said they didn't know.

"Sometimes," Jacob said, "when a painting hasn't ended up just right, Anna has destroyed it."

Rachel felt sick. Because of their closeness during the time they shared painting, she felt a huge loss. She actually felt the loss so severely she couldn't bring herself to paint, no matter how much Jacob encouraged her.

He also encouraged her to play the piano. But the first time she sat down, there in front of her was the music for "Sleigh Ride." She opened it and looked at it, and the memory of playing with Anna was too much for her. She laid her head on her arms on the keyboard and sobbed. Suddenly she felt someone beside her. When she raised her head, it was Jacob. He pulled her into his arms, and she sobbed against his chest as he leaned his head against hers. She could feel his tears falling into her hair and knew he was crying, too.

In late April, when the ground thawed enough to be worked, their two families started fixing up the little cemetery. Jacob wanted it nice for Memorial Day. They trimmed trees, put up a nice picket fence, planted lilacs and rose bushes around the perimeter, and planted grass inside. A lot of love and care was put into it. The last thing that was put in place was the headstone. Anna had picked it out and determined part of what she wanted on it. She had made it for three people, another indication that she expected Jacob to marry again. Jacob's name was engraved on the center position. On the back, across the section between their two names, was engraved the names of their children. Under that, Jacob had engraved the same words he had for Ina but changed the word "Mother" to "Sweetheart." It was a beautiful, touching indication of his love for her.

Rachel asked Jacob if she could plant, there in the cemetery, the beautiful rose bush that had grown from the flower he sent for her parent's funeral. He agreed and helped her dig the hole, and together they lovingly planted it prominently by Anna's grave.

By Memorial Day weekend, the little cemetery was beautiful. Rachel and her children joined Jacob's family for a wonderful breakfast that morning. They went first to the county cemetery, and Jacob again cleaned around the graves of his parents and Rachel's parents. When he cleaned around Matthew's grave, Rachel marveled at Jacob's love for a brother who was so spiteful to him.

Lastly, they spent the rest of the morning putting flowers on Anna's grave, and that was the hardest part for the two families. For lunch they had their annual wiener roast, and after dinner, the children gathered to watch a movie. Jacob disappeared, and Rachel knew just where he'd gone.

After he had been gone for some time, she became concerned and walked the distance along the ridge to the little cemetery. He was kneeling there, fresh tears on his face. Oh, how Rachel's heart ached for him. She walked over close to him and put her hand on his shoulder. "Jacob, would you like to be alone, or would you like some company?"

He sat down and patted the spot beside him. "If the company's you, I'd like it." She sat down beside him, and neither of them said anything as they watched the sun slowly set across Jensen Lake. The reflection of the orange and red in the water below them made the world tranquil, as if all of nature was at peace. As the darkness started to close in around them, Jacob rose to his feet and offered his hand to Rachel. He helped her to her feet and looked into her eyes.

"Thank you for being with me. This was a hard day, but it was better because I could share it with you."

"Jacob, I appreciate your company too. It is hard for me as well."

"Would you mind if I walked you and your children down to your house?" he asked.

"I'd like that very much."

They didn't say a word as they walked back to Jacob's house. John and David were playing a game, but Emily was sound asleep in Abraham's arms. Rachel retrieved her children's coats, and while the boys put on their own, Jacob gently worked Emily's around her, trying to disturb her as little as possible. He then lifted her off of Abraham's lap into his own arms.

Rachel and Jacob didn't say a word as they walked, though David and John prattled on about the game they had been playing. When they reached Rachel's house, Jacob carried Emily to her room, and Rachel helped him get Emily's pajamas on her. Emily woke and wanted a story, so Jacob read "Snow White and the Seven Dwarfs." When he finished, after saying that the prince and Snow White lived happily ever after, Emily was very sober.

"Uncle Jacob, are you going to marry Momma like Aunt Anna wanted?"

Rachel was aghast at Emily's bluntness. Jacob just stuttered his words. "I . . . I . . . uh, I don't know, Emily."

Rachel was concerned about what Jacob would think and said, "I didn't say anything about that to her, Jacob."

"I know. Anna talked about it a quite a bit, even to the children."

Rachel thought Jacob might feel more comfortable if she left, so she kissed Emily and excused herself, though curiosity wouldn't let her step away altogether. She stopped just outside the door to listen and watch, where Jacob, with his back to her, couldn't see her.

Emily wasn't satisfied with Jacob's answer, so she queried further. "Do you think my momma's pretty?"

Jacob reached up and lovingly brushed Emily's bangs from her face. "Yes, Emily. Your mother is very pretty. But even more importantly, she is a beautiful woman."

"What's the difference?" Emily asked.

"Well," Jacob said, "a woman is pretty when she is pleasant to look at. But beauty is much more. I had a friend who used to say 'Beauty is only skin deep, but ugly goes clear to the bone.' But he was wrong—really wrong. Beauty is really found in the depth of a woman's heart. I have seen gorgeous women who weren't very beautiful, and beautiful women who weren't necessarily pretty, but your mother is both pretty and beautiful."

Emily seemed to be taking this all in and thinking deeply for her young age. "How can you tell if a woman is beautiful?"

Jacob paused for a time as if thinking. Then, as he spoke, he did so as if his thoughts were coming from the depths of his soul. "The greatest indicator of a woman's beauty is seen in how she treats others. For a mother, probably the best reflection of that beauty is mirrored in the lives of her children. A lot of the beauty of your mother can be seen in how she has raised you and your brothers, despite the challenges she has faced."

Rachel could feel a strange feeling in her heart. She had never heard Jacob speak this way before, and especially not about her. She felt she needed to leave, and yet she wanted to hear more; needed to hear more.

Emily started to ask more questions, but Jacob told her she really needed her sleep, and Rachel wondered if he had heard her at the doorway. As he helped Emily say her prayers, Jacob helped her express gratitude for good friends, and Rachel wondered if he was in any way thinking of her. When he helped her pray for each family member, his voice seemed softer as he said, for Emily to imitate, "Bless Momma and help her."

When he started to help Emily close her prayer, she instead added, "And help Uncle Jacob love my momma so he can be my daddy like Aunt Anna wanted."

Jacob sat there quietly for some time after Emily finished. Then he pulled the blankets up around her and kissed her on the forehead.

Rachel slipped away and quickly wiped the tears from her face to avoid the appearance that she had been crying. She hurried downstairs so Jacob wouldn't know she had been listening. It was quite a while before he emerged into the family room, and when he did, his eyes were red, and Rachel knew he had been crying, too.

She walked with him as he headed to the door to leave. As he stepped out onto the doorstep, he turned to her. "Rachel, I understand there have been some men that have broached the possibility of dating you."

She nodded. "That's true, but I told them I was in love with someone already."

Jacob looked at her with surprise, so she continued. "Jacob, maybe it's wrong, since we both have been married and all, but I must admit that I have never truly loved any other man except you. Not Matthew, not anyone. I still love you, Jacob, and I suppose I always will, and I'm not going to make the same mistake twice—of marrying someone when I'm in love with someone else. Besides, Anna gave me permission to love you."

Jacob looked away, but not before Rachel saw tears starting to flow down his cheeks. He spoke quietly, and wouldn't look directly at her. "I just wanted to say that . . . "

He paused, and Rachel held her breath. She was so afraid he was going to tell her that if she was waiting for him to love her, she was wasting her time. She braced herself for those words and waited.

"Anna always wanted me to overcome the pain I had in my heart from what happened so many years ago, and I just couldn't seem to. But it's strange. It seems that the pain from losing Anna has wrapped itself around the pain I felt when I lost you, and as the healing is coming from her passing, it is gradually, slowly, taking the pain from losing you with it."

So instantly she couldn't stop them, Rachel felt the tears flow down her cheeks as he continued. "I just wanted to say that if you could be patient with me, I feel that it will eventually purge itself from my heart, and then maybe we could . . . "

He stopped, unable to say more, but he looked up at her, and his eyes said more than any words could. Through the tears and softness there, Rachel knew he was truly beginning to find feelings for her—feelings he had locked away for so many years.

She spoke in a voice that hardly sounded like her own. "Oh, Jacob. If there is any way you could possibly love me again, I would wait for you until my dying breath."

Jacob smiled, reached up and kindly touched her face, wiping away her tears. "I'm sure it won't be that long."

He smiled once more, then quietly turned and disappeared into the night.

Falling in Love Again

Jacob's words gave Rachel hope that perhaps, someday, he could truly love her once more. She was anxious for any sign, but it didn't come immediately. A couple of weeks passed, and he said nothing more about them. Once in a while, as they worked, she would glance at him and see him watching her, and he seemed deep in thought.

The children were out of school, and Jacob started working with them again. That seemed to revive his spirits a lot. His Saturdays became busy hauling wood, fixing fence, and taking the children out for lunch. He hadn't done it in all those months since Anna died. Rachel's children talked about how they missed it, and Marie had talked to her about it as well.

Jacob suggested that maybe Rachel's family would just like to work with his family on one garden instead of having two. Rachel jumped at the chance to spend more time with him. He prepared the spot, and they planted it together. In the middle of June, as they were finishing up the last planting of corn, he seemed to want to say something. He just kept looking at her, so Rachel just waited patiently until he finally spoke.

"Rachel, I was wondering if . . . " He paused, as if he felt timid and unsure, but eventually he did continue. "I was wondering if you might like to go horseback riding with me tomorrow."

A happy feeling permeated Rachel's whole being as she answered. "I would love to, Jacob. Would you like me to pack a picnic lunch?"

"I would love that. And maybe in the evening we could go out for dinner."

Rachel could hardly wait until the next day, and she spent the evening preparing the picnic lunch. After breakfast the next morning, she hurried with her children up to Jacob's house. He was ready and waiting. The two of them walked down to the horse pasture and called the horses. They gave the horses a few oats, and they let Star Bright and Lightning eat theirs while they saddled them.

Rachel retrieved the lunch from her house and handed it to Jacob to pack into the saddle bags. It wasn't long before they were heading off together. They followed a game trail that wound around the west side of Jensen Lake. They rode from there up to a small snow-melt lake in the hills. By the time they reached it, it was lunch time. Jacob took care of unsaddling the horses and tethering them where they could eat while Rachel laid out the lunch.

As they ate, they talked of many happy memories. When they finished, they took off their shoes and socks, rolled up their pant legs, and waded in the ice-cold water. Jacob laughed when she splashed water on him, and he splashed it right back on her. Soon they were both wet and shivering. Jacob reached out, took her hand, and pulled her to the shore so they could sit in the sun and dry off. His hand felt so good holding hers, and as they fell on the grass laughing, he didn't let go of her hand. They lay back, side by side and hand in hand on the sloping hill, and Rachel felt her worries and cares just slip away.

To Rachel, it seemed far too soon that they were packing up to head back, but she was happy to know they would go out for dinner together. The last time she had eaten out had been with Anna. As the thought of Anna crossed her mind, she wondered if Anna would be happy to see them together. Rachel felt she would indeed approve.

When they arrived back at the horse corral, they took care of the horses, and then Jacob hurried home to change. Rachel hurried to prepare as well. She showered quickly and put on a blue dress that came just below her knees. She knew Jacob liked to see her in a dress, and she wanted to please him. She was still finishing the last curling of her hair when she heard the doorbell ring. She looked out the window and could see Jacob's car, so she called down to him to let himself in. She was glad he still had a key because she didn't want to have to answer the door and have him see her before she was ready.

When she finally did descend the stairs, his eyes sparkled. "Rachel, you're beautiful."

Her heart fluttered at his compliment. He was dressed in nice suit pants, a blue shirt, a tie, and a handsome sweater. "Thank you, Jacob," she answered. "And you are very handsome."

He smiled shyly at her compliment and offered her his hand. He led her to his car and opened the door for her. The night together was wonderful. They went to a quiet restaurant where they had a small booth of their own and had a candlelight dinner. Her feelings for him were almost overwhelming.

When they arrived back at Jacob's house, it was quite late. Emily was asleep on Abraham's lap. Jacob took her into his own arms and put her against his shoulder. He took Rachel's hand in his free hand and walked with her and her children down to her house. After he had helped tuck Emily into bed, Rachel walked with him back to the door. He took her hand in his and squeezed it as he thanked her for the day together.

She squeezed his back. "Jacob, thank you. I love being with you."

He was so close to her. She wanted to grab him and kiss him, but she knew that wasn't appropriate for her to do. She hoped he would kiss her, and though he stood there so close, he didn't. Instead, he just smiled, dropped her hand, and was gone.

They spent a lot of time together after that. They went out for lunch a few times each week, and they went riding once or twice a week. They went out for dinner every Friday night, and sometimes other days, too. Sometimes they would go to a movie after dinner. She loved to sit by him with her head on his shoulder and have him put his arm around her. Other times they would just go for a walk and talk, but he would still put his arm around her as she leaned against him.

But no matter what they did, each night ended the same. He would get so close, but he would never kiss her. He had no problem taking her hand or putting his arm around her. Sometimes he would even surprise her from behind and sweep her into his arms as she was working in the kitchen or in his office. She loved it when he did that. But despite all of that, he couldn't seem to bring himself to kiss her. He might lean forward as though he intended to, but he always pulled back at the last minute.

After more than a month of spending lots of time with him, Rachel began to realize that a kiss was a barrier he just couldn't cross. She knew that even if he didn't think of it consciously, he was remembering Matthew kissing her. She understood that unless she could get him beyond that, their life together might always consist of wonderful times, but never as husband and wife.

Her thoughts went to the family room in her parents home and how Anna had said the bad memory needed to be replaced with something good. As she thought more about it, she felt a feeling, a feeling almost as if Anna was telling her what she had to do. She considered that she might be taking a big risk, but she felt she had to take the chance.

She talked to Marie, and they worked out the details of her plan together. July was coming to a close, and there was a community Summer Ball. As their date ended the Friday before, she knew it was time to put the plan into action.

"Jacob, will you go with me next Friday to the Summer Ball? I want to plan the dinner and everything just as if it were preference."

He smiled and nodded. "That would be fun. What color will you be wearing so I can buy the corsage?"

His eyes lit up when she said, "red," as if he suspected some of what she had in mind.

Next, she talked to Abraham and Isaac to get them involved. Her trepidation grew as the night approached, and she began to doubt whether she was doing the right thing or not. But when she almost canceled her plans, Marie gave her the encouragement to continue.

Friday came, and they spent the day riding horses together, which was the first part of her plan. When they got home, she told Jacob it would take her longer to get ready and not to come to get her until she called him. As soon as she was showered, she dressed in the red dress and hurriedly drove over to Marie's house. There, Marie helped Rachel curl her long hair until it fell in ringlets down her back. Rachel knew Jacob had always liked her hair that way, and that was how she used to fix it when they went to a formal dance. When she finally felt she was ready, she looked into the mirror.

Marie, standing behind her, said, "Rachel, you're beautiful. If you don't win his heart tonight, you never will."

Rachel's heart was beating fast as she implemented the next phase of her plan. She called Abraham's cell phone so as not to tip off Jacob. Abraham said he and Isaac were ready. She crossed her fingers, hoping Jacob would play along. Abraham and Isaac, dressed as gangsters, kidnapped their father, just as Anna's roommates had done for Anna. By the time the doorbell rang, Rachel's heart was almost pounding out of her chest, worrying whether it was all going to work out.

Marie's family were all out of the way in the back of the house, and Rachel stood in the foyer alone. She opened the door to find Abraham and Isaac in their gangster costumes with a blindfolded Jacob in front of them.

Abraham did his best gangster impression. "Aye, boss. We brought dat guy you told us to pick up."

Jacob's smile turned to a grin as Rachel tried to use a gangster type of voice to reply. "Okay, bring 'im in."

They marched him into the family room, and then Rachel told them they were excused so she could "talk to the prisoner alone." Jacob continued to grin. "Rachel, where am I?"

Suddenly Rachel could no longer play the humorous role as tears choked her voice. "Jacob, please don't be mad at me for what I've done tonight. Please know I did it because I love you."

Jacob suddenly became very serious. "Rachel, what is it? What's the matter?"

Rachel didn't answer him directly, but said almost the same thing. "Jacob, please just promise me that when I take the blindfold off, you will remember that I have done what I have done because I love you."

Jacob nodded. "All right."

She reached up and removed his blindfold. When Jacob realized where he was, the expression on his face and the look in his eye showed the emotion that Rachel had feared. She knew in this room, since that fateful night, she had lost every encounter she had had with those emotions and memories he held, but this time she wasn't going to give in without a fight, and this time she was determined to win.

"Jacob, in this room, I know you had one of the worst experiences of your life, and so did I. But in this room I have also had some of the best memories of my life. In this room you pinned on my first corsage. In this room you first took me in your arms and told me you loved me. In this room we sat together and watched the Christmas tree lights sparkle. And above all, it was in this room that I first fell in love with you."

When she had planned this, she hadn't thought that she would cry, but she couldn't help it now as she continued. "As I love you now, and I am hoping you are falling in love with me again, I hope with all of my heart we can again find some of that magic we felt here in this room."

By the time she finished, Jacob had tears streaming down his face, tears that seemed to be washing away the hurt that showed in his eyes and cleansing the pain from his heart. He pulled her into his arms, and they both cried for a time. She could sense some of the good memories flooding over him. Finally, after some time, she pulled back and looked into his face.

"Mr. Jacob Davis, I have a wonderful dinner planned, and I hope you're ready for it."

Hoping to bring another memory, she used the same language she had used on that preference night so long ago. Jacob smiled through his tears and seemed to sense what she was saying. "Are we eating in the tree house?"

Rachel nodded. Jacob's smile turned to a grin. "Eating spaghetti with spoons and chopsticks?"

When she nodded again, Jacob pulled her into his arms once more as he laughed. Shaking his head, he said, "Oh, Rachel!"

He held her for quite a while, and she was in no hurry for anything else. When he did finally pull back, he looked at her. He looked deeply at her in the red dress, and it was as if they were teenagers again and nothing had ever come between them.

After a moment, he laughed as he spoke. "Well, I suppose if we are going to ever get to the dance, we might need to get to dinner."

He reached for the corsage and realized it was still in the car. Rachel was not about to let him leave the room until he had pinned it on her, so she called to Abraham. He immediately poked his head in the door.

"Is dere someting youse needs, Boss?"

When she told him, he quickly disappeared to retrieve the flower.

Jacob laughed at his sons. "The gangster costumes were a nice touch."

"I figured that if Anna could kidnap you, then so could I."

Jacob smiled and nodded, and Rachel could see a look in Jacob's eyes as if he were thinking back on that night with Anna when she'd had her roommates kidnap him to make him propose. Rachel hoped he was. She hoped he could bring every good memory he had into this room to push the bad one far away.

When Abraham returned, Jacob pinned the corsage to Rachel's dress just as he had so many years before. He then stepped back and looked at her, and she saw that sparkle again in his eye that she had seen when they were young and she had descended the staircase. Her heart felt like it would melt as he said, "Rachel, you are so beautiful."

She couldn't help herself, and she threw her arms around him. Again he held her tight. As she laid her head against his chest and felt his arms tight around her, she said, "Oh, Jacob, I think you are the most handsome, wonderful man in the world."

Again she stayed there for some time before she finally decided she should get them to their dinner before it got cold. She had Jacob's boutonniere on a small table, and she pinned it on him. Then he put out his arm, she linked hers through it, and they started on their way to the tree house.

When they reached the foyer, she handed her keys to Abraham and told him and Isaac she would not be needing their services further. They both nodded as Abraham answered, "Whateve' youse says, Boss."

Rachel called to Marie that they were heading out to the tree house for dinner, and Marie answered that she would be there shortly. Jacob led Rachel to the tree house, and then he went up first. After he got to the top, he turned back to help her as she clumsily tried to hold her dress out of the way and climb at the same time. Marie arrived, and Rachel could hear both her and Jacob choking back their laughter as she worked her way from step to step. When she was close enough that Jacob could reach her, he pulled her swiftly into the tree house and into his arms.

He smiled and drew her close to him, and she thought he was

going to kiss her, but he didn't. As Jacob held Rachel's chair so she could sit at the candle-lit table, Marie stepped off of the ladder beside them. She was dressed like an Italian waiter, with her hair slicked back and a fake mustache glued to her upper lip, just as she had been many years ago. She came forward and spoke in a terrible Italian accent.

"I've a come to a take a your order. You a have a your choice a between a spaghetti, spaghetti, or a spaghetti."

Jacob grinned. "I'll think we'll have the spaghetti."

"Good-a choice-a," Marie replied, acting as if she was writing it down, and then she turned and headed back down the ladder.

The table was set with, of course, spoons and chopsticks. There were huge aprons, and they quickly tucked these around themselves to protect their clothes. They had just finished when Marie, with the help of a couple of her daughters, approached the tree house with their dinner. It took her four trips up the ladder to bring the spaghetti, drinks, and warm homemade bread. As Jacob and Rachel ate, they laughed at each other's attempts to get food to their mouths, and Rachel was glad they had on the big aprons. The laughter and fun felt good, and Rachel could have had the night go on forever.

When they finished dinner, they ate apple pie Rachel had made. When Jacob found out, he complimented her, and it warmed her heart. At one point, Rachel was quiet, and Jacob asked her if something was the matter.

"Oh, Jacob, I just wished our mothers could see us together again," Rachel replied.

Jacob agreed and added, "I wish Anna could see us, too. She would be pleased with what she started."

"Perhaps they do know," Rachel said.

When they finished eating, Rachel had to make the descent down the ladder, again to Jacob and Marie's amusement. Jacob drove them to the dance, and they talked and laughed all the way. They hadn't been at the dance long before Jacob invited her to the dance floor.

It was a swing dance, and they laughed as they awkwardly attempted it after so many years. When it ended, they stayed on the floor and a slow dance started. The song was one from many years before, and Rachel remembered dancing with Jacob to that song when they were younger. He seemed to remember it as well. As they floated around the room, Jacob's arms around her felt so good to her. The music seemed to meld their hearts into one, and as the song was coming to an end, Jacob slowed them to a stop. They looked into each other's eyes, and he leaned closer and closer until finally, he kissed her.

He pulled back and looked into her eyes again, and when she smiled, he leaned forward and kissed her again, much longer this time. The music ended, and they stayed looking into each other's eyes for a moment before Jacob asked, "Rachel, would you like to go for a walk with me?"

As they stepped outside into the moonlight, he pulled her into his arms and kissed her again. Rachel started to cry and felt foolish when Jacob asked her if she was all right. She held him tight as she answered.

"Oh, Jacob, I've never been better. It's just that I'm so in love with you, and I can't believe that I'm here with you again."

He kissed her again, and she could feel his tears, too. They walked in the moonlight and said very little, just enjoying the warmth of being together. They never did return to the dance, and Rachel didn't care. That night could have gone on forever just as it was, and she would have been happy. But the time finally came that they had to go home. When they arrived at Jacob's house, Emily was again asleep in Abraham's arms, and David and John were drowsing in front of a movie. Jacob walked home with them, but this time, when he said goodnight, he kissed her.

It took Rachel a long time to get to sleep because her heart was fluttering so much. She could hardly wait to see him again. When she went up on Saturday to make dinner, she didn't immediately see him. She hurried dinner and called everyone, hoping he would come, but he didn't. No one seemed to know where he was, but Peter said he thought he saw him go outside. Rachel told the children that perhaps they should go ahead and ask the blessing and eat, and she would go out to find him.

She was quite sure where he was, and sure enough, when she approached the cemetery, she saw him kneeling there. When she stepped through the little picket gate, he turned and smiled at her. He motioned her over. "Rachel, I'm glad you came. I was just talking to Anna about you."

"About me?"

"Yes. Oh, I know Anna isn't really here and that her spirit is in some place far better, but I feel when I come here that she joins me. Perhaps it's just the tranquility, but I like to talk to her, and somehow I feel she hears me."

Jacob stood to face Rachel and took both of her hands in his. "Anna always said that deep down I still loved you and that, when that pain in my heart healed, I would know that I did. I always told her I didn't, but I came here today to tell Anna about last night and to tell her she was right."

He smiled at Rachel, and tears glistened his eyes. "She was always right." He sniffled slightly and continued. "I came here to ask her what she would think if I asked you to marry me."

His voice started to tremble slightly, and the tears started to roll down his cheeks as again he continued. "But, really, I didn't need to ask, because we both know what Anna thought and wanted. She told me that if she had to share me with another woman, she wanted that woman to be you. She said if she was going to have a sister in marriage, she wanted that sister to be you. And she said that if she was going to have another woman raise her children, she wanted that woman to be you. I guess that means there is only one other person left that I need to ask."

Jacob put his arms around Rachel, and she put hers around him. Tears were now flowing down her face as Jacob continued. "Oh, Rachel, I haven't always been as good to you as I should have. Life has thrown us some heavy curves, and I haven't always hit each one perfectly, but I do want you to know that I love you with all of my heart."

With that, he pulled from her and knelt on one knee while still holding her hand. "Rachel, I would be the most honored man in the world if you would be my wife. Will you marry me?"

Rachel just started to sob and couldn't speak, so she just nodded as forcefully as she could. Jacob stood and pulled her into his arms. After a time, he leaned down and kissed her, and then he held her close again. When he pulled back and looked at her, he smiled as he spoke. "Perhaps we should tell the children."

Rachel nodded her agreement, so Jacob asked, "What do you think they will say?"

Rachel grinned as she answered. "I'm not sure what they all will say, but I know one little girl that will say she can hardly wait until the wedding day when you will be her daddy."

Jacob laughed. "She's such a sweetie."

As they walked back to the house with arms around each other, Jacob asked when they should set the date for the wedding.

"Jacob, I'd marry you this very minute if I could," Rachel answered.

They decided to set the date for the Friday in just under three weeks, just before Abraham went off to college. By the time they walked into the dining room, the children were just finishing dinner. The children were elated at the announcement of their parents' engagement, especially Emily, who ran to Jacob and threw her arms around his waist. Rachel was pleased that James did the same to her.

The next three weeks were busy ones. When they announced in

church that they were engaged, everyone congratulated them and asked what they could do to help. There was the wedding picture, the announcements, the wedding dress, the cake, a marriage license, and a million other things to do.

Rachel chose her reception colors to be red and white because of the memories of her red dress. Having plenty of money to buy what was needed helped a lot. When they went to get her a ring, Jacob told her they'd get whatever she wanted. She told him she wanted one identical to Anna's because if they were going to be sisters in marriage, they should have rings that matched. Jacob seemed pleased with that but insisted on buying a beautiful necklace to match.

She told him she wanted to do something special for his ring as well. With his permission, she took his wedding ring, which was yellow gold, and added a white gold band to it to represent both Anna and herself.

The wedding announcement was also fun. It started out, "The children of Rachel Henderson and the children of Jacob Davis would like to announce the wedding of their parents . . . "

When the big day finally came, Rachel met with Marie early in the morning. Marie helped her get ready, curling her hair just right. When it was finally time, and they were being married, Rachel looked at Jacob, all dressed in white, and thought he was the most handsome man in the world. She thought about the contrast to her first wedding. This time she was being married by a man of God to a man she truly loved, and her heart was so full of happiness and joy. All of her brothers and sisters were there, even Richard. All of Anna's family were there as well, and when they hugged her, she truly felt their love.

The reception was also wonderful. Since neither Jacob nor Rachel had parents who could be in the line, they asked Anna's parents to take that honor. They seemed very pleased, and both Harold and Mary beamed as they greeted people. Marie was the matron of honor, and Marilyn stood in the line in honor of Anna. Jacob and Rachel's sons were all in the line, though James seldom stayed there. Emily was supposed to be in the line but was never there unless she was in Jacob's arms. The rest of Anna's sisters and Rachel's sisters mingled at the reception center in identical red and white dresses.

Halfway through the reception, Jacob surprised her by saying he had written a song for her. He asked her to come up by him so he could sing right to her. He took out his guitar and sang. The chorus went:

Do you know that I love you.
Do you know I care.

Do you know I'm thinking of you,
All the time, every place, everywhere.
Do you know life is better, just because you're there.
Do you know you are my hero,
And I wanted you to know.

And the verses went:

And sometimes I try to tell you, but the words get in the way
And cause me to stumble and fall.
So I hope that my actions tell you what my words can't say,
That I love you more than anyone at all.

And often I am not the man that I would like to be,
And you probably wonder if I love you at all.
But I know that I am better just because you are here with me.
In my eyes, you're always standing tall.

And hand in hand and arm in arm we walk a road that's seldom paved,
And we've both grown stronger along the way.
And when the angels come to call for me you'll know in my heart's engraved
A love for you that's grown stronger every day.

He started with the chorus, sang it between verses, and ended with it as well. By the time he finished the last verse, especially as she considered how the road their lives had traveled truly had been far from paved, the tears started rolling down her face, and by the time he finished the last chorus she was crying openly. When he finished, she threw her arms around him and they kissed. Everyone applauded.

After Jacob held her for a moment, Abraham announced that he had a surprise. He brought in a big package covered in brown paper. Jacob and his children had talked, and since his children called Anna "Mom," they had all agreed to call Rachel "Mother."

As Abraham handed the package to them, he said, "Mother, Dad, Mom asked me to keep this for you until this day." He then turned to Rachel. "Mother, I'm sorry I lied when you asked if we knew anything about it, but Mom told me to."

Rachel gasped and knew immediately that it was Anna's painting. Rachel and Jacob pulled the brown paper off to find a beautiful picture of Rachel and Jacob that mirrored the one that hung in Jacob's home of him and Anna. Suddenly, Rachel understood why Jacob was not centered in it. In the background was the home on Pine Ridge, with Jensen Lake and the two of them riding horses. But what caught Rachel's eye more than anything, almost hidden in the picture, was Anna smiling approvingly. The painting was beautiful, and both Rachel and Jacob pointed out the different parts to each other.

When the reception was over, she and Jacob changed into regular clothes, and Jacob started helping clean up.

Marie scolded him. "Jacob, this is your wedding night. You and Rachel need to go, and leave the cleanup to us."

"But," Jacob protested, "there is so much to do and I . . . "

Marie looked humorously stern. "Rachel almost whipped you once. Do I need to have her try it again?" She then kindly patted his arm as she smiled. "You go on. We have plenty of help here."

Rachel grabbed his hand and pulled him to the door. It was wonderful to think she would never have to leave him and go home at night alone, but they would be together always. They climbed into his car and headed down the road with a string of cans trailing them.

A New Life Together: The Last Gift

Rachel woke with a start. As she lay there wondering what had awakened her, she could feel Jacob next to her. She was snuggled up with her back to him, and he had his arm around her. She could feel his warmth and hear his steady breathing. She felt such peacefulness.

They had been married almost a year, and what a wonderful year it had been. Oh, there had been little things that Jacob did that drove her crazy; there are always a few of those kinds of things a woman will see as a wife that she won't see otherwise. But after her terrible years with Matthew, they seemed so small and insignificant.

There were times that the memories of Matthew still haunted her, though they were getting more distant. One night she dreamed he had come back for her, and when Jacob tried to stop him, Matthew killed Jacob. She woke up screaming. Jacob had held her close, and she had trembled in his arms, unable to sleep the rest of the night.

But thankfully, Jacob's bad memories from their past seemed to have almost disappeared. When they visited Marie and Jason, he didn't even seem fazed to go into the family room. It was as if that night they had gone to the dance had washed it all away. She timidly asked him about it once, and he said it seemed like nothing more than a bad dream, and he almost never thought about it at all.

She thought of the wonderful things they had done together. They did a lot of horse riding, and Jacob made sure he took her out to dinner at least once a week. The day they were married she thought she could never love him more, but she found she loved him more every day.

She thought of the day they had hung Anna's picture together. They had moved the one of Anna and Jacob slightly so they could put the two pictures side by side, prominently in their home. Rachel was determined to always have Anna be an important part of their family. Rachel talked about her a lot, especially to the children. She didn't want them to forget her.

Another very special day to Rachel was the day Jacob adopted her children and she adopted his. They gathered in the judge's chambers, and the judge asked them questions. Her children were more than happy that Jacob was to be their father, but what pleased Rachel just as much was that Jacob's sons were happy to have her be their mother. She knew she could never replace Anna, and Jacob told her not to try. He told her to just be Rachel because he loved her for who she was.

She was proud to call Jacob's sons her own. There was so much goodness in them. But even more, she was happy to see David and John now emulating Jacob. In fact, except for the fact that their hair was dark and not blond like their new brothers, a person would have thought they had always been his sons.

Abraham had gone off to school, following in his father's footsteps, and was working in computer science. The family missed him a lot, and the reunion was great when he came home for the summer. Emily and James nearly tackled him when he stepped from the car.

Rachel thought of the wonderful holidays and family times they had spent together. Jacob always expressed his love for her, especially on special occasions such as Valentine's Day, her birthday, and Christmas. She knew she would never take it for granted.

She also enjoyed Memorial Day. In the cool evening, the two of them sat hand in hand by Anna's grave and watched as the sun set across Jensen Lake. Her marriage to Jacob made her feel an even stronger affinity and closeness to Anna. Their summer vacation was spent visiting Washington and Anna's family. They swung south when they left and went to the Grand Canyon. Jacob teased Emily that it was caused by someone leaving the water dripping in the sink, something Emily did often.

Their extended family had grown much closer. Rachel kept in constant contact with her siblings and Anna's family through e-mail and on the phone. She learned to love all of Anna's family even more. In addition, Rachel's sister Angeline and her family had moved into the old Davis home that had been Rachel's for so many years. Angeline's husband, Scott, lost his job when his company downsized, so they moved back. Scott was a hardworking farm boy, and Jacob hired him to be his ranch manager, so he could run his own cattle on his land instead of leasing it. The children still worked with Jacob, but now Scott helped direct them as well.

Rachel had grown much closer to Marie, and now Angeline had also become a wonderful friend. The three of them often went out for lunch together. All three of them planned their annual family reunion, and they planned to continue the tradition. Besides Rachel's own family, Anna's parents and two of her sisters also came to the reunion that summer.

But no matter how close she grew to others and how many friends she made, no one could ever replace Jacob as her best friend. Their wedding night together had been wonderful, and it just seemed to get better from there. Though she had been afraid of the intimacy because of the way Matthew had treated her, she found that intimacy is a beautiful, wonderful thing when it is shared by two people who truly love each other and have made commitments to each other that they plan to keep. And she truly loved Jacob, and she knew he loved her.

As Rachel was thinking about all of these things, suddenly a pain in her abdomen started building, and she realized what had wakened her. She was having labor pains. They weren't very strong yet, and she clocked them and found they were still about fifteen minutes apart. She wouldn't wake Jacob for a while. The baby squirmed uncomfortably at the pressure. Though she dreaded the thought of going through labor again, Rachel was so excited about this baby.

The ultrasound had shown it was a girl, so Emily would have a sister. And even more exciting, this baby would be Jacob's. Rachel knew she wouldn't love her anymore than she loved her other children, but the joy of having a husband excited about the birth of his child was something she had never experienced before. And, indeed, Jacob was excited. He had picked Rachel clear off of her feet in his excitement when he learned they were expecting. He could hardly contain himself and was always bringing home something new for the baby that he just couldn't pass up in the store.

They had decorated the room next to theirs, and in so doing, the two of them realized Anna had planned for it to be a nursery when she'd had it built. Rachel continued to be amazed at Anna's foresight and goodness. She and Jacob talked about it often.

Rachel's heart had been tender when she watched Jacob with Emily one day. For some time, Emily had been acting up and doing things she knew she shouldn't. On one particular day, when she was especially naughty, Jacob had pulled her, squirming and kicking, onto his lap. He refused to let her go until she calmed down, and then they talked. He asked her, "What happened to my sweet little Emily?"

It was then that the truth finally came out: Emily thought he wouldn't love her anymore when the baby was born. Somehow, as young as she was, she understood that the baby was truly going to be his baby, and she felt that would mean he would love the baby more than he loved her.

Jacob cuddled her up close. "But Emily, you are every bit as much my daughter as the baby will be."

She looked up at him in surprise. "I am?"

"Yes, of course. God knew you would be my daughter; he just

had to provide a different route to get you to me."

Emily's little eyes grew wide with wonder as Jacob continued. "And further, when the baby is born, you are going to be the most important person to her."

"Why?"

"Well, because you are going to be her sister, and she needs someone to show her how to be a little girl. I can't, and Abraham can't, and Isaac can't. None of the boys can. Not even James. And your mother hasn't been a little girl for so long, she surely can't do it as well as you. So we are counting on you to be her big sister and show her what she is supposed to do."

Emily grinned and nodded. "And I will, too!"

Jacob hugged her. "I know you will, Emily. You will be the best big sister anybody could ever have."

Emily was much better after that, other than annoying James by having an air of importance and bragging how important she would be to her new sister. Jacob ended up having to talk to James and tell him how important his role would also be in protecting his new little sister, and then he felt better. Rachel was always amazed at how much Jacob could make things better.

The whole family was excited about the baby. Abraham had planned to head back to college a couple of weeks early, but he put it off so he could see his new sister. The extended family was also excited. Rachel's siblings and Anna's mother and sisters called at least every other day to get an update.

As Rachel continued to think about these things, she realized that it had been more than an hour since she had awakened, and the contractions were getting close to five minutes apart and much stronger. She knew it was time to wake Jacob. She gently nudged him, and he groggily asked her what she needed. When she told him it was time for the baby, she had never seen someone come to full alert so fast. She had to laugh at his anxiousness, and told him he could calm down; there was still time.

He became very serious as he pulled her into his arms. "I just don't know what I would do if I lost you."

Rachel had felt his worry all along, but he almost trembled with concern now. They quickly packed and were ready to go. Jacob woke Abraham enough to let him know they were leaving, and then he pulled the car around front. He helped Rachel in, and they zoomed off to the hospital. Rachel had to keep reminding him she was fine and talk him into slowing back to the speed limit.

The labor was no picnic and took almost five hours after they arrived at the hospital, but Jacob was holding her hand the whole time, and she felt his strength and love. She wished that her mother, Jacob's mother, and Anna could know of the baby and hoped that somehow they did.

When the baby was finally born and cleaned and wrapped in a blanket, the nurse placed her into Jacob's arms. Jacob showed such tenderness with the baby that Rachel could barely contain her own emotions. He looked up at Rachel, and his voice choked as he said, "Oh, honey, she's so beautiful. She looks just like you." Rachel knew she had never loved him more than at that very moment.

As for Jacob, he wanted to start calling everyone. He didn't care if it wasn't yet even six o'clock in the morning. But he had to know her name first. Rachel had told him that she wanted to name the baby, but when he asked what the name would be, she had just said, "Not until the baby is born." She knew what she would name her, but Rachel couldn't bring herself to say what it would be until the baby was placed safely in their arms. After losing Anna, it would be too traumatic if they happened to lose the baby, too.

But with Jacob holding her snugly, she now felt safe telling him. "I want to name her Anna."

Jacob smiled. "I thought that's what you'd say." He then went on to say something that touched Rachel deeply. "If you get to choose her first name, I get to choose her middle name."

Rachel nodded, thinking he might choose his mother's name since Emily's middle name was already after Rachel's mother. But Jacob didn't choose what Rachel thought he might. Instead, he kissed Rachel and said, "I want her middle name to be Rachel. That way she will be named after both of the women I have loved most in my life." Rachel couldn't hold back the tears as she nodded her agreement.

Jacob started by calling Abraham. Abraham woke everyone to tell them, and Emily and James said they wanted to come to the hospital immediately. He then called Marie and Angeline. He didn't even wait to call Anna's parents even though it was only about five o' clock in the morning in Washington.

It wasn't even seven thirty before Emily had finally talked Abraham into bringing them all to the hospital. She was very possessive of Anna Rachel and didn't want to let anyone else hold her while she was there. That really made James mad, and Jacob had to intervene between the two of them and make sure they had equal time. Each person got their turn, and all of the boys were so cute holding her.

When Abraham held Anna Rachel, he said, "With all of her black hair, I'm not sure she looks very much like Mom."

Rachel just answered, "She may not look like her, but I just hope she grows up to be like her."

The children stayed a long time and were still there when Marie and Angeline came with their families just after nine o' clock. Rachel was getting tired, so they didn't stay too long, and when they left, Abraham suggested he should take his brothers and sister home, too, despite Emily's protests.

Jacob insisted that Rachel stay in the hospital as long as she needed to, but she just wanted to be home, so by evening, she was ready to go. Jacob took little Anna Rachel into his arms and helped Rachel into the wheelchair the nurse had waiting for her. Jacob was so cute with the baby and would talk to her and goo at her, and it just made Rachel smile.

Cards, flowers, and congratulatory e-mails came from all over, many of which were from people Rachel didn't know. But the best bouquet of all was a bouquet of a hundred roses from Jacob.

Jacob pulled the car to the door, put Anna Rachel in her car seat, and then helped Rachel in. He and the nurses had to make some extra trips for the flowers, which filled the trunk and the backseat.

When they pulled into their own driveway, Rachel felt happy to be home and happy to have a new baby with her. They had no sooner come to a stop than Emily was there wanting to hold her sister. But Jacob felt that both Rachel and Anna Rachel needed some rest, and he got them right to bed. Marie and Angeline had brought over lasagna for dinner. Jacob brought some up to Rachel, and the two of them ate together in their bedroom.

That night, Rachel got some much-needed rest. She did have to nurse the baby a couple of times, but Jacob would bring her and then put her back in her crib. Both she and the baby slept late, and Rachel enjoyed Jacob pampering her all day. By evening, however, she felt much better, and there was something she wanted to do. She told Jacob she wanted to take half of the roses he had given her and put them on Anna's grave. She also wanted to take Anna Rachel out there.

Jacob seemed to understand her feelings and prepared fifty of the roses and wrapped Anna Rachel in a blanket. He held the baby in one arm while Rachel held onto his other arm and carried the roses. They walked slowly out to the little cemetery as the sun began to drop in the sky. As they stopped in front of Anna's grave, Rachel knelt down and lovingly placed the roses there. Rachel was grateful that Anna had shared Jacob with her, and Rachel felt a desire to share her love and happiness with Anna.

When Rachel stood, Jacob put his arm around her. There, together in the little cemetery, they watched the sun set across Jensen Lake. Rachel remembered that evening so many years ago when she and Jacob had sat on this hill together watching the sunset and thought about all that had happened since then.

As little Anna Rachel made sucking sounds on her hand, Jacob tucked the blanket tighter around her, and Rachel thought of the full circle her life had taken. It was as though she was back to the point from which her life had digressed so long ago. Jacob often said that he felt God had taken his life on a wonderful detour where he could learn, grow, and know and love Anna, but eventually God brought Rachel back into his life.

Rachel thought of her own life and wondered if she would call the detour she had experienced wonderful. She, of course, had her other wonderful children. She had learned a lot and become stronger through her trials, but in the end, it was wonderful because she had been friends with Anna. Yes, even for her it had been a wonderful detour.

Jacob finished tucking the blanket around Anna Rachel, and, holding her lovingly in one arm, he put the other arm back around Rachel. She leaned her head against his shoulder. Tears came to her as she realized that when Anna had given her final gift to Jacob, she had given Rachel one at least as great. She had not only given her a loving husband and five beautiful stepsons, but she had given her a new chance at life, something she had only dreamed of during those dark years. That is probably the greatest gift someone can give.

As she stood there in the cool evening breeze, watching the last faint traces of sunlight on the horizon, Rachel said in her heart, "Thank you, Anna, my dear friend, for your last gift," and she felt as if Anna was smiling.

If you enjoyed our book, we would love to have you do a review on Amazon at:
http://amzn.com/1629860107

Read other stories, purchase more books, or sign up for a short story each week by going to
http://www.publishinginspiration.com

Other books
by
Daris Howard
Daris Howard Amazon page:
http://amzn.com/e/B004H76UGK

For inspiring plays and books, as well as discounts for book sellers, go to

http://www.publishinginspiration.com

About the Author

Daris Howard is an author and playwright who grew up on a farm in rural Idaho. He associated with many colorful characters including cowboys, farmers, lumberjacks, and others. Besides his work on the farm, he has worked as a cowboy and a mechanic. He was a state champion athlete and competed in college athletics. He also lived for eighteen months in New York.

Daris and his wife, Donna, have ten children and were foster parents for several years. He has also worked in scouting and cub scouts, at one time having eighteen boys in his scout troop.

His plays, musicals, and books build on the characters of those he has associated with, along with his many experiences, to bring his work to life.

Daris is a math professor, and his classes are well known for the stories he tells to liven up discussion and to help bring across the points he is trying to teach. His scripts and books are much like his stories, full of humor and inspiration.

He and his family have enjoyed running a summer community theatre, where he had a chance to premiere his theatrical works and rework them to make them better. His published plays and books can be seen at http://www.darishoward.com. He has plays translated into German and French, and his work has been done in many countries around the world.

In the last few years, Daris has started writing books and short stories. He writes a popular news column called *Life's Outtakes*, which consists of weekly short stories and is published in various newspapers and magazines in the U.S. and Canada, including *Country*, *Horizons*, and *Family Living*.